continued . . .

. . . and Kristine Kathryn Rusch

"A masterful writer."   —Orson Scott Card

"Whether [Rusch] writes high fantasy, horror, sf, or contemporary fantasy, I've always been fascinated by her ability to tell a story with that enviable gift of invisible prose. She's one of those very few writers whose style takes me right into the story; the words and pages disappear as the characters and their story swallows me whole."   —Charles de Lint

"Accomplished . . . exceptional."   —Edward Bryant

"Rusch's greatest strength . . . is her ability to close down a story and leave the reader feeling that the author could not possibly have wrung any more satisfaction out of the piece."   —*The Kansas City Star*

"Kristine Kathryn Rusch never stray[s] from the path of good storytelling as she dissects her characters and their situations for the reader's benefit. She integrates the fantastic elements so rigorously into her story that it is often hard to remember she is not merely recording the here and now."—Science Fiction Weekly

"[Rusch's] writing style is simple but elegant, and her characterizations excellent."   —*Beyond*

"Rusch's . . . stories are exceptional, both in plot and in style."   —Ed Gorman, *Mystery Scene*

"[Rusch] is already far better than should be allowed."
                    —*Nexus*

CONSEQUENCES

A RETRIEVAL ARTIST NOVEL

Kristine Kathryn Rusch

A ROC BOOK

ROC
Published by New American Library, a division of
Penguin Group (USA) Inc., 375 Hudson Street,
New York, New York 10014, U.S.A.
Penguin Books Ltd, 80 Strand,
London WC2R 0RL, England
Penguin Books Australia Ltd, 250 Camberwell Road,
Camberwell, Victoria 3124, Australia
Penguin Books Canada Ltd, 10 Alcorn Avenue,
Toronto, Ontario, Canada M4V 3B2
Penguin Books (N.Z.) Ltd, Cnr Rosedale and Airborne Roads,
Albany, Auckland 1310, New Zealand

Penguin Books Ltd, Registered Offices:
80 Strand, London WC2R 0RL, England

First published by Roc, an imprint of New American Library,
a division of Penguin Group (USA) Inc.

First Printing, April 2004
10 9 8 7 6 5 4 3 2 1

Cover art by Greg Bridges

Printed in the United States of America

PUBLISHER'S NOTE
This is a work of fiction. Names, characters, places, and incidents either are
the product of the author's imagination or are used fictitiously, and any resemblance to actual persons, living or dead, business establishments, events, or
locales is entirely coincidental.

BOOKS ARE AVAILABLE AT QUANTITY DISCOUNTS WHEN USED TO PROMOTE
PRODUCTS OR SERVICES. FOR INFORMATION PLEASE WRITE TO PREMIUM MAR-
KETING DIVISION, PENGUIN GROUP (USA) INC., 375 HUDSON STREET, NEW YORK,
NEW YORK 10014.

For Mike Resnick
with thanks for everything
(and there's a lot of everythings)

ACKNOWLEDGMENTS

The Retrieval Artist books have attracted a lot of attention, and I'm grateful to the readers who've followed me on these multigenre hybrid novels. Thank you for making it possible to continue the adventures of Miles Flint.

Thanks also goes to Laura Anne Gilman, who has such faith in this project and has taken such good care of it in-house. Thanks too to my husband Dean Wesley Smith, who got me through a difficult summer.

1

Kovac huddled against the edge of the crevasse. Below him, the massive rip in the glacier extended several hundred meters, narrowing as it deepened. He had no idea how deep the crevasse was, but he knew that a fall would kill him.

His white environmental suit, with crampons extended along its surface, clung to the smooth ice, leaving his hands free. One of them clutched the rifle, while the other remained at his side.

His feet dangled over the emptiness below him, but he knew better than to brace them. Too much pressure on the side of the crevasse could cause an avalanche, and then the month he had spent out here, scouting the proper location, would be in vain.

His head barely popped out of the crevasse; only his eyes and nose were exposed to the surface elements. He'd left the helmet off the environmental suit: He didn't have to worry about the oxygen content of the air, and, he hoped, he wouldn't be here long enough to expose his skin to the dangers of deep cold.

The part of the glacier in front of him angled downward, and with his far-range vision goggles, he could see the village nearly forty klicks away as if it were right next to him.

The village was laid out on a grid pattern, with buildings made of a local concretelike substance that could hold up to the valley's harsh winters. The buildings were white against the green of locally grown plants.

Vehicles weren't allowed there, so the streets were narrow, except for the market square, which filled every summer with makeshift booths and open tables selling handmade goods and produce, just like humans had done since time immemorial.

At the moment humans did crowd the square. That was the most unusual aspect of this place: the fact that only humans were here. No aliens of any sort visited—and the natives, if there had ever been any—were long gone.

Trieinsf'rd was the farthest Kovac had ever gone on assignment. Nearly two years' travel outside of Earth Alliance space, Trieinsf'rd was an outsider's paradise. The planet had been originally settled by a group who had rebelled against the Earth Alliance. Over the years, other colonies sprang up, none of them affiliated with Earth Alliance, and all of them containing people who wanted no contact with outside governments, for whatever reason.

The village below, called Nowhere by the locals, was as far away from anywhere as a person could get. It was in the only habitable valley in the northernmost continent on Trieinsf'rd—a valley that was hundreds of kilometers long and a hundred wide. But to get to Nowhere, a person had to cross three huge mountain ranges, most of them still covered by the glaciers that had carved the valley.

The mountains were so tall that regulation aircars couldn't cross them, and the glaciers were so fragile that most space yachts couldn't land anywhere near them.

To get here, most people had to rent a specially designed vehicle from one of the towns at the very edge of the first mountain range. Once one of those vehicles got rented, the leasor notified the authorities in Nowhere that someone was coming.

Kovac didn't want to notify anyone. He had bought his own vehicle off-world, and had one of his partners serve as a driver, launching illegally off his space yacht over Trieinsf'rd's Black Sea. Kovac had flown the vehicle low, landing it in a bowl about four klicks from here, then hiked to the crevasse.

The rifle felt sleek against his hands. The environmental suit sealed around his wrists, leaving his hands untouched by any fabric. He didn't wear gloves. Instead, he wore two layers of DuraSkin—enough to ensure that he wouldn't get frostbite, but not enough to interfere with his own delicate nerve endings.

He needed the sense of touch. The rifle was a fragile weapon, built for extreme conditions, and accurate only in the hands of an expert. The slightest thing, from the thickness of fabric to the infinitesimal vibration of a finger, could cause a shot to go wild.

Kovac had worked with rifles most of his career, and knew most of the hazards. Still, other problems could arise without warning, and in cases like this one, where he would get only one chance, he didn't dare make any errors.

He'd even made the bullets himself, something he had learned to do after the last disastrous job. Because this job was so important, he'd used a combination of water and a lightweight poison to create the pellets. That was the nice thing about ice: The evidence melted.

Not that anyone would be able to trace him. He was, as he had always been, a ghost. But he had learned long ago that there was no such thing as being too careful.

With his free hand, he adjusted the goggles, making certain that the glare from the ice field around him wouldn't affect his accuracy. He focused on the doorway that the Tracker had told him about. It was behind a booth selling Earth produce—strawberries, asparagus, red bell peppers, all obviously from a greenhouse.

If the Tracker's information was correct, the woman would emerge within the next five minutes. She would put a hand over her eyes, shading them from the thin sunlight as she surveyed the area around her. Then she would grab a basket from beside the door and begin her daily shopping.

Worried, yet not worried. Believing, deep down, that she was safe after all, not realizing that she had been found nearly a year before, and watched for six more months before the Tracker even contacted Kovac.

Kovac's heart pounded harder than usual, and he could feel the chill air sting his face. If she didn't come soon, he would have to retreat, set up again the next day, hope that his normally reliable source hadn't failed him for the first time.

Then the door opened. The woman stood inside the threshold, younger than he had expected. Her skin was soft, the color of the sand found on the Atlantic coastline of his childhood. Lines had formed around her brown eyes, but they were laugh lines, which he also hadn't expected.

Somehow he had thought she would be old and miserable, sorry she had been trapped in this godforsaken place. Sorry for the choices she had made.

She wore a dress made of material so thin that he could see her nipples through the cloth. No protective gear underneath, nothing to shield her from weapons fire. She had obviously adopted the credo of the community, the belief that they were so far away from human settlement that they were safe.

He used the suit's crawl circuitry to help him move upward. He set the crawl for a decimeter—enough to get his shoulders above the mouth of the crevasse. He had programmed the suit for a fragile ice field and hoped that the suit's actions would be as delicate as they had been in simulation.

As he rose, his perspective shifted. He was looking down on the village now, his view of the market square like one that a man would have if he stood on a rooftop.

Kovac didn't like it. He wanted a direct shot, not an angled one.

He waited until the suit finished its climb, then he adjusted the goggles again, but he still couldn't get the perspective right.

He glanced up, saw nothing except a pale grayish sky—the color Trieinsf'rd's distant sunlight created as it flowed through the planet's odd atmosphere. He shuddered, not from the cold, but from the isolation.

He hit the crawl again, and this time eased himself out of the crevasse entirely. He moved away from the opening, and sprawled on the ice field.

Then he lined up as he used to, decades ago, when he trained on Earth using conventional weapons—real rifles shooting real bullets, as they had for hundreds of years. He'd always preferred those weapons, thinking that a man couldn't truly be a sniper without one.

After he settled, he adjusted the goggles again. His angle was direct, just like he wanted.

Only he had wasted time. She had moved away from the door, mingling in the crowd, beginning her shopping by examining the strawberries at a nearby booth. She held up the little carton, apparently looking to see if any of the berries had been crushed, and as she did so, the little man behind the booth talked with her.

Kovac didn't know what direction she would move in after she finished with the strawberries. The Tracker's diagram of her day made it clear that she had only one routine—the one Kovac had just missed when she left the door.

But he didn't want to hurry. If he hurried, he risked making an even bigger mistake. He risked shooting and missing—warning her, allowing her to escape once again.

She set the strawberries down, shook her head
slightly, and turned, facing Kovac, exposing the front
of that too-thin dress.

He steadied himself, steadied the rifle, concentrated
on being motionless—motionless except for the flick
of his right forefinger, the one that controlled the
trigger.

He almost didn't hear the shot. The puff of air, the
slight sound vibration as the pointed piece of ice left
the rifle and zoomed down the glacier at a velocity
even his airglider couldn't achieve.

Velocity, the strength of the ice, and his aim would
cause her death. But he had the poison as a backup:
A trace of it in her system, from the outside edges of
the bullet, melting from the friction in the air, melting
even more as it absorbed her body temperature, would
kill her even if the bullet failed.

She moved toward the center of the market, just a
millimeter off, a millimeter that he hadn't anticipated,
that he could do nothing about.

Kovac held his breath, watched through the goggles,
his finger still wrapped around the rifle's trigger.

Then she staggered back, raised a hand as if warding
off a blow. The hole wasn't immediately visible, lost
in the drab brown of that dress.

People exclaimed around her, going through what
looked like from this distance a grim parody of panic.

She hit the wall behind her, hand still raised, and
slid to the ground, a red stain leaving a trail on the
white concrete.

Kovac let out his breath then. He'd hit her. Whether
she died now or later, whether they thought they could
save her or not, it didn't matter. Her life was over.

He had done his job.

2

Miles Flint placed his hand on Carolyn Lahiri's back as he took her up the stairs toward the private room above the Spacer's Pub. Her muscles felt rigid, her nerves evident not only in her posture, but in her stiff movements. She was taking quite a risk coming here, and they both knew it, no matter how many assurances he tried to give.

The Spacer's Pub was only a few blocks from the Port. Flint liked the pub. It was designed for clandestine meetings. The pub's upstairs room had one-way windows on all four sides, and it also had no closets, no storage, and no hidden areas. Only one door led into the room, and an open security system allowed guests to monitor the bar below.

Had Flint discovered the room when he worked his previous job with the Armstrong Police Force, he would have had to shut the entire pub down. Now he used the room for important meetings—not all of them, but enough to trust the room's system as well as he could trust anyplace outside of his own.

The stairs led to a trapdoor that opened into the room, giving whomever was inside a defensive advantage. As Flint reached the fifth stair from the top, he put a hand on Carolyn's arm.

"Let me go first," he said.

She nodded, the nerves he'd felt in her body not evident on her face. Her skin still had the dusting of color it had received from her time in Earth's sunlight, and the white highlights in her hair, she had once told him, also came from the sun. Those highlights took years off her face, made her seem like she was in her twenties instead of in her mid-fifties.

Flint reached up, unlatched the trapdoor, and eased it back. Then he climbed two stairs at once, popping his head into the private room.

The sheer size always surprised him. The room was hidden under an angled roofline, and he always thought that the floor space should have been smaller. Instead, it stretched almost as far as he could see.

He carefully scanned the walls, the ceiling, and the floor before going all the way into the room. The chairs that lined the back wall were empty. He latched the trapdoor open, then reached down to help Carolyn up the last few steps.

She ignored his hand.

She came up, her chin raised, her dark eyes focused on a point in the distance. Only when she stepped onto the black floor did she look around. Her shoulders relaxed visibly as she saw that the room was exactly what Flint had initially presented to her—a wide-open space, with no places for an assassin to hide.

"They're not here yet," she said, her English soft and accented, an affectation she had picked up while on Earth.

"We're fifteen minutes early," Flint said. "I wanted to make sure we had time."

"You wanted to make sure this isn't a setup." Carolyn clasped her hands behind her back and walked to one of the one-way windows. She peered down at the street below.

"If it were a setup," Flint said, "I would never have taken your Retrieval in the first place."

Carolyn was too exposed by the window, even though no one should have been able to see inside this place. People knew the room existed; all someone had to do was shoot out a window, and they could see inside.

Someone determined could attack this place easily.

He and Carolyn were trusting that no one determined still wanted to kill her.

"You need to sit," Flint said.

She glanced over her shoulder at the open doorway, realizing that she had her back to that and her front to a window, something that should have made any long-term Disappeared nervous.

Then she walked to the chairs, her rubber-soled shoes making no sound on the hard plastic floor.

Flint removed a small device from his pocket. He'd had it specially made only a few months before. It located most hidden spying equipment—and constantly updated its programming as new equipment hit the market.

He flicked the device on with his thumb, and then walked around the room, holding the device near the walls, the ceiling, and even the seemingly incorruptible floor. He found nothing, which didn't surprise him. He'd come here the night before and run the same scan, and then he had done so a few hours ago.

Still, Flint was uneasy. He had been uneasy since he accepted the job to find Carolyn. In his two years as a Retrieval Artist, he had Retrieved only four Disappeareds. He had found several more—people who had been on the run from various alien governments; who had somehow angered the Earth Alliance; and, in one case, a woman who had committed a crime—but, for a variety of reasons, he hadn't brought the Disappeareds back to the people who had hired him.

Disappeareds went missing on purpose, usually to avoid prosecution or death from any one of fifty alien cultures. Most of the Disappeared were guilty of the crimes they'd been accused of, but by human standards, those crimes were insignificant and often harmless.

Unfortunately, the Earth Alliance had agreed to

treaties with all of these alien governments. The point of the treaties was to facilitate trade, but the treaties also agreed to legal arrangements. Included in those were the instances in which humans could be prosecuted for crimes against the alien cultures.

The Multicultural Tribunals handled those cases. Humans sat on the tribunals as well as aliens, but usually the human judge had only one vote. So, often, humans were sentenced to death for crimes that would, on Earth, not have been considered crimes at all.

Carolyn Lahiri's crime was a bit more complicated. She fought in a war on a nonaligned world, and because of her actions had to Disappear. The government of that world had recently pardoned all of its war criminals and its Disappeareds.

Flint had investigated, and the pardons seemed legitimate. Still, after he had found Carolyn Lahiri, he warned her that returning to the family that raised her before she went off to fight in a foreign war might still result in her death.

She had been willing to take the risk, and now she was here, beside him in this pub, waiting to see parents she hadn't acknowledged for most of her life.

Flint moved to the center of the room and checked the laser pistol he wore on his hip, making certain that the charge was high. He also checked the smaller pistol he had given Carolyn.

She smiled at him as she watched him run the diagnostic.

"I already did that," she said.

He had suspected as much, but he wasn't going to rely on her. Yes, she had managed thirty years as a Disappeared, and another six years before that as a guerrilla fighter. But he had learned in his years as a police officer, first with Space Traffic Control and then as a detective, that people didn't always do things that were in their own best interest.

Flint handed her the small pistol, and watched her stick it in her purse. Then he paced the room again.

He hadn't told her a number of things about this meeting. He hadn't told her that he would smuggle her out of the building if need be, and take her to a new disappearance service if he thought anything was going wrong. He also hadn't told her about the crystal knife he had tucked in his ankle boot, or about the tracking device he had placed on her back as he helped her up the stairs—just in case Carolyn Lahiri proved as untrustworthy as the propagandists said she was.

So far, in all of Flint's dealings with her, she had seemed like the woman she had masqueraded as. She had enjoyed life as a small-time jazz musician in New Orleans, under the name Claire Taylor. Her income came not from the music, but from the jazz bar she had owned in that city's renowned French Quarter.

Flint had even asked Carolyn how she had enjoyed the quiet of her new life as compared with the violence of her old one, and she had given him a slow smile.

Anyone who thinks N'awlins is quiet, she had said to him, *obviously hasn't spent much time here.*

And he hadn't. He had spent more time in Florida and Mississippi than he had in New Orleans, following strange trails that had led him in circles before he realized he was following plants that someone had left decades before. Part of his confusion came from the fact that he had never investigated on Earth before, and he had found it a startling place, much more diverse than anything had prepared him for.

It took him nearly two weeks to get over his culture shock before he was able to do effective work. None of the other places he had visited in the course of his investigations had disconcerted him as much as his bright blue and green ancestral homeland, a place he had once thought he would visit only in his dreams.

His wristwatch pinged. Five minutes until Carolyn's parents arrived. Flint positioned himself at the windows, then activated his own spyware—equipment that he had installed earlier that afternoon. He would be able to monitor the streets around the pub, the pub itself, and the stairs.

He set a small disk on the windowsill, then pressed the disk's center. His collapsible screen rose, showing all the angles of his various surveillance cameras in tiny squares on the screen itself.

Carolyn folded her hands in her lap, but she kept her feet firmly on the floor. Most people would have tucked them behind the chair or crossed their legs, but Carolyn clearly knew that she might have to move quickly and that each precious second counted.

She shifted slightly in her chair. "I'm beginning to wonder what I'm doing here."

Flint was wondering if she felt that way. She hadn't seen her parents in more than thirty-five years. That fact had operated both as a red flag and as encouragement for him. The red flag seemed logical: Who would risk everything for a reunion after all this time? Yet the encouragement came from another place.

He would give anything to see his daughter again—even for five minutes—and she hadn't been an adult when she died. She hadn't even spoken one clear sentence yet when the day worker had shaken her to death. And yet he would give up everything he had to hold her in his arms one last time.

"You knew the situation when you agreed to come with me," Flint said.

Carolyn nodded. "I know. It's just—seconds away from seeing them—I feel eighteen again."

"As idealistic?" Flint asked.

She smiled at him. Her smile was soft and added faint lines to her face. "No, not as idealistic. I no longer think that's possible."

"You don't have to go with them, you know." Flint had told her that before. She knew her options. She could have chosen to remain in New Orleans, although he hadn't recommended it. As careful as he was, he had left a trail, and someone else might find her. She also could have come in now that her record was clear, and started a new life anywhere else.

He got a sense she hadn't been happy in New Orleans. Her marriage to a man named Alan Taylor had ended badly, and she no longer got to see her son. She wanted to escape more than she wanted to come here.

Flint crossed his arms and studied the screens, focusing on the aircars that passed on the streets below. The pub was nearly empty.

He took a deep breath—and suddenly realized he was as nervous as Carolyn.

Maybe more so, because he knew all the things that could go wrong.

3

Six months earlier, Flint lay beneath the desk on the uneven permaplastic floor of his office. He studied the circuitry built into the desk's back panels. He hadn't seen anything like it before, and he had worked in computer systems before he became a cop. Over the years he had studied hard to keep his knowledge current, and still he was stunned.

Someone had gone to a great deal of trouble to set up redundancies upon redundancies in his networks.

The office was hot, and his shirt stuck to his chest. He didn't want to command the environmental controls to boost the temperatures because he had the system partly disassembled.

He had bought the office, complete with all of its extremely sophisticated systems, from a Retrieval Artist named Paloma. In exchange for a large sum of money, Paloma had trained Flint in the esoteric art of Retrieving, as well as in all of the pitfalls that could trap someone who was operating just barely outside the law.

He had made a number of mistakes in his first years in business. The worst had been keeping Paloma's computer systems intact. He had trusted her not to have back doors and bugs throughout the network, and hadn't done more than a cursory check in all of the systems she had left him.

She hadn't set up any bugs or traces that he could locate, but she had made several mistakes in her own systems, mistakes that he would have avoided had he set up his own. She had also taken all of her records—claiming confidentiality—and, during a case six months before, he had found ghosts of those records remaining in the system.

He had had two cases in these last six months, and they had prevented him from finishing the overhaul. But now he had no cases—not an uncommon occurrence for a Retrieval Artist—so he figured he would have time to finish the last of the changes.

The computer system beeped and Flint cursed. Someone had set off his perimeter alarm. The alarm was probably nothing—it went off whenever anyone got within a half a block of his office. But he had to check. He didn't want to be surprised by a client with most of his systems down.

He pushed himself out from under the desk. Then he climbed to his knees, put a hand on the desktop, and stared at the screen that had risen when the alarm went off.

An older couple stood near a row of shops on the far side of his block. They wore clothing at least twenty years out of date. They stood side by side, staring at their surroundings as if stunned.

Flint's office was in Old Armstrong, the original settlement of the colony of Armstrong, and even though most of the buildings had been designated historic sites, few outsiders wandered in this direction.

This section of the dome was ancient, and the filters didn't work properly. The original permaplastic used to create the roads had long since broken down, and the main feature of this section of town was dust. Add to that the dilapidated buildings—most of which housed shady businesses like pawnshops and low-rent lawyers—and that led to little traffic, at least from people who had no reason to come to the area.

A seemingly defenseless couple had no reason to come to this part of Armstrong. Flint hoped they had come to see one of the other businesses. Still, Flint slicked back his hair, hoping he didn't look too disreputable. He hadn't had his hair cut in some time, and the curls, which always bothered him, now haloed his too-thin face. His clothes were covered with dust from the floor.

He brushed himself off and sat down at his desk.

"Computer," he said, "system override. Reestablish command structure alpha. And reset the environmental controls. It's getting damn hot in here."

The computer beeped a response, and Flint sighed. The beeps would have to go as well. He would have to save his work, then reset everything just because Flint thought there was a 30 percent chance the older couple would come to his door.

He pulled out the new keyboard that he had just finished installing two days ago. He used to prefer voice commands and touch screens. But Paloma had taught him caution: Voice commands could be overheard and compromised, and touch screens gave a hacker who ventured into the office a virtual map of the ways to break into the system.

He tapped a special key three times, and got a 360-degree view of the neighborhood. Except for the older couple, no one was on the street.

He sighed. They were clearly making their way to his office.

In one corner of the screen, he froze the frame on the couple's faces, then had the system search for identification. Paloma had left Flint with a system that recognized most of the registered faces in Armstrong, and he had recently hacked into the police database to get the classified faces as well.

It took only a moment for the system to identify these two: Mimi and Caleb Lahiri, two of Armstrong's most upstanding citizens. Mimi Lahiri was a well-known surgeon at Armstrong Unity Hospital. She often traveled all over the Moon, doing work on difficult patients and teaching at the various medical schools scattered throughout the domed communities.

Her husband, Caleb Lahiri, had spent the last two decades of his career working as a traveling judge in the Multicultural Tribunal system. Most of the judges in the Multicultural Tribunals were assigned a particular circuit, but forty judges from different alien races acted as traveling judges, moving from circuit to circuit, theoretically bringing new insights into the various areas.

Lahiri had retired nearly a year before, but he kept his hand in, writing articles, and speaking about Multicultural Law.

The Lahiris stopped outside his door. Judge Lahiri peered at the tiny sign that announced Flint's job, but not his name. Lahiri's face had a cragginess that didn't look natural, possibly the result of enhancements.

His wife's face was unenhanced, even though, as a surgeon, she could have undergone the procedures for free. Her features were delicate, her skin webbed with tiny lines. But her eyes were sharp; Flint had a hunch they missed little.

She glanced at her husband and he nodded. Then she reached for the doorknob.

Flint touched a second key, unlatching the door. Then he pressed a button, sending his screens down into the desk, so that the Lahiris didn't know he had been watching them.

He grabbed another shirt from his desk drawer, and was in the process of changing when the door opened. Out of the corner of his eye he watched the Lahiris enter. They both seemed startled as their links shut off—Flint's system automatically severed any contacts to the outside—but Judge Lahiri recovered quicker than his wife did.

Of course he did. The Tribunals themselves required the participants to be unlinked during the proceedings. He was used to the internal silence.

Flint slipped on the new shirt, leaving it untucked. Then he turned toward the couple. Dr. Lahiri was tapping the tiny chips on the back of her right hand, trying to regain the signal. Finally, her husband put his hand over hers.

No one said hello. The three of them studied each other. Flint had an entire spiel he usually ran through with new clients, but Judge Lahiri would have had experience with Retrieval Artists through his job. The usual methods of talking to new clients wouldn't work with him.

"The sign out front says Retrieval Artist, Judge, not Tracker." Flint kept his tone dry, but polite. He wanted Judge Lahiri to know what he was up against.

"I can read," Judge Lahiri said.

"I don't need the test," Flint said. "I've already dealt with two undercover representatives of the Earth Alliance, and I'll tell you what I told them. I used to be a police officer. I understand the law. I don't always agree with it, but I still see my job as working for the good of society. So I'll do my best to act within the law, even when the law is unjust."

Judge Lahiri clapped his hands together slowly. "Bravo. That statement wouldn't hold up in court, but I can see how it got the intergalactics off your back."

"Then you can also see that you're not needed here. I'm being monitored. I do the best I can. I don't need any more evaluations."

"We're not here to evaluate you," Dr. Lahiri said. "We've come about our daughter."

"Mimi." Judge Lahiri's voice held a note of caution. Flint could almost imagine the conversation they had before they got to his office: *Mimi, I've worked with these types before. Let me do the talking.*

"Find someone else," Flint said. "I don't work with officers of the court."

"You won't be breaking the law if you find Carolyn," Dr. Lahiri said. "She's been pardoned."

That caught Flint's attention even though he didn't want it to. He glanced at Judge Lahiri. The judge's expression was a mixture of annoyance and relief—annoyance at his wife for not following some protocol that he wanted followed, and relief that the situation was in front of Flint.

The judge might have been a good actor. It would be a good scam—bringing a judge into Flint's office to have him do some illegal tracing on a "pardoned" Disappeared, only to learn that the Disappeared hadn't been pardoned at all.

"You realize," Flint said, "that I don't accept cases on the basis of one meeting. I'll check, double-check, and triple-check everything you tell me. Then I'll dig into your backgrounds and I'll find all the dirt that exists. You'll pay me for that work, by the way, and it won't be cheap. If I decide you're being honest with me, then I'll take your case. Or not. It might not be something I believe that I'll be able to help you with. In that case, I'll keep the research fee and send you on your way."

"I know how Retrieval Artists work," Judge Lahiri said.

"From your legal experience," Flint said. "But if you're as pure as your title says you are, you've never worked with Retrieval Artists, only Trackers. And we're different from them. Trackers will use any means possible to bring a Disappeared back to face their legal charges or to serve their sentences. I might find your daughter, decide that her circumstances are too precarious to entrust to you, and never reveal her whereabouts to anyone—including the people I occasionally work for."

"You mean you might be successful, and she still won't come home?" Dr. Lahiri asked.

"That's right," Flint said. "I don't guarantee anything except my fees. You should know that hiring me automatically puts a Disappeared in danger. Many of the Disappeared have successfully escaped their former lives. Except in the most egregious cases, the governments can't afford Trackers to look for each Disappeared. So most get away with starting over."

Judge Lahiri was nodding. Dr. Lahiri watched Flint closely, as if she could verify his truthfulness just by the look in his eyes. He took his dirty shirt off the desk and stuck it in the now-empty desk drawer.

"The minute I start searching for a Disappeared," Flint said, "I expose that person to networks all over the known universe. My interest might arouse someone else's interest. A Tracker could piggyback on my work, find the Disappeared, and gain a finder's fee for the effort—automatically bringing a once-safe Disappeared back to face their past."

"I thought Retrieval Artists were too cautious to let a Tracker piggyback on them," Dr. Lahiri said.

"We are cautious," Flint said. "I would do my best to protect your—daughter, is it?—but that doesn't guarantee my success. Most courts have blanket orders that allow the tracing of any query about a Disappeared. My innocent queries might restart an investigation that's long dead."

"It shouldn't matter," Dr. Lahiri said. "Our Carolyn's been pardoned."

She spoke with such conviction that Flint felt his interest rise. He made a point of keeping eye contact with her, avoiding contact with the judge.

"Do all the parties involved know of the pardon?" Flint asked.

"What does that mean?" Dr. Lahiri again looked at her husband. As well known as she was for surgery, she clearly felt out of her depth in the legal realm.

"He wants to know if all the notifications have been sent to the various agencies, revoking our daughter's criminal status," Judge Lahiri said.

"More or less." Flint let his voice grow harsher. The nice thing about his job—the thing most people did not understand—was that he didn't need the work. A past case had left him independently wealthy, and he didn't ever have to work again.

Although he wasn't the kind of man who could spend the rest of his life pursuing pleasure. He would work, but only on cases that intrigued him.

"There's nothing more," the judge said.

"Actually, there is," Flint said. "Depending on your daughter's crime—"

That word made Dr. Lahiri wince.

"—she could be on the watch lists of Trackers, assassins, various alien groups, many of whom do not believe in pardons, even if the pardons are issued by a Multicultural Tribunal. There are aliens who believe that vengeance is the highest form of justice, and they will ignore pardons, even though their government recognizes them. So, Judge and Dr. Lahiri, even though the law may say your daughter is free to come home, it still might not be prudent for her to do so."

The judge's mouth was set in a thin line. He apparently didn't like to be contradicted.

Flint sat in his chair, the only one in the room.

"Maybe we should discuss this." Dr. Lahiri leaned toward her husband. She spoke so softly that Flint suspected her words were for Judge Lahiri alone. "I had no idea this could be so dangerous to Carolyn."

"It's not." Judge Lahiri spoke in a normal tone of voice. He didn't even look at his wife, clearly dismissing her comments. He looked at Flint. "My daughter's case doesn't deal with aliens. She got involved in a war—a human conflict—and the war's over. The exiles have been pardoned. Everything's done."

Flint shook his head slightly. "Wars are rarely over, particularly human ones. They often continue for centuries, with lulls. You haven't convinced me that your desire to find your daughter will protect her safety."

"She may not know that she's been pardoned," the judge said, ignoring Flint's last point.

"If she was part of a war, and things have changed, she knows," Flint said. "She might be enjoying her new life. She might not want to come home. Have you thought of that?"

Dr. Lahiri squared her shoulders as if she were steeling herself to talk with Flint. Then she turned around.

"She doesn't know she's welcome here," Dr. Lahiri

said. "That's the problem. She doesn't know we want her back."

Her gray-green eyes had tears in them. Flint clenched his own fists, careful to keep them below the desk. He didn't want this couple to know he had emotions, let alone understand that his emotions could be tapped.

"When she left for Etae, she was a teenager. A dumb, idealistic teenager who thought she could save people who didn't even know how to save themselves." Dr. Lahiri paused for breath, but neither Flint nor Judge Lahiri interrupted her. "She probably got that from us. Caleb and I, we believe in doing good works. We believe that one person can make a difference, and we've both acted on it. Carolyn saw that and she applied it incorrectly. She thought fighting on the side of the rebels in Etae was the right thing."

Flint frowned. He knew very little about Etae. The conflict on that faraway world had seemed unimportant to him, and difficult to follow as well, since the fighting had gone on for decades. All he remembered about the Etaen wars was that they had been bloody and expensive.

He thought it curious that an Armstrong native would fight in a conflict that seemed to have nothing to do with the Moon or the Earth Alliance.

"She was young," Judge Lahiri was saying, "and although youth is not a defense in a court of law, it is a factor we sometimes consider in making judgments. She has had decades to reflect on her actions. She might regret them. She might want to start again."

"Or she might still believe everything she did when she was a young girl," Flint said. "It sounds like you didn't part on the best of terms. Why are you searching for her now?"

The judge and the doctor looked at each other, a perfect moment of silent communication that Flint remembered enjoying with his ex-wife before his daughter's death. He made himself take a deep breath, trying to keep his own memories out of this. The longing for intimacy that he usually kept suppressed couldn't come to the fore, not right now. Otherwise he would envy the Lahiris' relationship and might fail to see the flaws in it or in their arguments.

"Our son died," Judge Lahiri said softly. "Last year. Killed himself. We'd been estranged from him too. We weren't the best parents."

Flint's eyes narrowed. His fists remained hidden and clenched. The thought that he was being manipulated rose again. Dead children—of any age—were one of the few emotional hooks that people could grab him with.

"We were terrible parents." The tears had worked their way into Dr. Lahiri's voice. "Judgmental and harsh and demanding. And selfish. We never gave up our careers, worked too hard, and rarely saw the children. And when we did, we were trying to make them into people they weren't. They tried so hard to impress us. I think that's why Carolyn went to Etae. I'm convinced—"

Her voice broke. She swallowed hard. Judge Lahiri put a hand on her shoulder and she moved away from him.

Flint found himself wondering if they both had been harsh and judgmental or if only one of them had. And if the apparent intimacy between them came from closeness or years of being together or was simply a façade.

"You want her back for you." Flint made his voice deliberately harsh. "You want a second—no, a third—chance. You want to get rid of the guilt you feel over her disappearance and the guilt you feel over your son's death. You're being selfish again, risking her life to make yourselves feel better."

The judge's eyes narrowed and he crossed his arms. But Dr. Lahiri nodded.

"We just want to see her one last time, to let her know that we love her." Dr. Lahiri's voice grew stronger. "And if we can't see her, if she won't come back, then we'd like you to tell her that. And it is for us, but maybe it's for her too. Maybe she'd want this. She's older now. She might have changed."

"And become someone you'd like," Flint said.

"That's enough," the judge said.

"No," Flint snapped. "It's not enough. I don't take work like this. This is precisely the kind of thing that costs innocent lives. Go home. Get counseling, talk to your religious leader, express your guilt to your friends. Leave your daughter alone. She's obviously made her choice."

The judge raised his head slightly, a movement designed to intimidate. It made him look down his nose at Flint. But Flint didn't flinch. Instead he waited.

Finally, the judge tapped his wife's arm—an imperial command—and left.

But Dr. Lahiri didn't move. She stared at Flint as if she couldn't believe he had spoken like that, a single tear running down her cheek.

"I believe you," she whispered. "I don't want to harm my daughter."

Then leave, Flint thought, but this he didn't speak out loud. He liked the doctor more than he had liked her husband, and he was beginning to suspect that she had less to do with her children's difficult lives than the judge had.

Flint resisted the urge to press the screens up so that he could see what the judge was doing. Instead, Flint waited Dr. Lahiri out.

"If I give you a message to take to my daughter, just a note, an apology, really, would you do it?"

"Dr. Lahiri—"

"After you do all the research, of course, and decide whether or not to take the case. I wouldn't want you to put her in danger just because we're . . ."

She waved her hands as if words failed her. Then she shook her head.

"That's what I've been trying to tell you," Flint said gently. "The initial research alone could put her in danger."

Dr. Lahiri bit her lower lip. Then she glanced at

the door. It didn't open. She took a step closer to Flint's desk.

"That's why you upset my husband so," she said. "You see, he thought because of his legal experience, he knew how to find a Disappeared."

Flint felt a shiver run down his back. "He's already started the research?"

She nodded. "If you turn my links on, I can download it to you—"

"I don't let any outside systems touch mine," Flint said. His suspicions remained, but if Dr. Lahiri spoke the truth, then she and her husband had just made matters worse for the daughter they claimed to care about. He could reverse some of that; he could plant false information, set up incorrect trails. If nothing else, he could protect the girl from the arrogance of her family.

Dr. Lahiri rubbed her links again. "I suppose I could get you hard copies—"

"No," Flint said. "You can download everything to a blind box."

He grabbed a small plastic card from his desktop. He had dozens of these cards, some with monetary links embedded in them, others with chips that opened an information node.

He handed her one that opened an information node.

"I'm not agreeing to anything," he said as she took the card from him.

But he was one step closer. Still, if Dr. Lahiri was telling the truth, then it didn't matter whether he did the preliminary research. The dangers had already started. He might be able to reverse the problem without even leaving Armstrong.

"What else do we have to do?" Dr. Lahiri asked, clinging to the card as if it were a lifeline.

Flint handed her a second card. "I need a retainer of two million credits. Deposit it into this account. I won't begin the research until I get confirmation that the money has arrived."

She nodded.

"If I decide not to take the case, the retainer is all that this will cost you. If I decide to take it, you will pay my expenses at the end of each week, and you'll also pay me an additional fee each week. This investigation will cost you a lot of money. Once we agree to work together, I can terminate at any time. You cannot terminate at all. If you cut off the funds, I stop working—even if I leave a wide-open trail to your daughter. Is that clear?"

Dr. Lahiri's breath caught. A lot of customers left right there, as they should. The investigation was outrageously expensive—or at least, Flint used to think so until Paloma reminded him that they were gambling with the life of a Disappeared and maybe even with the lives of the Disappeared's new family and friends. Looked at in that way, sometimes Flint felt like the sums he quoted weren't enough.

After a moment, Doctor Lahiri sighed. "It's clear."

She tapped both cards against her hand, then glanced at the door again. Flint wondered if she would tell her husband that she had hired Flint or if she was supposed to stay, to use her motherly wiles to convince him to take the case.

He would investigate the Lahiris first, before he ever looked into the daughter. If they weren't on the up-and-up, he would repair whatever damage the father had done, and quit, keeping the retainer.

"What do I do," Dr. Lahiri said softly, as if she thought someone could overhear them, "if my husband's efforts get Carolyn to contact us?"

"First, you make sure your husband stops whatever he's doing," Flint said. "He may have a superficial knowledge of my job, and that's just enough to get everyone in trouble."

Dr. Lahiri nodded.

"Second, you don't contact me. I'll contact you, in everything. But if it's an emergency, and you need me, you deposit two hundred and seventy-one credits into the account I just gave you. That number is a code, and it'll flag me. I'll know to get in touch with you."

She bit her lower lip, then nodded once.

"I thought," she said, "you know, once the war was over, once she was pardoned, this would be easy. I never expected all this."

"Your husband should have," Flint said. "He deals with large conflicts all the time. He knows how dangerous this universe has become."

"Knowing and understanding aren't the same thing," Dr. Lahiri said, and let herself out of the office.

Flint brought up a screen and watched her walk away.

Judge Lahiri was already gone.

4

Flint spent months researching, confirming that Carolyn Lahiri had indeed been pardoned. He also researched Carolyn's parents, still not quite willing to trust the judge.

Flint found nothing to convince him to stay away from the case. In the end, he decided that Carolyn could—and should—make the decision about her future.

When he found Carolyn and gave her the Lahiris' message, she had surprised him by asking if he could escort her back to Armstrong. Apparently she had done her research, had known that her little band of warriors had been pardoned, and she had a secret desire to return to her first home.

She had grown tired of Earth, she said, but he thought it was more than that. She had married and divorced since Disappearing, and in the divorce, she had lost custody of her son. Her parenting skills had been abominable—her word—and yet she sounded surprised by it.

Flint hadn't been. With parents like hers, years on the run, and years working as a guerrilla fighter, he would have been surprised if her parenting skills had risen to the level of bad. Part of him couldn't believe a woman like Carolyn had decided to have a child at all, but he had understood it.

After all, Disappearance Services promised their clients normal lives. What could be more normal than a marriage and a family, a life lived in happy obscurity?

And, of course, that life hadn't worked out. At her request, he brought her home, but he still wasn't willing to take her directly to her parents' apartment.

Instead, he brought her to the Spacer's Pub, where he could protect her if he had to.

Flint stood in the upper room, near the window, hands clasped behind his back. He watched the monitors, and occasionally glanced outside.

Carolyn sat across the room, her feet still flat on the floor, her hands clasped on her lap. If he didn't know her history, he would have thought her a demure woman.

The Lahiris entered the building. Flint did not warn Carolyn.

Instead, he watched them, saw the judge put his hand against his wife's back just like Flint had done to Carolyn. Saw Dr. Lahiri look around the pub as if it had a bad odor. Saw the judge steer her away from the bar.

The Lahiris walked to the door leading to the steps as if the couple knew where they were going. They followed Flint's instructions to the letter.

He said, "They're coming."

Carolyn raised her head slightly, a movement Flint had seen her father make. Until that moment, Flint had thought she had nothing in common with her father. She had gotten her looks from her mother, and her build seemed to have little to do with either of them.

She clasped her hands even tighter, took a deep breath, and squared her shoulders—that move from her mother.

Flint monitored the street. Nothing. He then examined the bar. No one followed the Lahiris to the stairs. No one even seemed to notice them.

He pressed a button so that the screen opaqued. The system was set up to scan faces for possible trouble—he had put most of Carolyn's old enemies into his system—the ones he could find—and had the system scan for known criminals. He also set up the warning buzzers to alert him should anyone start up the stairs once the Lahiris had entered the room.

Dr. Lahiri came in first. She was thinner than she had been, her face lined. She wore a gold blazer and a matching skirt, which made her seem older than she was. Her gaze caught Flint's and he saw fear in her eyes—the same fear that he had seen in Carolyn's.

He nodded toward Carolyn, and Dr. Lahiri nodded back, not looking in her daughter's direction. It was almost as if she were afraid of what she might see.

The judge followed his wife through the trapdoor. He scanned the room, his gaze passing over Flint as if Flint were little more than a servant.

When Judge Lahiri saw his daughter, he froze, swallowed hard, and seemed to shrink.

Finally, Dr. Lahiri looked in the same direction as her husband. She balanced precariously at the top of the stairs. Flint moved closer—whether to catch her if she fell or to prevent some kind of problem within the family, he wasn't certain.

"C-Carolyn?" Dr. Lahiri asked.

Carolyn Lahiri rose halfway off her chair, apparently uncertain as to whether she should sit or stand.

"Mommy?" Her voice sounded impossibly young.

Dr. Lahiri made a small noise in her throat, then nodded. She pushed past her husband, who remained frozen beside the trapdoor, and ran to her daughter.

Carolyn got off the chair, but didn't walk forward. Her mother reached her, wrapped her arms around her, and made a sound halfway between a sigh and a moan.

Flint moved back to the window, trying to blend into the wall. He didn't want to be here any longer, but he didn't know how to prevent it. He hated this part of Retrieving, the witness to the family reunion. At best, he didn't belong. At worst, he was needed.

"Caleb," Dr. Lahiri said, turning partway toward her husband.

Judge Lahiri nodded, but still didn't move. It almost seemed like he had been the one who had Disappeared; he was the one who had vanished somehow.

"Caleb!"

He glanced at Flint, and Flint thought he saw a plea for help. Then Judge Lahiri seemed to steel himself, and he walked, slowly, reluctantly, toward what remained of his family.

Dr. Lahiri stepped back, her hand clutching her daughter's, and grinned at her husband. "It's Carolyn. Look. She's just the same."

"Older and wiser, I would hope," Judge Lahiri said, and Flint winced. His assumptions from that very first meeting had been right. He had heard confirmation over the course of his investigation, but part of Flint had hoped that was all a myth, that beneath Judge Lahiri's gruff exterior hid a man who loved his family more than he could admit.

"Older at least," Carolyn said, her voice colder than Flint had ever heard it. "I thought from your note that you might be happy to see me, Daddy."

Daddy. Another of those words that sounded odd from Carolyn's lips.

Judge Lahiri dipped his head, the frailty back. "I am," he said softly. "I missed you, child."

Color rose in Carolyn's face, and Flint turned away so that the family could have some privacy. Still, he didn't entirely trust them, and so he watched the reunion on the opaque screen, trying to look at the body language and not any other details of the gathering.

"We're so glad you decided to come home," Dr. Lahiri said. "We have a room set up for you, and we really want to catch up. Carolyn, there's so much that's happened, so much we've missed—"

"I haven't lived the kind of life you reminisce about,

Mom." Even though her mother clutched her hand, Carolyn's fingers hadn't closed.

Flint leaned against the window, facing the family again. He wanted these things to go smoothly and they never, ever did.

"I know this isn't going to be happy or entirely pleasant." Dr. Lahiri hadn't let go of her daughter. "But we have a chance here to make amends to each other."

Dr. Lahiri looked at her husband. He didn't meet her gaze.

Flint kept his own gaze on Carolyn. She seemed impassive, as if the tense woman he had known from a few moments ago had never existed.

"So much has gone wrong," Dr. Lahiri said. "So much that we can put right, I think, if we just try—"

"I'm not Calbert," Carolyn snapped. She was referring to her dead brother. "I left when I was eighteen. You had almost no effect on me. Maybe you're responsible for his suicide, but you're not responsible for my life. There's not much that you can put right."

"I beg to differ." The judge finally entered the discussion. "You would never have gone to Etae if it weren't for us."

"Believe what you want, Daddy," Carolyn said. "But no matter how much influence you have, you can't change the past."

Her words hung in the room. Flint felt the tension in his own back, as if she had transferred all of her fears to him.

The Lahiris stared at each other, the conversation apparently over almost before it had begun.

Flint let out a small sigh. He was going to have to intervene after all, but not in the way he had planned. He would have to get Carolyn a room, offer to help her start again, since clearly she wanted nothing to do with her family.

The judge must have heard Flint's sigh, for the older man turned. His gaze was flinty, and not at all defeated.

"You can go now," Judge Lahiri said. "Send us your final bill, and we'll settle, as we always have. But we no longer need your services."

"I stay until this meeting ends," Flint said.

"It's private." Dr. Lahiri looked over her husband's shoulder. "Please, Mr. Flint. You've been good to us so far, and now Carolyn's here, and we're grateful. But we'd like to have this conversation alone."

"I'm sure you would," Flint said.

"So," Judge Lahiri said, "you're dismissed."

"Perhaps you've forgotten the contract you agreed to." Flint always had his clients sign an agreement after he did the preliminary research and decided to take the case. "I stay through the first meeting. Nothing changes that."

"Miles," Carolyn said, "it's all right. I'll be fine."

Flint shrugged. "If you want to continue in private, go somewhere else. I can't leave you alone in this room."

Even if he could, he wouldn't. His equipment was here, and Carolyn knew about some of it.

She nodded. The judge's eyes narrowed, as if Flint were a petitioner who didn't realize that his case had ended. The doctor looked down.

"Carolyn," Judge Lahiri said. "Will you come home with us and finish the discussion there? We'll put you up; we'll help you back into Armstrong's life. Even if you decide you no longer want anything to do with us, we'll make sure you're settled."

"I could bring my own funds with me." Carolyn's tone was flat. "I was pardoned, remember? I don't have to continue hiding."

"Fine," the judge said. "I was just—"

"Please," Dr. Lahiri said, but Flint wasn't sure if she was speaking to her daughter or her husband. "This isn't something we'll settle here or even in the next fifteen minutes. There's a lifetime of things we have to discuss, and I think we should. We should at least give it a try."

Carolyn looked at her mother for the longest time,

as if assessing her. Then Carolyn looked at her father. He met her gaze, but he still hunched, as if she had more power over him than he had over himself.

"All right," Carolyn said after a long moment. "I'll go with you."

"You sound so reluctant." Dr. Lahiri seemed disappointed. Flint wondered if she had fantasized in just the way that he had warned her not to, pretending that everything would go fine and they would have a perfect family yet again.

The judge jutted his chin forward and crossed his arms, apparently regaining his internal strength. "Why did you come home?"

Carolyn gave him a slow, cold smile. "I had nowhere else to go."

5

Amazing how sunlight varied from continent to continent, planet to planet, solar system to solar system. Honoria sat at a table in the very center of Binh's best-known outdoor café. The sunlight that fell on her arm had a reddish cast, almost like the reflection of a dying fire. It gave her skin a burnished quality, as if she had been made of copper instead of flesh.

She had dressed carefully for this day. She had piled her golden hair—also looking reddish in the odd sunlight—on the top of her head, allowing only a few strands to fall about her face. Her dress, expensive, purchased outside of the Vekke system, had originally been white, but the light changed everything.

Only her black bag, which matched by virtue of her black-and-white shoes, remained unchanged.

She nursed a califf tea, the liquid untouched by sugar or milk. Califf tea was one of Vekke's exports, but here, on the planet itself, the tea had an exceptional flavor. Something about the water, or the atmosphere, or the air.

Something about the afternoon.

Despite all her plans to the contrary, she was nervous. She had planned to be calm—after all, this was the most important day of her life, and she had to do everything properly.

But perhaps that awareness of the day's importance added to her own nerves.

She hoped they didn't show.

Around her conversations flowed in dozens of languages. Binh was a cosmopolitan city. Because of Binh's location in the galaxy—and because of its port, which was one of the best in this solar system—groups met all over the city to discuss business and interstellar relations. Unlike the rest of Vekke, unlike even the country that housed it, Binh tolerated all kinds of aliens and worked to make them comfortable.

At this café, Disty sat on the tabletops, long feet pressed against each other in a sign of relaxation. Two Peyti had a conversation in their own language, their faces only partially visible behind the masks they had to wear to cope with Vekke's atmosphere.

An Ebe paced near the door, all five legs hitting the ground at the same time—a sign of concern. The Ebe was probably worried about the Umnifant that someone had left corralled across the street. The creature, half the size of one of the buildings, had a doglike intelligence and was kept all over this galaxy as a pet.

Honoria resisted the urge to tap her fingers against the tabletop. It was just like Femi to be late. Inconsiderate, difficult, the woman had many attributes that no one else seemed to notice.

Femi had made herself one of the best-known jewelers in Binh, specializing in all sorts of rare gems, settings, and designers. Humans came from all over to buy from her—she refused to sell on any kind of network, only in person—and she also did work for the Peyti, the Ilidio, the aausme, and others.

Honoria had had this appointment set for nearly nine months. She had prepared for it carefully, actually going to gemologists to get some unusual pieces to offer Femi, spending a small fortune simply to convince Femi that Honoria was on the up-and-up.

The committee hadn't believed Honoria had this kind of wherewithal. They had wanted to use one of their own people, the soulless ones they had used countless times before.

But this moment was about passion, not rationality. And perhaps, if she thought about it this way, Honoria's nervousness made sense. It was a sign of her passion, a sign that she was doing everything she had been trained for, everything she believed in.

A human woman entered the outdoor section of the café from the indoors. She was tall and thin, but not very elegant. She wore spacer's pants and a shirt that had several holes across the top.

Honoria dismissed her even before she sat with the group of human students at the large table beneath the flaring dew plants. The dew plants absorbed the sound of their conversation, but not their laughter. The students seemed to be on holiday, spending nearly an hour drinking and having animated conversations.

Honoria wished they would leave.

Finally, a silver-haired man wearing the gray sunglasses common to humans in Binh entered from the interior of the restaurant. He examined the outdoor tables, his gaze stopping at the three tables with humans—the students, a male couple having a heated discussion about their relationship, and Honoria.

When he saw her, he inclined his head toward her. She inclined her head back, feeling it proper to acknowledge him, whoever he was.

Then he disappeared into the darkness of the interior. A robotic waiter floated past and extended its mechanical arm, picking up Honoria's califf tea and replacing it with a fresh one. Her table lit up, asking her in twenty different human languages if she wanted anything else to eat.

"I'm waiting for a friend," she replied. "We'll order when she gets here."

The robotic waiter did not respond. Instead, it floated off, and the language lights on the table's surface disappeared.

At that moment, two more silver-haired men entered the café. They sat at a table next to Honoria. Another silver-haired man—the first one? Honoria couldn't tell—accompanied a heavyset woman wearing a dress made of flowing scarves.

As the woman drew closer, Honoria realized that the point of each scarf was adorned with a waterbead, a rare silver-blue shell-like sustance found only in the rainwater mollusks of CeeDwarDo. Honoria wouldn't have known what a waterbead was without all the study she had done for this meeting.

She was glad she had done the work now, because Femi looked nothing like Honoria expected. Honoria had seen only old holos, and few of those could be made life-size. As a young woman, Femi had been tall and slender, like the spacer who had entered a few moments before.

Femi made her way to the table, engulfing Honoria in a perfume that smelled faintly of mint. Femi's dress rattled softly, the waterbeads touching each other as she sat at the table.

"You're Lyli D'lap?" Femi asked.

"Yes," Honoria said, pleased that she could answer to the false name without her voice shaking. "I'm so glad you met with me."

Femi turned to the silver-haired man who had accompanied her. "Get me some califf tea and two slices of nutbread along with a salad—whatever their specialty is today."

The silver-haired man bowed, an oddly formal response that seemed appropriate somehow. He retreated to a nearby table. Instead of going inside, he used the tabletop menu to place Femi's order.

Bodyguards. Somehow Honoria had expected more.

But they weren't really guarding Femi's person so much as the jewels she wore on it, and the jewels she might carry back to her office with her if this meeting went well.

"You realize that I deal only in the rare and unusual," Femi said to Honoria.

"Yes." Honoria swallowed. Femi had always dealt in the rare and unusual. And with the same sensitivity she was now showing Honoria.

Femi leaned back in her chair. Her waterbeads clicked even more. "I am not pleased when anyone wastes my time. So, if you're uncertain, call it off now."

Honoria smiled faintly. "I will not waste your time."

The robotic waiter floated over and set Femi's tea down. A light flared on the table, probably telling her about her food, but Honoria couldn't read what the words said. Apparently the restaurant was familiar with Femi, and didn't have to use all available human languages to communicate with her.

As Femi dropped bits of imported apple into her tea, Honoria leaned over and removed the jewel display case from her bag. She set the case on the table, opened the lid, and took off the velvet top.

The gems she'd purchased with all that remained of her own money glittered on the surface. Femi leaned forward, clearly intrigued.

"Prices?" she asked.

"Which are you interested in?" Honoria's mouth was so dry that she could barely speak. She had to avoid looking at the hunk of uncut turquoise in the center. Instead she watched Femi's fingers.

If they didn't touch the turquoise, then Honoria would have to, and oddly, she didn't want to.

"Well, I need to look at the pieces. Do you mind if I pick them up?" Femi had already taken out her jeweler's loupe. She was reaching for a ten-carat ruby before Honoria could even answer her.

"Please do," Honoria said.

Femi sorted through the gems, picking up some, setting them down without looking at them through the loupe, and then picking up others. She avoided the turquoise.

"The oldest piece I have is the turquoise," Honoria finally said, unable to stand the suspense.

"Turquoise is low-end." Femi's voice held a sneer.

"Not in the Earth Alliance," Honoria said, trying to keep the panic that was swelling in her out of her face.

Femi shrugged. "We're not in the Earth Alliance."

She reached for the glitterstone next to the turquoise, and as she did, one of her waterbeads clicked against the turquoise's shell.

Honoria stiffened.

"Interesting sound," Femi said, her fingers moving away from the glitterstone. "Are you sure it's turquoise? Each precious gem has a tone, you know, and that just doesn't seem like the one I'd expect."

"It's turquoise," Honoria said.

"I don't think so." Femi's thumb and forefinger clamped onto the rough edges.

Honoria's breath caught. She thought of her mother and her father and her little brother, barely a year old when he died, and even with their images in her head, she realized she was terrified.

She did not want to die terrified.

She bowed her head, willing herself to remain calm, as the bomb went off.

6

Arek Soseki stood in the center of the Armstrong Cultural Center, his hands on his hips. The great hall was cold, as if someone had turned the environmental controls to frigid.

Above him, the ceiling blended into the dome. The designers of the center had decided to replace the official dome with material of their own. Even though Armstrong's dome changed color throughout a twenty-four-hour day, mimicking the light on Earth, the dome in the cultural center followed the Moon's day, and soon the two weeks of sunlight would begin.

Soseki would have preferred the two weeks of night. The great hall, which had been designed to bring out different features in the extremes of light and dark, looked better under the blackness of a Moon night.

But he had no choice in the timing of these meetings. In one week, diplomats from Earth Alliance would hold their own meetings in this building.

Soseki had to make certain the place was secure.

He hated the fact that the diplomats had chosen his city for their meeting. It meant extra police presence, more work for the Port Authority, more work for the dome patrol. He had to monitor for troubles coming in on the bullet trains as well as any possible crazies with political motivations.

And not just crazies from one culture but crazies from dozens of cultures. Humans who might hate the Alliance, Distys who might not want the Peyti evaluating the scenario, the Rev, who seemed to believe that the Alliance wasn't strong enough, and hundreds of others, all of whom had their own agenda.

He hadn't planned for any of this when he had run for mayor of Armstrong. Naïve him, he had thought the job would entail running the city, not dealing in intergalactic politics.

Of course, if anything did go wrong, he would get the blame. Just like he would get the blame for the high price tag on all the security, the extra money these handful of diplomats were costing his city. A few extra press would show up, but only for a few days. This was being billed as a routine negotiation, nothing the citizenry of the Alliance needed to pay attention to.

Of course, if this meeting went well, then more diplomats would come, the meetings would continue, and no one else would be able to use the cultural center for more than a month.

Soseki paced the room, gazing at the walls. All of the great Moon artists had work here. The fragile pieces came out during the night phase, replaced by works specifically designed to hold up against the powerful sunshine coming in the dome. The art was part of his problem with the timing—he didn't care for most of the day pieces.

He passed a sculpture made from discarded permaplastic tiles. The sculptor had taken the tiles, cut them, and used them like bent straws. Soseki passed the work quickly, moving on to an oil depicting one of the first astronauts staring at the Earth. The oil had been placed so that when the Earth was visible through the dome above, the viewer mimicked the position of the astronaut on the regolith. A person looking at a painting of a person looking at the Earth, with the real Earth in the background.

He let himself into one of the side rooms. It smelled stale and musty. Normally, he would set this room up for press, but he had been assured no press would cover this meeting. The door at the back of the room led to a cafeteria. He pulled that door open, and stopped.

Half a dozen people stood inside, many of them lifting wire shelves.

"What's going on?" Soseki asked. He had thought he would have the building to himself this afternoon, except, of course, for the people who always staffed the place.

A tiny woman approached him. She was wearing all white, which accented her golden skin and her dark brown eyes. Her black hair was tucked under a nearly invisible net.

She stuck out her hand. "Nitara Nicolae. You hired me to provide lunches for the upcoming Earth Alliance conference."

He took her hand. Her skin was dry and smooth, and unusually warm.

"Arek Soseki," he said, even though she clearly knew who he was. "And I think 'provide lunches' is an understatement. I wanted you to show them the best of Armstrong cuisine."

She smiled, which added laugh lines to her small face. He wondered how old she was, knowing it was impossible to really figure out her age. With enhancements and genetic upgrades, people could look nearly a century younger than they were.

"I'll do my best," she said, "given this primitive kitchen."

He studied it. It didn't look primitive to him. The stove alone was beyond anything he could handle. Five times the size of the stove in the mayor's mansion, this one had cooling trays and heating units and an actual oven in the center, just like the old-fashioned stoves he'd seen from early colonial pictures.

Nicolae put her hands on her hips and studied the long, rectangular room as if she hadn't seen it before. Her assistants set down the steel shelves, and one man leaned against a long steel table. Another leaned against the double doors leading into the refrigeration and freezer units.

The city had already spent a lot of money on this kitchen—the equipment in here was so high-class that the designer of the center had had to defend his choices in a series of public speeches.

"This place is designed for cooks, not for chefs," Nicolae said.

Soseki, at least, knew the difference between the two. "Yes. It's a cafeteria kitchen."

"I suppose I could work in my own kitchen and bring the items here. But they'd lose their freshness."

"If you make changes here, I'll have to authorize a new inspection," Soseki said, hoping she wouldn't take him up on the offer. "It's not very convenient."

"Neither is cooking in two different locations." Her words were soft, as if she were speaking to herself instead of him. "Let me consider my options, and I'll contact you."

Then she turned toward him, a look of bemusement on her face.

"Although," she said, "I suppose you are not the person I should be dealing with. I'm sure the mayor's office has some sort of liaison for this?"

He nodded. "I'll have her contact you."

Nicolae smiled. "You're just here because . . . ?"

Because his entire career could rest on this one meeting, and the whole damn thing was out of his control. He wanted to cancel it; he wished it had never happened; he wished these outsiders would simply go away and leave him alone.

But he said none of that.

"I'm a hands-on mayor," he said. "I like to know what my people have planned."

"Hmm." Her smile faded a bit. She was less interested in his answer than she was in fixing her kitchen.

He almost felt as though he didn't exist—something that hadn't happened to him in years.

"I'll leave you to your work," he said, and went back through the press room to the great hall of the cultural center.

Many of the sculptures had been moved from their usual places in the center of the room to accommodate the large table that the diplomats had insisted on. He didn't like that change either.

In fact, visiting the center had made him grumpier. He had thought it might calm him.

The last thing he wanted was for Armstrong to lose clout under his reign. This meeting was going to be about him and his city whether he liked it or not—most accords carried the names of the places in which they were made—and he wanted history to be kind to him. He did have ambitions that extended beyond this dome. He had to make certain they weren't thwarted by an economic scandal, a political debacle, or a failed diplomatic event.

Somehow, he had to show himself to be a leader equal to or greater than the politicians and their minions who were coming to Armstrong.

He just had to figure out how.

7

Assistant Chief of Detectives Noelle DeRicci pulled up at the crime scene with a sense of anticipation. It had been nearly a year since she had worked a case—a real case, not just visiting a scene to rubber-stamp what her subordinates had done. When she had accepted the promotion to assistant chief (and it really wasn't a promotion; it was more like an elevation: She had flown over dozens of people who had gone up the ladder one rung at a time), she hadn't expected a desk job.

After all, she wasn't the only assistant chief. She was one of six, and at least four of them still worked in the field.

But DeRicci was a celebrity now. She had, in the words of her boss, Andrea Gumiela, "single-handedly saved the city of Armstrong from sheer disaster." Only it hadn't been single-handedly, and it really hadn't been her.

The promotion had its good and bad points. She got paid a lot more, so she was able to move to an apartment that actually had windows. She also got a lot of free meals and some free travel, since she was going all over the Moon, talking to civic groups and other domed-community leaders about the crisis at the Moon Marathon.

She had become an authority on dome living and crime prevention in the enclosed city, and she rather liked it. She hadn't realized how vain she was—she actually liked the nice clothes (provided by the city and purchased by a woman whose job it was to make sure city spokespeople reflected well on Armstrong), and the makeup, and even the expensive haircut.

Despite the perks, she missed the hands-on work, the way she had to think on her feet, the challenges that being in the field actually brought.

So when Gumiela poked her head into DeRicci's office—a corner office with windows that had an excellent view of the entire city—and gave her the assignment, DeRicci's heart did a little flip-flop, since she didn't dare dance for joy.

She had gotten the assignment because two of the victims were respected members of the community, one a well-known doctor and the other a big-time judge. Gumiela wanted someone who would handle this with efficiency and aplomb—words that Gumiela would never have used about DeRicci eighteen months ago, but seemed to associate with her now.

I'd have taken the case myself, Gumiela had said, *but I really do believe you're the better detective.*

Which was true, but it was also a heads-up to DeRicci. This case could have problems associated with it, problems that might cause her to lose this lovely post with all its strange little perks.

She was parking one of the perks now, a state-of-the-art aircar, imported last month from Earth. Only senior officials got these things, and then only the senior officials who insisted on driving themselves. DeRicci always drove herself. She liked the solitude, and she really hated having to rely on someone else.

Which she would have to do anyway on this case. The moment the primary detective identified the victims, Gumiela informed him that he would have a new partner.

DeRicci knew that if she had received that message from Gumiela, she would have resented it. Had resented it, in fact, the two times Gumiela had done it to her in the past.

The parking protocol was programmed into the air-car. She just had to state aloud the name of the street, and the car found the best place for a person in her position to park. Apparently that was right in front of the sidewalk leading to the building's main door.

The other police cars were parked a block away—no obvious official presence was allowed in this neighborhood—but apparently that didn't include people of DeRicci's rank.

The car landed with a bump. DeRicci waited until the engine shut off and the exhaust released, having learned from startling experience not to get out until the last of the air was discharged. She took this moment to study the neighborhood.

Upscale, but she'd known that when she got the assignment. She'd worked a few cases here before, but it had been a long time since she'd been in the area.

The neighborhood was known as the Edge, even though the name no longer applied. Once upon a time, the neighborhood had bumped up against the newest section of the dome—back when the city engineers had toyed with making the dome rectangular instead of circular. That experiment had failed rather spectacularly, if DeRicci recalled her history right, nearly causing a full-scale collapse of the dome itself.

The engineers had redesigned, the dome had gotten bigger, and the Edge moved closer and closer to the middle of the city, what would have been an unremarkable place if the neighborhood hadn't been able to maintain its character.

But it had, partly because no one wanted to tear down these magnificent old apartment buildings. They had been built more than a century ago, using imported Earth materials—brick made from Earth materials, not Moon regolith, so the color was an unusual white, stone taken from quarries, and even, DeRicci had heard, wood, which was the most expensive material of all.

Nothing in these buildings was fake; nothing was made of plastic. All of the materials were Earth-based and imported, expensive and impossible to replicate.

DeRicci felt a sense of anticipation as she opened her car door and put one expensively booted foot onto the pavement. She wasn't dressed for a crime scene; she was dressed for her desk job.

She adjusted the jacket over her shoulders, buttoned the top button so the damn thing wouldn't fall off, and headed up the cobblestone sidewalk—another affectation, apparently, of the old neighborhood.

No one stood outside, but then again, she wasn't sure if unis were allowed on the lawns of these grand old buildings. She hurried across the cobblestone, amazed that anyone would choose it to line a walkway, and reached for the brass handle on the larger-than-necessary front door.

The door swung open, somehow missing her, but not startling her. A tall, broad-shouldered woman wearing a bright red uniform that DeRicci didn't recognize frowned.

"State your business." The woman's voice was low-pitched and filled with a subtle threat.

A doorman. DeRicci had never encountered one before. She had heard that there were buildings throughout Armstrong that still kept that affectation—usually a redundant system, since most expensive places had security that made Dome Security seem like they were amateurs.

"Assistant Chief of Detectives," DeRicci said loudly enough to be heard by every busybody on the street. "I understand you allowed a murderer inside?"

The doorman blanched. She held the door open, and DeRicci stepped in.

The air was cooler here than dome standard, but the coolness had an odd edge to it, as if something other than the environmental systems caused it. The lobby itself was surprisingly small—about twice the size of DeRicci's office—and had a row of metal rectangles on one wall with numbers marked in script

along the top, and a large black desk that nearly hid
a bank of elevators. Staircases curved upward on either side of the desk, flowing like a stream. They were
the lobby's most dominant feature, and built cleverly
to hide the elevator banks. Artwork covered the walls
on each stair, and gold-covered (or were they brass?)
banisters ran along the inside edge.

The effect was breathtaking, partly because of the
lobby's close quarters, and DeRicci struggled not to
show that she was impressed.

"Where do I go?" DeRicci asked the doorman, who
seemed to be the only person manning this amazing
room.

"Fourth floor." The woman seemed to have recovered from DeRicci's rudeness. "And on your way
down, use the back exit. This entrance is for owners
and guests only."

"Owners and guests," DeRicci repeated. "Guess
you'll have to count me as a guest of the deceased. I'm
not using any servants' exit just because you have to."

The doorman's rather expressive skin flushed this
time. "I will be reporting this to your superior,
Officer—?"

"See?" DeRicci said. "That's where you fall down
on your job. I am the superior, and I told you that
first thing. I'm here to check on my subordinates.
There will be a lot of police, and even more official
types coming to do forensic analysis and crime-scene
investigation. You will treat them kindly and you will
not force them to use the back door. Otherwise, I will
speak to *your* superior. Do you understand?"

The doorman nodded, the color fleeing again. She
seemed smaller than she had when she had pushed
the door open. DeRicci would have thought that a
person like that would have been used to terrible
treatment from the folks who lived here, but apparently not.

DeRicci skirted around the desk and headed for the
elevator banks, which looked more imposing the
closer she got. They had a cage in front, made of some

kind of black wire twisted into a floral pattern. De-Ricci had never seen anything so strange or useless before, but then she supposed that was what extreme wealth was all about—finding new and even more ridiculous ways to impress the neighbors.

As DeRicci stepped onto the shiny black area in front of the elevator, the cage door opened. Or rather, it folded against itself until it no longer blocked her way.

She shook her head slightly, sighed, and stepped inside, commanding the elevator to take her to the fourth floor.

The elevator bounced to a stop. The door on the fourth floor was not a cage (for which she was quite grateful), and it slid back the way elevator doors were supposed to, revealing a long, narrow hallway lit by globe-shaped artificial lights.

Half a dozen doors marked the hallway, like doors in a cheap hotel. Only the artwork on the walls—all of it original, none of it familiar—took away the hotel illusion.

To DeRicci's surprise, none of the doors were open. Usually, in an investigation, the door to a crime scene remained open for hours, maybe even days, as the police and the techs filed their way through. But here, no one stood in the hallway and no door revealed which apartment she needed, giving DeRicci a moment of worry that she had gotten off on the wrong floor.

She blinked twice, checking the download that Gumiela had given her link. The information ran along the bottom of her vision, confirming that yes, indeed, DeRicci needed to be on the fourth floor. At apartment 4011, to be exact.

That apartment was at the very end of the hall, directly across from the elevator. The door was unlocked, but closed. Only the bolt from an old-fashioned (and, DeRicci guessed, mostly decorative) dead bolt kept the door from closing entirely.

She reached into the pockets of her skirt and removed the thin gloves she'd remembered to bring. That was the other problem with the new work clothes—now that she was back at the old job, she had to remember things she had once carried automatically, or that had been part of her daily outfit.

When she reached the door, she knocked once, then eased it open and stepped inside.

The smell hit her first—blood, feces, decay. The bodies had been here awhile. Her eyes watered—she was out of practice—but her gorge didn't rise.

The entry was as narrow as the door, and then opened into a wide living room. A plant had been knocked over onto what looked like a real wood floor, leaving a water trail that had whitened against the polish.

People crowded the interior, two backs she didn't recognize, clothed in detective black, and several more wearing uniforms. A few techs had already arrived, and they were standing near the wall, apparently waiting for someone to tell them it was their turn.

"Hey!" DeRicci called, amazed no one had heard her knock. "I'm looking for Detective Cabrera."

All the people she could see turned toward her, their faces registering the same amount of surprise. She could have given them the same look in return—after all, she'd never seen such a lack of attention at a crime scene before.

A whip-thin man with a narrow face was the only person who turned all the way around. He took a step toward her. He was wearing detective black, clothing that wouldn't show the wear from a crime scene.

"I'm Sergio Cabrera," he said.

He had a deep voice with just a hint of an accent, something that suggested he wasn't an Armstrong native. His eyes were a dark brown, and turned downward, as did his mouth. Lines that ran from his nose to his chin made him seem even sadder than he probably was.

"Noelle DeRicci." She stuck out her gloved hand. "I'm the assistant chief assigned to this case."

His expression cooled even more.

"The hero," he said with just enough sarcasm for her to hear it, and yet still wonder if she had made a mistake.

She shrugged a single shoulder. "I'm supposed to partner with you on this."

"I don't need an overseer," he said, and she heard echoes of her own voice in that.

"I agree." She clasped her hands behind her back so that she wouldn't be tempted to touch anything. "However, Andrea Gumiela believes this one is going to be political, and she always likes to have a hand in when something is political. Be glad it's my hand and not hers."

Cabrera turned away from DeRicci, not even acknowledging her last statement. She suppressed a sigh, finally understanding what it was like to be on the receiving end of that treatment.

"Detective," she snapped, "I am going to be primary on this case. You will have to partner with me, and we will work it together."

He looked at her over his shoulder. "I already have a partner."

"Who will assist," DeRicci said.

He stared at her for the longest time. She knew the next sentence she'd have to utter, and it was one she didn't want to speak. She'd have to relieve him if he was going to be difficult.

"All right then," he said after a moment. "Let's get to work."

DeRicci pushed past Cabrera and into the ring of people looking at the mess in the living room. And it was a mess. Three bodies, a man and two women, sprawled on the polished real-wood floor. Blood had congealed everywhere. Spatter had hit the sofa, the antique chairs, the wall.

"The scene's already been recorded," a woman said beside her. "We've got all the angles and the layouts, as well as the trajectory analysis and the spatter patterns."

DeRicci didn't even look to see who was speaking. She didn't care how many times the scene had been recorded. That was nothing like actually observing it, seeing what really happened through all of her senses.

"Everyone vacate the room," she said. "I need some time alone here."

"Ionia already told you that the scene's been recorded."

DeRicci didn't have to turn around to know who was talking to her. She already knew Cabrera's accented sarcastic tones as if she'd been listening to them for months.

"I don't like giving orders twice," DeRicci said, without referring to Cabrera. "I'd like some time alone with the scene."

"It's not procedure to leave one person in the room with the bodies," Ionia—who had to be the partner—said. She was standing beside DeRicci, one of those thin, intense women who wore her intelligence like a shield.

DeRicci had a few tricks of her own. "You are?"

"Detective Ionia Vasco," she said with just enough crispness that DeRicci half expected a salute.

"Cabrera's partner."

"Yes, sir."

DeRicci nodded. "Well, Detective Vasco, I'm Assistant Chief DeRicci, and I'm your partner's new partner. You've been demoted, for this case only, to gofer. It's not a fun position and it's not one I would have chosen for you, so if you have any complaints, bring them up with Chief Gumiela. Until then, you don't get to lecture me on crime-scene behavior. Is that clear?"

Vasco drew herself up so that she stood even straighter. DeRicci didn't think the human back could be so straight without some kind of artificial aid.

"Yes, sir," Vasco said.

"Good." DeRicci looked at the crime scene again. No one else moved. "I ordered everyone to leave. Must I take badge numbers?"

This time Vasco sighed. She nodded to the rest of the team, and they filed out.

DeRicci closed her eyes for a moment, shut down all but her emergency links (she'd been forbidden from ever shutting down her emergency links again—apparently she'd done it too much in the past), and then took a few deep breaths to calm herself.

Then she opened her eyes and really looked at the scene before her.

Expensive, comfortable room, which she hadn't expected. She had always thought the two things were mutually exclusive. The art on the walls was Earth-based, showing a preference for centuries-old Japanese prints. DeRicci wouldn't have recognized them if it weren't for a smuggling case she'd had years ago, which had taught her more about Earth-based art than she ever wanted to know.

Most of the prints were reproductions—valuable in their own right—but a series across the wall to the left of the window appeared to be original. The perp hadn't touched the art. Maybe he hadn't known how valuable it was, or maybe it hadn't interested him.

But, DeRicci had learned, each detail at a crime scene could be important. She wouldn't know which detail solved the case until she was deep inside it.

She pressed a chip on the back of her hand, starting her own vid of the crime scene. She was going to make a contemporaneous log of her observations, partly so that she wouldn't have to remember what she thought was important, and partly so that she'd have a report for Gumiela long before returning to the office.

The spatter rose above the art on the far wall. The windows were covered with light spray, and the spray arched against the ceiling. The couch and the reading chair below the nearest window had indentations on them, apparently from someone's weight, but those indentations were covered with spatter.

And the spatter contained more than blood. In at least one area, she saw gray debris—brain matter—and something white that was probably bone.

She hadn't examined the bodies yet—they were always last because they trumped everything else in the room—so she didn't know which, if any of them, had a gaping exit wound.

The tabletops had several items on them. A few bronze sculptures, which also seemed Earth-based but not Japanese. American Indian, unless she missed her guess—and she very well might, considering how cursory her knowledge was. There were also boxes, some of them nesting boxes, and most curiously of all, books.

The books were thick and heavy, their paper edges yellow with age. DeRicci peered around the corner, looking down a long, narrow hallway that led to the rest of the apartment. Sure enough, the hallway was lined with bookshelves. The books themselves looked like nothing DeRicci had ever seen before. They were all thick, with the same color cover and gold lettering on the spine. They seemed to be some kind of matched set.

She turned her attention back to the main room. Four books, one on each of the four tables, and no obvious screens. No holo matrices or security screens or even group vid screens. It was as if this room hadn't been touched by modern technology.

The thought made her uneasy, although she wasn't sure why. She'd heard of people who lived like this, and she'd seen vid tours of retro homes whose inhabitants had reverted to primitive precomputer styles, but she'd never actually seen one before.

She'd have to search later to see if her assumption was right. She also knew that a lot of people bought faux retro furniture with screens built in but hidden. It might tell her a lot about these victims just to see if they chose to be truly retro or only pretended to be.

DeRicci closed her eyes again, only this time not to reset, but to concentrate on her other senses. The smells she'd noted when she first entered the apartment—blood, feces, decay—were still here, still present, but not as powerful because she had grown used to them. She sniffed, hoping to sense other odors, ones that weren't as expected or as obvious.

She caught a hint of something acrid, like smoke or

burned food, and the scent of singed hair. She took a deep breath and tried to filter the smells out. Her link could do that—she'd been given some very expensive equipment with her promotion—but she preferred not to use it. She wanted to get the information herself.

Acrid smoke, singed hair, and perfume—faint, but only in the context of the other overpowering smells. The perfume had a heady, musky odor, one that seemed embedded in the room. She suspected if she went deeper into the apartment, that perfume scent would return to its dominant status.

The apartment was amazingly quiet. Two windows across from her overlooked the street, and yet' there was no traffic noise, no conversation. Of course, this street had more regulations than most—she'd figured that out before she'd even parked—but still, she should have heard sirens or horns or the other every-day sounds of Armstrong, amplified by being this far up. Sound bounced against the dome.

Yet there was nothing. She couldn't even hear the conversation Cabrera's team had to be having outside the apartment, and she would wager that they hadn't closed the door all the way. Maybe that was why they had all seemed so surprised when she entered.

The apartment was soundproofed.

How very odd. She had encountered soundproofing only a few times outside of the docks, and it surprised her every time. Why live in a city if you wanted to block out all of its noises? She had never understood that part of human nature.

The apartment had no real sounds of its own either. The silence was so intense that she could hear the raggedness of her own breathing. She held her breath and listened, hearing nothing more than a slight hum and the ever-so-faint thud-thud of her own heart.

DeRicci opened her eyes and finally looked down at the corpses. They had fallen in interesting and unex-pected ways. None of them was near the furniture, which meant that they were standing in the center of the room at the time of death.

The man was closest to DeRicci. He was older. He only had one wound—in the center of his torso, leaving him with a hole instead of a chest. His hands had been flung back. They were open, palms up, the fingers curled, and they rested next to his face.

His eyes were open and clouded over, suggesting—like the smell—that the bodies had been discovered a long time after death.

One of the women had fallen near him. She was also older, her features seemingly unenhanced. She had landed on her side, her arm extended, her feet bent unnaturally backward. Her wound was also in her torso, large and open, revealing a few intact ribs.

One of her feet had landed in the third corpse's hair. That hair was some kind of brownish silver, and shiny, seemingly untouched by blood, even though DeRicci knew that couldn't have happened. She just couldn't see the spatter from where she stood.

The hair belonged to a woman—DeRicci could tell that by the corpse's relatively untouched body, her clothing, and her legs, but certainly not by her face.

Her face was gone.

The wound seemed bigger than the wounds on the other two, which led DeRicci to believe it might be an exit wound. She couldn't tell, not without examining the corpses up close. Before she did that, she would call Cabrera and his pompous little team back into the room, so that they could see her do hands-on analysis of the bodies.

First DeRicci turned her links back on and downloaded the information Gumiela had given her.

The apartment belonged to Judge Caleb Lahiri and his wife, Dr. Mimi Lahiri. Their only son, Calbert Lahiri, had committed suicide more than a year before. They had a daughter, Carolyn Lahiri, who had recently been pardoned by the government of Etae for war crimes. She was listed as Disappeared.

The corpses, Gumiela surmised, belonged to the Lahiris, although no one knew who the third corpse was. Even before she downloaded the visuals on the

Lahiris, DeRicci already knew that they were the elderly couple before her.

The person without the face was the one whose identity she didn't know. Had someone wanted to keep it that way? Surely that person would understand that DNA would provide the answers.

DeRicci stared at all three of them for a long moment. The bodies hadn't been moved, and they weren't in any ritual death positions, like she might find with a Disty vengeance killing or a Guine death ritual.

Sometimes she could tell what happened at a scene just from body position—a parent's body cradling a child's, or one corpse covered with the blood of another.

But there was so much blood here—all of it pooling and coagulating—that she couldn't tell what belonged to whom. And the wounds were so broad and vicious that spatter wouldn't help in these instances either, not until the medical examiner did the proper testing.

She couldn't even tell from body position who had died first. None of the three corpses had fallen against the others. They didn't touch one another, and nothing on the floor had splattered upward, coating one corpse and not another. It would take tests and studies and computer models of splatter patterns to figure out who had died first and why the others hadn't tried to stop the killer.

DeRicci frowned. Perhaps the answer was here after all. Killers didn't usually change methods of operation in the middle of a crime scene, not without sending some kind of message.

She wasn't sure what it meant that two of the corpses had been shot in the torso and one had been shot in the face. She had assumed, at first, that the victim had been shot in the face to avoid identification, but the only way that could have truly happened would be if the entire body were removed.

She slipped her hand in her pocket to grab a bag for her shoes—she wasn't wearing the kind that coated automatically—and then she realized that she hadn't carried any of those bags. Either she would have to go out front and get some from the team, or she'd have to quit right here.

But she wasn't ready to quit. So she backed away from the crime scene, then turned in the narrow entry—which had no spatter, as far as she could tell—and leaned out the main door.

"Shoe bags?" she asked one of the nearby techs.

The woman started as if DeRicci had surprised her. So even the area around the door was soundproofed. That was interesting. The killer would have had to know that, just as he (she? it?) would have had to know how to get around the doorman downstairs.

The tech frowned at DeRicci as if she hadn't understood the question. DeRicci extended her hand.

"Shoe bags," she repeated.

The tech's frown deepened. Then she nodded once and reached into her kit. She removed two very old, very crumpled bags.

DeRicci hoped they would do.

She bent down, wrapped them around her shoes, hit the "fit" chip at the edge of the bags, and watched them mold to her. Then she nodded and headed back inside.

The smell of feces and old blood hit her again, but this time she recognized the perfume scent beneath it. Little trickles of light came from the lights recessed into the ceiling, but no dust motes filtered through.

This place was startlingly clean, except in the living area, where the victims had died. DeRicci made a note to check the cleaning system; she wondered what it had picked up in the time that the bodies had been left alone.

Then she stepped back into the main room. The light was slightly different here—a bit came through the windows, that almost too-bright light that simulated Earth's midday. She walked around the area where she had stood before and headed toward the side of the faceless body—she wanted to get as close to it as possible.

Uncarpeted floors were usually slick, and even though this one appeared to be made of real wood, it was no different. DeRicci picked her way across it, trying not to step in spatter and trace, but knowing she probably was. She did not touch the furniture to keep her balance; instead, she moved very slowly.

The slickness actually pleased her—it fit into a theory she was just beginning to develop.

She stopped as close as she could to the faceless corpse without stepping into what she was beginning to think of as the sacred circle. The furniture had been set up so that each piece faced another, leaving an opening in the center, the place where the Lahiris and the woman had died.

DeRicci crouched between two of the chairs, and then, carefully, peered beneath them.

More spatter, which did not surprise her, and little else, which did. There was something that had cleaned this apartment—be it a person (which might make sense, given this neighborhood's emphasis on old-fashioned living), a robotic cleaner, or automatic cleaning programs built into each surface.

There were problems with all three systems, but none of them should have failed on this catastrophic a level. Since the Lahiris and their guest had been dead for a few days, the cleaning system—all except a human one—should have gotten rid of the spatter and the rest of the mess.

Or, in the case of the most sophisticated systems, called the police to deal with the crime scene.

Yet this system seemed to have cleaned up the dust and avoided the corpses in the center of the room. The cleaning pattern made no sense to DeRicci at all.

From her crouched position, she peered as best she could under the rest of the furniture. Each piece had curved legs that raised the furniture a few inches off the ground. She could see shapes, mostly, or the flat floor, although one or two pieces were simply dark underneath.

What she couldn't see—at least from this vantage—was a weapon. She had thought there was a good possibility one would be on the floor somewhere.

Because she might have been wrong when she initially arrived. The third corpse might not be the victim of another killer. The third corpse could easily be a suicide.

She'd seen that before—people shot in the torso or abdomen, and then the killer shooting herself. Usually the shooter pointed the gun at some part of the face—inside the mouth, against the temple—and often, given the strength of most weapons available in Armstrong, blew the face (or the head) right off.

DeRicci's legs had started to ache. She was no longer used to remaining in this position for a long time.

Still, she remained crouched. The unknown corpse's hair sprawled away from her as if it had a life of its own. Her face was gone, and she had fallen backward, her legs curled slightly as they no longer had to support her weight.

Her hands were flung outward. Any weapon held in them would have slipped across the floor.

Unless she dropped the weapon as she fell. Unless she had landed on top of it.

DeRicci stood. Her thighs ached.

Time to bring in that second investigator. Time to bring in the entire team.

She had to start moving furniture and corpses.

If there was a weapon in this room, a weapon that had fallen near the unknown woman's body, then DeRicci's first theory of the crime became the working theory.

She felt a surge of excitement and willed it away.

The investigation had begun.

8

Four days after Carolyn Lahiri left with her parents, Flint came back from lunch to find a strange woman outside his office.

She was sitting on the makeshift sidewalk, her legs extended across the dirt-covered permaplastic, her back against the door. His alarms hadn't gone off, so she hadn't tried the knob, but he suspected that his security system was flashing all sorts of warnings inside.

Flint studied her from half a block away. She didn't appear to be aware that he was watching her. She had a hat pulled down over her face, her hands folded across her stomach.

If he didn't know better, he would have thought she was sleeping.

He could use the back entrance, search through the last few hours' recordings, plus the perimeter alarms, and see who she was. But he suspected that she wanted him to go around, wanted to see how he got inside without using the front door. He wasn't going to give her that advantage, particularly when he could get the same information with a bit of patience once he let himself in through the front.

He headed down the street, feeling a bit loggy, wishing he hadn't eaten both halves of the sandwich that he'd bought at the neighborhood grocery.

From several meters away, he deactivated the door's main locks and set the security system on standby. He didn't want the woman to see how he did that either. The system changed silently, so she wouldn't know what he had done.

She didn't move as everything changed behind her, so nothing in her links told her about the change—at least, nothing that she let on to.

He stopped a meter away from her. "Can I help you?"

She didn't move. For one brief moment, he wondered if she was dead. He resisted the urge to go closer, to push her with his foot.

"Miss," he said, "are you okay?"

This time, apparently, he spoke loudly enough for her to hear him. Or to figure out that she should pretend to be awake. She slid her hat back with a single pointed finger.

Her face was familiar, angular with dusky skin and uptilted, almond-shaped eyes. Her nose was broad and delicately tattooed with faint snakelike lines. The overall effect was funky and attractive.

She smiled at him, a reaction he hadn't expected.

"Miles Flint," she said.

He hadn't been at this kind of disadvantage since he'd become a Retrieval Artist. It felt odd not to know whom he was talking to. "Have we met?"

She shook her head, brushed her hands on her tan pants, and stood. "I'm Ki Bowles. I work for Inter-Dome Media."

InterDome Media, the biggest media conglomerate on the Moon. InterDome specialized in information programming for every form of media in dome use, from vids to net-text to links.

"Doing what?" Flint asked.

Her eyebrows rose, then she smiled. The smile was warm and genuine—something that seemed to surprise her more than it surprised him. "You honestly don't know? I thought you knew everything."

"I can open my link and pretend I know everything," he said, "or we can have a conversation, like people used to do before everything was downloaded for them."

"Mmm." Her eyes twinkled. Definitely attractive. "You have an edge."

More of an edge than she realized, especially with someone who played games.

"I asked you a question," he said.

"One which no one has asked me in nearly ten years, and it's refreshing to hear it." She took off her hat and shook down her hair. It was silver, black, and purple, with curls that seemed too perfect to be real.

The hair clinched it. She looked familiar because he'd seen her on the vids. But he wasn't going to let her see that he'd finally recognized her.

Her smile slowly faded. "I work for InterDome as an investigative reporter. I do have my own show, but it's weekly. However, I do stories daily, and I do the work myself."

As if that were unusual. But maybe it was for investigative reporters. It certainly wasn't for Retrieval Artists.

"And you thought I had enough time to watch the vids."

She shrugged. "I had heard that Retrieval Artists—the good ones—didn't work much."

True enough, but he wasn't going to comment. For all he knew, he was being filmed, which was something he didn't want.

"You're blocking the door to my office," he said.

"Oh." She moved aside. "I didn't mean to."

He mounted the half sidewalk that someone had installed decades ago, then opened the office door. As Bowles started to follow him, he pulled the door closed.

He had been right: The warning lights were whirling

all through the interior. All of the screens on his desk were up, and as he went around, he saw that images had piled on top of images.

She had been waiting for a while.

He pulled out his keyboard, tapped the code, and the warning lights went off. Then he saved the material on the screens, and let them slide back into the desk. Only one remained up, and on it, he watched Ki Bowles in real time as she stared at the closed door.

She seemed perplexed, as if she had never had a door slammed in her face.

Her head moved as she searched the sides of the door for some kind of ringer or intercom. She wouldn't find one. After a moment, she knocked.

"It's open," Flint said, enjoying this more than he probably should have.

She grabbed the knob and stepped inside, then stopped just like he expected. She was so hooked up that two more warning systems went off—one on the screen already up and another buzzing through his own link.

He tapped three more keys, setting the security system as high as it went, hoping it would shut off all her links.

The last one shut down and the warning systems vanished.

She touched her right ear, turning slightly. In the artificial light, chips winked all along the ear's lobe and outside edge. Her visible links. She had to have dozens of others that weren't visible.

"What did you do?" She sounded stunned.

"I disconnected you," he said.

"You can't do that." She bit her lower lip, drawing blood.

"Seems I just did."

She shook her head, touched her ear again, then slapped her hand against it. The sound of flesh against flesh was loud and startling.

"Christ," she said. "Why the hell did you do that?"

"Because everything in here is confidential."

"I would've signed a waiver," she said.

"And then I would have had to trust you." Flint pressed one more key and the final screen recessed. "This way, I don't have to trust you at all."

She looked at the door and swallowed hard. She was thinking of running. He wondered how long it had been since she'd been unlinked, and realized it had probably been decades.

"The links'll reboot when you go outside." He expected that to give her enough impetus to leave.

But she didn't.

"I don't do interviews, and I'm not real fond of the media." He leaned back in his chair and folded his hands behind his head.

"I understand that Retrieval Artists really don't want their pictures broadcast all over the known universe."

He nodded, wondering if that was a segue into a threat.

"So I'm not going to do a story on you or any of your colleagues. I'm here because I'd heard that you were the best."

Ah, the familiar flattery. He was getting tired of it. There was no such thing as the best Retrieval Artist. There were just degrees of ethics, degrees of competence, and degrees of desire. He was more ethical than most, more competent than most, and had less desire.

"Yet you recognized me," Flint said.

"You have quite a history with the media," she said. "You had a few high-profile cases for Space Traffic Control, and you gave some interviews. There was coverage of your promotion to detective, which was—is—considered unusual for a traffic cop, and then there were the stories that hit the links when you left the force to join the other side."

"The other side?" he said, not altering his position. Yet his shoulders tensed. He could feel the muscles shift.

"Well, being a Retrieval Artist isn't exactly on the up-and-up, now, is it? If you wanted to find people who've skipped out on their legal obligations and do it for the right reasons, you'd be a Tracker."

"That's a matter of opinion," Flint said. "And, by the way, if you're thinking of writing any of this down when you leave, I consider this entire conversation off the record and confidential. I'll sue InterDome Media, and I have enough money to hire lawyers comparable to InterDome's. I'd win."

"No doubt," she said. "I'm not here to interview you or get information from you. I might be here to hire you."

"Ki Bowles, investigative reporter, needs a Retrieval Artist?" Flint rocked his chair down and leaned forward, elbows on his desk. Now he was intrigued. "I'm not searching out a Disappeared for some story or to help you make a career."

"I'm not sure if this is a career maker," Bowles said. "It's just something that intrigues me, and I have enough knowledge to realize that going after any kind of Disappeared is a dangerous proposition."

"Too dangerous for an intrepid reporter?"

She shoved her hands in pockets. "You know, you're not treating me very fairly. I don't want to get someone killed—or a bunch of someones killed—just because of my curiosity."

That was, he knew, the exact right thing to tell him. Appeal to his integrity, let him know that she shared the same values.

"Yet you were willing to come in here, links on full-tilt, to have this discussion."

She straightened, raising her chin slightly, as if his words stung. "I meant what I said. I don't use material that can harm someone."

"But you let it float around the corporate links so that another person might find it."

Her eyes narrowed. "You don't trust people, do you, Mr. Flint?"

"Should I?"

"You did once," she said. "I saw the footage after your daughter died. Quite the eloquent speaker, getting the day-care center closed down, getting the proprietors arrested, making sure it didn't happen again to any other parent."

His entire body froze. He hoped his expression remained neutral. No one had the right to discuss Emmeline. No one.

But he wasn't going to let Bowles know she had gotten to him.

"Well, then, if you really studied the footage, you'd know that I had already failed. It took a second death for me to understand the pattern. And there was one before Emmeline. A very small, very mundane story when you come down to it."

But painful. So painful that it took work for him to sound calm and dismissive as he spoke to her. He kept his gaze on hers as well, hoping that the pain didn't appear in his eyes—or, if it did, that she wasn't intuitive enough to see it.

"Ah, but fascinating." She took a step toward him, apparently feeling that she had the upper hand now. "It would make a great human-interest piece. The grieving father, driven from his corporate job into the dangerous world of police work, rising through the ranks through passion and desire rather than with a formal police education, and finally achieving the brass ring—a detective's position, where he might actually save other lives just as bright, just as shiny as his daughter's."

Not as bright, not as shiny. Not even close.

But he said nothing.

"And then he lets it all go for reasons no one understands, just walks away, buys a business with money no one knew he had, and starts yet another career, this one to find Disappeareds. Why? What changed, Mr. Flint?"

"I thought this wasn't an interview," he said.

"But you can see my interest." She smiled, and this time the smile was fake. It didn't reach her eyes.

"I can see the amount of work you put into research—or that your assistant put into it."

Her smile faded. "You're not an easy man, Mr. Flint."

"And you're not telling me what you want, Ms. Bowles."

"As I said, I'm thinking about hiring you."

"Not interested. But thanks."

"Hear me out at least."

That he would do, just to satisfy his curiosity.

She bit her lower lip again, a nervous habit that seemed to almost be a tic. He wondered if she had some kind of neurolink that subverted the tic, something he'd shut off.

"I know that Retrieval Artists find Disappeareds," she said, "but I have something a bit more complicated."

"I doubt that's possible," he said.

She walked over to his desk and perched on the edge. He'd had a few potential clients do that before, but never with such ease.

"If I know someone who was raised by a loving family, who grew up believing that she came from one place and had a long history, but through a series of circumstances discovered that all of that history was a lie, could she hire you?"

"Theoretically, I'm sure she could," Flint said. "But there'd be no point. You could handle this, Ms. Investigative Reporter, or some private detective somewhere or an off-duty detective who needs a few extra credits. She certainly wouldn't need me. I'm about as expensive as an investigator gets, and I doubt she'd get the proper return for her money."

"Even if she believes that she might be a Disappeared?"

This time, he let the surprise show on his face. "She doesn't know?"

"She has no memory of her life before she came to her family."

"And now she has this fantasy that she was put into hiding for a reason. Rather like those secret princess stories that children like."

"You're being snide, Mr. Flint."

He nodded. "I don't believe fairy tales. I don't like

them, and here's why. Let's say she's right. Let's say she is Disappeared. Then her parents probably crossed a rather vicious alien race like the Wygnin, who take the firstborn as punishment for a crime against them. The Wygnin have warrants that allow them to take that child until the child's death—and sometimes those warrants extend through generations. If you had me investigate to satisfy this girl's curiosity, then I'd be putting not just her life, but her sanity in jeopardy."

"Sanity?" Bowles asked.

"The Wygnin aren't taking the children out of malice," Flint said. "It's their way of handling problems. In the Wygnin system, someone who is criminal enough to warrant this punishment isn't good enough to raise a child. From what I understand of their system, they often take all the children out of the household."

"I understand the Wygnin system," Bowles said.

"Not if you're asking me about the possibility of this hurting your prospective client's sanity. The Wygnin will take the firstborn, whatever age that child has become, and try to make that person into a Wygnin. Apparently it works with infants, but fully formed humans get broken. No adult has ever come back whole."

Bowles visibly shuddered. "You can't know that she's wanted by the Wygnin."

"I can't think of many reasons to disappear a child," Flint said.

Bowles sighed. "But how could looking hurt?"

"Looking could alert the Wygnin to her presence. Trackers do piggyback on Retrieval Artists, you know. A number of Trackers just follow Retrieval Artists' signatures through the nets, see which case they're hunting out, gather the information at the same time, and sell it back to the authorities."

Bowles raised those magnificent eyebrows again. "And you don't approve of that."

"Of course I don't."

"Because they steal your work?"

"Because they often destroy people who are guilty of nothing more than crushing a flower petal."

"That's a myth," Bowles said. "The aliens we do business with don't kill us because we stepped on a flower."

"The Stlaety do and have," Flint said. "Check the records."

She smiled at him, that phony, glitzy smile she had learned for her job. "I think we're off topic. You were explaining to me why seeing if my friend is a Disappeared is a bad thing."

Flint sighed. He doubted he would convince this woman of anything, but he had to try.

He stood, something he usually didn't do when he was talking to a client.

"Let's assume that your friend is a Disappeared, one who was sent away as a child," he said, wondering if *friend* was truly the right term for the person this reporter knew. "That means that her parents feared for her safety—for her very life—and were willing to give her up rather than lose her to some alien group who threatened her."

"You're sure it was aliens?"

"That's what the disappearance services are for, people who've crossed strange alien laws and don't want to be punished for a minor infraction like—as you said—stepping on a flower."

Bowles frowned. She clearly didn't believe him.

"Other people use the services," Flint said. "Some of them criminals that have committed crimes we consider heinous, but for the most part, the services only deal with helping humans survive an alien punishment."

"For a price," Bowles said, as if that were a bad thing.

"For a price," Flint said. "And, if this woman is a Disappeared, I can tell you a few things about her parents' crime. First, they committed the crime against one of the nastier alien groups—the Wygnin, the

Kafor—the ones that target the children of the so-called criminal instead of the criminal himself."

"What if the parents were dead?"

It was Flint's turn to shrug. "Same thing. Only certain alien groups target the entire family—especially when the offending members are dead. This isn't a small crime, and it's not a small punishment. If your friend was Disappeared, then any contact with her past could get her killed."

Bowles stood too. "This all seems so melodramatic."

Flint glared at her. "It's not. I've seen the effects of these laws. If anything, I'm underestimating the problems here."

"I guess it would be redundant to ask you to take this case. You're going to say no."

"Any reputable Retrieval Artist would," Flint said.

Bowles shook her head. "It seems odd to turn down money like this."

"If you want the information, hire a Tracker," Flint said. "Your friend will die or go to prison, but you'll all know what happened to her and why she's in Armstrong."

"So tough." Bowles grinned at him. "That edge just peeks out from every sentence."

Flint walked around the desk and leaned on the other side of it, just like Bowles had. "This isn't something to play with lightly, Ms. Bowles. Researching a disappearance like this one—if, indeed, that's what this is—could cost not just your friend's life, but several other lives as well. And for what? To satisfy curiosity? That doesn't sound very reporterlike."

"It is very reporterlike," Bowles said. "That's what we do. We ask questions because we're curious. Then we search for answers."

As if it were that noble. Maybe she thought it was. Maybe that was how she went home night after night and slept, thinking her conscience was clean.

"What's your interest in this case?" He used that

edge again, finally getting to the question he wanted answered.

"Friendship." Bowles finally had an edge too, one that made it clear she was willing to take on a verbal battle if she had to.

"If it were friendship," Flint said, "you would have accompanied the mystery woman here, let her ask her questions while you waited outside, and then you would have hugged her as she left. Instead, you're inquiring without her, and you want too many details."

Bowles tilted her head, as if he were a curiosity. The movement made her seem both fascinated and condescending.

"Don't worry," Flint said into her silence. "I'm not going to steal your story. I don't have those kind of connections."

"Then what do you want?" Her voice was cold.

"I want to know why you're following this story. It could be important."

"Of course it could be important," she snapped.

"In ways you don't see." This time he tilted his head and raised his eyebrows.

"I see just fine."

Flint shook his head. "There are a lot of dangers in this business. Let me give you one more. If this woman's family did cross one of the more vicious alien groups, and you do some research in those alien communities, you could become a target too."

"Is that a threat?" Bowles asked.

"No," Flint said. "A fact. And the way the law works, certain aliens are protected even though they're on Armstrong soil. So you could get in trouble with alien laws without even realizing you've done it."

"Why do you care about me?"

"I don't, really." Flint found that he rarely lost anything when he was blunt. It usually helped him. "But I do care about all the people you might put in harm's way."

Her lips thinned. "I'm not insensitive or incompetent."

"Good," he said. "Then tell me your story. Remember, everything discussed in this room is confidential."

"Only your systems are on," she said. "So I have to trust you."

Touché. Obviously, his comment about trust had hurt her. Flint shrugged. "I'm very trustworthy."

She stared at him for a long moment, and then she let out a small laugh. "You're incorrigible, you know that?"

"Yes," he said.

"You're not going to help me, are you?"

"No," he said.

She sighed. "That's it then. Thank you for your time, Mr. Flint."

He didn't say anything as she walked out the door. He stared at it, wondering what she really wanted, and who the possible Disappeared was.

Then he shrugged. He would probably never know.

9

Her first memories are of mud and incredible, powerful
rain. She's chest-deep in the water, arms raised, waiting
for someone to rescue her, to lift her to safety, when
she hears a voice behind her.

"What the hell is that?"

She turns toward the voice and cries piteously—she
doesn't have language yet, or if she does, it has abandoned her—and she sees a big man, broad-shouldered,
a hat dripping the rain around his face.

She cannot see his features—they're a blur of water
and movement—but she can hear his voice as if it's next
to her.

"My God, is that a child?"

Then he steps forward, his boots sloshing in the mud,
his coat dragging behind him. He swoops down, grabs
her by the armpits and lifts her against his cold, soaking
slicker. The water from his hat hits her face, and it
seems cooler somehow, fresher.

"God," he says, indignation in his tone, "who let
this happen?"

And for the first time, she realizes they're surrounded
by Idonae. The aliens are tall, with feelers running
down each side like teeth of a comb. Their chubby
torsos are the only solid thing about them, their feelers
having turned the color of the rain.

"Ain't nothing happen." The Idonae who spoke has a typical raspy dry voice, and it sends shivers through her. *"Nothing happen here."*

The man waves his hand toward the mud he has pulled her from. *"That's not nothing. I count five bodies and a river of blood."*

"Not Idonae," the speaker says and the aliens turn away.

The man juggles her as if she is an already forgotten burden. *"I know they're not Idonae. They're human. They're probably her family, for crissakes."*

And then she looks, really looks, and it is as if her brain works for the first time. Hair floating on top of the mud is long like Mommy's, and a hand with Daddy's ring clasps the edge of the muck as if he's trying to pull himself out.

She groans, and buries her face in the man's shoulder. He puts a hand on her back, holding her in place.

"Not Idonae," the alien says again, with that tone, the one that implies the listener is stupid. *"Perhaps Ynnels done."*

"Ynnels did this?" the man asks, and maybe he is stupid. He sounds stupid, dumbfounded, as if the information is—has to be—somehow false.

"Not Idonae," the alien says again, and walks away, leaving the bodies in the mud.

The man puts his finger beneath her chin and lifts her head toward his. She can finally see his face. He is leaning toward her, and for the first time since he picked her up, his hat shields her as well.

"Child." His voice is gentle, but his face is not. It is flat, skin taut against bone, eyes narrow and dark. Later, she realizes he has allowed the damage to his skin—scars, heat, strange sunlight—to remain, but then she thinks he looks as alien as the rest of them. *"Who did this?"*

She studies that strange face, and for a moment, other faces—softer, rounder, more like hers, beloved faces, with voices that are as gentle as his—come to her mind. She can almost reach them, almost touch them. . . .

And then she buries her face in the man's shoulder, head shaking, and he pats her back, thinking she is crying. But she is not crying. She is waiting for him to decide what to do with her, waiting to see if he will place her back in the mud where she belongs.

Anatolya Döbryn shook the memory away. It always rose when she waited, as if it were her default program. Her brain returned to that moment, the moment she gained consciousness or regained consciousness, since she was pretty certain she'd had it before.

She had been four years old when Leon Döbryn saved her life. He told her later that he feared she would have drowned there, too shocked to realize she could stand and climb out of the mixture of mud, water, and blood that she had been sitting in since her family was murdered.

That moment was as real to her as the current one—more real, perhaps, because if she shut her eyes, she could still feel the cold rain, the warmth of the liquid around her, the safety she felt in Döbryn's arms. In contrast, the bench she sat upon seemed almost sterile, Armstrong's port decontamination room like all the other decontamination rooms in the known universe.

She had been here nearly an hour. It hadn't taken that long to go through the decon unit and have it declare her free of germs and other contaminants the residents of the city of Armstrong feared. Armstrong insisted that newcomers go through decontamination alone—an Earth Alliance wrinkle that she did not approve of—but she had no say in the matter.

She might have been one of the ruling council on Etae, but here, she was a stranger, just like everyone else.

Anatolya got up and paced the small room, peering only once through the webbed window in the door. They were checking her identification, examining her papers, making certain she had the right to come to this pesky moon.

Even though the Earth Alliance had invited her here, they still treated her as if she were a fugitive.

And, God's truth, she felt like one. She shivered in the chill of the decontamination room. The ambient temperature in the Alliance was several degrees lower than what she was used to. She had dressed for it—a long-sleeved shirt and pants instead of her usual skirt and tank top—but she was still chilled.

She rubbed her hands on her arms and walked to the mirrored glass across from the decon chamber. The woman who stared back at her was thick, with long hair piled on top of her head and wrapped with seed pearls Döbryn had brought her from his last trip to Earth. He had been dying then, and willing to spend his meager fortune on the only person he'd ever considered a child of his own.

She sighed and smoothed the blouse over her pants. Just from that record alone—the way her people managed to turn Etae around in such a short time—the Alliance should welcome Etae with open arms.

But she knew they wouldn't. Her government was young, and it had rebelled against the first human government of Etae, overthrowing them. The name Etae had become synonymous with *bloody* in many, many places.

The civil war was over now—had been for more than a decade. Her government was actually making a little progress in improving the country, but the government couldn't do it alone. This had been their first chance to apply to join the Earth Alliance, and she had championed the cause.

She had expected difficulties, but not from the moment she had landed in the port. Being trapped in this small room was one of those difficulties. If the Earth Alliance considered her important, she would have been able to bypass the decon units and head directly to the diplomatic headquarters.

She'd argued as much with the traffic police who had escorted her here. At first they had ignored her. Then their leader had the courtesy to explain that all must go through the procedures at Armstrong Dome. Even the heads of the Earth Alliance.

Anatolya did not believe this police officer, but she did not argue. Arguing with underlings was a waste of breath. If the rudeness continued, she'd bring it up with the Alliance delegation, and, she hoped, they would change their behavior.

If they did not, there was little she could do to change it for them. She was here as a supplicant. She needed the Earth Alliance more than they needed her.

Finally, the door swung open. A slender woman wearing one of the traffic police's dark uniforms stood before her.

"I'm sorry it took so long," she said. "Your decon had some suspicious reads."

Anatolya tilted her head slightly. It was her only visible reaction to the other woman's words. Long ago, Anatolya had learned to control her physical responses.

"Suspicious?"

"You carried some unidentified microorganisms, a few toxins that we have banned, and immunities to some diseases we have never seen. So we had to run the scan twice, then take it to some of our experts."

The woman smiled. Apparently the look was meant to be reassuring. Anatolya did not find it so.

"They reread the scans, filtered them through some other equipment, and compared them to some scans done with others from your region of space. Apparently, your reading was quite normal in that setting."

Anatolya wasn't sure what to do with this wealth of information, not certain how it applied to her or why she should care about it. She wasn't even sure if it was an excuse.

"We're not used to getting people from so far away." Anatolya's lack of response was clearly making the woman nervous. "We're a port, but we're so close to Earth that it's rare we get anyone outside of the Alliance or the approved trading partners. You understand."

"Actually," Anatolya said, "I do not. But all I truly care about is whether or not I'm free to go."

The woman blinked, stepped back, and held the door open. "Yes. I'm sorry. I thought I said that. You're welcome to continue. There's someone waiting for you at the end of the isolation units. He'll take you wherever it is you need to go."

Anatolya nodded, then she headed out of the room, taking her time. The woman fluttered near her, even more nervous, as if this had all been a mistake.

"You do know that we had a close call about six months ago," she said as Anatolya walked past her into the corridor. "We nearly had a lethal virus released into the dome."

That caught Anatolya's attention, but again, she didn't let it show. "A bioweapon?" she asked, keeping her tone dry, as if she were merely making conversation.

"I was never sure," the woman said. "No one really explained it. Kinda scary all the same."

The corridor was even colder than the decon chamber. Anatolya didn't like the dark walls, the matching black floor, the signage that rotated words in various Earth Alliance languages.

She was lucky Döbryn had insisted she learn English, Disty, and Peytin, as well as six of the Etaen languages. No matter what part of space she found herself in, she was able to get along.

Finally, she reached a set of double doors. The woman officer hung back, as if she were not allowed to pass through them. The doors slid open, their movement silent, and sent a blast of cool air toward her. This air was fragrant with perfumes and sweat and some kind of relaxation coolant, added to the mixture to keep anxiety levels low.

The area she stepped into was a waiting room, and it was filled with peoples of various races and species.

A human male, age indeterminate, stood when he saw her. He had silvering hair, clearly an affectation, and a narrow face, the kind the Alliance thought trustworthy. His eyes were a silver-blue that matched his hair, and his skin was a pale, almost orangish brown. He wore a long black tunic with an embroidered edge over black pants, and as he walked toward her, he extended both hands.

"Ms. Döbryn?" he said, his voice silky and warm. He spoke Alkan, the main language of her people. "I am Gideon Collier. I've been assigned to you for your stay."

"My police escort?" she asked in English.

He raised his oddly silver eyebrows in surprise. Apparently he hadn't known she spoke that language.

"No," he replied in Alkan, "nothing like that. I'm your guide and your majordomo. I understand you've never been this deep in Alliance space before, and I'm to help you with customs and language—although it doesn't seem you need that—and anything else that may occur."

"Like being stranded in a decon unit for the better part of an afternoon." She was still using English. The time in the decon unit had left her feeling stubborn.

"We're sorry for that," Collier said. "Armstrong is phobic these days about anything coming through the dome. We should have prepared you for that."

She gave him her coldest gaze. "If you had asked for permission to search for bioweapons, I would have given it to you."

The crowd in the waiting room turned toward her, and all of them wore an identical expression of shock. Collier moved in front of her, as if he could block their gazes.

"This really isn't the place to discuss bioweapons," Collier said in Alkan. His voice had reached the level of a hush, almost as if he were afraid of being understood.

"Why not?" Anatolya finally answered in the same language. She was beginning to feel childish using English because she had been annoyed. "I thought you people prided yourselves on your openness."

"Openness has limits," Collier said.

She let her true reaction show. A slight frown creased her face. "Yet one of the hallmarks of the Earth Alliance is its free speech, its willingness to embrace new cultures and new ideas, its willingness to tolerate—"

"We are careful in the docks," Collier said. "You never know who might be listening."

She felt a slight shiver run through her that, for the first time, had nothing to do with the cold.

"You'll have to explain the differences to me," Anatolya said to Collier.

He started to speak, to tell her—again—that he couldn't converse in this place, and she held up her hand.

"When we're away from here, of course," she said.

He looked relieved.

She gave him a begrudging smile, then glanced at the walls, struggling to read the various signs as they rotated through the languages. She saw nothing that referred to remaining silent. But then, she hadn't seen the full rotation.

"There will be a reception in a few hours," Collier was saying. "I'm to bring you, if you're not too tired to attend."

She was tired, but it was the exhaustion of a woman who had traveled a great distance for something she wasn't sure she believed in.

"Let me meet with the rest of my delegation," she said, "and I'll tell you what we decide."

"Delegation?" he asked.

It was her turn to raise an eyebrow. "You didn't think I traveled alone, did you?"

"We knew you came in your own ship. It's just that clearances were only for you. No one had informed us that there'd be others who needed to leave the port."

Human or not didn't seem to matter. Customs apparently varied greatly from Etae to the Alliance.

"You had my name because I planned to speak to your conference." She continued to speak in Alkan because it sounded haughtier than the other languages she knew. "It should be understood that I travel with an entourage. Do any of your ambassadors travel without one?"

Collier sputtered, then shrugged. "It's just that we are required to name our traveling companions so that their credentials can be approved by the host government. The fact that you haven't means that they can't enter the city without going through the entire entrance procedure."

"Which can't be long," she said. "Obviously people do it all the time."

He cleared his throat, then glanced nervously over his shoulder. The people still in the waiting room had stopped looking directly at her, but several were still watching her from the corners of their eyes.

Did they recognize her? Did news of Etae make it this deep into Alliance space?

"Um, Ms. Döbryn, surely you know that Etae has been on the Alliance watch list for almost a century." He had finally looked at her again, his expression taut.

"It's one of the many things I'm here to discuss," she said.

"Armstrong is a domed city." He licked his lower lip, a nervous habit that no one in diplomacy should have. "It doesn't allow anyone from a watched state inside."

So that was why the Alliance had chosen the major city on Earth's Moon, instead of a major Earth city, as the meeting place. The dome, just by existing, gave the diplomats a level of control they didn't even have to think about.

"Well," she said airily. "That's your first job then, Mr. Majordomo. You'll get my entourage approved. And you'll do so before this evening's reception, so that I can attend."

She walked to the nearest chair, crossed her arms, and sat down. Collier looked panicked.

"I'll just wait here," she said, "until we're ready to leave."

"Ms. Döbryn, there's no way I can get all the clearances in time," he said.

"Perhaps not on your own," she said. "But I'm sure someone in your delegations can help. You are diplomats, after all."

He studied her for a long moment, then gave her a tight smile. "I'll see what I can do," he said in English.

"Yes," she answered in the same language. "By the end of the day, we'll both know what you can do."

10

"How many of these people are there?" Arek Soseki stood at the wall of windows in his office, staring at the rooftops of Armstrong and their matching reflections in the dome. He had hooked his thumbs in the back pockets of his pants, ruining the lines of his suit and probably wrinkling it as well.

"She gave us a list of two dozen, but she'll settle for six," said Hans Londran, Soseki's assistant. Londran was a small, dapper man who seemed to know everything from proper attire for political functions to the details of internecine conflict between tribes in small cities on far-off worlds.

"She brought them all with her, I assume," Soseki said.

"Yes, sir."

Soseki shook his head. No one had told him that the purpose of this Earth Alliance meeting was about Etae. If they had, he would not have allowed the conference to take place in his city. He would have even contacted the Moon's governor-general, and argued that the conference shouldn't be held anywhere near the surface.

Etae's civil wars may have ended ten years before, but Soseki didn't believe the bitterness was over. He had studied Etae when he was getting his Intergalactic Relations degree from Harvard, back when Soseki believed he would rather be a diplomat than a politician. This was one non-Moon issue that he probably knew more about than Londran.

"Who did they send to talk to me?" Soseki asked.

"The Earth delegation sent one of their junior diplomats. He's quite apologetic."

"I'll bet." Soseki shook his head slightly. What a mess. Not only was Anatolya Döbryn here, a woman rumored to be one of the greatest mass murderers of all time or one of the greatest military minds, depending, of course, on which of the many sides a person took in the Etaen conflict, but she had brought an entourage without clearing them first, and now refused to leave the port without them accompanying her.

"Do we have a list of names?" he asked.

Londran shrugged. His suit's lines were never ruined, and always looked as fresh as they had when it hung in his closet. His hair—colored half a dozen shades of black—had been cut in layers, going from dark to light. The effect made him seem youthful, even though he was nearly two decades older than Soseki.

"She provided names," he said. "Half of them do not show up in any database."

"And, of course, she doesn't want us to do a DNA ident," Soseki said.

"Mr. Vallin does not know," Londran said. "He hasn't spoken to her directly. The problem was relayed to him by the attaché assigned to escort Ms. Döbryn from the port to her hotel."

"Where they registered her under a fake name, I assume." Soseki let the bitterness he felt come out. He knew that Londran would be discreet about it.

"They didn't have to register her under a fake name, sir," Londran said. "The Alliance has blocks reserved at four of the main hotels. Apparently, they were going to put her up in a suite."

"And none of these people thought it curious that a member of the ruling council of Etae, a government that's not exactly the most stable in the universe, would come without bodyguards or assistants?"

Londran shrugged. "I only report what they told me. I can't vouch for their intelligence or lack thereof."

"I don't suppose we can contact the governor-general and get some of the Guard here," Soseki said.

"The whole idea of the meeting was that it would get no publicity," Londran said. "If you so much as request the Guard, then the publicity will start, and that violates our agreement with the Alliance."

Soseki bit back a curse, a habit he'd gotten into since he ran for office. Better not to ever swear than to let the voters think his mouth was as foul as it was.

"I can't approve this quickly," Soseki said. "I'll have to meet with the governor-general, and we'll have to do it in person and in private. That'll take time to set up."

"Döbryn is waiting in port," Londran said.

Soseki shrugged. "That's not my problem. Send her back to her ship. She can stay there. Or, if she complains, have Space Traffic Control send them out of Moon space. They'll have to apply for reentry."

Then he paused, feeling odd. He leaned against his desk.

"How did she get through Space Traffic in the first place? Who approved her landing?"

"Again, blanket issue for the diplomats," Londran said. "They had her ship's name and its codes amongst theirs."

"Bastards," Soseki said, breaking his own rule. "They were sneaking her in."

"It seems that way," Londran said.

"Well, if they complain about this, remind them of that. We have strict rules in this dome, and they're done for the safety of the dome. The rules apply to everyone. Make sure the Alliance knows that from now on."

"Yes, sir." Londran spoke with an automatic obedience, which implied that he felt the job he had to do was a waste of time.

"And send that list to my desk, would you?" Soseki would look over the names himself. Even though his knowledge was decades old, it might still be valuable.

"Right away," Londran said, and then let himself out of the office.

Soseki leaned against the desk for a moment longer, trying to restrain his fury. He had known that the diplomats would be a problem. He had made a calculated choice, and it had bitten him in ways he hadn't even suspected.

The risk to the dome infuriated him. The fact that he had been played infuriated him even more.

He pushed away from the desk and paced the room, wishing he were more than a mayor, wishing he were the governor-general, a person with some clout in the Earth Alliance. He would make this into a public incident, let the Alliance and its peoples know that they couldn't threaten domed cities with their special interests and ways around the rules.

Maybe he'd bring this before the governor-general at the meeting as well. She had a second home in Armstrong. She understood the threats to the dome, and she knew that what affected one dome could affect the entire Moon. Maybe she would step forward and speak out to the Alliance.

Although he doubted it. To speak out against the Alliance would take political courage that the governor-general did not have.

Soseki walked around his desk, and was about to sit when the doors to his office banged open. A man he had never seen before stormed in, Londran scurrying behind him.

"You cannot be here," Londran was saying. "You are not cleared to meet with the mayor. You—"

"I don't give a damn," the man said. "Mayor Soseki?"

Soseki took his hands off the arms of his chair and

rose to his full height. "No one's allowed in this office without Mr. Londran's approval."

The man ignored him. "You are causing an intergalactic incident."

So this was the junior diplomat the Alliance had sent to negotiate with him.

"If you don't leave," Soseki said, "we'll have security arrest you."

Londran put his hand on the man's arm. The man shook him off.

"You won't," the man said. "I'm Locke Vallin. I'm a diplomat with the Earth Alliance. I was sent here to get Ms. Döbryn's bodyguards approved through your customs. You can't arrest me."

"I can," Soseki said, even though he knew the charges wouldn't stick. "The situation could be embarrassing for all concerned."

"Particularly a young mayor of a major Alliance city, a man with political ambitions," Vallin said.

Soseki raised his eyebrows. He hadn't thought this square, broad-shouldered man with thinning hair that even enhancements couldn't improve would have this much fight in him.

"Are you threatening me?" Soseki asked.

"I'm merely stating facts." Vallin raised his chin slightly. He was shorter than Soseki, but heavier and more tailored. He also had a deceptive blandness, one that probably hid every thought. "A man with political ambitions should not take on the Alliance."

"A man with political ambitions does not let two dozen unknown people into his dome without the proper background checks, particularly if those people are from as unstable a world as Etae."

Vallin turned with the precision of a military man, and looked down his nose at Londran. "You can leave us."

"He's my assistant," Soseki said. "He takes orders from me. Escort Mr. Vallin out of the office, please, Hans."

Londran's hands hovered near Vallin's arms. "Come with me, sir."

"No," Vallin said. "I need to have this discussion with Mayor Soseki in private."

"Call security," Soseki said to Londran. "Have them standing by."

"I've already done so through my links, sir."

Soseki loved how efficient his assistant was. "Then wait for me outside. I'll let you know if I want security in here."

Londran blinked once, a sign of surprise, and then nodded. He backed out of the room, keeping his gaze on Vallin, almost like a warning.

So Londran didn't like the man and didn't trust him. It was unusual for Londran to be so blatant about his reactions.

"What's so important that my assistant can't hear?" Soseki asked.

"I need you to shut your links down," Vallin said. "This is a confidential conversation."

"I don't know you, Mr. Vallin. I'm already giving you considerable leeway. I'll leave my links intact, and should I decide later that this conversation is off the record, then I'll delete it, with a copy of these two statements covering the deletion. That's the best I can do."

"It's not good enough," Vallin said.

"Fine." Soseki sat down and slid his chair into his desk. "This meeting is over."

"Mr. Mayor, please. This is important to the entire Alliance."

"My concern, as a mayor with political ambitions"— he stressed the last six words, to let Vallin know that the insult had sunk in—"is my apparently insignificant city. I don't care about the Alliance or its politics. So, if you want to talk with me, you have exactly one minute. Or I will call security and have you escorted from the building. And, since I am a mayor with political ambitions in a city that doesn't always like Alliance policies, I will call the media to record your humiliation. Is that clear?"

"You're out of your league, Mr. Soseki."

No "Mayor" this time.

"But you're in my office, Mr. Vallin, so you clearly need me for something."

Vallin let out a disgusted breath. "All right. Swear to me this will be deleted."

"If I deem it confidential, I most surely will," Soseki said. "You have my word."

He spoke laconically, as if he weren't as angry as Vallin. In truth, Soseki was probably angrier. He hated being treated as insignificant.

"You have to let Döbryn and her company out of the port," Vallin said.

"I have to?" Soseki crossed his arms. "Really? Why?"

"She's the reason for our meeting."

"You're negotiating with Anatolya Döbryn?"

"She's an important member of their council," Vallin said.

"She's one of the most ruthless generals in the history of warfare," Soseki said, "and, frankly, not someone I want in my dome."

Vallin gave Soseki a slow smile. "So you consider yourself an expert on Etae?"

"I didn't say that."

"And yet you believe her to be a problem," Vallin said.

"Alone, probably not," Soseki said. "But with two dozen of her henchmen, people whom I can't run though the proper background checks, yes, I do believe her to be a problem."

"What do you fear?" Vallin asked. "That she'll attack your dome? She wants her world to join the Alliance. She won't hurt any of us."

"The current leadership of Etae used to express contempt for the Alliance," Soseki said. "Why would they want to join now?"

"That's what we're here to find out," Vallin said.

"I don't even understand why you're interested. Etae has been at war for so long, the planet can't have many resources. It's impoverished and too far away to be of much strategic use."

"Yes," Vallin said. "I can see how someone in your position would think that."

"Care to enlighten me?" Soseki asked.

"I would," Vallin said, "but you refuse to shut down your links, and I cannot risk the confidentiality issues."

Soseki couldn't take any more. For a diplomat, Vallin was not very good at negotiation. "And I can't risk my dome. So I'm going to refuse entry to Döbryn and her people."

"You can't refuse entry to Döbryn," Vallin said. "She's under our blanket."

"I had no idea you were trying to smuggle in known terrorists," Soseki said. "I'm of a mind to rescind your entire blanket permission. Who knows what other kinds of people you have brought into my dome?"

"Is that a threat, Mr. Soseki?"

"No, sir," Soseki said. "It's a bit of policy that I'll be considering with the help of my advisers. Your group has abused your diplomatic privilege. I'm sure, if tried in the court of public opinion, your case would lose."

"But diplomacy isn't tried in the court of public opinion," Vallin said. "Of necessity, we deal in secret. If we didn't, we wouldn't make the headway that we do."

"I don't see headway. All I see, given the information you've shared with me, is a serious threat to the safety of my dome and of the Moon herself. So I stand by my position, Mr. Vallin."

"You may lose that position, Mr. Soseki."

Even the "Mr." was beginning to annoy him.

"I'm an elected official," Soseki said. "No matter how much I irritate you, you can't get me out of office."

Vallin smiled. The look did not reach his eyes. "Don't tempt me, Mr. Soseki."

Soseki sat down at his desk. He tapped a screen and it rose, blocking the view of Vallin's face. "You may leave us now, Mr. Vallin."

Soseki used the same tone that Vallin had when he gave that order to Londran.

Vallin inhaled sharply. He started to argue, and then he spun, clearly furious, and headed out the door.

Soseki counted to ten, then leaned forward, resting his forehead in his hand. This would have tremendous repercussions—not just for him, but for the dome, and maybe even the Moon itself.

But he couldn't, in good conscience, let that woman manipulate her entourage into Armstrong. And Soseki didn't want her there in the first place.

He pressed a chip on his hand, opening his audio link to Londran.

"Get the governor-general for me, would you, please?" Soseki asked. "Tell her it's urgent."

Time to do damage control. Somehow he had to protect both his dome—and his career.

11

DeRicci didn't explain her thoughts on the crime to anyone. The theory was still young, and subject to change. And she'd found that explaining a theory might make everyone look for evidence to fit that theory. It was dangerous enough that she had one—she certainly didn't want the others to form around her.

All she had told them was that she wanted to see if the perp had dropped the weapon. The techs began by rolling the furniture back so that DeRicci and Cabrera could peer under it.

DeRicci crouched. She found nothing beneath the chairs, just like she had expected.

This case already intrigued her. Why hadn't one of the victims sent an emergency message through the links? There had to have been time; all it took to send such a message was a brief instance of thought. Even with the others dying, one of these people should have had that instant to send for help.

"Done," Cabrera said as the techs set the last chair down.

DeRicci straightened, heard her back crack in three separate places, and walked to one of the techs.

The woman was half DeRicci's size. She was slight and muscular, and had more link chips glittering on her skin than DeRicci had ever seen on one human being.

"Let's lift the body," DeRicci said.

"Which one?" the tech asked.

"The one without the face."

DeRicci caught Cabrera's wince out of the corner of her eye. He looked away, as if he couldn't stomach the idea of touching one of the corpses.

"We'll do it, sir," the other tech said. "It's part of our job anyway."

"Fine." DeRicci said, and stepped back, careful to avoid as much of the blood pool as possible, and to stay away from the furniture.

The two techs flanked the faceless body, and paused.

"What part do you want us to lift?" the woman asked.

"Roll her to one side, and then the other." DeRicci wanted to see all of the floor beneath that particular body. If there was no weapon beneath it, she would have to revise her theory. Then she'd have the techs move the other two.

The techs rolled the corpse toward the windows. The corpse's back made a sucking sound as it separated from the floor.

DeRicci crouched again, her knees creaking in protest. The floor beneath the corpse was a black mess of blood and tissue. Most of the fluids from the head had seeped downward, congealing in an obvious dip in the floorboards.

It took a bit of work to separate the congealed blood from the bits of hair and fabric. Lumps that looked solid were not—they were simply places where the fluids had gathered.

DeRicci was about to stand when she looked at the back of the corpse. A small laser pistol, barely the size of DeRicci's hand, had adhered to the corpse's spine.

Before calling attention to it, she said, "Detective Cabrera, if I let you return to the station, what'll you do to further this investigation?"

She looked up at him. He blinked, looked at De-Ricci in surprise, and then said, "I'd . . . um . . . investigate the histories of the couple here, and see if the building's security keeps the coded entry logs. I'd wait for the DNA on the mystery corpse before identifying her and her relationship to the Lahiris."

"And the theory you'd use as the basis for your investigation?" DeRicci asked.

"That there was an outside intruder, one who knew the family well enough to get in, and was calm enough to leave without leaving a trace of himself," Cabrera said.

The female tech was shaking her head, probably warning Cabrera not to go on. He didn't notice, but he had stopped anyway.

"Why?" he asked.

"Because," DeRicci said, "I always figure hands-on examples are better than lectures."

She pointed at the corpse's back. The tech who had been shaking her head stopped, and gave Cabrera a look of pity.

"See that?" DeRicci asked.

"What?" Cabrera didn't move. It was clear he didn't want to get any closer.

"Come here," DeRicci said, patting just above the ground next to her. "You can see better from down here."

"I'm fine standing," Cabrera said.

"All right." DeRicci suppressed yet another sigh. "Do you see what I'm pointing at?"

"I'm not sure what you want me to see," Cabrera said. "It's pretty clear she's been here awhile. The . . . materials have gelled. Maybe I haven't been doing this long enough, but that doesn't seem like a surprise to me."

"What else?" DeRicci asked.

Cabrera took two large steps, ostentatiously stepping over a trickle of blood, so that he was directly beside her. Then he bounced downward, the sign of an in-shape body.

He squinted at the corpse and started to shake his head. Then he stopped, closed his eyes for just a moment, and swore as he reopened them.

"That's the weapon, isn't it? On her back. She fell on it."

DeRicci wanted to give him a sarcastic cheer, but that wouldn't help anyone. Now she had to see if he was going to get angry at her for showing him how to do his job.

"Possibly," DeRicci said. "That's where the techs come in. They'll see if the weapon fired the shots, or even could have created the damage in those wounds."

"If she fell on it—"

"She might have been pulling it out to save herself when the perp shot her. And the perp might have shot her quickly, so he didn't have time to go for the torso. She might have been bending down to get that weapon when he shot. He aimed for the torso and hit her in the face."

"You think that?" Cabrera asked.

"All I think at the moment," DeRicci said, "is that the weapon fell shortly before she died. She clearly landed on it, and her weight, along with the coagulated blood, made the weapon adhere to her back."

"It might be a cheap pistol," the female tech said. "It might have fired hot. Then it would have burned into her back when she landed on it."

"All questions we need answered." DeRicci still wasn't going to explain her theory, even though the gun added weight to it.

Cabrera hadn't left his crouch. If anything, he leaned farther forward, as if he were trying to see more clearly.

"You don't think she killed them, do you?" His question was soft, almost as if he were embarrassed for thinking of it.

DeRicci turned toward him in surprise. She hadn't expected him to make an intuitive leap. "I think murder-suicide is an option."

He nodded. "You already thought of it. That's why you wanted the floor searched, why you wanted the body moved."

DeRicci liked him better and better. "That's one reason. But I also think the more we find out at this crime scene, the faster we'll solve the crime, and the faster I'll be out of your life."

He was still staring at the gun, as if he couldn't believe it was there. "You actually think we'll solve this fast?"

DeRicci considered the question.

"No," she said after a moment, "I don't."

He sighed, then shook his head. DeRicci felt sympathy for the movement. So many cases never got closed. So many mysteries never got solved.

She stood and nodded toward the techs. "This part of the scene's all yours," she said.

She was going to look at the rest of the apartment, to see if these people lived the way that their front room said they did. So many people had clean front rooms and sloppy bedrooms, or respectable art in the living areas and pornography across from the bed.

She headed down the hall, past bookshelves lined with matching books. She glanced at them; they were legal tomes—Earth case law from the United States—probably collectible.

The first bedroom and bathroom didn't tell her much. Either they had been cleaned or they weren't used. She headed into the master bedroom, and stopped.

It was the largest room in the apartment. The walls were covered with some kind of silk, and the floor was carpeted with a thick white shag. Two chairs were pushed against the floor-to-ceiling windows—also covered with that heavy silk—and two more chairs sat on the other side of the room, like two separate groupings designed for reading.

A large bed with a real wood headboard and matching frame leaned against one of the walls. The coverlet was a thick gold brocade that somehow accented the silk in its own gaudy way. Pillows four and five deep leaned against the headboard, making the bed look soft, at least, although not inviting.

DeRicci had concentrated most of her attention on the end tables. They were a dark wood—real wood again—that matched the headboard, and in their upper drawers, she found all sorts of burned chips, discarded info nodes, and ancient hand-helds. She would tell the techs to take all of that and test it, hoping to find something.

In the end, though, it was the armoire that dominated one side of the room that yielded the only truly viable clue that DeRicci found outside of the living room.

The double doors were heavy, made of that same dark wood, and very old. She had no doubt that the piece had been imported from Earth. The interior smelled strongly of the same perfume that floated through the apartment.

Only a woman's clothes hung inside, and DeRicci almost closed the doors. Then she changed her mind. She used an old-fashioned search, the kind the techs didn't even do anymore, and touched each article of clothing, seeing if anything was hidden beneath it.

She also stuck her gloved hand in every pocket. In the past, she had found a lot of items in pockets, usually lost chips, broken jewelry, and a few slips of very expensive paper, usually on someone who had just come from Earth.

This time the pockets gave her little. She was about to give up when her fingers found the edge of a stiff card. It was in a golden blazer in the right-hand pocket, which was pressed against the back of the armoire.

DeRicci pulled out the card and stared at it for a long moment. It was blank except for three chips along the middle, and a number handwritten on the side. Pressed into the paper itself was a watermark with a design she recognized:

MF

Miles Flint. This was the card he gave prospective clients so that they could shovel money into one of his many accounts. If she took the card into processing, she'd find accounts on each of the chips, accounts that would only have a small amount of credits in them so that Flint could keep them active.

He transferred the money out and filtered it through several other accounts, finding untraceable ways to get it to his main accounts. At least, that was what he told her the one time she had asked him. He'd even given her a card of her own, just in case she came across any more Disappeared cases as bad as the one that made him quit the force.

Miles Flint. He even had the money to waste on paper cards.

She slapped this one against her hand. So Flint had had something to do with these people. Since they were so established in Armstrong society, she doubted they were Disappeareds themselves. Flint wouldn't have given them a card in that instance.

They had asked him to find a Disappeared. Or at least one of them had—the woman, judging by the blazer.

And that changed the entire nature of the case.

DeRicci let out a sigh and stared at that very faint watermark. She would find no other information in the apartment. She was lucky to have found this.

The question was whether she told anyone else about this or not. Armstrong law enforcement had strict orders not to work with Retrieval Artists. If anything, the police were to hire Trackers to find Disappeareds, and even that took channels upon channels upon channels.

Flint had been involved in the Moon Marathon case,

but on his own. His connection to DeRicci had never come up, for which she was grateful. Gumiela had complained too many times about the fact that it was Flint, and not her detectives, who had ended that case. At least he hadn't wanted public credit.

But he had been DeRicci's partner. Of all the rookies she'd had to train, he had been the best. She still missed him, although she would never admit that to him.

And he owed her. For her silence, for her support, and for her willingness to look away when he had used a few codes that he wasn't supposed to know in that Moon Marathon case.

She slipped the card into the pocket of her own blazer. She would talk to him first, see if he would break confidentiality for her.

After all, they were dealing with a murder here. And it was on a case that Flint had worked.

Maybe he'd be interested enough to get involved.

12

The great hall of the Armstrong Cultural Center had pretensions to art. Orenda Kreise had positioned her chair so that she wouldn't be subject to most of the things hanging on the walls. She still had to stare at the still-lifes of the famous footprint, theoretically left by Neil Armstrong himself, in Moon regolith however many centuries ago, but at least she didn't have to look at the other things passing as quality Moon art.

The building itself was beautiful, however, and Kreise appreciated the sunlight flowing through the treated dome above her. She had lived most of her life on Earth and couldn't get used to the artificial light most of the humans in this solar system suffered through. Dome lighting and its sophisticated imitation of an average Earth day simply didn't work for her.

She had arrived ahead of the rest of her colleagues, early enough to move the tables away from that wretched art, and to take her seat at the head of the table. She was the senior ambassador for the Council of the Governments of Earth. Her position as the chief representative of Earth made her the leader of this meeting of the executive committee of the Earth Alliance.

Earth had formed the Alliance, first with human

colonies off-Earth, many of them nonaffiliated to Earth member countries, and then with various alien governments.

The agreements between the member planets and the Alliance could probably fill this dome, and most of those agreements had to do with ways to balance the various cultural systems with each other. Of course, there were rules that applied to all member planets—the greatest being that each member planet had to have some kind of ruling body that spoke for all of the planet's peoples and/or governments, just like the Council of the Governments of Earth.

Kreise sighed and blinked so that the time would appear in her left eye. Five minutes until the meeting. She was relieved that the Etaen representative was still delayed in port. That gave her one last chance to stop this farce before it began.

The faint scent of garlic and onions floated through the large hall, matched by the smell of baking bread. Armstrong had promised excellent meals, which was one of the many reasons Kreise had picked the largest city on the Moon for the meeting with the Etaen representative.

Kreise had several other, sneakier reasons for choosing this site—one of which was in play at the moment. She knew that Armstrong's recent dome crisis had led to stringent reforms. Armstrong wouldn't change its entrance rules for anyone—although she'd had some moments of concern early on, when the Alliance booking committee managed to get blanket entrance immunity for the members of the committee and their entourage.

Still, they'd all had to go through decon, even people like Kreise, who was from a planet that had been cleared for general decon sixty years before, and ident records were still checked against watch lists as an extra security precaution.

So far the Etaens had been caught in that snare and, she hoped, the problem would continue, making this series of meetings impossible. Someone would suggest a new meeting place, of course, and she had an entire list programmed into her links of places just as stringent as Armstrong, if not as deep within Alliance space.

The main door opened and she heard voices. The bodyguards and attachés all waited in the outer rooms. Sometimes the diplomats liked to have "their people" in the meeting room with them, but Kreise did not allow it. The talk was freer in meetings without underlings, simply because the diplomats knew there wasn't even the potential for leaks.

Pilar Restrepo came into Kreise's view. Restrepo was a short, pear-shaped woman who wore flowing robes to conceal her figure. She had a former spacer's view of enhancements: Enhancements to improve performance—particularly of a job—were fine, but those designed to improve appearance were silly luxuries that wasted both time and money.

She smiled at Kreise. Restrepo also had the air of a friendly matron until she got down to business, and then she was the most ruthless of all of them.

"Are the others boycotting?" Restrepo asked without even saying hello.

"They're not late yet," Kreise said, although she did double-check the time again, this time downloading from a different server. It was only a minute later than the last time she'd checked.

Restrepo placed a handbag on the table. The bag matched her flowing clothing, and even seemed to be made of the same ethereal material.

Kreise did not comment on it. She hated carrying everything with her, feeling that her links and downloads were more than enough. Restrepo didn't trust anything wired, so she would shut off all but her emergency links whenever she interacted with someone.

Kreise felt that she should probably do the same. After all, Restrepo had decades more experience in the diplomatic corps than Kreise had. Restrepo represented Jupiter and her moons, but her first job had been a junior attaché on Mars, just before the Disty took over.

"If we're going to meet," Restrepo said, "perhaps we should compromise and use Döbryn's ship. Then her people won't have to be cleared by Armstrong."

Kreise folded her hands together and rested them on the tabletop. "I don't trust the Etaens."

"It's been more than a decade since the war ended," Restrepo said.

"On Etae." Kreise kept her voice level. "There've been suspicious deaths all over the known universe, all of them with ties to Etae."

Restrepo shrugged. "Such things happen with many Alliance members, some of them longtime Alliance members. If you use that standard, even Earth is not immune. Centuries-old religious and tribal disagreements that began on Earth are still being enacted in outlying colonies."

Kreise had heard that argument before and hated it. She didn't even dignify it with a response. "The Port Authority won't let us board that ship. If the ship's inhabitants aren't welcome in the Port, then no one from the city itself may board."

"All of which is probably relevant to Armstrong natives, but that doesn't include us," Restrepo said. "I'm not fond of the games the city is playing. These provincial politicians have no idea how many lives they're tampering with."

The door opening at the end of the great hall saved Kreise from having to answer. Uzval, the Peyti representative, stopped just inside the door, her long fingers clasping the edge of the door like three tails wrapping around the frame. She appeared to be speaking to someone outside, but Kreise couldn't tell whom.

That was one of the many problems of having a Peyti on the executive committee. Their conversation was quiet, partly because of the breathing masks they had to wear to survive in any kind of oxygenated atmosphere.

Uzval nodded once, let go of the door, and crossed the room. Her translucent skin caught the sunlight, making her glow from within. It was such a startling image that Kreise stared at Uzval as if she had never seen her before. Usually the Peyti's skin looked gray, but the direct sunlight made it come alive.

"Wow," Restrepo said. "You look stunning."

Uzval nodded her head in acknowledgment. As she drew closer, it became clear that the direct sunlight also made the fluids than ran beneath her skin phosphoresce.

"That's not going to hurt you, is it?" Kreise asked, pointing to her own skin.

Uzval looked down, and then shook her head. The movement seemed so brittle. The Peyti always seemed as if they were going to break.

"It is good for me. Better, in fact, than the human-made lights." She bent in the center of her torso, folding herself into thirds as she sat in her chair. Then she leaned upright, an unnatural position for the Peyti, but one they had adopted in their interactions with humans. "The others are missing, I see."

"They'll be here soon," Kreise said.

"Perhaps they are boycotting in protest against the treatment of the Etae representative," Uzval said.

"Then I'll cancel this conference altogether." Kreise didn't care if that sentence tipped her hand. She wouldn't tolerate uncivil behavior in the committee.

"No matter whether the Etaen representative speaks to us or not, this will be a difficult session," Uzval said. "I do not think we can conquer our differences."

Uzval's use of the word *conquer* made Kreise frown. She was never certain whether Uzval's command of English had some faults in it or if she was excessively precise.

"The advisory committees sent the petition to us," Restrepo said. "We should consider it with open minds."

As if Restrepo had one. The Jupiter colonies liked

her representation because her firm beliefs coincided with their political philosophy. Many of the Jupiter colonies were founded by the intergalactic corporations, and a lot of the residents were fifth- and sixth-generation employees of those corporations. The educational systems and the living conditions did not value the free exchange of ideas, nor did they like a lot of clear dissent.

In those ways, Restrepo was an excellent representative for them. As a negotiator and diplomat, someone who should consider all sides, find the one that was best for her homeland, and sometimes compromise, she was perhaps the worst that Kreise had ever seen.

"I have read the reports," Kreise said, "and I don't believe that the Alliance gains enough from Etae to justify the risks."

"Risks?" Restrepo asked. "We routinely work with the Disty, whose vengeance killings are both legal and legendary. We allow the Rev free access to all Alliance ports, and they're exceedingly violent when provoked. What's to fear about the Etaens? They're human, for heaven's sake."

Uzval's long fingers bent upward, a sign of discomfort. Usually Uzval hid her emotions. The fact that she was communicating them clearly meant that she was very upset.

"Humanity does not automatically confer virtue," she said, her voice growling through the breathing mask.

The door opened again, and this time the Nyyzen entered, two because Nyyzen always operated in pairs. At first, Kreise believed the pairs rule was simply a custom. Then she worked with the Nyyzen, and realized that compatible Nyyzen created a third entity between them.

The third entity actually had substance. It was transparent, although its outlines were often visible in strong light. The Nyyzen sat one chair apart from each other, and the third entity—the actual ambassador—

occupied the chair. The Nyyzen had let Kreise touch the ambassador once. It—these entities had no real gender—felt like hot, slime-covered rubber, a sensation she had not expected.

But the ambassador was not with them now. The Nyyzen were "in transit," and the ambassador wouldn't appear until they literally put their minds to the task before them.

The Nyyzen were square creatures, with flipperlike feet and heads shaped like isosceles triangles. Their mouths were at the tip of the equal sides of the triangle, which was, from a human perspective, in the back of their heads. Their eyes were on the triangle's short-sided base—on the opposite side of the mouth.

Dealing with Nyyzen actually took training for humans, even those Nyyzen who didn't create third entities, because humans had trouble looking at someone who saw from one side of the head and spoke from another.

"You have not started without us, have you?" one of the Nyyzen asked. Kreise couldn't see the mouth move, and the Nyyzen did not use any other speech indicators. Even though they had arms and hands like humans—their bodies did conform to the human idea of two hands, two feet, two eyes; one torso—they did not use their hands or any other body part in communication. Only the mouth.

"We've been discussing Etae's rights," Restrepo said, knowing that her comments would cause the Nyyzen to go into an immediate panic.

"We must set up!" one of them said.

"You should not have started without us!" the other said.

"We need the ambassador!"

"It's fine." Uzval's voice was soft and soothing. "Not everyone's here yet anyway."

"And not everyone will be," said Restrepo. "We still haven't gotten approval for Etae's representative."

Kreise gave Restrepo a hard look. Apparently Restrepo was set on causing trouble at this meeting.

The Nyyzen sat next to Kreise, leaving an empty chair between them for the ambassador, and immediately started to hum. The crests on the top of their heads rose.

Restrepo shut her eyes. She had once confessed to Kreise that she hated watching the aliens and their strange ways. She tolerated nonhumans only because they were the gateways to the rest of the universe.

The final member of the committee let himself in the door. Hadad Foltz represented the Outlying Colonies, which were outlying no longer. They had been named when the known universe had been much smaller, and humans actually believed that the Outlying Colonies were as far as the human race could travel.

Foltz was a tall man who moved with an athletic grace. In the custom of Outlyers, he kept his head bald and covered with tattoos, complex designs done mostly in sky blue, a color that accented his dark brown skin.

He saw the Nyyzen humming, and shook his head. "You've panicked them," he said, assessing the situation with a clarity that Kreise envied.

"Ambassador Restrepo panicked them." Uzval was rigid with disapproval. All three of her fingers on both hands were bent upward. She was angry, and the meeting hadn't officially started.

"It smells like garlic in here," Foltz said. "Is someone cooking?"

"We've been promised lunch," Kreise said.

"By someone approved, I trust," Restrepo said.

"Take it up with the city of Armstrong," Kreise said. "They know our rules."

"As if they've been paying attention," Restrepo muttered.

"The rules sometimes clash with local law." Foltz took the seat at the other end of the table, so that he faced Kreise. He was wearing a blackish-blue suit that gave him a suggestion of even more height than he already had.

"I know," Restrepo said.

"If you knew it, then why complain about it?" He smiled at her and she smiled back.

Kreise was the one who bristled. She hated the way her colleagues taunted each other.

The humming beside her rose to a buzz. She resisted the urge to cover her ears. Restrepo rolled her eyes. The Nyyzen didn't notice, of course, because theirs were closed while their minds combined. No one else seemed to notice Restrepo's lack of respect either.

"We were discussing the merits of the petition," Uzval said. "Informally, of course."

"But enough to upset the Nyyzen." Foltz raised his voice so that he could speak over the buzz.

"We weren't certain who would come," Restrepo said. "This meeting is silly, considering the fact that Döbryn is still stuck in port and Ambassador Kreise refuses to let us vote on whether or not to hold the hearing on Döbryn's ship."

"I thought the Port of Armstrong wouldn't allow that." Foltz looked at Kreise for confirmation.

"Since when do port guidelines affect intergalactic relations?" Restrepo asked.

[WHEN THEY INTERFERE WITH LIFE, HEALTH, AND SAFETY OF THE SENTIENT BEINGS THE PORTS ARE SWORN TO PROTECT.]

The Nyyzen Ambassador finally arrived. The buzz disappeared as it spoke, but Kreise always took a moment to notice. The buzz would echo in her ears for a good five minutes.

The Nyyzen Ambassador's voice didn't really sound like any other voice Kreise had ever heard. It rasped and echoed and doubled back on itself, and yet, even though it didn't sound like speech, it was easy to understand.

"I thought you supported the Etaens' claim." Restrepo crossed her arms. Bangle bracelets that she wore on both wrists jingled.

[I DO. BUT WE ARE UNDER NO TIME PRESSURE TO REVIEW THIS APPLICATION, SO THERE IS NO REAL REASON

TO UPSET THE CITY OF ARMSTRONG, WHICH HAS BEEN KIND ENOUGH TO HOST US.]

Kriese folded her hands together, her fingers digging into her skin. She worked to remain silent, even though she wanted to argue.

"There's time pressure," Restrepo said. "We do have our own lives and schedules."

[BUT THAT SCHEDULE IS IRRELEVENT. IF WE CANNOT HOLD A MEETING IN ARMSTRONG, WE SHALL FIND SOMEPLACE ELSE AT SOME OTHER TIME. IT MIGHT GIVE US AN OPPORTUNITY TO CONVINCE OUR MORE RELUCTANT COMRADES OF ETAE'S IMPORTANCE TO THE ALLIANCE.]

"It'll take a lot of convincing," Kriese said before she could stop herself. "I see nothing positive in allowing Etae into the Alliance."

"They would be subject to our laws," Foltz said.

Kriese frowned at him. "And we would be subject to theirs. If they have any."

"That's unfair, Orenda, and you know it," Restrepo said. "They have laws."

Kriese glared at Restrepo. When they gathered, they were to talk to each other formally. But Kriese had never officially called the meeting to order, an argument that she knew Restrepo would make.

"Laws they don't enforce," Kriese said.

"Actually," Uzval said, "they enforce those laws stringently, within certain segments of the population."

Her fingers had flattened on the table. She was, apparently, calmer.

"Yet another reason not to let them into the Alliance," Kriese said. "The peoples of a planet should be treated with equanimity on that planet before anyone applies to the Alliance."

[NYYZE HAS NEVER APPROVED OF THAT RULE. IT IS HUMAN-CENTRIC.]

Kriese suppressed a sigh. "We note that every single meeting, Ambassador."

"The rule exists," Uzval said. "It is something you

agreed to within the Alliance. Stop changing the subject."

Her voice seemed even raspier than it had earlier. Kreise wondered if she was getting enough air.

One of the side doors pushed open. A woman whom Kreise had never seen before stuck her head inside. "I have lunch. When would you like it served?"

Everyone at the table, with the exception of the Nyyzen Ambassador, looked at Kreise. She stood.

"No one informed you about protocol?" she asked in her haughtiest voice.

"I was told to ask—"

"One of the assistants," Kreise said. "Even they are not allowed in this room."

The woman bowed her head.

"I'm sorry," she said, and eased the door closed.

There was a long silence before Foltz spoke. "Is anyone else uncomfortable here?"

"In the building?" Kreise asked.

"In Armstrong," he said. "Doesn't it seem to you that a lot of things are going wrong?"

Kreise sat down slowly. It did seem that way. But sometimes meetings went poorly.

"I have never understood," Restrepo said, "why we didn't set this meeting up on the Earth compound. After all, we're on our own ground there."

"Nonaligned aliens are not allowed on Earth," Uzval said.

"At least in the Earth Alliance compound," Foltz said.

Kreise sighed. She hated correcting them. "Actually, that's just a guideline. In the early days of the Alliance, potential new members always made their pitches at the compound."

"Which is my point," Restrepo said. "You know that, and you set up this meeting. Why here?"

Kreise made certain that her surprise didn't show. Did Restrepo know what Kreise was doing?

"Armstrong is as close to Earth as we dare get. I

wanted to see if the Etaens would enter the heart of the Alliance," Kreise said.

"Now you know they will," Restrepo said. "If the Ambassador is right"—whenever anyone referred to someone that way, they meant the Nyyzen Ambassador—"then we can reschedule this thing somewhere else. Maybe even at our headquarters in the Outlying Colonies."

Foltz was shaking his head.

"What's the matter?" Uzval asked. "Don't you want Etaens there either?"

"We'd have the same problems that Armstrong is having. Etaens have been known to bring their disagreements—and their enhancements—to other planets."

"Yet you back them for the Alliance," Uzval said.

"I never said that." Foltz kept his voice calm. He had an amazing ability to avoid seeming provoked. "I said I believed they deserved a hearing, just like any other petitioner."

"Just not in your homeland." Restrepo spoke with bitterness.

Foltz inclined his head toward her. "Indeed."

"Not in any of our homelands," Kreise said. "That's another reason for Armstrong. I'd like to give this a chance here."

She hoped that they'd have enough time for discussion before Armstrong cleared Döbryn and her colleagues, if the city ever would.

[I CANNOT HELP BUT FEELING THAT THERE ARE SUBTLE PREJUDICES AT PLAY.]

As usual, the Ambassador's words silenced the argument. The group turned toward the shape outlined in the chair.

[ALL OF OUR HOMELANDS HAVE A HISTORY OF GENOCIDE. WE HAVE ALL OVERCOME IT. OUR PEOPLES STILL MAKE ERRORS, WHICH IS WHY WE HAVE LAWS. SURELY WE SHOULD LOOK AT ETAE'S RECORD, AND REALIZE THAT HAD THE ALLIANCE EXISTED WHEN WE WERE IN

THE SAME POSITION, WE WOULD HAVE APPLIED—AND
WE WOULD HAVE BEEN TURNED DOWN.]

Kreise's breath had left her body. The Ambassador
had said so many things that offended her, she wasn't
sure which one to object to first.

"You're calling genocide an error?" Uzval's fingers
had bent upward again. In fact, she was leaning
slightly backward in her chair, her upper torso bent
back at the shoulder, another sign of upset.

"The Ambassador was making several points," Restrepo said. "Don't work them all together into one."

"Then the Ambassador shouldn't have said them all
at one time," Uzval said. "Genocide is not an error.
It is not an unfortunate occurrence. It is not a footnote
in history, nor is it easily forgivable."

[YET YOUR PEOPLE COMMITTED IT AGAINST THE
QAVLE AS RECENTLY AS A CENTURY AGO, AMBASSA-
DOR UZVAL.]

The Ambassador seemed to be enjoying itself. Kreise's observation over the years, was that the Ambassador lived—literally—for intellectual debate and
argument. So it seemed to relish the moments when
things became tense in the meetings.

Uzval was about to answer the Ambassador, but it
kept speaking as if it didn't notice her attempts to
interrupt.

[WHAT FASCINATES ME THE MOST, HOWEVER, ARE
THE HUMANS. THEY HAVE TAKEN GENOCIDE TO AN ART.
I KNOW THAT MOST OF US WHO HAVE DEALINGS WITH
THEM BELIEVE THAT THE HUMANS HAVE NOT PARTICI-
PATED IN SUCH THINGS IN A LONG TIME, BUT WE DO NOT
COUNT TRIBAL DEATHS WITHIN OUR OWN SPECIES AS
GENOCIDE. THE HUMANS DO. THEY HAVE SUCH VARIED
CULTURES AND THEY HAVE WIPED THOUSANDS—
PERHAPS MILLIONS, IF YOU COUNT ALL OF HUMAN
HISTORY—OUT.]

Kreise clenched her fists. The Ambassador probably
wanted to anger her. If so, it was doing a good job.

She had to turn the attention back to Etae, and

then chastise the Ambassador for the assumptions it made in its earlier arguments.

"That's precisely why we don't want Etae in this Alliance," Kreise said. "They have committed genocide—human against human genocide—and—"

"That stopped with the Child Martyr incident thirty years ago," Restrepo said.

Kreise's fingers dug even deeper into her skin. "It did not. We have records that the killings continued during the civil war. Just because so many people sympathized with the rebels when it became clear that the then-government was murdering children doesn't mean that the rebels stopped their own killing of families. The rebels just got smarter about it."

"I have not seen this evidence," Restrepo said. She had always defended the rebels, who, in the end, had won the civil war and become the current government of Etae. No matter how much evidence of unjustified killings Kreise had shown her, Restrepo believed that the current government could do no wrong.

"You also ignore the murders of the indigenous peoples," Uzval said into Kreise's silence.

"That was done by the Idonae," Restrepo said. "They conquered Etae first, exploited it, stripped it of resources and the Ynnels, and then the humans came. Humans had nothing to do with the death of the Ynnels."

"That's not the history that I have read. I've seen evidence of human-Ynnel slaughter with my own eyes," Uzval said. "I will bring it to our next meeting."

"You should have given it to the various approval committees." Foltz's voice was soft.

"I did," Uzval said.

"If they ignored it, then they didn't think it relevant," Restrepo said.

"I think they had other reasons for ignoring it," Uzval said, "reasons you're quite familiar with."

"Are you making some kind of accusation?" Restrepo asked.

"The intergalactic corporations," Uzval said, her

breath raw in the mask, "want the Etaens—the current ones, the human ones—to train them in the art of guerrilla warfare, intergalactic style. They want to buy Etaen enhancements. They want all those subtle little weapons that can get past scanning, and they want the murderous techniques. You pretend to speak for your people, but you speak for the intergalactics. We all know they're tired of playing by the rules, tired of reporting all of their activities to the Alliance, tired of—"

"They do none of those things," Foltz said. "Stop accusing Ambassador Restrepo of being in bed with them. She is her own woman."

"She is," Uzval said. "She represents the Jupiter colonies well because she believes the lies the corporations that run those colonies tell. She has to realize there is more to life than trade and economics. She has to understand that a certain morality—"

[IF THE ALLIANCE TEACHES ANYTHING, IT IS THAT ONE SPECIES'S MORALITY IS ANOTHER'S IMMORALITY. DO NOT LECTURE US ON LIFE, AMBASSADOR UZVAL. YOU HAVE NO STANDING. AS I SAID, ALL OF OUR PEOPLES HAVE MADE MISTAKES, AND ALL OF THEM WOULD NOT, AT ONE POINT OR ANOTHER IN THEIR HISTORIES, HAVE QUALIFIED FOR MEMBERSHIP IN THE ALLIANCE.]

"Precisely," Kreise said as quickly as she could. "And that doesn't excuse the Etaens. Just because we once had a similar history doesn't mean we should look at a decade as if it's a significant amount of time."

[IN THE HISTORY OF ETAE, IT IS. THE ETAENS—THE CURRENT ONES, AS AMBASSADOR UZVAL SAYS—HAD NOT MAINTAINED PEACE FOR LONGER THAN AN EARTH DAY BEFORE THE CESSATION OF FIGHTING A DECADE AGO. TEN YEARS, THEN, IS QUITE A SUCCESS. WE MUST LOOK AT THEIR HISTORY IN THIS CONTEXT.]

"I think we should look at it in the context that you presented earlier, Ambassador," Kreise said as quietly as she could. "Humans are experts at genocide, particularly of a type that many other races do not recognize. Now Etae is populated almost exclusively by humans, and two decades ago, they were slaughtering each other. A decade may be a long time in Nyyzen history, but in human history it's a nanosecond. We need to deny the petition."

"We need to let them make a petition before we deny it," Restrepo said.

"There is no rule that states such a thing," Kreise said.

Restrepo stood. "Then I'll invent one. Because I declare this meeting over. I will not converse with you people again until I hear Döbryn's speech—whatever it is."

And she stalked out of the room.

"Someone get her," Kreise said. "We must continue this."

"I don't like considering things without all the evidence," Foltz said. "I'm particularly intrigued by Ambassador Uzval's statements and the Ambassador's rather twisted logic about history. I'd like to see the evidence Ambassador Uzval mentioned and hear more from the Nyyzen Ambassador. Perhaps an informal gathering would be possible?"

Kreise let out a small breath. She had lost control of this meeting from the moment the Ambassador appeared. And she didn't know how to regain that control.

"First, let me speak to the city," she said. "Then we can all decide how to proceed."

Especially her. She needed time to come up with another plan of her own.

13

Nitara Nicolae stood beside the stove, looking at the mushrooms in garlic sauce that she had created especially for the ambassadors. The entire lunch was ruined because no one had informed her that the meeting would last only an hour.

Bread filled with her own blend of meats and spices was still baking, and a berry cobbler, made with berries grown in Armstrong's greenhouses outside the dome, cooled on a side table.

When she had poked her head into the meeting, she had been startled to see that her tables had been moved. The ambassadors were closer than she had expected them to be, and they were uninterested in any type of food.

She also did not see Anatolya Döbryn. The woman was supposed to be addressing the ambassadors, and she wasn't even present.

Nicolae would have to start over. She would have to find something to do with this food, first of all. Her fists clenched, and she turned around and around in the badly designed kitchen.

She had already dismissed her staff for the day. She didn't want them to see her losing her temper, and she was very close. She wasn't sure what she should do next—confront Mayor Soseki, who had wanted her to represent Armstrong and its cuisine, speak to one of his deputies—the one who had told her that the meal service would be part of the meeting and she should act accordingly—or talk to the ambassadors themselves to see if they even cared.

She was half tempted to have the food delivered to their hotels, but she wouldn't do that. Instead, she would contact one of the centers for the poor. The indigent would have an excellent meal this afternoon.

All of that took care of her food issues. But they didn't deal with her pride or her reputation. She was a renowned chef, and she had been treated like a cook.

She hadn't been a cook since she had left the merchant ships, and she hadn't been subject to someone else's bidding since she had opened her own restaurant.

Still, she wanted to be here. She wanted to look on the face of Anatolya Döbryn, to see how the Butcher of Etae would look just before she died.

14

DeRicci's aircar stopped two blocks away from Flint's office. The dang thing landed with some fanfare in a parking lot marked *Private,* and refused to go any farther. When she tried to disconnect the autonavigate, the car informed her links that she was not allowed to do so—she didn't own the thing, after all, and it was subject to the laws of Armstrong, which she should consider before trying to violate them.

She damn near started to argue with the car, then realized the ridiculousness of it all, shut the vehicle down, and got out. She stood in the lot, feeling grimy from her hours in the Lahiri apartment, and stretched, letting the annoyance of losing her vehicle to rules slip away.

Then she stared at the car, looking ungainly as it sat on its airjets on the dirt-covered permaplastic, and smiled almost involuntarily. How ridiculous her life had become. Not only did she worry about her new clothing and keeping her new apartment and not hurting the status of her somewhat dull job, but she was also at the mercy of a car.

She shook her head, then walked toward Flint's block. When she reached the cross street, she waved. At some point along this route he had set up perimeter alarms. He would be watching her approach. She always liked to let him know she was aware of his spy techniques.

She fingered his card in the pocket of her blazer. She felt the small piece of paper there, as if it were twenty times heavier than it was. She felt almost guilty about it, partly because she was walking away from a crime scene with evidence that the techs and her so-called partner didn't know about.

When she had come out of the master bedroom, she had almost told Cabrera about the card. But then he went on some tear about the collectible law books. He thought looking around them a waste of his precious time.

When he started that, any ideas she'd had about sharing her Flint discovery vanished. Instead, she had sent Cabrera back to the detective unit to discover all he could about the Lahiris—especially the stuff not on the mainstream databases—and she had come here, leaving the techs in the apartment to gather the last of the evidence and, with luck, discover who the mystery corpse was.

DeRicci stepped onto the ratty sidewalk outside Flint's office. If anything, the place looked more decrepit than it had a few months ago. The dirt clung to it, creating rippled lines in the ancient permaplastic.

She reached for the doorknob and heard it click open. The door swung back. Flint was leaning against his desk, his long legs crossed at the ankles. When he saw DeRicci, he waved.

She grinned and he grinned in return. At least he looked better than he had when he was on the force. Then his face had been lined and he always had shadows under his eyes. Now his skin had more color to it, and his blond curls seemed even lighter than they had before, almost like a halo of hair. His eyes were a radiant blue, and when he grinned, like he did now, he had a cherubic handsomeness that belied the ruthlessness she had come to rely on.

"To what do I owe this visit?" he asked her.

"You don't think this is a social call?" She stepped inside. The air was cooler here, and fresher. She wondered if he had some illegal filters. The interior air should match the air in this part of the dome, for better or for worse.

"Not the way you're dressed. Don't tell me. Gumiela put you on a case because you're new, it's political, and she can fire you if things get out of hand without worrying about any interdepartmental backlash."

None of that could have been in any database. Flint obviously guessed some of it because he used to work in the department, but the rest was just an example of how intuitive he was.

"Nonsense." DeRicci started as her links shut off. There was an unnatural hum in her ear, then a white line ran across the bottom of her vision. Finally she got a *System malfunction* warning before it all faded away.

Usually she remembered to shut down her links before she came into Flint's building. But this was the first time she had come here since that command to keep her emergency links on.

And the comptechs in the department had told her that nothing—not court, not anything—could shut down those emergency links.

Obviously, those techs hadn't encountered Miles Flint.

His grin widened. "You know better than to come in here with your links on."

Damn his observative nature. "Forgot," she said.

The door had shut behind her, leaving the office in that dim light that Flint seemed to prefer. She suddenly felt uncomfortable, and realized, for the first time, how his clients felt when they stepped into his office.

"You were telling me why my guess was nonsense," he said.

She made herself smile and walk over to him, shaking off the unease. "Haven't you been following the news this past year? I'm a hero. Heroes can't be fired."

Only Flint truly appreciated how ambivalent De-Ricci felt about the Moon Marathon. She'd seen a lot of death that day. He'd seen a lot too, and hadn't been comfortable with his role either. They'd actually had a few dinners together in some of Armstrong's more private restaurants, talking about how unhappy that case had left them.

Those conversations were the only time the two of them were able to talk about the case. Because of the traumatic nature of the whole thing, DeRicci had been required to go to a departmental shrink—which she had—but she'd talked only about superficial stuff, and the shrink, not nearly as intuitive as Flint, hadn't even noticed.

"Yeah," Flint said, "that hero stuff lasts for the rest of your life. But jobs under Andrea Gumiela don't. I would've thought she'd be jealous of you."

DeRicci shook her head. "She's relieved. I saved her ass."

"Which'll only get you so much currency for so long."

"I know." DeRicci walked to the other side of the desk and grabbed Flint's chair. "Mind if I sit?"

"Be my guest, so long as you move the chair away from my desk."

She carried the chair to the center of the tiny room. Flint watched her, making no move to help. Then she set the chair down, pulled off her stupidly expensive and wonderfully attractive shoes, and rubbed her aching feet.

"Sorry," she said. "They're not made for standing."

"The feet or the shoes?" Flint was in a good mood. He must not have been working on a case. Although his mood had improved considerably in the years since he had left the force.

"Don't make me choose," DeRicci said. "The feet and the shoes have become one."

Flint laughed appreciatively. DeRicci felt her own

mood lighten. She liked him so much better now that they were no longer partnering. Maybe she was the kind of cop who wasn't made for a partner. Maybe, no matter who the partner was, she would find fault with him.

Flint's smile slowly faded, and he looked her over. "You're not dressed for fieldwork."

"You're beginning to make it sound like I'm not dressed for anything," she said.

He stood and lightly brushed her arm. She looked at the sleeve of her blazer. A streak of blood ran from the hem to the elbow. She had touched those pools of blood after all.

"Damn," she said. "This is new."

"You can afford it."

She sighed. She would have liked to let the banter continue a few moments longer. Maybe she should spend more time with her friends, talking to them and relaxing with them. Maybe she should get a few friends—at least ones who weren't work-related.

"Noelle?" Flint returned to the desk. "Did I say something wrong?"

She shook her head, slipped her hand into the pocket of her blazer, and removed the card. Holding it between her index and middle fingers, she handed it to him.

He took it, ran his thumb over the edge where the numbers were written, and frowned. He clearly recognized the card.

"You didn't find this with the blood, did you?" There was an edge in his voice. If DeRicci hadn't known better, she would have thought it fear.

"You ever hear of the Lahiris?" DeRicci asked.

Flint looked at her, his blue eyes no longer sparkling. "Just tell me where you got the card, Noelle."

"Gumiela gave me a case with three corpses in an apartment. Two of them are very prominent citizens: Dr. Mimi Lahiri and her husband, Judge Caleb Lahiri. We can't identify the third."

Flint continued to watch her, his expression unchanging. She couldn't read him. He didn't used to be that good at covering his emotions. He had learned a lot in the last few years.

"I found this in the master bedroom, in a woman's blazer. I recognized the card and brought it to you. No one else on the force knows about this, Miles. Everything we discuss will be off the record."

"There's nothing to discuss."

Masterful. Not a denial and yet not an affirmation either. As if he knew nothing.

"Miles," DeRicci said, "if there's one tie to you, there will be others. If one of those three people came to see you, someone will have a record of it, even if it's on the public surveillance cameras scattered around the dome. And it might be in their links. Tech thinks one or two of the chips might be intact."

Still no change in his expression.

"Miles," she said, "you might have to talk to me or you might have to talk to a judge. It's better to talk to me."

"I don't talk about my business to anyone," he said.

DeRicci shook her head. "You know that's not always possible in a murder case."

His expression didn't change this time either, but his body grew tenser. "You're certain this is murder?"

"The Lahiris were murdered," DeRicci said. "I'm not sure if the woman we can't identify is a murder or a suicide."

"Woman," he muttered as he braced his hands on the desk.

"Does that mean something to you?" DeRicci asked.

But of course he didn't answer. He lowered his head as if he were thinking about something.

She let him. Sometimes Flint made choices that no one expected him to make, but only if he wasn't pushed into them.

His silence made her nervous. He didn't move for the longest time. She wanted to shift position, but didn't. She watched him, waited for some kind of change, and hoped she had enough patience to out-last him.

Finally, he said, "I can't talk to you as a Retrieval Artist. Not about my life or my work or anyone who has come to this office."

He didn't say *clients,* which disappointed her. But she also knew he was cautious. The Lahiris or that woman might have been clients, and he wouldn't tell her.

He wouldn't tell anyone.

"However," he said, "Retrieval Artists sometimes hire themselves out as private detectives. I'll act as one in this case."

DeRicci leaned back in his chair. She slipped her sore feet back into her shoes. "You know I can't do that. The more I work with you, the more trouble I'll get into."

"That's not your main reason, Noelle." He said that with warmth.

"Well," she said, "there is the budget. The City of Armstrong can't afford you, Miles."

"I knew that when I made the offer," he said.

She swallowed, not wanting to state what he must have already figured out.

"Miles," she said softly, "you know that anyone who had contact with the Lahiris is a suspect in their deaths. And if I find out that you had contact with them, I have to report that card, and I have to investigate you."

"You can't," he said. "Conflict of interest. We were partners once."

"Two years ago. We're already outside the rules. I'll be required to investigate you."

"And what happens when the department finds out you warned me?" Flint asked. "Retrieval Artists know how to disappear."

A chill ran through her. He wouldn't do that. Flint had integrity. He wouldn't run out on her if he was involved in this case.

She said, "I know you better than that," and was

happy that her voice didn't reveal the sudden doubts that she felt.

Did she know him well? She had discovered so much about him after he had left the department that it made her feel as if she hadn't known him at all. But they had become friends in the meantime.

Hadn't they?

Flint stood, the movement obviously the beginnings of a dismissal. "Run your investigation the way you always do, Noelle. Follow the leads; follow the book as best you can."

She squinted at him. "Why are you saying that?"

"Because," he said, "if you don't hire me, I'll have to treat you like I would any other authority. I can't talk to you about anything I've done, anyone I've met, or anyone I haven't met. No exceptions, Noelle. Not even for friends."

She hadn't heard him be so harsh, at least not to her. Not to Paloma, either, his mentor. Something was changing for him. Something had made him different.

She wondered what it was.

"That single card can cause a lot of trouble for you, Miles," she said.

He gave her a small smile. "I'm not worried."

She stood and extended her hand. "I need it back."

He studied the card for a moment, ran his thumb along those numbers again, and then slowly, reluctantly, handed it back to her.

That surprised her. She hadn't expected him to do so.

She took the card and slipped it in the pocket of her blazer.

"How're you going to explain that?" Flint asked. "You didn't report it at the scene."

"It's in my personal log," she said.

She shouldn't have told him that, but she felt that she owed him that much. As a friend and a former colleague.

"You'll get in trouble for coming here," he said.

She shook her head.

"Think about it, Miles," she said. "Consider cooperating with me."

"Consider hiring me, Noelle."

She handed him the chair. He took it and put it behind the desk.

"I hope we can settle this without bringing you in," she said.

"Me, too."

She nodded at him, feeling awkward, feeling like their friendship might have changed.

And then she let herself out.

It wasn't until she was half a block away that she realized his words—his *you'll get in trouble for coming here*—might not have been meant as friendly advice.

He had been warning her.

Not to watch out for her colleagues.

Flint had been warning her to watch out for him.

15

Flint watched DeRicci's departure on all five of his main screens. He double- and triple-locked his doors, feeling as if he had somehow been violated.

The Lahiris were dead. The unidentified body—which obviously hadn't gone through a DNA scan yet—was probably Carolyn. And Flint certainly hoped that the weapon used in the crime wasn't the one he had given her.

He sank into his chair, put his face in his right hand, and rubbed his eyes. He knew the law. He knew how public this case was going to be, and how ruthless DeRicci would have to be.

All the factors—the judge, the family politics, and Etae itself, not to mention the fact that Carolyn was a newly recovered Disappeared—would play all over the media. DeRicci's involvement, as much as she wanted to joke about it, gave the case cachet.

And Gumiela already had a sense of what a political nightmare this case was going to be when she assigned DeRicci to the case. DeRicci's record this past year or so had been impeccable. Before, it was filled with reprimands and demotions and citations.

Poor thing. She knew what a mess she was in, and in typical DeRicci fashion, she let her dry sense of humor speak for her. But he had seen the stress in her body, the way that the old exhaustion was reaching for her. By the time this case was over, she'd be as destroyed as she always was by cases.

Maybe more so, because she had found a link to him.

She had played fair with him. More than fair. And she would get in trouble for it if things went badly for her. She had given him a chance to run.

He knew how. Every Retrieval Artist did. And he had more than enough money to survive for the rest of his life.

Unlike most Disappeareds, he wouldn't even have to change his identity or his lifestyle. Even if something went horribly wrong, and he got charged in this case, all he had to do was go to a world outside of the Alliance. Unlike many of the alien cultures he interacted with, humans did not track their ordinary criminals to the ends of the universe.

Only the really dangerous ones—the mass murderers—got that treatment. And, he'd learned, not even all of them.

It would be so easy. All he had to do was clear the accounts he had in Moon banks, and take the *Emmeline* wherever the spirit moved him. He could travel for the rest of his life, finding new places to live, having adventures that would take his mind off Armstrong forever.

If he were that kind of person.

He raised his head. DeRicci had reached her car. She stood outside it, staring at it as if she didn't see it.

She had sensed the change in their relationship. Had she heard his warning? Because if he stayed, he would fight, and he would fight dirty. He knew more of her weak points than she knew his.

He would survive, if he could. And he would do what it took.

He had learned that side of himself a long time ago. He had a ruthlessness that most people didn't expect to see in him. A ruthlessness that enabled him to survive the loss of his daughter and his wife, and to go against some of Armstrong's laws in the first place.

A ruthlessness that allowed him, in DeRicci's presence, to slide a chip off his desk, hide it in his hand, and then use it to erase that card DeRicci had handed him. He had destroyed the information on all three chips in the card.

He left the watermark and the handwritten number, although he could have deleted those as well. He had figured, even before she told him, that DeRicci had made a record in her personal log.

She was a good detective, and she was meticulous. He didn't want to be on the wrong side of her.

Finally, she opened the car door and got inside. Then she leaned her head against the steering wheel.

She knew, then. She knew how difficult this would be.

Only she didn't know the depth of his involvement. That he'd worked with the Lahiris for more than six months, that he'd found their daughter, that he'd reunited them—in a public place.

She would find all of that out, and she would have the beginnings of a case—not necessarily for murder, but as an accessory. Particularly if she could show that the death of the Lahiris happened because Carolyn had returned to their life.

He leaned back in his chair and stared at the ceiling. He felt an overwhelming urge to talk to Paloma, but he knew better. He had learned, in the last year, not to trust anyone, not even his mentor.

To get through this one, he would have to rely on himself.

16

The bullet train took Soseki from Armstrong to Littrow in thirty-five minutes. Littrow was the dome nearest Armstrong, just over the Taurus Mountains. The Moon's governing council had its seat in Littrow, a fact that had annoyed the citizens of Armstrong since the Moon's domes unified.

An aircar had been waiting for Soseki when he got off the train, and had taken him directly to the governor's mansion. The mansion sat in the exact center of town, only a block from the executive office building, and two blocks from the council chambers. The mansion had—like so much else in the domes—been built from a Moon-based concretelike substance made of regolith. Only the regolith found in the Taurus-Littrow valley was the darkest on the Moon, and this building wasn't the gray of most Moon-based concretes, but almost black.

The mansion made Soseki feel small. He hated walking across the ceremonial sidewalk, next to the thick green lawn (planted centuries ago, and maintained with precision), to the tall front door. In the very center of the door—just above his head—was an old-fashioned brass knocker, imported from some famous building on Earth, and everyone who came to the mansion was expected to use it.

Soseki hated grabbing the brass bar, pulling it back, and hitting it against the knocker's frame. The action always made him feel like a child, holding something above his head and pounding with all of his might.

The mansion's door eased open—apparently it had known he was coming and had been instructed to let him in—and a digitized voice bade him welcome.

Soseki stepped into the hallway, which was almost as wide as his office, and waited until a bot floated up to him, told him in a preprogrammed voice to follow it, and led him up the winding staircase to the second floor.

Soseki had been here several times. The second floor housed the governor-general's office. The entire floor had been turned over to the business of Moon government; Soseki doubted the governor-general even went to the nearby executive office building most days.

She was waiting, standing in the center of her office, dwarfed by the ceremonial mahogany desk that had been a gift from the Council of the Governments of Earth when the United Domes of the Moon had been formed.

The blue-and-gold rug beneath the governor-general's feet had been woven in Glenn Station; the paintings on the wall behind her—of the Taurus mountain range—had been completed in Armstrong; and the rest of the furniture had all been hand-built in Tycho Crater. Soseki was certain that everything in the room came from various other domes, but those were the only things he recognized.

The bot veered off. Soseki stepped into the large room and resisted the urge to wipe his feet before he stepped on the beautiful rug.

"Arek," the governor-general said, hand extended.

He didn't like the informality. He was here as the mayor of Armstrong, not as one of her political cronies. "Governor."

She smiled. He'd always thought her smile impish and insincere. "Whatever happened to Celia?"

He almost answered, *Whatever happened to Mayor?* but thought the better of it. He wasn't here to antagonize her. He was here to get her to work with him.

"I'm afraid I'm only here on business, Governor," he said, keeping the formality in his tone.

She assessed him for a long moment. She was a tiny woman who barely came up to his shoulder, and yet when she studied him with her large black eyes, he always wanted to back away.

"You're that disturbed by the Etaen hangers-on?" she asked.

"Did you look at the documentation?" He regretted the question the moment he asked it. It sounded too harsh and critical.

"Of course," she said, turning away from him and heading to her desk. "We've let in other suspect peoples."

"The names Döbryn gave us are from known watch lists, and many of these people had some association with crimes committed off Etae," he said.

"I said I read the documentation." The governor-general walked behind the desk and sat down, looking suddenly taller. Apparently someone had put the chair at intimidation height.

"Then you know that these are people whom we can't trust," Soseki said.

"Whom we *couldn't* trust," she said. "Now the Alliance wants to meet with them to determine if their petition for membership is legitimate. And a mayor from a rather unimportant city from a moon—not even a planet—wants to interfere with decisions made by representatives from various parts of the known universe. Somehow I don't think that's right."

He felt the muscles in his shoulders tense. She had brought him here to reprimand him, not to listen to his arguments.

"Governor," he said, walking toward the desk, "she didn't even give us the names of all the people traveling with her. For all we know, they could be assassins, hired to get rid of the Executive Council of the Earth Alliance. I wouldn't put it past the Etaens."

The governor-general templed her fingers and stared at him over them. "You wouldn't put it past them?"

"No, sir, I wouldn't."

"You, the interstellar expert. The man who has a history of working in the diplomatic service, the man who of course has traveled all over the known universe so that he could form these opinions."

Her sarcasm was great because she knew that he hadn't been outside of the solar system. She also knew his history. She was the one who had approached him to run for mayor of Armstrong when the position became available. But she hadn't liked the fact that he was an independent thinker, that he didn't always follow her lead when it came to Moon business.

"I have studied the history of Etae," he said, "and—"

"Studied the history of Etae." She tapped her templed fingers against her chin. "Of course, you did so on the nets and in databases and through other people's writings. The Alliance makes a point of visiting the places that petition for membership. The evaluation process includes months, sometimes years of hands-on work before a determination is made. Your 'study' is, of course, more valuable than theirs."

"I'm not saying that." Soseki had to struggle to keep his voice level. "My complaint is that Döbryn is trying to bring a group of unknowns into my city without following protocol or the rules. She even caught the Alliance by surprise. They thought she was coming alone."

"They've already determined that she can enter with her security team. You're the one holding things up, Arek."

He stared at her. Her return stare was cold, her features impassive. He wasn't going to convince her with polite logic. He doubted he would convince her at all, but he had to try.

"Do you know who Anatolya Döbryn is?" he asked.

"Of course," she said. "Everyone has—"

"They call her the Butcher of Etae," he said, talking over the governor-general. "It's said that she personally killed one hundred Enison in retaliation for her father's death. Whether she did or not, she ordered the death of all the Enison in custody, and destroyed entire cities—"

"Enison?" The governor-general tilted her head up. She had clearly never heard the word.

"The humans who formed the Etaen regime," he said. "You've heard them called usurpers and rebels, but they actually controlled the government for nearly forty years."

"I really don't care about the history," the governor-general said. "I've found political conflicts on other worlds are simply too esoteric for me. The details of Etaen politics belong with the Alliance, not between you and me. And you, Arek, are interfering with Alliance politics. If you don't cease, I'll have to override you."

He felt a desperation that he hadn't felt since the days after the Moon Marathon, when he realized just how close to a disaster that event could have been.

"All I want them to do," he said, "is give their names and their DNA ident, and open up all of their backgrounds. If they have criminal records or are on watch lists, I don't want them in my city. Everyone else has to play by those rules. I don't understand why these people should get a pass."

"These people get a pass precisely because they're trying to play by the rules." The governor-general let her hands fall flat on the desktop. "That's what you're missing, Arek. They can't fit into Armstrong's rules precisely because their world has been at war for so long. The watch lists aren't infallible."

"And neither are the decon units and the security filters and the weapons monitors. None of the Alliance members will have to stay in the dome after their meetings are done. But what if these people let another virus loose? What if they bring weapons in with them, ones we can't detect? The Etaens are renowned for their weapons-making abilities, particularly for their abilities in subverting the standard security features of any port, and getting weapons into places that normally don't allow them. And you want me to allow people like that into my dome?"

"Our dome," the governor-general said, "and yes, I do."

Soseki waited for the explanation, but she didn't give him one. She simply expected him to leave here, and let those people into Armstrong.

"They could be killers," he said.

Her smile was slow. "You claim to know your history, Mayor Soseki."

Now she was being formal, and he wasn't sure why. Perhaps because she was ordering him about.

"But what you fail to remember is that terrorists often become statesmen late in life. Rogue states break away, fight for their independence, and then are forced to make a government. It happened here on the Moon."

Soseki shook his head slightly. "You're talking about colonies breaking away from parent states. And yes, that did happen to us. But Etae wasn't anyone's colony. It didn't break away."

"Really?" The governor-general leaned back as if she had caught him in a lie.

"Not among the humans, anyway. The Idonae lost their battle for Etae. They killed the indigenous population and then the humans took over. No one broke away from any parent state."

"And yet a government was formed where there hadn't been one before," she said.

"There was a government. They had a civil war," Soseki said.

The governor-general shrugged. "That government, if I remember right, slaughtered children. It—"

"A child," Soseki said. "It was a political tool. Other children died, on both sides—"

"It doesn't matter," the governor-general said. "Your problem is that you're used to living in the established solar system. We deal with different issues. Someone decided to bring a young state into our world, and we'll have to deal with it. *You'll* have to deal with it, Arek."

Back to his name again. She was trying to cajole him.

"I won't," he said. "I won't take responsibility for them entering the dome. If you want to release the Etaens from port, you have to come to Armstrong to do it. And believe me, I'll be all over the media opposing it."

Her entire body froze. The tendons in her hands showed against the skin. He had never seen her so tense.

"Do that," she said quietly, "and you'll never hold political office again."

He shrugged. "Depends on whether you survive the battle, doesn't it? I'm arguing for people's safety and security. You're not."

"Safety and security are illusions," she said. "Right now, as we're talking, someone who has met all of the safety protocols of the port is walking into Armstrong and going to commit some kind of crime. And if they aren't walking in now, they will. I can guarantee it, Arek. The more we pretend otherwise, the more we get surprised by attacks."

"We live in an enclosed community. If something happens to that community, we only have ourselves to blame," he said. "I will not take risks with Armstrong."

"You're not," she said. "You're taking a risk with the Alliance. We need the Alliance, and your actions jeopardize our relationship with it."

"We're all independent states. They can't dictate how we conduct our day-to-day living," he said.

"They can and do," she said. "To believe anything else is to be very naïve, Arek. We live in an intergalactic community, and it's better to bring in outsiders so that we can control them than let them run amok all over the known universe."

He stared at her for a long moment. She actually believed that. She believed that the Wygnin and the Disty and all the other alien groups would do worse harm to the members of the Alliance if they didn't belong.

He knew better. He'd seen the damage that interaction with groups so different that they couldn't understand the same concepts had done, not just to humans, but to the aliens as well.

"I'm going back to Armstrong," he said. "I'm telling the ambassadors that if they want Döbryn to speak to their group, they'll have to do it without her security people."

"And if she dies while in Armstrong because she doesn't have the protection she needs, what then, Arek?" the governor-general asked. "Have you thought about all the reprisals her government will take—all the illegal actions they'll conduct against *your* dome because you've been so unreasonable?"

He gave her a small smile. "If we continue to follow my rules," he said, "they won't get into my dome. No one from Etae will ever be allowed to land in our port, let alone cross through its doors into Armstrong."

She stood, studied him for a moment, and then shook her head. "I always thought you were a good politician, Arek. I thought you'd be an asset—a man like you, with your education, your sophistication. But it's a veneer, and you don't even realize how wrong you are."

"Funny," he said. "I've been thinking the same thing about you."

"I'm sending the order to let them out of the Port,"

she said. "By the time you get back, Döbryn and her people will be inside Armstrong, meeting with the ambassadors. You shouldn't go head-to-head with me, Arek."

"It doesn't matter when they get in," he said. "I'll publicize the meeting. I'll publicize your action, and I'll tell everyone what kind of killers you let into 'our' dome. See whose political career survives then."

He didn't wait for her reaction. He turned, digging his foot into that beautiful rug, and hurried out of the office. As he walked, he sent messages through his links to Londran, asking him to prepare a press conference.

Soseki would need what little background they had on the "security" team being let into his dome. He would also need a history of Etae, a biography of Döbryn, and a history of Etaen-sponsored terrorism throughout the known universe.

He wanted Armstrong—hell, he wanted the entire Moon—to know the danger that the governor-general and the Alliance had put them in.

17

Flint kept his screens up. As he watched DeRicci get into her car and sit while she clearly mulled over what to do next, he moved money through his various accounts. He had several dummy accounts that allowed him to transfer funds until they could no longer be traced. He went through four accounts that were numbered only—no names on them, no way to trace back to him—before he hit one of his emergency accounts.

He moved a large amount of his fortune into that account, just in case he decided to disappear. If he left, he would be able to do it on his own, without an agency, and he would have his own money.

He also downloaded twenty thousand credits into one of the chips on his hand, so that he would have traveling money if he needed to run right away.

His mouth was dry. He felt more nervous than he ever had. Even when he had defied Armstrong's laws and gone against the police department itself, he hadn't felt this nervous.

Paloma had warned him this would happen. She had told him that he would break laws he wouldn't normally dream of breaking. She had also told him that he would become a person he didn't recognize.

If Flint ran, he would become that person.

DeRicci finally started her car and pulled out of the parking lot. Flint wondered what kind of decision she had come to.

He guessed he would find out soon enough.

He took a deep breath and focused on the computer in front of him. Before he came to any decision about his own future, he had to have more information. He opened the files he had made on the Lahiris. When he was considering their case, he had tracked them for a long time.

He had even put tracing devices into their apartment's systems. His devices had been—at the time—state-of-the-art and untraceable. But they might not be now.

The Lahiris had excellent home systems. The systems were well hidden, in keeping with the old-fashioned air, but they existed. Their apartment cleaned itself, and they used robotic equipment to serve them when necessary.

Each movement, each command, left a trace within the system, and if Flint wanted to, he could see what the Lahiris did for every second of every day since he first loaded his spyware into their equipment. He even saw the security scans their system did, searching for security breaches.

Now he needed to use those tracers to view the current scene inside the apartment. He also had to download the system history, and do so before the police scanned the system. He doubted the police could trace him either, but he had to be cautious nonetheless.

He brought up a second screen, and turned on the cameras throughout the apartment. That screen also handled sound. On a third screen, he ran the sensory information: He needed to know what the smells were—the system could give him only component molecules, but his own settings would identify the odor—and if anything had changed in the apartment—

had the temperature gone up, or were there other molecules in the air, ones that had not been there before?

Their system would also inform his of any breakdown, and give him an account of the routines and the changes therein. He hoped that the Lahiris would have used audio/visual continually for security's sake.

He hoped there was a recording of the murders itself.

As their system downloaded into his, his second screen went blank. Then the Lahiris' apartment filled the screen. Each room had its own window, small and square, and he could see people moving inside the bedrooms, the kitchen, and the living area.

Techs. They were still on-scene.

Flint had his own system record them. Their conversation might provide him with information; their actions certainly would.

He searched the windows for the bodies and found them in the living room. He enhanced the window, making it fill the screen.

The room looked like it had on his visits to the Lahiris. The furniture was fussy, the lighting was too dark for his tastes, and the tables had old legal tomes on them, as if Judge Lahiri had been too snobby to use a link for his legal information.

Flint had found the place stuffy and repressive, and that sense came through the window, almost as if he were there.

Only two bodies remained on the floor. One had already been loaded into a SmartBag by the medbot, but the other two lay near each other.

They were recognizable, their faces slack in death. Dr. Lahiri was covered in blood, her hand open, looking surprisingly vulnerable. Judge Lahiri seemed even frailer than he had in life—an elderly man with no hope of defending himself.

Too much had been moved. Flint couldn't tell where the bodies had been, if the blood around them had come from all three or only one, and if anything had been moved prior to the police's arrival.

Another large bloodstain covered the floor a few meters from the couple. It had soaked into the hard-wood floor, making the wood seem black.

Flint had no idea how that happened. Dr. Lahiri was phobic about cleanliness. She even had a cleaning bot sweep Flint's chair when he had stood to leave. Flint had once asked her why she hadn't bought self-cleaning furniture, and the judge had answered instead of his wife.

We prefer antiques, he had said with such precision that Flint wondered why the couple had any modern conveniences at all, much less so many. Apparently appearances were more important to them than the actual simpler-era lifestyle.

The bots should have cleaned, even if the Lahiris were dead. The bots should also have called in the emergency information when they encountered bodies.

And the apartment itself should have called for police when the first shot was fired, unless the weapon wasn't recognized by the system. If the weapon had been similar to the one he had given Caroline (or, worst case, if it had been that weapon), the system would definitely have recognized it and sounded the alert.

Something had failed here, and failed spectacularly.

The techs really weren't discussing much. Occasionally, they'd ask one another to verify something or move an item. But mostly, they worked in silence.

Flint left the audio on and studied the sensory information. The air was thick with the smells of decay. It also had a lot of perfume in it. Dr. Lahiri used some natural odorizers in her home, so that the place often smelled of flowers or wood smoke, and she also wore a lot of perfume.

He found nothing else unusual, at least in the first readings. He would check again, and cross-compare to his old records. If Flint had managed to break into the system, then he had to logically assume that someone else could have, especially someone else on-scene. If that someone else changed the apartment's computer command structure, that would explain the lack of bots, the dirt, and the failure to note an emergency situation.

Flint then downloaded the remaining files off the security records. He wanted to see if there were vids, but he wasn't willing to do so in real time, while his system was open and vulnerable.

He left the tracking on, set the chips he had planted when he first took the case to record the techs so that he would have a double backup, and then he logged off.

He had several things to do before he really got deeply involved in this investigation. He had been thinking about it while he had been watching the Lahiri place, and he realized he needed more than their records.

DeRicci would keep concurrent records of her investigation. He knew she wouldn't confide in him—not after the way he had dismissed her—but he would need her information if he was going to solve this case.

Flint leaned back in his chair. He hadn't realized that he wanted to solve it until now.

He had the skills for it. He also had more information than DeRicci ever would. Unlike her, he wasn't bound by Armstrong law or even Alliance law. He would hack into systems with impunity, find out what he could, and then move on.

He also wanted to know his own culpability—he had been honest with himself about that. And the only way to discover how liable he was—or wasn't—was to find out the extent of Carolyn Lahiri's involvement.

If he did solve it, and found out that this case actually had nothing to do with him, he would somehow send the information to DeRicci. He would even try to make it seem like she had put the information together herself.

Then he smiled. As if DeRicci would fall for that. She would know where the information came from, even if she couldn't trace it, and she would double-check it herself.

And if she believed him, she would act on it.

But he was getting ahead of himself. First he had to find out who killed the Lahiris, and who the third body belonged to, and, with luck, clear himself.

18

She was about to give up. Anatolya Döbryn couldn't handle the waiting any longer. If she paced this suite much more, she would literally go insane.

She was still in the Port, still in the same section they had brought her to shortly after her arrival, only now they had moved her to a suite of rooms.

Apparently no one liked her pacing in that public waiting area. And no one liked the constant questions she asked.

She was given a choice: Return to her ship and go through the entire decontamination process again, or stay in a private suite at the Alliance's expense until the matter was settled.

She had chosen the suite, expecting it to be outside the Port. But Armstrong's Port had been here forever, and apparently had had time to think of every inconvenience. There were, one of the officials had informed her, several hotels built into the Port itself.

It almost felt as if she were moving backward, as if all the progress she'd made getting to Armstrong had been for nothing.

She would have complained to the attaché, Gideon Collier, but he had vanished long before that little

Port employee had banished her from the official waiting area.

Anatolya didn't even have Collier's link so that she could inform him where she was going. She had to trust the Port to give him that information.

For all she knew, this could be an embarrassment set up by the Alliance, to show to her how unworthy Etae's petition to join was. She had missed the reception they had planned for her, and would probably miss the first meeting as well.

The suite was nicely apportioned, done in human proportions instead of Disty, like some of the suites she'd seen on Mars. The furniture was made of a plastic she didn't recognize—it probably predated the plastics used on Etae—and seemed unusually durable.

Three rooms composed the suite: a living area, with all sorts of entertainment—almost enough to make a person forget that she was cut off from everyone around her, a bedroom, and a kitchen.

Anatolya's off-world links had shut down the moment the ship entered Port—standard procedure in any large port. But she also couldn't link with anyone outside a small prescribed area within the Port—and that area did not include the dock where her ship waited.

Nor, apparently, did it include anyplace Gideon Collier was. A simple page of the area brought no response at all.

She wasn't sure how long she'd have to stay here. She peered into the bedroom with its small bed and cheerless gloom, and hoped she wouldn't have to sleep there. The fact that the tiny kitchen, attached to a larger dining area, had provisions also unnerved her.

It made her feel like she would be here for the rest of her life.

Perhaps the problem she had with this treatment was that she wasn't, by nature, a supplicant. She never had been, and she never would be. She liked to be the one in charge, the one making the decisions, the one in control.

She sat down on the couch and drew her knees to her chest. Etae was ready to join the Alliance, and Etae needed the Alliance. Nearly a century of war had destroyed the planet. The oceans were so heavily polluted that the fish were dying, and none of the decrystallization equipment worked.

Half the arable land was covered with land mines or had been fallow for so long that it would take a decade of work to revitalize the soil—at least with Etaen technology. And there wasn't enough food to feed her own people, let alone the ones who had now become subjects under the Etaen accords.

She had gone from being a military leader to the ruling member of a peacetime council, and she had learned something startling: Commanding armies was easier.

Yes, some of the problems were similar. Soldiers, supply routes, food—food was always an issue. So was water and so were maintaining systems—lights, heat, military equipment.

But she had been trained to run armies, and her government had always placed a priority on its soldiers. That was one of the reasons she was in power and the previous government was not.

One of the many reasons.

But she would lose that power soon if she didn't find some solutions, and she wasn't sure she was going to. The only solution that seemed reasonable was joining the Alliance. Alliance members helped each other, and sometimes deferred payment or forwent it altogether.

And she needed them to forgo that money.

Because one of the many things that Etae lacked was capital. The money had fled the planet long ago, afraid that they'd lose what little they had left.

No resources, no food, barely enough water, and nothing to sell. She was amazed she had gotten this far.

And now the Alliance would let the very rich, very comfortable city of Armstrong turn her out without a hearing. They couldn't judge her people on their backgrounds: Etae had been at war. If her security team were labeled terrorists, she would never get inside Armstrong.

If they had known that her deputy, Gianni Czogloz, was here, they would never have let her in. Gianni was the man who had ordered the massacre of a thousand then-government soldiers in retaliation for the Child Martyr attack. Gianni hadn't picked up a weapon in nearly a decade. He now went to the temple every day, asking for forgiveness, trying to find a way to become a man of peace.

All of her advisers and every member of her security team had terrible pasts. But these people, her friends, had lived a peaceful life since the war ended. She wanted them judged for the past ten years, not the decades before that.

She envied the established governments; she really did. They went through these crises so long ago that they didn't remember what it was like. They all had their military leaders—the ones who became great peacetime leaders, whose reputations were rebuilt. Not just the humans, although she could cite example after example from Earth alone, but also the Disty and the Nyyzen, and even the high-and-mighty Peyti.

All of them had once let reformed killers run their government, and those killers had succeeded.

She would fail.

At least on this attempt.

She stood and was about to contact the port on the wall link when the door opened. Collier hurried in, his hands clasped together and a smile on his narrow little face.

"Your security team may join us," he said as the door slid shut behind him.

She had been so prepared to give up this plan that she wasn't sure she understood what he had said. "My security team?"

"Yes," he said. "I'm sorry that the whole delegation can't come, but who's to know which of your two dozen are security and which aren't? At least you'll have some."

"Who approved them?"

"The order came from the Moon's governor-general a few moments ago."

"The governor-general," she said, sounding stupid. Feeling stupid too. She hadn't expected this after her treatment in the Port.

"Apparently the mayor wasn't going to let you in. It's a big to-do, but it's Moon-based. We don't have to worry about it." Collier moved his hands as he talked—the first time he had really done that. He also grinned at her—the first time he had done that too.

"The Moon's part of the Alliance," she said.

"But this is internal, an argument over procedures and policies. By the time it's settled, we'll be long gone." He inclined his head toward the door. "Are you ready?"

Past ready. But she didn't say that. Instead, she smiled at him. "Of course," she said, and walked to the door.

As it slid open, she asked, "What about my team?"

"They're going through decon and the standard entrance procedures just like you did. We'll wait in a portside restaurant. One of my assistants will bring them to us."

Assistants of assistants. Another sign of long-established and long-peaceful civilizations. Döbryn doubted Etae would ever achieve that in her lifetime. But they would get to it someday; she would guarantee it.

For the first time since she landed on the Moon, she had hope.

19

Flint sat in the back of the Brownie Bar, a bowl of turkey noodle soup beside him. The soup was made with real turkey special-ordered from one of the small farms near Tycho Crater, real noodles, handmade on the premises with flour imported from Earth, and real vegetables, grown in the greenhouses outside the dome.

The Brownie Bar could afford real ingredients at all levels of its cooking, and sell that food for a reasonable price, because of its clientele. The Brownie Bar catered to marijuana users.

The party section, located up front, was reserved for large groups of people who planned to spend the evening eating marijuana-laced brownies and laughing. By the end of the night, the people in the party section usually ordered (and ate) more food than most restaurants served in two days. The party section kept the Brownie Bar in expensive ingredients.

Casual users filled the main section of the restaurant. They often sat in groups of two or three, and had quiet conversations and a brownie or two, before having a full dinner. The Brownie Bar tried to keep the atmosphere there low-key, figuring most people wanted a relaxant before a quiet meal.

But Flint wasn't there for the dining experience or the marijuana. He wanted the public-access ports. In the section he preferred, the Brownie Bar had placed screens on the tables, so that regular customers and hard-core users could come in during their workday, get some work done, and enjoy a brownie or a good meal.

This section was walled off from the others so that the raucous laughter from the party section didn't filter in, nor did the conversation from the main section.

Flint had started to come to the Brownie Bar when the city slapped it with expensive fines for the pipes the Brownie Bar originally allowed in one of its private rooms. Most domed communities had stringent laws against anything that polluted the air, including various kinds of cigarette smoking and pipe usage.

Flint had grown to love the Brownie Bar after the air got clear. He had his favorite table in the back, and the waitstaff—they still hired actual people here—knew not to give him the complimentary tray of brownies to start his meal and not to peer over his shoulder while he worked.

In return, he tipped well and made certain that at least once a week he ordered a large meal to make up for his long table use.

This afternoon, the bar was quieter than usual. Just Flint, with his turkey soup and his home-brewed ale, and a young woman who sat across the room from him, slowly working her way through a plate of brownies, staring at the screen in front of her, and crying softly.

Flint had asked the waitstaff if there was anything he needed to do, but they had shaken their heads. Apparently she came in as often as he did, ate an entire plate of brownies, cried for a while, and left. She'd been doing so for nearly a decade. It was, they guessed, her form of release.

He bent over his screen, bought time with a credit account he'd never used before (and wouldn't use again), and got to work. Even though he normally didn't wear gloves here, he had put on a pair this afternoon. If the police came to trace what he had done, he didn't want to leave any part of himself— except maybe the image of him on the Brownie Bar's security system.

Even that he could thwart, though. He didn't need to deny being here. Instead, he rerouted his access code through several of the access terminals, until the system believed he had logged on from the crying woman's table.

Some systems were remarkably easy to hack. The Brownie Bar's was one, which was why he loved to work here. He sometimes just came in to update his skills, try things he hadn't tried before, so that he wouldn't lose his abilities to alter programming in most systems that existed around Armstrong.

He worked for only a few minutes to get into the police department's systems, and took even less time to find the detective files.

He used to work for the department, and he had had access to the system then. He had left himself several back doors, and after his last major case with the police, he had also given himself a few fake identities with some security protocols so that he could get the day's passwords and use those to enter any police-encoded system.

Fortunately, the Lahiris' system hadn't been encoded when he downloaded off of it. He would have to stop at another public terminal before going back to his office to see if anyone had tried to trace his actions in the Lahiri system. If he found evidence of that, he would wipe it out, making absolutely certain no one could trace the actions back to him.

He decided to tap into DeRicci's files. From there, he would be able to tap into everything the Detective Division did. That might be useful. It would also give him access to the crime-scene division and the medical examiner's offices. He wouldn't have to contact De-Ricci about anything.

As he did this, he left himself a few other back

doors, creating more entities. If he left these other entities floating in the department computer, using their own software so that his tampering wouldn't show up as spyware or as ghosts in the system, he would always be able to access files if he needed to.

Slowly, he was learning how to think ahead.

He paused and ate some of the turkey soup. It was rich as always—the broth had flavor that he rarely encountered in Armstrong restaurants, and the turkey had texture instead of that soft, almost tofulike pseudomeat that passed for poultry in most of Armstrong.

He savored each bite, then set the bowl down again and continued his work. It wouldn't take him long to finish, but he had to do so in a way that he could access the departmental files from anywhere, not just the Brownie Bar.

Fortunately, he'd never told DeRicci the extent of his skills as a hacker. She had known that he was better than most. She just never learned that he was once one of the best in Armstrong.

Now he hoped she'd never learn it.

He paused again and finished the soup. He felt almost dirty doing this, as if he were betraying every friend he had made.

He was certainly betraying DeRicci. But he couldn't work with her—and he couldn't stop the investigation, not without hurting himself.

20

DeRicci had a headache, and she wasn't going to spring for some automatic endorphins. She deserved this headache, and it was only going to get worse.

She shouldn't have seen Flint. She had known that when she drove over, but the feeling grew worse during the meeting. And then, when he had refused to work with her, the feeling had grown even stronger.

These impulses were the reason that DeRicci hadn't been promoted for nearly two decades, the reason that the only promotion she'd ever received came after some political heroism that could be revoked as easily as it was achieved.

She felt some sort of loyalty toward Flint that he didn't feel toward her. Or, worse, she had a death wish of her own, a desire to screw up this case so that she'd be back on the street, forgetting all about the desk and the nice apartment and the even nicer salary.

All those thoughts went through her head as she stood outside the medical examiner's office, talking to Armstrong's chief coroner and one of the senior techs. Gumiela had ordered an express on this case, so the DNA of the third victim had been run at the scene, then rerun here three separate times. Information that sometimes took days because of verification and reverification this time took hours.

And the news wasn't good.

The body belonged to Carolyn Lahiri, a woman who was thought to have Disappeared three decades ago. DeRicci hated that news. First the link to Flint, and now an actual returned Disappeared.

Flint had taken the Lahiris' case, he had found their daughter, and now they had all ended up dead. No matter what happened, he was mixed up in it.

And DeRicci had given him a heads-up. Her prime suspect and she had all but told him to flee the city.

"A Disappeared's going to cause all sorts of problems in this case," the coroner was saying. DeRicci had to force herself to listen. She didn't like Ethan Brodeur, even though she'd worked with him countless times. Her dislike wasn't rational—he was good at his job, and he'd helped her with innumerable cases.

But she found everything about him irritating, from his baritone voice, which he modulated even lower than normal in an attempt to sound sexy, to his enhanced hair, so thick that it looked like he was growing enough for eight people.

He smiled too much, too. No man who cut up dead people for a living should smile that much.

"I'm sure I can get the computer guys to make sure the records are accurate," the main tech, Barbara Passolini, said. She was too thin and looked sickly—the kind of person who never took enhancements because she had seen too many of them go wrong in her job. In fact, DeRicci could remember when Passolini had all of her enhancements removed. She had been on a campaign to make everyone in the department enhancement-free.

"You haven't worked a lot of Disappeareds, have you?" Brodeur asked.

"Usually they don't end up as homicides." Passolini glanced around the hallway. The three of them had decided to meet there to prevent too many leaks in this case. They had also decided not to use their main links for fear of being tapped.

"Actually," DeRicci said, "a lot of Disappeareds end up as homicides. I get them all the time."

Brodeur and Passolini looked at her as if they had forgotten she was there. She shrugged.

"I send them to you, Ethan, and you verify that they're vengeance killings or core deaths or all the other sanctioned murders that go on around here. It just takes a while to find out who they are and why they died."

Brodeur sighed. "We always assume with an alien killing, especially by the Disty or the HD, that it's legal and work our way from there. We don't make that assumption with human-on-human deaths."

"We don't know that this is a human-on-human death," DeRicci said. "We don't know much of anything yet."

"She is right about that," Passolini said, as if DeRicci's being right were an unusual event. "We have a lot of trace and no time to process it. That apartment was oddly cleaned, as if the Lahiris had a cleaning service that quit the moment of the murders."

DeRicci frowned at that. She started to say something, but Brodeur interrupted her.

"We have a Disappeared and we have her parents. We have a weapon on the scene, and wounds—at least in the Disappeared—that could have been made by that weapon."

"But you haven't confirmed that yet, right?" DeRicci asked. "There hasn't been time to verify if that weapon caused the murders."

"It seems likely," Brodeur said.

DeRicci gave him a cool smile. "I'll figure out what's likely and what's not. You just tell me the facts as you discover them. We work better that way."

"Touchy," Brodeur said, but he didn't disagree. He knew better than to get involved in her part of the job.

"Well," Passolini said, facing DeRicci, "you have to

tell me where to start. This case has so many angles that I could pursue all of them and never have free time again."

"We have two obvious anomalies and they're wrapped up in the same corpse." DeRicci had to work to keep her tone level. Passolini should understand this. But techs never really did get their heads out of the details. Usually DeRicci liked that.

She had a hunch she wouldn't in this case.

"First," DeRicci said, "we have the problem of the corpse herself. If Carolyn Lahiri is a Disappeared, what's she doing back in her hometown? How long has she been here, and why is she visiting Mom and Dad, where she's easy to find?"

"I thought of that," Passolini muttered.

"Second," DeRicci said, not believing Passolini, "her face is gone. The other faces are intact. Killers usually use the same MO. This one shot two people in the stomach and one in the face—the one who had been hiding her identity. I want to know if the killer was sending some kind of message."

"Good luck," Passolini muttered.

DeRicci ignored that as Brodeur whistled softly. "So you think she was killed by an outsider?"

"I don't think anything at the moment," DeRicci said.

"You were the one who discovered the gun," Passolini said. "I figured you already know she was a suicide."

"I don't know anything," DeRicci said. "I just make a few guesses. And judging from the layout of the bodies, I made an educated guess. If I had known that the third body belonged to a Disappeared, I might have made a different guess."

"Do you think she's a suicide?" Passolini asked Brodeur.

"I haven't done much more than run her DNA," he said. "You just brought her here. I'm going to need a lot of time with this body. I want to do her autopsy right. Gumiela has made it pretty clear that this is a do-not-screw-up case."

Which was good and bad. It meant that some parts of the case would end quicker than others, but it also meant that most of the case would take longer as people checked and rechecked their work.

"I'm going to need to know several things as quickly as you can get them to me," DeRicci said. "First, I want to know if that body was moved."

"Aside from the trip here, you mean," Brodeur said.

DeRicci nodded. "You had techs on-site. I want to know if Carolyn Lahiri was shot there or shot somewhere else."

"You don't care about the parents?" Brodeur asked.

"I don't know about them either, but they died in a similar method, and if you had gone inside that apartment, you would have realized that someone had died there. There was spatter all over the walls. The question is, of course, who does it belong to—all three corpses or two or maybe even just one?"

"We'll find that out soon enough," Passolini said. "We test the spatter first in cases like this."

"Then," DeRicci said, "I'm going to need to know if that weapon killed her, and if she used it herself."

"Provided, of course, that she wasn't moved," Brodeur said with a smile.

DeRicci didn't smile back. "I'm also going to need to know if there's anything alien in the trace. If she lived off-world, then maybe she was killed by someone who lived off-world. I want to know who or what that someone is."

Passolini nodded.

"I'll check body chemistry then," Brodeur said. "Certain chemicals get into the bloodstream and into the skin that don't exist here. They might tell us where she's been living."

"We'll do all that as a matter of course," Passolini said. "But I don't think you understand, Detective, how messy this case is."

DeRicci hated it when people told her she didn't understand something. "Politically? I have a clue."

"No," Passolini said. "Scientifically. We have a judge, a doctor, and a Disappeared. The Disappeared presents problems you've already listed. But the doctor could bring home a lot of trace if she's not careful, and since she lived and worked in a port city, she saw a lot of people just off the boat, so to speak. That place can be full of more false evidence than you realize."

"Wonderful," DeRicci muttered.

"Then we have a whole different issue with the judge. He was on the Multicultural Tribunal. My great-aunt served on one of the Tribunals. These judges work with aliens all the time, and they have to travel for their cases. Depending on what circuit he was in, he might have had to go from planet to planet to hear appeals and cases."

"I'm assuming he was based here," DeRicci said. "It should only take a moment to check."

"Well, so far, no one's taken that moment, and we need to know," Passolini said. "Because if he was based somewhere else, then we have even more odd trace in that apartment."

"So you're telling me that the scientific evidence in this case might lie?" DeRicci asked.

"It's going to be tough separating the good evidence from the bad," Passolini said. "Building a case for court, if that's what you end up doing, might be difficult."

"Let's just hope it's a suicide, then," Brodeur said.

DeRicci glared at him. "You want a daughter who has been estranged from her parents for I don't know how many years to come home and shoot them for no apparent reason? You want that to be what happened?"

"You want it to be some outsider we haven't caught yet?" Brodeur asked. "One we might never catch if the trace is so iffy that we can't read it?"

DeRicci let out a sigh.

"Best case," Passolini said, speaking directly to Brodeur, "is that these people were killed by the daughter's enemies, the ones who made her Disappear. Then we probably have a legal death and—"

"And two murders," DeRicci said. "If that's the case, then the parents didn't deserve to die. Or they would have Disappeared too. It's not like they weren't prominent people. They were visible. They would have been targets if they were implicated in her crime."

"You don't think this has anything to do with her disappearance?" Brodeur asked.

DeRicci let out a sigh. Her headache was getting worse, and Brodeur's inane questions weren't helping. "I don't make assumptions when I start a case, and you both have to stop doing so now. If this evidence is as messy as you say it is, Barbara, then we have a lot more work than usual. And since Gumiela wants this case to be letter-perfect, we have even more work. The worst thing we can do is go into this with our eyes closed and our minds made up."

The other two were silent for a moment. Then Passolini said quietly, "We're not beginners, Noelle. We know what we're doing."

"Let's hope so," DeRicci said. "Because all of our careers rest on what we do in the next few days. And I, for one, don't want to be demoted."

At least not for the mistakes of others. The mistakes she had already made in this case were another matter. If she got demoted because of Flint, she would accept it.

She rubbed the bridge of her nose with her thumb and forefinger. Maybe she would take the endorphins after all.

"You going to be all right, Noelle?" Brodeur asked.

"This is going to be a son of a bitch," she said. "Once the press get hold of this, we lose what little control we already have."

"I don't think we have to worry much about the press," Passolini said.

DeRicci frowned at her. "Why not? Did Gumiela scare them off?"

"That's not in character," Brodeur said. "If anyone loves the media more than Andrea Gumiela, I have yet to meet her."

"The death of a doctor and a judge would be major news normally," Passolini said, "but not today. Haven't you had your links on?"

DeRicci had forgotten to turn the main links back on. Brodeur shook his head. She wondered what his excuse was.

"The governor-general and the mayor are going head-to-head about letting some known terrorists into the dome for a political meeting. The mayor just issued a statement disagreeing with the governor-general's decision." Passolini shrugged slightly. "It's already a feeding frenzy. I had to shut off the news links because I don't need the distraction."

"But the city does," DeRicci said. She was more relieved than she would have thought possible. "Good. That buys us some time. Let's make the best of it."

"Any objections if I assign some of my best assistants to help me finish quicker?" Brodeur asked. Normally he wouldn't have to check, but DeRicci was glad that he had. This case was messy enough without accusations of incompetence coming their way.

"So long as you review their work," DeRicci said. "And by that, I don't just mean reviewing the reports. I want you to look over their shoulders before you sign off on anything."

"All right," Brodeur said. "I'll have as much as I can as early as I can."

"And I'll do the same with the trace," Passolini said. "You might want to assign someone the site. The more good people we have working on this, the better off we'll all be."

DeRicci fingered the card in her pocket. They were right. Everything had to be by the book.

She pulled out the card and handed it to Passolini. "I found this in one of the woman's blazers in the master suite," DeRicci said. "Have your computer techs see what they can get off of it."

Passolini studied DeRicci for a moment, as if trying to decide to speak up. She finally did.

"You know you should have given this to a tech on-scene," Passolini said.

DeRicci nodded. "I know. I could lie to you and tell you that I forgot that part of procedure or that I took it and forgot about it. I recognized it. It belongs to my old partner, Miles Flint. He's a Retrieval Artist now."

"It's not even properly bagged," Passolini said. "I hope it's not an important piece of information."

"Why would it be?" Brodeur asked, his sarcasm evident. "We have a newly returned Disappeared and a Retrieval Artist in the same case. Of course they're not connected."

DeRicci felt her cheeks heat. "I didn't know she was a Disappeared when I was in the apartment."

"So you thought you'd protect your old partner," Passolini said.

DeRicci shook her head, even though that thought had been on her mind. But she decided to tell these two the other part of the truth.

"I asked him to give me his confidential files," she said. "I actually thought he might, given our past. He didn't. So now I'm turning in this evidence. Flint and I are no longer partners, and he made it very clear that we never will be again."

"Angry, DeRicci?" Brodeur asked, the sarcasm gone from his tone.

"Disappointed," she said. "It was a good partnership. But now, I guess, we're on opposite sides."

Even though she didn't want to be.

21

Kreise hunched in front of her wall screen, staring at the image flat against the paint. She hadn't expected this. She hadn't expected to be outmaneuvered by a regional government—and so quickly.

Döbryn and her security team, as the press was calling them, would be allowed into the dome—might already be in the dome, for all Kreise knew.

She was trapped in her suite on the fifth floor of Armstrong's nicest and oldest hotel, the coyly named Lunar Lander. She had come up for a nap after the tense meeting that afternoon, not expecting any decision from the city on Döbryn's status—at least not that fast.

Normally she would have thought that an official had been bought off. But the governor-general of the Moon had many other, more important things on her agenda than some visitors to Armstrong, and the mayor, well, had a reputation for complete honesty.

Apparently that reputation was correct. It had been his press conference that she had watched, not the governor-general's, and he had been mad. Soseki had even tipped off the press that the Alliance's Executive Council was in town, and then he had mentioned Etae and Döbryn's name.

If anything was guaranteed to bring out the crazies, that was.

Kreise stood and shut off the wall screen by hand. She had only a few choices. She could cancel the meetings now that Soseki had breached security. However, if she canceled the meetings, the others might claim she was being petty—having lost her chance to silence Döbryn, she was going to stop Döbryn's opportunity to speak—which she would love to do, without the accusations, of course.

Her other choices included continuing the meetings and allowing Döbryn to make her case; not calling a meeting until the Armstrong political situation settled down; or calling the press and having them show up at the meetings, effectively destroying the meeting's privacy and its main purpose.

She wanted out of this mess, which seemed like it was getting larger by the minute. Soseki had said that he would protest the release of these terrorists—his word—into the dome. He was informing his citizens now that the dome was no longer a safe place, and they would have to watch out for any kind of troublemakers.

He had also said that he didn't have the information on all of the Etaens being allowed into the dome, but the moment he had it, he would release it. In the meantime, he was going to have his office prepare video documentation of what he did know about the Etaens, just so that the people of Armstrong would be informed.

Theoretically, Kreise should have approved of the anti-Etaen attitude. But it didn't help her much. Soseki's methods were crude, and the very opposite of the diplomacy that she practiced.

Soseki had placed himself in a political war with the governor-general, pitting the city of Armstrong against the Unified Domes of the Moon. He had also exposed the Etaen-Alliance meeting, which was supposed to have occurred in secret.

Now everyone would be debating the merits of

Etae's joining the Alliance, and most of that debate would happen out of ignorance.

Whenever ignorance ruled, the correct decision—no matter what it was—got buried in a flood of irrational responses. This situation could quickly escalate into something unpredictable.

At least Soseki hadn't announced the location for the meetings, although anyone with some sense should be able to figure it out. Very few buildings in Armstrong had the size and the security measures already in place to handle diplomats—at least outside of the port. And anyone who was watching live news would now know that the meetings weren't in the port.

Kreise sighed. Her own tricks had backfired and now she was in a mess. From now on, she was going to have to play this one straightforwardly. She was going to have to let the entire Executive Council make its own choices on where to go next.

She opened her private Executive Council links, and sent a message to all the ambassadors. They had to have an emergency meeting, and they had to have it now.

22

When Flint came back from the Brownie Bar, he brought up all five screens on his desk, ran a quick debugging scan, and had the system search for new spyware. Then he double-checked what he had done, made certain that the outside links were still off, and called up the information from the Lahiris' apartment.

He was most interested in their security and cleaning systems. He had the cleaning system run its findings on the screen farthest to his left. That run he started two months before, first letting his computer find the everyday patterns. Then he would have it search for anomalies in the month, starting with the week before Flint contacted the Lahiris to tell them that he had found their daughter.

The system should find differences when Carolyn Lahiri entered her parents' apartment. Even though she went through decon, no system was perfect. She would be carrying a bit of Earth and maybe something of some of the other places she had been before she went to the Lahiris' apartment—maybe even some kind of trace material from Spacer's Pub.

To find that sort of material was extremely detailed work, best done by computer. While his machines cross-compared trace findings, he searched the security protocols for the audio and video recordings.

He should have found them easily. Theoretically, they should have been the first option—the thing he found as he opened the security files.

Instead, he had to search for any kind of audio or visual record at all. People like the Lahiris, who spent a lot of money on their security system, always thought aurally and visually first. Some people even forgot to buy the other systems—the ones Flint considered even more important—the smells, the cleaning records, including the components of the dust and dirt picked up every week, and the history of who entered the apartment and when.

He would get to those things after he found the audio/visual. According to the records he had in front of him, the other systems stayed on until the day of the murders. Then something had changed with them too.

But there had been no audio or visual record for nearly a month before the murders—and that bothered him. He had double-checked the Lahiris' security account a number of times before he actually accepted their case, and their audio/visual was always running.

It never ran in the bedrooms, bathroom, or kitchen—something he had found frustrating, because that meant the Lahiris had places to have private conversations and often used those places, but at least he had seen who entered and exited their apartment.

In those months, the Lahiris had had few visitors. Mostly, their visitors consisted of food delivery personnel—usually bots who had special serving trays to keep the food warm—and the occasional colleague. If one or the other Lahiri had to discuss business, it was always done off-premise.

Judge or Dr. Lahiri would greet the business colleague, exchange pleasant chitchat for a moment with the other spouse, and then go out the main door.

But that got Flint thinking. Both Judge Lahiri and Dr. Lahiri were in professions in which confidentiality was a major component. If either one of them had to discuss business at home and for some reason couldn't do it in the back bedroom or even the kitchen (although some of the kitchen conversation floated into the living room), then the Lahiris would have to have a way to shut off the audio and visual portions of the security system—usually before the guest arrived.

If it had been Flint's system, he would have kept a visual link to the hallway, but the apartment complex itself probably covered that. He would have to check their systems.

In the meantime, he was going to look for the on/off toggle—if indeed there was one.

By the time he had found the on/off switch, he had gone through six different layers of code. Finally he had traced Judge Lahiri's command sequences. The judge had shut down the audio/visual portions of the security system nearly two weeks before Carolyn joined them in the apartment. Either he forgot to turn that part of the system back on or he wanted it off.

Flint studied the information for a long time. As phobic as the Lahiris were about security—rightly so, given that their daughter had been a Disappeared—they wouldn't have left the a/v off that long. Something was wrong with his findings.

So Flint kept tracing Judge Lahiri's command codes, and found that the judge had reactivated the full system the next day. But the a/v records never made it into the security's archives—and that seemed even odder to Flint.

He paused, stood, and stretched, feeling the muscles groan. He hadn't exercised all day, except for his walk to the Brownie Bar, and his body felt it.

But the stretching gave him enough time to recall that security systems were redundant by design. If something didn't make it into one part of the system, it would be backed up in another part, and maybe even backed up again in a third part.

He sat back down and set to work, hoping he would find exactly what he needed.

23

The restaurant just inside the north exit to the Port was ancient. Anatolya Döbryn wasn't sure she had ever seen a restaurant so old, let alone eaten in one.

The booths were made of a plastic designed to look like fake wood. They had metal bases that were bolted into the floor, just like booths on a commercial space yacht. The seats encircled the booths in a giant U shape, making each booth large and somewhat uncomfortable.

Even though the booths were set up for a kind of privacy, the sound still carried. Conversation became muted echoes that mixed with the clang and clatter of dishes. In the distance, she could hear an androgynous voice calling various arrivals—public transport ships that had come in from Earth or Mars.

Collier sat beside her, his fingers tapping on the table's fake-wood surface. He had ordered coffee and then pushed it away when he realized it wasn't real. Anatolya had confiscated it; she didn't care if the coffee was real so long as it had caffeine.

She also ordered a sandwich and some soup. The sandwich's bread was made of Moon flour—always identifiable by how thick, pasty, and tasteless it was— and the meat wasn't real. Still, the sandwich was one

of the best she'd had in years, and the soup, thin as
it was, was even better.

Collier watched her eat with distaste. He probably
thought she was some kind of heathen, enjoying this
food. Probably saw it as one more sign that she wasn't
worthy to lead her people into the Alliance.

She didn't care. Collier was lucky; he'd never
starved or coped with dwindling resources. He probably ate well and richly every day of his mediocre little life.

He could judge her all he wanted, so long as his
prejudices didn't influence his bosses. She needed the
Alliance, and she was pleased they'd given her this
second chance.

She was trying not to fidget. The wait for her people
seemed to go on forever, even though she knew it
hadn't been. She just wanted out of this port. She was
ready to give her speech and leave Armstrong, heading back home, where she was in control.

As she ate, she glanced up at the old etched-glass
windows that separated the restaurant from the rest
of the port. Humans and aliens of various types filed
outward, heading toward the exit. Some were chatting;
others looked serious as they pushed their luggage forward. Still others seemed harried, as if they were running chronically late and would never catch up again.

She looked away. At least Collier wasn't trying to
make small talk. That would irritate her. She didn't
like exchanging pleasantries with minor officials.

She finished her coffee and then his. And at that
moment, Collier stood.

"Here they come," he said.

She glanced around the restaurant, but saw nothing.
Then she looked into the corridor and still saw nothing. Just the same sorts of people—wearing different
clothing but the same expressions—and the same sorts
of aliens heading toward the exits.

Collier beckoned her to stand. Apparently, he had
gotten notification through his links.

"Let's go out front. We'll be less conspicuous." He

pressed his fist into the slot on the side of the table, connecting his payment chip with the collection chip embedded into the fake wood, then extended a hand to help her up.

She ignored it, standing on her own accord, and walked toward the door, stepping gingerly over other people's luggage, scattered across the floor as they ate their quick meals. Her legs felt shaky, mostly because she felt shaky.

As she stepped out of the restaurant door into the corridor, she looked for her team. She had asked for, not her security team (even though that was what she had called them), but her main advisers.

Collier had moved away from the door, standing against the wall, almost blending in. His head was turned toward the right, watching the people exiting the main part of the port.

She stood next to him, her hands folded in front of her, trying to blend in as well.

This was the dangerous moment. If anyone was going to attack her, they'd do so now. They'd expect her guard to be down while she was waiting: That relief she had felt in the restaurant would be her enemy if she let it.

So she didn't look in the same direction as Collier. She scanned the entire corridor, and stood with her back against the wall. She made certain that anytime someone stood close, she moved just a little away.

She protected herself as best she could.

Collier didn't notice. Secure little man—he was oblivious to anything and everything that had any danger attached to it. If she had planned this—and if she wanted the person in her position dead—she would have sent a flunky just like Collier, in case he got killed in the crossfire.

To her left, the corridor turned slightly, and people vanished as they rounded the corner. She wished that Collier had stood closer to that bend so that she could see anyone who came around it, but he hadn't.

And she didn't want to call attention to her nervousness by moving away from him, closer to the exit.

"There they are," he said again.

This time, she turned slowly, scanning everyone before looking to her right. Her team was walking toward her, their strides long, their hands at their sides.

Her deputy, Gianni Czogloz, walked in front, as he always did, as if he had nothing to fear. He was a large man with a full head of thick silver hair. Years ago, he'd been the first to get the new enhancements, and now the muscles made him look doughy, as if he weren't quite made of flesh.

But his walk was smooth and elegant, his scarred face familiar and trusted. The relief she had felt in the restaurant grew, and because of it, she kept her place, unwilling to walk to him.

He nodded to her.

The rest of the team—six women and two men—followed closely behind. They were surrounded by port officials and other people she didn't recognize.

"Dismiss the employees," Anatolya said to Collier.

"What?" He glanced at her, startled. Apparently he hadn't expected her to speak.

"The people who flank my team," she said. "Dismiss them."

"I can't," he said. "They don't answer to me."

"Then I'll make them leave." She took a step forward, hoping that would be enough. She didn't want to leave her perch near the wall.

"Wait," he said, catching her arm. "I'll see what I can do."

She nodded, just once, and leaned against the wall again. His mouth was pursed, as if he had eaten something sour. He was clearly sending through his links.

One by one, the port employees stopped, all of them looking confused. But her team kept walking.

Gianni stopped in front of her, taking her hands into his own. "Anatolya," he said gently.

Her eyes burned. She hadn't realized just how panicked she was. Odd that she could be so strong on Etae and feel so weak here.

"Did they treat you well?" he asked.

"It depends on your definition of well," she said. "I felt like a prisoner, and thought I'd never see you again."

Collier shot her an angry look, apparently deciding that he no longer needed to hide his emotions.

"But they did feed me and keep me in nice quarters," she added, as if she hadn't seen the look at all.

Gianni nodded. "We'll make certain none of this happens again."

Collier's chin went up, and Anatolya felt rather than saw his fear. She could see him rethinking his choices, wondering if he had done the right thing in setting her team free on Armstrong.

Let him wonder. She needed them to give her strength.

"Are you well?" she asked not just Gianni, but also the remaining eight members of the team.

The other eight looked to Gianni for the answer. They knew better than to respond for themselves.

"I too dislike being held prisoner," he said, "even if it is on our own ship. Perhaps we should rethink this, Anatolya."

"We'll issue a protest," she said. "If we don't get the response we need, we'll stand aside."

He nodded again and she felt an almost irrepressible urge to smile. She and Gianni were a good team. They both knew they wouldn't give up the meeting with the Alliance, not now, not after they had already suffered through the humiliations of the wait.

But they were still going to issue the protest, still going to make Collier—and anyone he was linked to—squirm.

Collier cleared his throat. "Your ride is waiting at the south exit. I think we should go."

Gianni didn't look at him. Instead, he kept his gaze

on Anatolya, as if waiting for her to decide if indeed she wanted to enter the City of Armstrong.

She let the silence spin out between all of them for several seconds. Around them, conversations continued in dozens of languages. She saw no one she recognized, no one who seemed to care about her or her team.

Collier shifted his weight. He *was* squirming, and it pleased her. She finally turned to him, holding herself as if he were a servant almost beneath her notice.

"Is there enough room in that ride for my entire team?"

He glanced at the ten of them—Anatolya, Gianni, and the rest of the team—and seemed to be sizing them up. So Collier played games as well. He just wasn't as good at them as she was.

"Yes," he said.

"Excellent," she said. "I assume we'll have an armed escort."

He looked panicked. "We don't do things that way in Armstrong."

She froze. "My people are not allowed weapons. If something goes wrong, we cannot defend ourselves."

"Nothing will go wrong," Collier said.

Anatolya bit back a curse. On Etae, such phrases were considered bad luck.

But she didn't rebuke him. Instead, she gave a silent signal to her team—a small movement of the hand farthest from Collier—so that they'd be ready for anything.

Anything at all.

24

It took Flint nearly four hours to find what he was looking for. Buried in the redundant systems, deep inside the code, he finally found the video for the past two weeks.

The audio was gone or buried even deeper. No matter how hard he searched he couldn't find it.

But the video went from the day after Judge Lahiri stopped it to six days before Flint downloaded. The file then cut off abruptly, but not because someone had altered it. Someone had destroyed the program that caused the redundant backups—probably deleting most of the other files or compromising any chain that would allow him to find them.

At that moment, he let out a breath that he hadn't even realized he'd been holding. He had been worried that his download was incomplete or that the police were monitoring him. Instead, he realized that someone had tampered with the Lahiris' system—perhaps the same someone who had killed them.

He had to rebuild the file, add links and code so that it would play on his machines. First, he isolated the file from the Lahiris' download. The last thing he wanted to do was alert any bug in their system that one last piece of video existed.

Then he took the isolated file, copied it, and moved

the copy to a different machine, one not attached to the network that was analyzing the information he had gotten from the Lahiris'.

Finally, he instructed that new machine to repair the files before beginning playback.

The repair took another hour; the file had been badly damaged. He only hoped it was playable.

When the playback was ready, the computer beeped at him. Flint pressed a button on his keyboard so his other screens receded into the desk. Then he instructed the remaining screen to play the download in six-hour increments, beginning with the last six hours first.

The beginning was unremarkable. Judge Lahiri walked in and out of the main room, often talking to someone behind him. Dr. Lahiri worked in the kitchen—not cooking, but arranging food on a tray that she then brought to one of the back bedrooms.

Flint felt a shiver run through him. In that back bedroom, he suspected, Caroline lay.

He watched the vid in fast-forward, slowing it only when someone flitted across the screen. Generally that someone was either Judge Lahiri or Dr. Lahiri, although, curiously, he never saw them together.

He got a sense, even from the two-dimensional soundless vid, that a chill had fallen on the relationship, probably in the intervening months since Dr. Lahiri had decided to hire Flint on her own.

After three hours vid time, he finally saw Carolyn. She crossed the hallway wrapped in a robe, her bare feet peeking out from the hem. Her hair was tousled, her eyes sleep-weary. She let herself into another room, probably the bathroom, and vanished for another half an hour.

Dr. Lahiri joined Judge Lahiri in the living room, sitting in the uncomfortable-looking antique chairs and having an animated conversation. Occasionally either the judge or the doctor would wave a hand toward the hallway. Obviously, the conversation was about Carolyn and was evolving into a disagreement.

Flint sighed, and leaned back in his chair. If he wanted to, he could have his system decipher as much of the conversation as possible. The system had been set up to read lips in a variety of languages, so if the vid provided a clear view of the Lahiris' faces, then he would be able to get much of the conversation.

But he would wait to see how the vid ended before he made that decision.

Then Carolyn appeared. She was dressed as she had whenever he had seen her—neatly, carefully, her body squared by the long blouse she wore over loose-fitting cotton pants. The same rubber-soled shoes that she had worn at the Spacer's Pub graced her feet.

Carolyn didn't sit across from her parents. Instead she stood, the tension in her body as obvious as it had been when she had climbed the stairs in front of him the day she was going to meet her parents.

Something had gone wrong in their reunion—or perhaps the reunion had never gone right. Dr. Lahiri kept her head bowed during the conversation, her hands clasped on her lap, her thumbs tapping against each other in irritation.

Judge Lahiri didn't speak much either. His lips had thinned, his hands gripped the arms of his chair, his knuckles turning white. Carolyn's head bobbed slightly, as people's heads did when they were speaking emphatically, but Flint couldn't see her face.

That was when he realized the vid should have showed the room from all angles. All he had managed to find was one. Apparently what he had found was simply the remains from one camera; the record from all the others had been destroyed.

The conversation went on for an hour, and then all three people jumped. Obviously, they had heard a noise and it had stopped the conversation.

Judge Lahiri turned to his wife. She shot him a look of pure hatred, then stood and walked to the foyer.

There she disappeared from the camera's view, and Flint wished that he could see what was going on at the door. That part of the system should have had the most redundancies—troubles that arose in private apartments often came through the front door—but clearly whoever had gotten rid of the security videos had known to double- and triple-check for the door vids.

Carolyn turned, the fear on her face so palpable that Flint wanted to step in. Her lips moved, the words so clearly formed that Flint could read them.

Do you have a weapon in this house?

Her father looked shocked. He rose from the chair and reached for her, but Carolyn moved away. She scurried down the hall, the judge gazing after her as if she had been a vision.

He pressed one of the chips on the back of his hand, and then looked directly at the camera that provided this video.

Get help, he said, followed by another word. Immediately? Quickly?

Flint couldn't tell, but he could see the urgency. He wondered what was going on at the door that sent the remaining two into a panic.

Then he saw it—Dr. Lahiri being held in a man's arms. Her eyes were wide and tear-filled.

The judge's hands fluttered, a helpless move, and he started to glance toward the hallway, but caught himself.

The man wasn't yet fully in the camera's range, but his arms were. And they didn't look like normal arms. They seemed too long. They were digging into Dr. Lahiri's stomach.

As she moved past the camera, all Flint could see was the man's back.

Judge Lahiri spoke, his words lost to the blur of the vid. His hands fluttered again, the movement of a man who wanted something bad to end quickly. He was making promises, begging, stalling for time.

Only once, he glanced toward the security system, but once was enough. The man looked too, the back of his head making a sharp, aware motion.

He might have spoken, for suddenly, the judge looked even more terrified.

Dr. Lahiri's entire body was hidden by the man's. He was large and moved with a deliberation that made Flint's skin crawl. The man had done this before, often enough that he had no real reaction to the fear around him. It didn't anger him or excite him. If anything, it made him calmer.

Judge Lahiri stepped in front of the man, reaching for his wife. The man's head shook, and the judge stopped, his body also partially blocked by the man's.

Flint wished for the other cameras—for sound, for anything that gave him a clue as to what was going on.

The camera panned back a little—obviously the Lahiri security program was very good—so that the man's body didn't block everything.

Still, Flint couldn't see much more than he had before—just the man's legs, Dr. Lahiri's barely visible between them, and the judge's hands, still fluttering.

Then the judge's hands stopped fluttering. He looked toward the hall, and his face filled with chagrin.

He hadn't meant to look. It had been an involuntary movement that would probably cost his family their lives.

At that same moment, the man whirled and shoved Dr. Lahiri forward. She caught the blast to the stomach that had been meant for the man.

The judge screamed, the horror on his face distorting it to unrecognizability. He fell on his knees beside his wife, touching her face, her wound, her shoulders.

But it was too late: She was obviously dead, her eyes open, her hands flung back as they had been when the bodies were found.

The man's face was in full frame now. Flint had never seen it before, but that meant nothing. He didn't know all the criminals in the universe. He didn't even know all of them in Armstrong.

The man's mouth moved. His eyes glittered, almost as if he were playing a game, and had somehow won.

Flint didn't understand why Carolyn didn't shoot again, and then the camera panned back one more time.

The man's strangely enhanced arms had elongated. He had grabbed the weapon in her hand, and was trying to tug it away from her with his right hand.

She was struggling, avoiding the weapons that his left hand had become. The fingers had become knives.

Flint's entire body turned cold. His mouth was dry, and he wanted to look away, but he couldn't.

The man had enhanced himself into a killing machine: a walking weapon that somehow had more tricks than Flint could imagine. Carolyn did not seem shocked by it. She had moved her body sideways, somehow anticipating the man's changes.

Flint froze the frame and studied the man for a brief moment. He appeared human, except for his magical arms. But Flint knew that enhancements could make a variety of changes—keeping people young, repairing limbs, regrowing eyes.

Why wouldn't they be able to cause a human being to become a walking arsenal?

Flint separated out the freeze-frame, then rewound to that perfect image of the man's face, and separated that as well. He set them aside, planning to plug them into one of the criminal databases he kept constantly updating.

Then, reluctantly, he started the vid again.

Carolyn lost her grip on the weapon. The man's arms snaked back against his chest. He whirled and shot the judge, just like he had shot Dr. Lahiri, in the torso, wiping out the center of his body.

The old man remained on his knees for just a moment, then fell backward, his heels digging unnaturally into his spine.

Carolyn did not scream. She didn't even look. Instead, she ran for the door.

The man's arm elongated again, caught her, and pulled her toward him, as if she were a lover. His arm wrapped around her several times, like a rope, the weapon still clutched in his right hand.

He spoke to her, close up, his face away from the camera. Her expression remained impassive. His other hand, the one with the knifelike fingers, rose, and still she didn't flinch.

The blades threatened her eyes, and she didn't even close them.

Finally the man shifted her to his left hand, which had become human again, and then shoved her far enough back that she was in the range of the small pistol Flint had given her days before.

The man spoke, his chin moving, but his lips hidden.

Carolyn stared at the weapon, not moving.

The man spoke again, but she still didn't respond.

Finally, he shot her in the face.

She slammed backward, hitting the wall and falling to the ground, her body sliding down slowly, leaving a smear against the wallpaper.

That smear hadn't been at the crime scene. None of this evidence had been there.

Flint swallowed hard, staring at her body. It didn't move. It didn't even make the involuntary shudders that sudden death sometimes caused.

He froze the frame again.

His hands were shaking, and he had to stand up. He paced around his small office, making himself breathe.

Had he caused that? By finding her, had he made it easier for that man—that *thing*—to track her down?

She had been visible from the time Flint brought her on the *Emmeline*. Sure, she had traveled by her Disappeared name, but she was in the presence of a Retrieval Artist. Anyone with brains could have figured out that she was a Disappeared.

A bit of research, and they would have discovered who she was, just like he had.

This man—this thing—had waited until she was in her parents' home, waited until she had been there for a few days, before attacking all of them.

Perhaps this vid had been planted for the police to find. Perhaps they were supposed to think the three Lahiris died this way when actually something else happened. The evidence didn't match the crimes, and that had to count for something.

Unless . . .

Flint returned to his desk. He unfroze the image, and the vid continued to play.

The man was studying Carolyn as if he found her corpse fascinating. As he stood there, cleaning bots slid into the room from the kitchen. He slipped his hand into his pocket and removed a small device. He held it up, and the bots stopped moving, hovering in midair.

Flint's breath caught, and he knew without watching the rest what had happened. The man had reprogrammed the bots to clean only what he wanted cleaned. Then he had shut down the security system and the cleaning system so that nothing else would be touched, so that his carefully staged crime scene remained exactly as he wanted it.

Why stage a crime scene, though? What exactly was he trying to hide?

Hopefully Flint could get a clue by watching the man clean up. The man walked to the closest bot, opened its chip storage, and replaced two of the chips with two of his own. That bot bobbed for a moment; then the man spoke to it.

Again, Flint couldn't see the man's face. But the bot lowered itself to the ground and waited in a corner, unmoving. Flint certainly hadn't expected that.

The man ignored the other bots, which remained floating, as if they knew he would command them, given time. Instead, he picked up Carolyn's body as if it weighed nothing and carried it to the center of the furniture arrangement.

The corpse dripped fluids across the hardwood floor, but the man didn't seem to care. He set the body down, then stood back as though he were creating a piece of art.

He fanned her hair around what remained of her head, except for the strands in the very back, which

were matted with blood and tissue. Then he let her
hands drop, as if they had fallen naturally. He studied
her for a moment, shook his head as if he were dissatis-
fied, and moved away from her.

He went to Dr. Lahiri next. He rolled her on her
side, so that only part of her wound was visible. Then
he dragged her a little closer to her daughter's corpse.
He bent Dr. Lahiri's feet behind her back in an
unconscious—or was it conscious?—imitation of the
position the judge had landed in.

One foot fell against Carolyn's hair. The man
reached for it, then stopped himself. He smiled, as if
he liked the serendipity; then he tucked the doctor's
hands together and stepped away.

Once more he studied the corpses. Finally he
grabbed the judge's legs and straightened them. The
man spread them slightly—as if the judge had fallen
from a standing position—and flung the judge's
hands back.

The bodies flopped easily; it was too soon for rigor
to take effect. The mess on the floor was another matter. At that moment, all of the man's actions were
visible—the bloody drag marks, the drips from the
wall, the way the blood had pooled in Dr. Lahiri's
back.

Flint bit his lower lip, wondering what this man was
about. He continued to watch, stunned, as the man
finished staging the death scene. He rolled Carolyn's
body to the right, set the gun beneath it, and rolled
her back as if she had fallen on the weapon.

Then he reset all the bots, giving them verbal direc-
tions about cleaning specific areas. They took care of
the drag marks and the long stain down the wall, the
drips and his footprints.

They even cleaned his shoes and clothing.

The scene looked almost like the image Flint had
on the other computers, except for one thing: The
walls were mostly clean. Only the wall that had been
behind Carolyn when she had been shot was covered

with blood and brains, and that wall, according to Flint's notes, hadn't had a bit of trace on it.

The killer had used most of the time remaining to clean up the room. He moved toward the security panel—recessed behind one of the pictures—and opened it.

Then he paused as if he had gotten an idea. He turned his back to the camera. His hands moved, however. He was obviously speaking again.

The bots that had done the cleaning spread around the room. They spewed the trace at the furniture, the walls, the floor. The spatter fell the way it would if the Lahiris had been killed in their positions now.

Gooseflesh rose on Flint's skin. He'd never seen anything quite like this.

Then the man gathered up the bots, removed the chips from their wiring, and threw the bots in a pile against the kitchen door. The one remaining bot still floated, as if nothing had happened around it.

The man reached up into the security system's main board. As Flint watched, the vid flickered, then went dark.

Flint had never seen anything quite so brilliant. The remaining bot would be reprogrammed to clean all but the staged areas—that was why the place was so clean, and yet the bloodstains stayed on the walls. The bot also probably gathered the damaged bots and sent them into recycling. The program wasn't designed to get new bots—that would be a choice that the Lahiris, had they lived, would have had to make.

So that one little bot had spent the last few days in the apartment, cleaning up trace, wiping away evidence of the killer's visit, and helping perpetrate his lie.

Flint shook his head slightly. He wanted to tell De-Ricci. She needed this information if she was going to solve the case.

But he couldn't figure out how to do so. His own signatures were in the Lahiris' system, buried as

deeply as this vid was. For all the police knew, Flint
had set this up as a false vid to exonerate himself.

That would be what he would think if he found
the vid at this late date, especially with his long-term
spyware inside the Lahiris' system.

All he could hope for at the moment was that the
techs in the Detective Division were as bad at taking
apart computer systems as they had always been. The
last thing he needed was for them to find more evidence of his presence.

The computer screen before him still showed the
vid, even though the visuals had gone blank. He had
no audio, so he didn't know what had been on the
recording.

Still, he told his machine to try to clean up, to see
if it could find any imagery at all. He didn't hold a
lot of hope, but attempting something was better
than nothing.

He also ran the translation program, hoping it
would get something from the lipreading—at least
more than he had. And he took the captured image
of the killer, moved it to his other system, and used
it as a template, running it against all known criminals
in the solar system.

If he didn't get a hit on that, he would run it against
the remaining criminal database, and then any other
facial files he might have within the computer.

Even though the computers did the work swiftly,
there were still millions of faces to compare this one
against. And he was going to have to search to see if
this kind of enhancement was available on humans.

If not, he was going to have to see if some of the
alien species could disguise themselves as human.

He hadn't heard of any, but that meant nothing.
Most of the aliens within known space weren't members of the Alliance, and as a consequence, didn't
travel to the Moon. He had never had cause to exam-
ine non-Alliance databases before.

He wasn't even certain what he got from the vid. If
it had been unaltered (and he would have to run a

check for that too), then it confused matters greatly. The killer had spoken to Carolyn, but there was no guarantee that she was the main target.

After all, the killer had come to the Lahiri home, a place she hadn't lived for decades. Judge Lahiri worked with aliens. So did Dr. Lahiri. The judge had looked defeated before the killer had done more than hold his wife hostage.

Perhaps the killer had come for the judge and not Carolyn. Or the doctor herself. Flint never did see her initial reaction to the killer's arrival. For all he knew, this death could have been revenge for some kind of medical procedure gone wrong.

But, as DeRicci used to say, a good detective looked at the anomalies. And the anomaly in this case was Carolyn herself. She hadn't been in the apartment in decades, and the Lahiris had been fine. She showed up, and within days they were all dead.

If only he could get this last bit of information to DeRicci. But he couldn't, not without compromising himself further. He couldn't even send it through the spyware he'd set up in the Detective Division.

He had to find this killer on his own, and he wasn't even sure where to start.

25

Anatolya heard the sound first.

She stood in the wide Port hallway, surrounded by her team and Collier. The team had just finished the link tests; they were back up and running, and she had never felt so relieved in her life.

Then she heard the noise. Voices rose in a low hum—not angry, but not calm either. Like people disgruntled with a turn of events, discussing, and egging each other onward. No one voice rose above the din, no words seemed to stand out.

Gianni moved closer to her. The rest of the team glanced at each other. The voices unnerved them as well.

Collier stayed at her side. His face had gone a ghostly pale.

"I think we should turn around," he said.

But Anatolya shook her head. They couldn't play these kinds of games with her. They had released her from the Port, and now they wanted to scare her back into it.

She started to walk, and the others followed. The signs, blinking against the upper walls, informed her that she had only a few meters left before she reached the exit. She had to make certain that her papers were in order, the signs warned her, because she would not be allowed back into the port if they were not.

Generic messages for generic travelers—none of whom were at this exit of the Port. They had all veered off toward the main exit when she and her team started to leave. The Port Authority tried to be circumspect about it, but they had failed; Anatolya had trained herself early to observe everything that happened around her, and she watched as travelers were deflected, told to take other exits, or had similar messages sent through their links.

The handful of travelers who persisted were met by Port security and moved aside. Apparently the Port or the city of Armstrong wanted no one near her or her team as they exited the building.

That had disturbed her as well. She almost did turn around when she saw that and the empty corridor ahead of her. In some ways, the growing sound outside the Port's exit doors reassured her: yes, there was a plan; yes, it focused on her; and yes, it was something she could handle.

She'd been half expecting an assassin waiting in the hallways. If that had been the plan, she—or the assassin—would be dead already.

The corridor made one final turn before the double doors opened into the street. Gianni was as close to her as he dared get. His massive frame did not block her view of the upcoming corridor, but he did block her view of the right wall. He was half a step in front of her, ready to block anything that came at her if the need arose.

Collier leaned closer to her left. "Please, Ms. Döbryn," he said, his voice as low as it could be without a whisper, "we need to turn around."

"I'm not going back into this port," she snapped.

Her team moved faster, and Collier had to jog to keep up with them. He was breathing hard. None of the Etaens had even broken a sweat.

"There's a problem at this exit," he said. "Please. Let's go out a different one."

"Only to discover a problem there?" Anatolya asked. "I don't think so, Mr. Collier."

He winced. "You're the one who said your team had no weapons. Perhaps if we go back, we can get some Port security—"

"My team can defend itself with or without weapons," Anatolya said, and wished she hadn't. She didn't want to sound threatening or difficult. She also didn't want to reveal too much to this flunky who had thwarted her from the beginning.

"Please, Ms. Döbryn. My people are warning me that a crowd has gathered and they're very upset."

"At what?" she asked, still moving forward. Light poured in the double doors at the end of the corridor. It took her a moment to realize that light was as artificial as the interior light. Armstrong was a domed city. She wouldn't see real light again until she got into her ship.

"They're upset that you've been let into Armstrong." This time, Collier's words carried.

The team glanced at him, even the three members who walked in front, breaking rank—breaking the rules—that Anatolya had established for defensive formations long ago. She would reprimand them later. So far, there was no one in the corridors to defend against.

But those voices had grown louder.

How brilliant of her opponents, whoever they were, to notify the residents that Etaens were coming into the dome. Let someone else protest. Allow no one to take the blame, and yet have the same outcome.

Anatolya Döbryn's meeting would be a disaster for the Alliance, one that would be reported on the nets. Armstrong was known as a civilized, peaceful city. If the team she brought with her upset the good citizens of Armstrong, well, then, no other city should take the chance of allowing her and her thugs inside.

She sent a command through her team link, and everyone stopped. They stood at attention, guarding her flanks with military precision.

"How would anyone know I am coming into the dome?" she asked. "My meeting with the Alliance Executive Committee was supposed to be classified."

"I don't know, sir," Collier said. "I only know what I've been told. The Alliance is worried about a scene. If we can avoid it, by using another exit or waiting until the turmoil dies down, then—"

"The turmoil will not die down." Gianni spoke not to Collier, but to Anatolya. Gianni had a gift for public disobedience. He knew how to make crowds do his bidding, and she usually loved him for it. "If these people do not have some kind of satisfaction, they will take matters into their own hands. If they believe you have sneaked through, they will attack the port."

"Such things don't happen in Armstrong," Collier said.

"Which is why the Alliance wanted to meet here," Anatolya said, biting back anger. Of course they wanted to meet here. They wanted to meet here, and ruin any chance she had of ever approaching the Alliance again.

She knew she had allies on the Executive Committee, but she also had enemies. And at the moment, her enemies were winning.

"You may find another exit, Mr. Collier," she said with an imperiousness that she hadn't used since she left Etae. "But my team and I, we'll be leaving from this exit. And if we get injured or killed, the government of Armstrong, the Moon, and the Alliance itself will have to answer for our treatment. Send that along your links, along with your observations about my stubbornness."

He started. Apparently, he had been complaining about her stubbornness, with probably exactly that term.

Gianni was good with crowds. Anatolya could be good with people, when she wanted to be. Not so much at persuading them, which she could do if she had to, but at analyzing who they were and what they thought.

That, more than anything, was why the Etaen ruling council had sent her. There were better speakers, better analysts. But no one was better at seeing through people's masks to their real intents.

"Ms. Döbryn," Collier said, "please. I truly think you're making a mistake. Don't exit from here. We'll find a better way."

But she had turned away from him. She sent a forward command through her links, along with a command to defend only, to get her through that crowd as efficiently as possible.

The team started forward again at a quicker pace, a military pace, and this time Collier didn't try to join them. The team's rear had to go around him.

I don't like that, Gianni sent Anatolya through the links. *He's afraid to come with us.*

It's a setup, Anatolya sent. *We have to use it as best we can. We have to survive without giving away much of our position.*

Gianni nodded. At that moment, the front members of the team flung the double doors open. Sunlight poured into the corridor, blinding Anatolya.

The voices, which had sounded like a hum only a moment ago, grew into a roar. The doors had blocked most of the noise.

The team stepped out. Anatolya blinked, her eyes adjusting to the light. The team was on a platform, two meters above the crowd. The crowd spread before her like a sea, filling the space between the port and some of its outbuildings.

Signs flickered throughout the crowd in all the languages of the Alliance, stating the same kinds of things:

TERRORISTS, GO HOME!!
NO MURDERERS IN ARMSTRONG
KILLERS STAY AWAY FROM OUR CHILDREN!

A few courageous airtaxi drivers floated above the

crowd, and several cars—all with news-department logos—filmed from above.

She was probably live on a dozen different media outlets. How she handled the next few moments would change everything.

You want to speak to them? Gianni sent.

Hell, no. Anatolya put as much force as possible into the words. *The last thing we need are all these news reports to start with me talking and the crowd surging to shut me up. The reports'll blame my words if anything goes wrong.*

We can turn around, Gianni sent.

I haven't turned away from a fight in my life. Anatolya surveyed the crowd. Most of them were angry citizens. A few, scattered throughout, were simply there for the violence.

They were the ones she had to watch, because they'd incite the others.

"Let's go," she said, and as one, her team started down the stairs.

26

DeRicci sat down at her desk for the first time in hours. Her hair was a mess, her suit twisted and worn, and her shoes covered with dirt. She felt like an impostor, not like an assistant chief of detectives.

Her own office intimidated her. The large corner windows, which she had been so proud of, almost seemed to be watching her. The soft chairs and end tables looked like they belonged to someone else.

She was investigating again. Strange that something that had thrilled her only a few short hours ago upset her now. The deeper she was getting into this case, the more she hated it.

All because of Flint.

Carolyn Lahiri, a Disappeared, and Miles Flint, a Retrieval Artist. DeRicci shook her head. Gumiela would tell her that she should have known Flint had the capacity for breaking the law when he decided to quit his detective position to become a Retrieval Artist.

Retrieval Artists had no respect for the law. If they respected the law, they would have become Trackers, looking for Disappeareds and turning them in.

This afternoon, after going through police archives on Carolyn Lahiri, DeRicci was no longer certain that she believed in letting some Disappeared slip past justice. Lahiri had been a mercenary, fighting for the rebellion in Etae. She had killed countless people in a quest to overthrow a legitimate government, and she had done so with no emotional involvement at all.

She hadn't even joined up after the Child Martyr incident. She had joined up before. Etae's conflict hadn't had universal attention until that incident.

DeRicci didn't remember it, but she had studied it in school, and her research on Lahiri brought it back. Awful footage of a child being slaughtered by government troops—deliberately killed—had leaked into outside media. The effect of this brutal—and pointless—killing was immediate: Reasonable people in the known universe started supporting the rebels against Etae's established government.

Those rebels got the arms and the monetary support they needed to overthrow that government, and now, decades later, they were in charge.

DeRicci would have understood if Carolyn Lahiri, like so many other idealistic young people, had joined up in the Etaen rebel cause after that famous incident. But she had gone to Etae nearly a year earlier.

DeRicci found that all the stranger, considering that Lahiri had never even been to Etae before she left the Moon. Yet she had traveled with four other mercenaries to the outside edges of the known universe to fight in a war that had no consequences for her, her family, or her friends.

All DeRicci could think was that Lahiri had gotten involved for the love of danger and, eventually, for the love of killing. That she had Disappeared at all was a surprise. The fact that she had stayed out of the news also seemed to be a surprise.

But DeRicci would have DNA records shortly, and once she had them, she would know for sure if Carolyn Lahiri had indeed stayed out of the news. For all DeRicci knew at the moment, Lahiri had gone from identity to identity, fighting wars. With luck, the DNA would reveal her history for the past thirty years.

DeRicci rubbed her eyes and made herself lean forward, concentrating on the case. Carolyn Lahiri was a mystery, but her parents also had ties to unsavory people. Dr. Lahiri was known for treating anyone who came through her door: so many doctors took only Alliance patients or human patients. If Dr. Lahiri had thought she could save an alien, she would try—often using a link with a doctor on an alien's homeworld to conduct a virtual consult.

And Judge Lahiri was known for his harshness, his willingness to uphold the legal traditions of the Alliance to the letter. If a judge could be considered conservative, not interpreting the laws at all if he could avoid them, then Judge Lahiri was that person.

The suicide of the son bothered DeRicci as well. The son had never succeeded at anything, and finally had ended it all in an unremarkable fashion, notable only for its cruelty toward his parents, who discovered the body. He had set up a meeting with them, and had killed himself only minutes before they arrived.

DeRicci knew she would have to reopen that case as well.

She tapped the screen on her desk to see if there were any updates from the techs. She got several. The techs had finally finished at the crime scene. A few of them had left early to start examining the wealth of evidence.

Their preliminary reports sent a shudder through DeRicci: The spatter wasn't making sense.

She read carefully, then pressed a corner of the screen for audio presentation. The information was the same.

The way the spatter had fallen, it should have been isolated to each victim. The direction of the shots should have sent the spatter to specific places for each victim. But the initial results were surprising: the brain and blood had mixed—each spatter pattern held material from all three victims, instead of just one.

The techs told DeRicci that they would make sense of the evidence; it would just take them more time.

But this was precisely the kind of news she didn't want to hear.

And she didn't know what to make of it. In all her years as a detective, she'd never had the visual evidence—the spatter pattern so obviously belonging to only one victim—contradict the DNA evidence. Usually those two things matched, and they contradicted eyewitness statements.

Only there were no eyewitnesses here, at least not yet.

She continued to dig through the preliminary reports. Most of them were simply a record of each tech's experience in the apartment—something now required by law. She scanned those, and also the notifications of when the techs planned to finish the lab work, and the early guesswork at the dates when the techs would finish their final reports.

DeRicci knew those deadlines would change—nothing ever worked the way it was planned, at least not in the detective business.

Then she found a few other newly filed notes.

The weapons specialist had already completed a preliminary report. Since he hadn't been at the crime scene, his report was an examination of the pistol and test-firings of it, as well as a cursory comparison between the weapon and the wounds on the corpses.

Aside from the things she already knew—that a small laser pistol like that could make those wounds—she didn't expect to find anything else of interest in the report.

And she was wrong.

The weapon had been fired, probably on the day of the murders. It had a distinctive signature. It had been modified from its original specifications to emit a stronger laser pulse—one that could do more damage at closer range.

That pulse left burn marks at less than two meters, marks that showed up on all three corpses. At point-blank range, however, the weapon could cause a fire. And none of the victims had been burned, not even

Carolyn Lahiri, whom DeRicci had initially suspected of suicide.

The suicide theory was officially gone now. There had been a fourth person at that crime scene, a person who had managed to get away from the bloody living room without leaving footprints, handprints, or any other trace of itself.

DeRicci wasn't willing to consider the killer human, at least not yet. So the killer could have escaped in any one of a variety of ways. Several alien species living on Armstrong did have wings and the ability to fly.

She would have to check the apartment's records to see if any of those lived nearby.

She also wondered if an alien's ability to fly or to travel by alternative means—using the sticky part of its legs or feet to adhere to surfaces and walk on walls—could have caused the mixture in the spatter. She made a mental note to ask the techs that when she acknowledged the receipt of their reports.

The weapons specialist's report went on in great detail, mostly talking about trajectories and wound edges. He wanted thorough autopsies, because the preliminary information he got also didn't match up.

Dr. Lahiri seemed to have been shot at close range, but Judge Lahiri had been farther away from his killer. He had also been fired at from above, while Dr. Lahiri had been fired at from a direct horizontal angle.

So, from the preliminary autopsy information, had Carolyn Lahiri. Which also raised questions of spatter and trace evidence, and whether or not there had been more than one killer in the room—one who was taller than the others, who had shot Carolyn and her father, while the other killer—the shorter one—had killed Dr. Lahiri.

DeRicci's headache was growing. She closed her eyes for a moment, wishing she had someone to discuss all of this information with. Someone who had a solid detective's mind, who would help her sift through the evidence as if it were a puzzle that the two of them could put together.

She wasn't willing to do that with Cabrera. At the moment, considering the delicate nature of this case, she wasn't sure she wanted to discuss it with anyone.

She opened her eyes again, and sighed. The words on the weapons specialist's report still blurred together. She blinked and the words finally separated.

She scanned ahead, past the discussion of trajectories and multiple killers and laser shot angles. She had to keep that information in the back of her brain, but not let it influence her, since it was all preliminary and could be wrong. She kept looking until she got to the end of the report, and a history of the weapon itself.

A weapon used in a murder shouldn't have had a traceable history. She rarely got enough information from the guns she found to know where they were sold, who had initially owned them, and how they had gotten into the killer's hands.

But this weapon had a history, and it told her more than she wanted to know about how it had gotten into the killer's hands.

Either he brought it to the apartment or it was already there, in the hands of Carolyn Lahiri.

DeRicci closed her eyes again, feeling the old demons of failure and loss rise within her.

She should have known that the gun belonged to Miles Flint.

27

There were aliens in the crowd.

That was what struck Anatolya first as she plunged headlong into the sea of bodies. The supposedly peace-loving Peyti, their breathing masks grotesque against their elongated faces; the Disty, short but violent, always around when there was trouble; and oddly, a few Rev, large, cone-shaped creatures whom she had never seen away from their own kind.

Gianni pressed against her—the rest of the team flanked her—and she barely walked. She almost floated toward the hired car, supposedly at the other end of the crowd.

She had only Collier's word for that—Collier, who was too much of a coward to walk with them.

Shouts and screams in a variety of languages caught her ears. All the voices competed for her attention. She saw people only in bits and snatches—through shoulders, around heads, bobbing up and down as they tried to see her.

Or were they trying to see her? They were shouting about terrorists, shouting about aliens, shouting about murder. They didn't seem to know about Etae and its struggles. All they knew was that this group—Anatolya's group—didn't belong in Armstrong.

"Criminals!"

"Murderers!"

"Baby killers!"

That last caught her. She turned her head toward the voice. It sounded familiar, but how could something sound familiar in this cacophony?

The stench was almost unbearable—human sweat mixed with fear, the cloying odor of ginger rising from the Rev, the putrid smell of aausme hiding somewhere in the crowd.

Gianni shifted against her—he had seen something and it made him nervous. She felt his entire body go into alert.

Don't do anything, she sent. *We can't afford to do anything.*

We have to defend ourselves, he sent back.

Only if attacked. She was hoping that they wouldn't be attacked, but even she was not confident. Nothing had gone their way since they had arrived on Armstrong.

Signs floated around her, deliberately untouched by human hands. Signs that were illegal on Etae, anonymous protests sailing above the crowd.

Etae = Mass Murder
The Deaths of 18 Million Idonae Will Be Avenged
Terror & Alliance Don't Mix!

Someone had leaked the information about them. Someone had told the good citizens of Armstrong who she was, who her team was, and why they were here.

"Oh, no," Gianni breathed.

At least, Anatolya thought he breathed the words. He might have sent them across the link, but it felt real. Yet she wasn't sure how she could have heard him over the noise of the crowd, which had grown deafening. She could barely hear herself think.

Look.

That word came from the three team members in front of her. They had sent the command in unison.

She followed the tilt of their heads, and felt herself grow cold.

On a makeshift ledge, cobbled together from chairs and scraps found nearby, a group of Idonae stood. They had their arms woven together like a tapestry, their fat brown bodies looking like cocoons trapped in a spider's web.

They stood like they used to at the entrance to all of their cities on Etae, in the first war—the one before the humans started fighting each other. The Idonae's fragile limbs entwined together in an attempt to be strong, to hold out the invaders.

She shivered, and for a moment, she thought she felt rain fall on her, her feet slogging in mud. Then she shook the image away, and continued moving forward, trying not to look, and unable to stop herself.

She had always found the Idonae hideously ugly, but never more than now—their lack of a conventional face made it impossible to see where they were looking, understand what they were thinking.

They blamed all Etaens for their plight, not realizing that they had been the first invaders. The humans had only repeated the Idonae's actions.

And were being cursed for it.

At the end of the line of Idonae, the last Idonae let its limbs flow like feelers in water. Then its tiny hands opened in unison and released yet another sign.

ETAEN USURPERS SHALL PAY FOR THEIR CRIMES

Anatolya gasped in spite of herself.

Her team moved close, pressing against her. Or were they being shoved against her by the crowd?

The cries had turned to angry shouts, and she couldn't make out the words—she didn't dare.

We have to defend, Gianni sent.

No, she sent back, and hoped she was right.

28

Flint's facial-recognition program couldn't identify the killer. At least not from all the databases he had swiped from the Detective Division, focusing mostly on the Moon.

He expanded the search to include the entire Alliance, but knew that would take time, and his instincts were warning him that time was running out.

He wasn't quite sure why he felt that way—Armstrong police investigations, even ones of well-known victims—had their own pace, and it was usually slow. But DeRicci's visit had come right on the heels of her trip to the apartment, and her disappointment in his unwillingness to cooperate had been palpable.

Because he was thinking about it, he checked the spyware he'd been running in DeRicci's computer. In the last hour, it had downloaded a significant number of reports.

Flint flipped through them and cursed. The weapons specialist had already gotten back to her: DeRicci knew that the gun had initially belonged to him.

She hadn't contacted him either, when she discovered it. His instincts had been right. She was done with him. Still, he hoped that she would try to reach him when she left the office.

Sometimes DeRicci didn't do things in the order that he expected her to.

He blanked that screen and returned to work on the killer. The system was sorting through millions of faces. But Flint had set up other scans as well, and those seemed to be getting better results than the name and face search.

His databases had information on the killing method, but it came from an unexpected source. He was expecting to find a single killer's modus operandi.

Instead, he found an entire army's.

The Etaen army's. Or at least one branch of it.

Flint felt cold. These murders were obviously tied to Carolyn Lahiri, and to her past.

He leaned forward as he read. The killer had been human, but enhanced in ways that had been forbidden throughout the Alliance. His DNA had been altered with Idonae DNA to give his limbs an elasticity that they wouldn't normally have. The other alterations—the knives for fingers, the added strength—came from experiments done off-world with human children.

Although there were rumors that these experiments had yielded the ultimate physical weapon, the Alliance had no proof of it. Because Etae wasn't part of the Alliance, information on this sort of enhancement—how to achieve it, the benefits (and problems) of the alterations, and the uses of it—wasn't available, at least through legitimate channels.

Several intergalactic corporations had been lobbying the Alliance for approval of the techniques, claiming that corporate security guards needed the alterations to survive the opening of new worlds at the edge of the known universe.

"History has shown us," one corporate exec argued before the Alliance's main governing body, "that the security corps for major businesses die in record numbers in the first years of a colonization. Laser weapons often don't work in intended ways on different alien species. However, if these species believe that we have morphing powers and can become any sort of weapon we want, they will leave us alone, allow us to establish our businesses on the planets, and work with us diplomatically—provided, of course, the alien species has enough intelligence to understand the delicacy of diplomatic negotiations."

Flint shook his head. The only reason he had a job was because of the stupidity of intergalactic corporations. If they had researched planets before colonizing them, then the errors that caused people to Disappear would never have happened. But corporations didn't work that way; they went in, colonized, stripped the areas of the goods the corporation wanted, and dealt with the consequences.

Now the corporations wanted to alter the very makeup of their employees' bodies, just to provide a measure of security for their colonizing executives.

The computer to his left beeped. The facial recognition scans had found a match—or what the computer considered a match. Sometimes the program came up with false positives, and he had to weed through them to find what he was looking for.

He called up the image on the screen, and studied it. It was a hologram crammed into a two-dimensional picture.

The picture looked close enough, but he couldn't tell, not with the two-dimensional image. Faces got mashed sometimes when they went from a hologram down to 2-D.

He would download it, but before he did, he wanted to see what database the computer had found the image on.

As he stared at the web trail, he felt a shiver run through him. This image hadn't come from any law enforcement database. It had come from a soldiers-for-hire site, under the subheading of *Unattached*.

Flint lifted his hands from the keyboard and frowned. He should, he knew, return to the Brownie Bar or some other public dataport to download the rest of the information about the site. But he felt crunched for time, and, for the first time since he started in this business, he didn't want someone looking over his shoulder—not to protect his clients (a feeling he had all the time), but because he was afraid that simply by looking at the site, he might get himself arrested.

The same problems existed within his own system, but he knew how to clean it up well enough that the police couldn't trace it. Also, he knew, if the police were inside his system, they had enough information to arrest him on a variety of other illegal activities. They didn't need his viewing of a soldier-for-hire information board as proof that he was breaking the law.

Soldiers-for-hire had a long tradition within the Alliance. Corporations hired them for new world security. Sometimes entire teams went with the corporate diplomats to negotiate terms (read: threaten) with new natives on nonaligned worlds.

But this little corner of the database worried Flint more than others. *Unattached* meant more than a mercenary. Mercenaries tended to hire themselves out in groups. They fought wherever the money led them—and they got good money for their work.

But in this circumstance, *Unattached* meant working alone. And a soldier-for-hire who worked alone was simply another term for assassin.

If this was indeed the killer of the Lahiris, he had been hired to kill them. Which would explain his calmness, his lack of enjoyment or upset, and his methodical ways of cleaning up the scene.

Flint captured the holographic ad. Then he paused the programs he was running, shut down his outside links, and set his entire system on Emergency Scrub. That program, of his own design, would get rid of anything any outside link had planted within his system.

He made certain the building was locked, set the soundproofing on high so that his neighbors and anyone passing on the street had absolutely no chance of overhearing this broadcast, and commanded the hologram to play.

It was an attractive little package that made no real promises. An anonymous voice spoke while the hologram itself shimmered on Flint's floor, unassembled, waiting until the voice was done before showing Flint what he had downloaded.

The voice said, "Blind Box six-five-four-eight-nine has worked unattached for the past decade, satisfactorily completing four hundred and thirty-two jobs. References available on request. A specialty soldier, six-five-four-eight-nine has no need of conventional weapons. Enhanced to free himself from tight situations, six-five-four-eight-nine will use those enhancements to take care of any serious problems you may have.

"Especially useful in Old Universe areas where security is high, six-five-four-eight-nine's weaponry will not attract the attention of law enforcement or Port Authorities. Able to cross into any colony, even the most heavily guarded ones, six-five-four-eight-nine is best used in the most difficult cases, since he provides our most expensive service. Six-five-four-eight-nine and the others in the six-five-four series have our best records and our most efficient workmanship. If you want the best, order six-five-four-eight-nine.

"See Proceedings for ordering information. All transactions confidential."

The hologram continued to shimmer in front of Flint. It hadn't coalesced. He would have to order it to start, which, if he had kept his links open, would have given the soldiers-for-hire site his voice imprint. He wondered if the hologram would start without his links being open, and decided there was only one way to find out.

"Start," he said.

The hologram coalesced, forming a see-through image of the man Flint had seen in the security video. Statistics ran on a 2-D screen alongside him:

Height: 6'4"
Weight: 260
Alterations: 165
Updated: Every five years
Original Service: Classified
Home World: Classified
Name: Classified
Capacity: 6 adults at one time

It took Flint a moment to figure out what that last meant; then, as he realized it, his hands clenched into fists. The man could handle no more than six adult humans at once.

Handle was probably the wrong word. The man could kill as many as six adult humans at once.

"Create hologram from my file of killer in Lahiri apartment," Flint said. "Do a point-by-point comparison."

He had already indicted and convicted the man before him in his own mind, but he wasn't 100 percent certain this man was the killer. He needed the computer verification, and then he needed more.

He needed to break into the system to find out who this killer was—and who had hired him.

The hologram from the site continued to turn. As it did, the "alterations" revealed themselves. In addition to the elongated arms and the fingers like knives, the killer could do a handful of different, small things like change his eye color at will, and carry chips in small pouches hidden in the pads of his fingers.

His sight had been augmented to see movement a split second before the movement registered on the average human eye, and his hearing had also been augmented to include an upper range that very few mammals heard. His vocal cords had been enhanced to produce a sound that blocked most computer usage within several meters of him.

He wasn't really human, not any longer, if he had ever been. What kind of person would request these alterations, anyway?

Finally, the hologram stopped its insane little sales program. Flint kept it on while his system finished its point-by-point comparison.

Then he would purge any reference to this from his system. He would keep the information, however, and access it from a public port if he needed to.

He hoped he would be able to get information on 65489 some other way. He really didn't want to dig through the records of the soldiers-for-hire site. Somehow that made him feel like he was setting himself up for surveillance of a kind as sophisticated as his own.

The points-of-comparison check finally ended. According to every measure his system had—and his was more advanced than all but the strictest intergalactic corporations—65489 was the man who had been in the Lahiris' apartment.

Hired by someone to kill all three of them. Or one of them and whoever else happened to be there.

The rest—the cleanup, the destruction of the evidence—was simply business as usual.

And somehow that offended Flint even more. He had wanted this to be personal. If these people had to die, he wanted it to be in a crime of passion, not as an act for hire, by someone who had never met them and had no reason to value them as people.

Flint owed them. He owed all three of them. And he would solve this, no matter what it would take.

29

In the end, Anatolya's own people caused the riot.

The banner unfurled from the Idonae's tiny hands and floated over the crowd:

ETAEN USURPERS SHALL PAY FOR THEIR CRIMES

And when it reached Anatolya and her team, it blared the words in all six Etaen languages, English, Peyti, and every other language she knew. The sign lit up and followed them like a tracking dog.

This has to end, Gianni sent, and started to reach for the sign.

She grabbed his arm, feeling its strange softness. *No,* she sent again.

The others on the team sent more arguments to her. They agreed with Gianni. They had stopped moving forward, and the crowd surged against them, pressing them tight into each other.

It's an insult, yes, she sent, *and we have to take it.*

They had to realize, all of her people had to realize, how important this moment was, how much they needed the support of the Alliance. If they started something, then the Alliance would have nothing to do with them.

Nothing at all.

She stumbled and someone caught her arm—a member of the team. But she shouldn't have stumbled in the first place. The crowd was getting rougher.

Another team member reached for the sign, and she felt a surge of panic.

No! she sent across their links, wondering how anyone could miss her point. *No! Stop! Think! It could be a bomb!*

The hand went down, but too late. Someone in the crowd screamed, "Murderers!" and the sound carried across all of the noise.

Anatolya stumbled again. Her team was being shoved.

"Murderers!" the voice shouted again.

It took Anatolya a moment to realize the voice was shouting in Alkan.

"We are no worse than you!" Gianni shouted in the same language, and Anatolya felt her breath catch. The bait had worked, and her oldest friend, her protector, had been caught in it.

The man with the most guilt let it flare up, and it snared him. How long had it been since he had seen an Idonae? Two decades? Three?

The Idonae let out a shriek, a unison sound that blared over the crowd and silenced them. Then the Idonae scattered, screaming for protection from the evil Etaen.

"We haven't done anything," Anatolya said, but as she spoke, she saw that her team had broken up. The reason she had been stumbling was because she had lost her left flank. They were pouring forward, out to get the traitor Idonae, the liars that had stolen Etae's reputation from the beginning.

The crowd plucked at her people, then slammed into them trying to stop them. But it would be no use. The weapons came out—hands swirling, arms stretching—and Anatolya glanced up at the news cars hovering overhead.

It was a disaster, a horrible disaster, and she was losing everything she had ever worked for.

She reached for Gianni, but he too was gone, in pursuit of the Idonae who he would swear had ruined their chances of joining the Alliance.

But the Idonae were simply bait, and her people had risen to it, just like someone had known they would.

Anatolya let the crowd jostle her, sweep her along— apparently without her team, no one recognized her— and she stumbled forward, always forward, each step blind, alone, and terrified.

30

Flint didn't want to hack into the soldiers-for-hire site, at least not from his own office. If any organization had the skills to trace his work, it would be that one. So he decided to see if he could find the information he needed some other way.

He had dozens of searches running on all of his newly scrubbed machines. He'd spent the better part of an hour making certain that nothing had been left in his system, not even a fragment of code. He'd gone as deeply as he could into the system itself, looking for ghosts, for echoes, for anything suspicious, cleaning off all he could find, destroying information in an effort to be cautious.

He'd even destroyed the hologram—deleting it wasn't enough for him. He knew how to bury signals in holographic software; if he knew it, the soldiers-for-hire people did as well.

But he kept the image he had made from the security vid. He was running that image against port arrivals, not just here, but all over the solar system. If he needed to, he would branch out to other parts of the galaxy before broadening the search even more.

At the moment, he had limited his search to the

past three months. The amount of information his system had to sift through was staggering.

He had more hope for the other scans he was running. He was searching for the surgeons who performed these augmentations, and this time, he didn't have to limit his search to the solar system.

As he ran these searches, he also kept an eye on DeRicci's files. She had downloaded more reports—all of them preliminary, many of them expressing confusion over the mixed-up spatter.

Those reports inspired him as well. He looked for other unsolved homicides where the scenes had an odd mixture of cleanliness, multiple victims, and impossible-to-decipher spatter patterns.

So far, he had found none in Armstrong, and even though he had expanded that search, he had a hunch he would find none on the Moon.

Finally one of his searches stopped and seized a screen. It bleeped at him, informing him that it had found some of the information he wanted.

He swiveled his chair and studied the center screen, backlit now so that he could easily read the data before him.

That combination of enhancements, creating elongated arms, fingers like blades, increased vision and hearing, as well as a host of other things, had become a science in the outer regions of the known universe.

Only one place needed that exact combination:
Etae.

The information he had discovered on the Etaen army, the information he had seen earlier that day, now tied directly to the man who had killed his clients.

Flint had incontrovertible proof. No longer could he lie to himself and say that the man had gotten his enhancements elsewhere.

Flint made himself take a deep breath. The contracts he had with his clients—contracts ably drawn up by Paloma over decades of work as a Retrieval Artist and modified for his own use—absolved him of any responsibility in the death of the Lahiris. Everyone knew, long before they had gotten involved with one another, that reprisals were possible. Otherwise, the Disappeared wouldn't have had to leave in the first place.

Usually, though, a found Disappeared hadn't been pardoned. Carolyn had. She had fought with the resistance, which had become the current government. No one needed her dead now.

She had been free to come home. Even she agreed with that. She had inspected the documents, done some research on her own, was even expecting Flint when he showed up.

He froze.

She had expected him. She had known she could leave. Still, she waited for a Retrieval Artist to find her.

That fact had bothered him then; it bothered him now, but didn't seem suspicious in and of itself. Nothing was. The case had been straightforward until everyone involved in it died.

He set up a new scan, this one for murders connected to Etae. The list he got back was immediate and so long that it made his eyes hurt. Thousands and thousands of deaths, all occurring off Etae, all of them within the last few years.

He tried to refine the search, uncertain of the best way to do so. Finally, he decided to search only for unsolved cases that were somehow tied to Etae— either in method of the killings or through the victims.

That narrowed his field to a thousand entries. Then he looked for possible assassinations. Five hundred. And finally, he realized that he should search for non-Etaens killed for being mercenary soldiers in that far-off place, just as Carolyn had been.

And, as an added measure, he threw in *possible pardoned Disappeareds*.

The search slowed. For a moment, he thought he'd get no results at all.

Then his screen displayed three—one on Trieinsf'rd, one on Esterwk, and one possible in the Vekke system.

Trieinsf'rd was obvious: The woman had been in hiding in a place called Nowhere for ten years. She had been killed by some kind of pellet weapon at long range—the pellet passed through her, leaving a trace of poison in her system.

It was a clear assassination, one with a signature of a well-known and very selective assassin named Kovac. He had no ties to Etae, but she had. The victim had gone to Etae at the same time as Carolyn Lahiri.

The killing on Esterwk proved, after a bit of study, to be a simple crime of passion—a murder that the local police believed to be an assassination since the victim was a Disappeared. Apparently, the victim hadn't known that the leadership of Etae had changed since she had been exiled, and she had died at the hands of a brother-in-law who had been jealous of her attentions to her own husband.

The final killing had just appeared in the database he'd been searching. It had occurred in the city of Binh, a cosmopolitan area of the conservative Vekke system. A bomb had gone off in a crowded café, killing dozens of people of various races, from Disty to human.

One, however, closest to the blast, had been a Disappeared. She had been identified from DNA records and, like Carolyn and the Trieinsf'rd victim, had fought as a mercenary in the Etaen wars for independence.

He let out a small breath. He was searching for coincidences. He shouldn't have been surprised to find them.

Still, all three deaths had occurred after the pardons had been announced. He wondered what other events were occurring at the same time.

Why had Etae announced pardons anyway?

He decided to run a news scan on Etae and was startled when a live feed poured into his screen. He was even more startled to see Ki Bowles reporting with an earnestness that she had lacked when she visited his office.

Behind her, people swarmed in a small space identifiable to him only as one of the anonymous streets near the port. He saw hands raised, Revs with their emotion collars flared, Disty struggling to stay on top. Signs floated all around, but remained unreadable.

He turned up the audio.

". . . peaceful demonstration that turned into a riot." Ki Bowles's voice had an urgency that led Flint to think her own adrenaline was pumping. She must have been very close to the action. "Shortly after Mayor Soseki's angry speech about the governor-general's action allowing Etaen terrorists into Armstrong's dome, various protestors gathered. The terrorists left the building a short time ago without a guard. It seemed as though nothing was going to happen, when suddenly the entire place erupted."

Footage of the screaming crowd interrupted her narrative. Flint could make no sense of any of it—he couldn't tell who were Etaens and who were human residents of Armstrong. Only the alien residents of the city were clear, and they seemed just as angry as everyone else.

"The streets around the port are blocked off. The city has dispatched police and police robots trained in riot suppression to the scene, and they hope to have the situation contained within the hour."

Flint didn't like the sound of that. If it was going to take the police an hour to contain the crowd, then the riot was extremely violent. A lot of people were going to get hurt.

He left the feed running in a corner of his screen, but turned the audio back down. This riot was not a coincidence. The Lahiris died because something connected to Etae was going to happen in Armstrong.

But he had looked specifically for ties between Etae and Armstrong and had found none. That had been nearly two weeks ago. How could things have changed so quickly?

He recorded the names of the other two Disappeared victims, assassinated off-world, and decided to see if he could find their ties to Carolyn.

Something was going on here, something that was very important, something DeRicci and the police likely wouldn't catch.

If he acted quickly, he just might find out what that something was.

31

The arm movements were not natural. The cameras focused on them—long, swinging, fingers sharp as blades as a tall man scythed his way through the rioting crowd.

Orenda Kreise turned away from the live scene. The image was displayed on the clear screens the cultural center had dropped from the ceiling throughout the main room. The only way Kreise could avoid seeing the disaster at the Port was to bury her face in her hands.

Which she did.

She no longer felt like a leader, an ambassador, or one of the most effective diplomats in the Alliance. She felt like a fool.

Someone had certainly played her for one.

[I BELIEVE I SAW IDONAE.] The Nyyzen Ambassador spoke, its odd voice sounding like echoes in Kreise's ears.

"You did." Hadad Foltz seemed tired.

"This is a disaster," Uzval said, her voice muffled by her breathing mask.

"Something certainly went wrong." Pilar Restrepo wasn't trying to hide her anger. It filled every single word. "Stop hiding your face, Orenda. You set this up, didn't you? You wanted the entire solar system to remember all the problems on Etae."

Kreise closed her eyes. Her lashes brushed against the palms of her hands. She didn't want to look at anyone. She was tired of seeing, tired of making decisions, tired of this entire game.

"Orenda," Restrepo snapped. "Look up."

Another voice filled the room. It came from a screen behind her, a deep chilling voice. A narrator's voice.

"Oh, no," Foltz said. "They're running the history of Etae concurrent with the riot."

At this, Kreise did raise her head. On every other screen, a program—hastily made—started recounting the known history of Etae. At the bottom of the feed, a tag line read:

> *Courtesy of Arek Soseki*
> *Mayor*
> *the City of Armstrong*

"The little weasel." Restrepo stood. "What's he hoping to accomplish?"

[HE HAS TOLD YOU. HE DOES NOT WANT TERRORISTS IN HIS DOME.]

"Then he shouldn't let anyone in or out. For God's sake." Restrepo moved her heavyset body to the nearest screen. "One person's terrorist is someone else's freedom fighter."

"Not now," Kreise said. She didn't want to hear those arguments again.

She was staring, mesmerized, at the screen closest to her. Even though the package was hastily put together—the production footage was raw and unchanged from its original forms—it was compelling.

But the history of Etae was compelling, from the moment the Idonae decided to wipe out the Ynnels and strip the northern continent of *vorgefur,* a mineral that had no real use to anyone in the Alliance, but powered much of the Idonae's technology, to the hideous death of the Child Martyr, which had brought the current government into power, the entire history of Etae had behind it great storytelling compressed into a very short period of time—decades, instead of centuries.

Kreise turned her head slightly so that she could see the screen showing the riot. All she could see were heads and backs and bodies, and the occasional elongated arm, the fingers hidden as they sliced their way through the crowd.

Kreise had wanted the Etaens to be discredited, but not like this. Not at the cost of lives.

People were screaming, but the screams were barely audible. Someone—thankfully—had kept the sound down.

Armstrong police were shoving their way toward the center of the melee. Kreise hoped someone had warned them about what they'd encounter, or this situation would get even worse.

"We cannot meet with them now," Foltz said.

"We have to," Kreise said. "All this death can't be for nothing."

[BUT IT WILL BE FOR NOTHING. NO MATTER WHAT HAPPENS, WE CAN NO LONGER APPROVE ETAE'S INCLUSION IN THE ALLIANCE. SOMEONE HAS THWARTED US IN THIS.]

The Ambassador sounded disappointed, but Kreise had learned not to read much into its tones. The two Nyyzen whose linked minds created the third gave her no clue either. They sat in their chairs, facing straight ahead, their eyes glazed.

"Yeah," Restrepo said, her back to the table. "It was Orenda."

Kreise shook her head. "I would never do this."

She worked in diplomacy. Diplomacy, the art of forging alliances—or of breaking them—without the loss of life.

Had she caused this failure?

She didn't even want to think about it.

"You're the one who wanted the meeting inside the

Alliance," Restrepo said. "You're the one who prevented it from happening on Earth. You knew that Armstrong had tough port laws, and your people handled the booking of the hall as well as the hotel. Didn't they know that Döbryn's people would need approval?"

"Stop it, Pilar." Uzval's voice had gained strength. Her long, thin fingers were bent backward, as they had been in the last meeting. "We accomplish nothing by bickering. We have to figure out a way to save this situation. I believe the only way we can do that is meet with the Etaens. Otherwise, we look as foolish as the city itself."

"Are you looking at that?" Restrepo extended a hand toward one of the screens. "They're probably killing innocent Armstrong citizens right now."

"I thought you were one of their backers," Foltz said.

"I *am,* and they were provoked. We all saw the Idonae—nice touch, Orenda. Anyone with brains knows that seeing an Idonae will set off even the sanest Etaen. It's almost as bad as showing the footage of the Child Martyr's death, which will probably show up"—Restrepo glanced at one of the other screens—"oh, any moment now."

[WE MEET WITH THEM. WE JUST DO NOT EXPLAIN OR JUSTIFY THE MEETING. WE REMIND THE PRESS THAT THIS MEETING WAS TO BE CONFIDENTIAL AND WE FINE THE MAYOR OF ARMSTRONG FOR BREAKING OUR AGREEMENT.]

"I'm sure that'll go over well," Kreise said. "The mayor has already shown how malleable he is."

Foltz glared at her. He never did appreciate sarcasm. "We have to do something. If we abandon Döbryn now, we look like cowards, and all this damage is for nothing."

"We are cowards," Restrepo said.

"Yes, we are," Kreise said and looked pointedly at Restrepo. "But you and I speak of different things. I think we're cowards for not standing up for our principles. If we had done that, we wouldn't be in this mess in the first place."

"We have different principles." Restrepo's tone was flat.

[PRINCIPLES ARE NOT THE ISSUE. DAMAGE CONTROL IS. WE HOLD THE MEETING. WE LISTEN TO ETAE'S CASE. WE MAKE OUR DECISION. THEN WE DO NOT REPORT OUR DECISION FOR A YEAR OR MORE. BY THEN, THIS ENTIRE CRISIS WILL BE FORGOTTEN.]

"A year?" Restrepo whirled. "We don't have a year."

[WE HAVE ALL THE TIME WE NEED.]

"We have corporations who are trying to go through channels right now. They want those medical procedures that Etae perfected, and they'll get them, legally or illegally. Let's at least make this legal." Restrepo had her hands flat on the table.

"We're watching those medical procedures at work now." Uzval's fingers were still raised. "Look, Pilar. Is that what you want for your corporations?"

Kreise felt her breath catch. She hadn't expected Uzval to be so blunt.

Restrepo did not look at the screen.

Uzval tilted her head slightly. "We sacrifice much for some corporations' desire to step outside the law."

Restrepo crossed her arms. "Etae's entrance into the Alliance is inevitable. They'll join us eventually."

"Perhaps," Kreise said. "Decades from now, when they've shown they're civilized."

"Let's hear their case," Restrepo said, "and then decide. They may be more civilized than you think."

Kreise looked at the screen. She couldn't even make out what was happening. "I don't think they're civilized at all," she muttered.

"You are ignoring the risks." Uzval's voice was almost inaudible in her breathing mask. She was speaking to Restrepo. "They are considerable."

"We take those risks with all the alien groups that have come into the Alliance," Restrepo said.

"Really?" Uzval extended her long fingers toward

the screen. "The fact remains that much of Etae's current population has been enhanced in unacceptable ways—"

"By current standards," Foltz said.

"—and," Uzval said as if the interruption hadn't happened, "the fact remains that we would let walking weapons into our cities, into our once-safe ports. Are we willing to do that?"

Everyone turned toward the monitors—everyone except the Nyyzen. Kreise wasn't sure about the Ambassador.

She sighed. This group would continue fighting until someone took the lead. And that someone was always her, even though she wasn't certain why.

"The Ambassador is right," she said. "We hold the meetings. We report a little bit to the press so that they feel satisfied, and we withhold our decision until the furor from today's riots dies down."

"Provided, of course, that the Etaens even survive those riots." Restrepo's voice was bitter.

Kreise ignored her. "I'll put the motion on the table. I'll need a second."

"I'll second," Uzval said, surprising her.

"Then I'll call the vote," Kreise said.

"Divide it into two parts," Restrepo said. "The meeting and withholding the decision."

"I already made the motion," Kreise said. She glanced at the second screen. Just as Foltz predicted, the scenes of the Child Martyr's death were playing.

The little girl, her face a mask of agony as conventional weapons sliced her in half, dominated the screen.

Kreise had to look away. "All in favor?" she asked, and as the voices rose around the room, she knew she wouldn't even have to call for opposition.

They would have their meeting, and it would be toothless, just like she had initially wanted.

Only this vote didn't feel like a victory. Diplomacy had not worked.

She had failed, and her failure had cost lives.

32

Anatolya's arms were wrapped protectively around her head, and she plunged forward, bent at the waist so that she could avoid the blows raining on her from above. Her team had vanished, lost in the crowd. She didn't even try to look for them.

The shouts had become a blur of sound, the hands reaching for her, grabbing her, pushing her, slapping her had become a blur also. All that mattered was moving forward, getting away, if indeed there was an away.

She thought she might die here, in this horrible dome on this sterile land. Her heart rose and she thought of Etae—how much she'd lost for Etae—and this time, this would be an unworthy sacrifice.

She hadn't even made it to the Alliance. She had no chance to press her case, and she wouldn't now.

There was a curb ahead of her, and a parked—and now damaged—aircar that she slammed into because she hadn't been able to see it over the mass of bodies. The stench gagged her—she hadn't been around so many frightened humans in a long time, not since the riots after the Child Martyr's death.

Riots she had sometimes started.

A blow landed in the center of her back, knocking

the breath from her. She had to extend a hand to keep from falling—she wasn't enhanced, even though her team was, but she sure wished for enhancement now.

If she fell, she would be trampled to death. She knew that as clearly as if it had already happened. She would die and no one—

A hand grabbed her arm, then another, and an arm wrapped around her back. A normal arm, a human arm, not an elongated one. Bodies crowded around her, not hitting her—protecting her.

She looked up, saw a uniform, saw an unrecognizable face—young, male, professional—underneath a cap that had Armstrong's city symbol on it.

Police? Saving her? What was this?

They couldn't talk to her, probably didn't know she was linked or didn't want to risk having the message intercepted by the crowd. Another police officer put her arm around Anatolya too, and they whisked her forward.

This time, they actually moved ahead—plowing through the crowd as if it were made of water. There were no hands on her, besides the officers', no blows, no slaps across her face.

She could not see her people. They had vanished into the crowd. She caught the faint copper scent of blood, human blood, and shuddered.

"It's okay, miss," the cop, the human cop, the human cop from Armstrong in the Old Universe, said to her, right in her ear so that his voice rose above the screams and the cries and the shouts filled with anger. "We'll get you out of here."

"My team . . ." she said, but even she could feel the futility of speech. Unless her mouth was right beside his ear, he couldn't hear her, and neither could anyone else.

Cameras floated above her, taking in the mess, aircars, and glaring faces—some of them, she knew, reporters, all trying to make things worse.

Anatolya wanted to close her eyes, to slip away

mentally, never to return. But Döbryn would never have allowed that.

You have to fight, little girl, he would say to her when things got difficult—when memories got too difficult. *You have to fight.*

She didn't want to fight. She was tired of fighting. She had listened to him all her life, and even now, years after his death, she still listened to him.

He got her to place one foot in front of the other, to help the officers, to keep her eyes open so that she would know when that final fateful blow hit her and stopped her heart.

The crowd parted, revealing more officers. They were using some sort of stun weapon to keep the rioters back. She could hear its electric crackle over the unbearable din.

Behind the officers was the airlimo that Collier had promised her in what seemed like another life. Coward. Bastard. He was still in the Port, safe, when her people were struggling with the crowd.

The back passenger door to the limo opened, and the officers forced her inside. It was cool there, the interior smelling of real leather and some kind of perfume. Her stomach growled, a mind of its own despite the trauma.

Her officer—he had never introduced himself—had his hand on the outside of the door. He was going to slam it shut, but she caught it just in time.

"My people," she said.

He shook his head and leaned in. "I can't hear you."

He shouted those words and they seemed extraordinarily loud. The airlimo was soundproofed. Already the noise from the riots had faded. Only what came in the door reached her at all.

She crooked a finger, making him lean in so that he could hear her.

"My people," she said again. "Where are they?"

He shook his head. "Our instructions were to get you."

"Instructions from whom?"

"Dunno. Orders get filtered. Someone in the city. I'm sure your people will be all right."

"No," she said. "They won't. You have to get them. I won't leave without them."

But he was already backing out of the car. He slammed his open palm against the hood, and the limo rose.

"Close the door!" he shouted.

She pushed to keep it open. "My people," she yelled. "I can't leave them."

But the door slammed itself closed. She had to move away to keep from being caught in its mechanism.

She leaned forward and pounded on the opaque plastic between the back and the driver's compartment. The plastic cleared, revealing no driver at all.

She cursed, trying to find a way to stop this thing. But technology wasn't her specialty. She had no idea how to change out the chips and reorder the car.

Hey! she sent through her network. *I'm in the air-limo. Stop it! Then you can board. Stop it—*

You are too far away, Gianni sent back. *We're—*

The connection snapped. She didn't know if he was silenced or the link was broken or both. She tried to send again, and then again, but she got nothing.

She slammed against the smooth leather seats, her arms crossed. Damn them. The Alliance had gotten what it wanted after all.

She was approaching them alone, without backup, her mission in question.

She had lost, even before she had begun.

33

Even though she had been cursing Gumiela all day, DeRicci realized that her promotion still held perks.

She stared at the riot playing on the wall screen that opened up whenever the department had an all-points emergency, and read the message that flared red along the bottom.

All detectives junior grade and below report to the Port office. Bring standard-issue weapons and riot gear. All detectives . . .

She had been junior grade before Gumiela had made her assistant chief, although very few people knew that. Each demotion had cut back her seniority. She often held the same rank as her partners, most of whom were fresh out of school.

And now she didn't have to report. She could stay at the comfort of her desk and ignore the out-of-control citizens fighting in the streets below.

She had been in enough of these brawls to last her the rest of her life. She didn't need to get in another one, especially centered on an issue she couldn't even pretend to understand. Etae? She hadn't even heard of the place before this morning. And terrorists? The good citizens of Armstrong would have been better off worrying about the criminals already in their midst.

Eventually, she would have to investigate—see if the current troubles with the Etaens in Armstrong had any connection to Carolyn Lahiri—but for the moment, she could remain at her desk and look through files.

Bless those perks.

She couldn't shut off the wall monitor—it had an emergency control that kept it running so long as a police presence was needed—but she could decrease its size, which she did.

Now the image covered only part of the wall—a nuisance, rather than a problem. She turned her attention back to the screen on her desk.

She had been examining the file on the suicide of Calbert Lahiri, Carolyn's brother. The reports had been thorough and up-to-date; the file was complete as well. Apparently, politics had influenced this file as well; since Calbert's father was one of the most respected judges in the Tribunal system, Calbert's death had been investigated with a thoroughness usually reserved for the most gruesome murders.

Calbert had been several years younger than Carolyn, and had gone in and out of therapy for nearly a decade. The cause of his death, one of his therapists said, was that he had never left home.

Perhaps if he had left Armstrong, even for a trip to one of the other domed cities, he might have learned that the universe was bigger than the one controlled by his parents. But he never had, always saw himself in their light, and never did find his own reflection. He was lost, almost before he had started.

DeRicci found all of that interesting, but irrelevant. If the brother was a suicide—and she had no real reason to believe otherwise—then the cause of his death was important to him and routine to everyone else. She had investigated dozens of suicides, and almost all of them blamed their families for their inadequacies instead of looking to themselves.

More preliminary reports had come in—short on details, long on speculation, even though she had warned the team against that. She scanned through them, finding nothing that she didn't already know. Then she looked at the attachments. The crime scene techs had included a security vid from the hallway—apparently they were still trying to get information from the front door and the entry, at least at the time they wrote the report.

The hallway vid, according to the crime-scene techs, confirmed the presence of a fourth person somewhere near the time of the killings.

She opened the vid file, commanded the play to go to her wall screen—a secondary screen that wasn't playing the emergency feed—and leaned back.

The image appeared life-size on her far wall. The hallway looked realistic enough, even though she could see the white paint faintly through the image. Still, it seemed like she could walk down that corridor and get into the elevator at the far end.

The view of the elevator wasn't that good; she could see only a corner of the door. The hallway, at the beginning of the vid, was empty, and looked nothing like the hallway she had found herself in a few hours ago.

It seemed wider, for one thing, probably because it wasn't crammed with police and crime-scene technicians. For another, it seemed cleaner and better lit, but that could have been a function of the tape itself.

There was a soft ping as the elevator door slid open, and she saw movement at the very edge of the screen. The camera wasn't mobile or no one was watching it, or it hadn't been set up to focus on movement, because whoever had gotten off stayed at the bottom of her screen.

She got a sense of thinness and height, also saw a dark coat and a black hat. The techs had made notes that ran concurrently along the right side of the image, planning to expand the visuals so that they might extrapolate the visitor's appearance with computer modeling.

DeRicci let out a small sigh. That meant they never got a good view of the visitor, not from these cameras.

She glanced at the report to see if there were other security vids from this floor, but found nothing. Then she looked back at the person standing in front of the Lahiris' door.

He had moved from the side of the image to the very center of it. She rewound, watched his progress, and caught only a few details—a blond curl catching the light, a bit of white skin, long lashes hiding bright blue eyes.

She had known only one man with that coloring. Flint. He was blond and unusually white-skinned. Humans had intermingled so much over the centuries that the standard color had darkened, leaving pale people like Flint in the minority.

Only a handful of them lived on the Moon.

There were pockets of pale people elsewhere, some going to faraway planets to preserve their heritage, but they rarely traveled back into what they called the Old Universe. Their cultures had been denounced by the Alliance, and they were rare in this solar system. Even rarer than people like Flint himself.

Her hand had tightened into a fist, sending shooting pains up her arm. She forced herself to relax.

The man got in the center of the camera's range when his back was to it. She no longer saw the curl, no longer saw the skin. Only broad shoulders that tapered into narrow legs, a head hidden by a black hat, and a long coat that covered most of the rest of the clothing.

The man clearly knew where the camera was, and had done everything in his power to avoid it. Perhaps that was why the techs had run the notes alongside— to prove to DeRicci that they would try to discover his appearance while covering their butts in likely event of failure.

A bell sounded in the distance, and for a moment, she thought it was the elevator on the vid. But it was the Lahiris' bell. Somehow the man had rung it without revealing his hand.

DeRicci chewed on her lower lip, wishing she could

make all of this go away, wishing that it would be as easy to rewind life as it was to rewind the vid.

But it wasn't, and she watched as Dr. Mimi Lahiri opened the door, her squarish face animated.

DeRicci hated seeing the victims as they had been in life. It made them into people and it made her care too much about them. But she still watched, entranced, as Lahiri spoke.

May I help you?

What an odd thing to say to someone who had come to your door. If she hadn't known him, she wouldn't have opened the door. So opening the door suggested that she had known him, and yet her words were those someone would utter to a stranger.

The man's words were garbled—probably deliberately—and DeRicci couldn't even get a tone of voice from them. They'd been scrambled by something— something on his person? Or something that simply scrambled the vid's recording of the incident?

She glanced at the running commentary from the techs. They suspected a disruption in the feed. The voice had sounded different to Mimi Lahiri, probably like a normal voice. The distortion that DeRicci was hearing was part of the vid, not the way that the man spoke.

Lahiri turned, said, *Carolyn?* as the man shoved his way into the apartment. Lahiri looked back at him with a mixture of fear and anger.

Then he kicked the door shut.

DeRicci froze the frame on the closed door.

Obviously the man had claimed he was there for Carolyn. If the man was Flint, as DeRicci suspected, the request and Dr. Lahiri's response to it made sense. She would let him into the apartment to see a woman he had helped rescue from her past.

But Dr. Lahiri wouldn't have treated him so coldly, would she? In addition to being something someone said to a person they didn't know, *May I help you?* was also a polite way of telling someone that they weren't wanted.

DeRicci rewound the vid and watched the sequence again. She hadn't known Dr. Lahiri, so she didn't know if the woman was reacting the way she would when a friend was at the door or if she treated everyone that way.

And now there were no members of the family left alive to help her sort this out. DeRicci would have to go to friends—if the Lahiris had any—and colleagues to get some of these questions answered.

Something wasn't right here, and it wasn't just the suggestions of Flint in all the evidence. If he had decided to target this family, he would have been more careful—wouldn't he?

Police and former police liked to think they were sophisticated about evidence, but they made mistakes like everyone else. And perhaps the family had provoked him somehow, perhaps they had found out the one thing that would really upset him.

DeRicci shook her head. Even if the person at the door was Flint, there was nothing here that proved he had killed the family.

DeRicci leaned back in her chair and folded her hands together. If she hadn't been friends with Miles Flint, she would have brought him into the station for interrogation based on this evidence.

She was giving him leeway again.

Her stomach twisted. She hated this case.

But she would do it her way. Before she brought Flint in, she would make certain she had all her evidence together. She didn't want to set him free on any kind of technicality. She didn't want to tip her hand.

After all, Retrieval Artists knew how to Disappear—and that was the last thing she wanted Miles Flint to do.

34

Flint watched the security vid concurrently with De-Ricci. She had no understanding of her computer networks and links, leaving that to the techs, so Flint was free to piggyback onto her system, to watch even as she watched.

He didn't like what he saw. The killer had stayed at the edge of the camera range, showing that he knew exactly where the building's security was.

Like he had done inside the apartment, the killer had planted evidence, all of it false. The killer had dark hair, dark skin, and dark eyes. When he had entered the apartment and killed the Lahiris, he had looked like his image on the soldiers-for-hire site.

Somehow, he had tampered with the vid here or had worn some kind of costume to gain entry to the apartment.

Flint studied the hallway security vid. There were a number of problems with it. First, it seemed to start only moments before the elevator opened. Granted, the techs could have sent it to DeRicci that way, but the opening seemed static—the kind of static that came from a fixed image, not from a camera studying the same spot for long periods of time.

Besides, most building security measures had

sensors—sound and motion detectors or heat monitors, something that would trigger the on cycle. This vid had been running *before* the elevator opened, which didn't seem right.

Flint couldn't work with this copy of a copy of a copy. He glanced at the screen that monitored De-Ricci's work: She was still reading reports.

So he moved to another screen, used his links, and probed the police files, going into the tech files as deeply as he dared. He used the code generated off the report the techs had sent to DeRicci, hoping to find the real copy of the vid before the backup alarms went off.

He had already deactivated the main alarms; those were easy. The backups, which he'd insisted get installed in the system when he moved up from Traffic, were the ones he didn't trust.

Because he had seen the killer tamper with the cleaning bots, because he knew some of the tricks built into the man's systems, Flint knew what to look for.

It took him about ten minutes to find it.

The original had been altered. A chip had been added to the pile that ran the building's security. Someone had added the chip, and if Flint had time, he would hack into the building's security system and see if that someone showed up in the twelve hours between diagnostics.

At the moment, he concentrated on the chip itself. It had its own self-sustaining program, and didn't seem to blend with the other chips. Yet it hadn't set off the diagnostic's sensors, probably because it had been designed to lurk.

In spite of himself, he had to admire the ingenuity the killer used. Flint backed up the security vid, watched the original from the beginning, and saw what he was searching for: the slight bounce that indicated the start of a recording.

He froze the bounce, then zeroed in on it, slowing it down to microseconds and watching each tiny frame. The security vid showed the elevator, but with the door already open. Apparently something had triggered the vid—movement or the door itself—and then the new chip cut in.

In a split second, the elevator door went from open to closed; the altered version of the vid ran, and no one would be the wiser. Unless they knew what they were looking for.

His hands were shaking. The techs had missed this, and would continue to do so if he didn't do something. He hacked deeper into the system, found one of the tech's digital signatures, and flagged the bounce—highlighting the open elevator door and then the fact that it was closed, as well as the odd diagnostic.

Then he added a message: *Anyone else catch this? Got a clue what it means?*

He quickly scrubbed his own prints from the system—at least as best he could, without removing the traces he'd planted in DeRicci's net—and backed out, hoping that the backup alarms hadn't gone off while he was doing his good deed for the day.

Then he shut down the links into his office, and studied the security vid one more time. Blond hair, curls, light skin. He touched his own skin. How many people had commented on his coloring over the years? How many had smiled at him and asked if he was from off-world or mentioned how very old-fashioned he looked?

The chances of someone else with the same combination of skin color, hair color, and eye color approaching the Lahiris was slim.

Someone was setting Flint up to detract attention from the killer himself.

His palms were damp. He wiped them on his pants legs, then stood. He paced around the small room. The fact that someone brought him in as a decoy bothered him—and not just for the fact that he might be implicated in the crime.

This killer had to know that Flint was working on the case and had to observe Flint enough to know what Flint looked like.

Flint frowned. If the killer had known Carolyn was on Earth, he would have killed her there.

So that meant he had stumbled on her—and Flint—later.

Which actually gave Flint a time line. Because once Carolyn agreed to come back to Armstrong, she didn't leave Flint's side. In fact, Flint had guarded her (without her knowledge) while she was deciding what to do.

The killer had to have found them after Flint had contacted Carolyn. The killer had come to Earth looking for her, saw Flint take her away, and followed them back to the Moon.

Flint supposed the killer could have seen her in Armstrong and followed her to the apartment, but that was less likely—how would the killer have known when (or even if) she would return to the Moon?

At some point, the killer had piggybacked on Flint's work, and Tracked Carolyn, waiting for the best moment to assassinate her.

Flint sat back down at his desk, reopened his links, and copied the picture he had of the killer. Then he let the computer compare it to Port records on Earth during the week he'd been there. The killer would have had to go through security and decon—Earth was the strictest of all the planets in this galaxy with its decon procedures: The place had never had a foreign-brought plague. It also kept records of all outsiders entering Earth, and the records were on file for seven years before they went into the back archives.

It was a nifty system and one he had once argued for Armstrong's Port to adopt. Because if someone had the same physical ID and used a different name at different times, it automatically red-flagged the system. Several people got slowed down unnecessarily, but a number of criminals had been caught that way—often on years-old data.

Armstrong's Port archived its information for only a year, claiming it had too much traffic to keep the information much longer. Armstrong had a point: The Moon was a hub for most of the solar system—

particularly for aliens who didn't want to go all the way to Earth, since Earth had so many other restrictions—on weaponry (you couldn't carry any), on currency, on the amount of off-worlders let onto the planet for more than a few weeks—and there were fewer ports on the Moon. So the information was concentrated in one place.

Which made it useful for Flint, since he needed information from this year only. First he hacked into the Earth records, picking ports closest to New Orleans, where he had found Carolyn.

He also looked for information on the space station that orbited Earth, where a lot of larger vehicles chose to dock instead of using the older and more dangerous ports or attempting to go through Earth's atmosphere.

It didn't take long for him to get a match. The killer, using the name Hank Mosby, had entered via Cape Canaveral two days before Flint had located Carolyn, and had left the same way on the same day that Flint and Carolyn had come to Armstrong.

Apparently, Flint and the killer—Mosby—had been looking for her at the same time. Flint had found her first, and by staying beside her, had protected her.

Her death in her parents' apartment had probably been the first chance Mosby had gotten to go after her since he arrived on Armstrong.

Flint examined the Port records on Armstrong. Mosby had arrived just after Flint had and had left right after the murders. He had taken a transport back to Earth.

Flint's breath caught. Had Mosby been going after more than one person on Earth? Or was he hiding out there?

Then Flint glanced at the records again. Mosby had never brought his own ship to any of the ports. Every single time he'd been on a transport, where the security was even tighter than it was in the ports.

Of course. He could get through because he seemed to have no weapons. And being on the transport meant he didn't have to go through the extra level of decon and genetic examination that Earth required; transport companies certified their passengers, even though it was common for the companies not to do the double-checks that Earth required.

It was a loophole for Earth's stringent no-hidden-weapons policy. Earth knew about creating weapons out of the human body and often scanned for it at the ports. But no one had thought to add that into the age-old transport scanning.

An alarm buzzed through his office. Flint tapped his third computer screen and it rose, showing him the source of the buzz.

Someone in police headquarters had discovered his trace in DeRicci's machine.

He cursed. Right now, things did not look good for him. And no matter how much he counted on DeRicci to believe him, no matter how much goodwill he had established with the department, he would lose it all by having an illegal trace in their system.

DeRicci might arrest him just to teach him a lesson. It might have been one he deserved, but it wasn't one he wanted to learn.

Since he was made, he downloaded his information and sent it through his private links to his space yacht, the *Emmeline*. Then he shut down his office system, removing two specialized chips so that no one could start it back up except him.

He was heading to Earth, and he wasn't sure he was ever coming back.

35

Nitara Nicolae pressed against the building, her hands behind her. She tried to disappear. The riot continued around her, but it had lost its momentum. The moment Anatolya Döbryn had escaped in the airlimo, the riot had lost its heart.

Nitara's breath was coming in short gasps. She hadn't moved from this spot, not since the crowd started to gather. She had thought herself far enough away from the center of the crowd to stay out of the action—and she had been right, for the most part.

But she had forgotten how violence felt, even if she wasn't exactly a part of it. The air got a charge to it, made up of the shouts, and the smells of fear and anger and blood. Add to that the physical pounding, the movement of thousands of feet, the actual vibration from people's heads hitting the ground, and she was in the world of her childhood—one she thought she had escaped a long, long time ago.

The Idonae hadn't helped that feeling. She had been the one to recruit them—she had sent word to one of her associates that the Etaen terrorists were here and perhaps the Idonae would want to protest—but her involvement didn't matter. Seeing those feelers, watching those squishy bodies press together in protest, made her queasy.

She glanced up at the media cars floating above her. They hadn't gotten close to her; in fact, so far as she could tell, no one had filmed her face.

Which was a good thing. She was well-known in Armstrong, and she didn't want people talking about her. Although they probably were now that she had been fired from her work at the cultural center. She had handled the diplomats badly. If only she hadn't been so fixated on Döbryn, she would have paid more attention to her own behavior. But between her personal plans and the meal plans as well as running the restaurant, she had had little time for sleep—

And that was an excuse too. She hadn't slept since someone had let it slip that the Alliance meeting was about letting Etae into the organization. She had tried not to ask too many questions, but it was difficult. It became even more difficult when she learned that Anatolya Döbryn would be speaking to the committee.

A body flew past her—someone tossed by the crowd. The body—male, she thought—landed on the pavement and skidded into a corner of her wall.

She didn't move. If she moved, she would call attention to herself, and then she would be next.

Nitara closed her eyes. She was not a child any longer. She wouldn't get caught and she wouldn't die. She took a deep breath, willing herself stronger.

Then she eased toward the man, keeping her back to the wall and her hands pressed against it.

In front of her, more people surged and fought and pushed against each other. The shouting continued, the police voices rising above all the others, amplified and evil, like authorities who had no idea who they commanded.

She willed her ears to hear nothing, just like she used to do when she was little. Her parents had fought in the war on the wrong side, and her father had been captured.

And then her mother had found her transport, sending her off Etae to relatives. Eventually, Nitara had found a home and learned a trade, and buried the memories as far as her nightmares would allow her.

But she never forgot the woman who had ordered her father's capture: Anatolya Döbryn. And Nitara had watched Döbryn's rise within the ranks even when she didn't want to keep track of Etaen politics.

Döbryn was the one who had presided over the slaughter of the former government officials and their families. No one talked about them, the people slain because they'd done nothing more than live in the same house with a government employee.

Like her mother had. And her cousins. And her entire extended family, all of whom remained on Etae after Nitara had left.

Nitara slid down the wall to the man. His face was covered with blood, his eyes closed, his breathing shallow.

Döbryn's visit brought all this back, and now, her presence caused even more turmoil. The riot had little to do with Nitara and her friends. It was Döbryn's fault, like everything else.

Döbryn and her people couldn't come into the Alliance, not after all they had done. At first, Nitara had planned to stop that simply, using her own skills. A badly cooked meal, the loss of a reputation. An accidental death by food poisoning—not common anymore, but not unheard of, especially for someone from the outlying colonies, someone whose stomach wasn't used to certain processed flours, certain reengineered meats.

But the meal was off, and she had to come up with a new way.

She crouched beside the man, smoothed his hair back, thought how young he was—maybe the age her father had been when he'd been captured. Someone shouted near her, and the bodies kept surging, people kept fighting, and somehow she ignored them.

The man's skin was clammy. He would die without her. She wasn't a child any longer. She was an adult who lived in the Old Universe, who knew other ways.

"It's all right," she said to him, hoping he could still hear her. Then she sent an emergency message across her links, warning the authorities that this man—and so many others—might die. She sent his image with it, letting them know he was badly injured and in need of help.

But she didn't send any more messages. Instead she looked at the crowd, fighting to save Armstrong, fighting to save the Alliance, fighting for her new home.

She couldn't go back to the cultural center. They wouldn't allow her there. She even had to wait until the meetings were over to get her equipment.

But Döbryn had escaped. She might still make her plea before the imbeciles who had decided to hear her case.

The riot might be enough to incite public opinion, but it wasn't going to be enough to let those fossilized Ambassadors realize they were making the wrong choice for the Alliance.

She had other skills, taught to her by nervous relatives who thought she was going to have to go back to Etae. Other skills that would help her now if she so chose.

If she could make a decision that had a price attached to it.

Her freedom, her reputation. Maybe even her life.

She smoothed the man's hair back, then lifted her hand. She had blood on her fingers. Slowly, carefully, remembering the rituals she had learned as a child, she painted that blood across her face.

36

Flint got into the Port easily, despite the riot. He knew all the Port's back entrances—a benefit of having been a Traffic cop once upon a time—and he knew all the employees. An old friend helped him get in.

And the very fact that he had a yacht docked in Terminal 25 gave him special privileges. They were one of the many things he paid an extraordinary storage fee for.

As he hurried to his ship, he realized he'd have no trouble getting off the Moon. Although the roads heading to the Port were closed, the traffic flowed in and out of the Moon's orbit, just like normal.

The *Emmeline* lived in Terminal 25, along with all the other rich people's space yachts. He had trouble thinking of himself as rich. In fact, he had trouble thinking of himself as the sort of man who owned a space yacht.

But the *Emmeline* was his only indulgence—and he spared no expense for her. He had named her for his daughter, and somehow his affection for them both crossed in his mind.

Terminal 25 was one of the largest terminals because the ships docked there were among the largest privately owned ships allowed in Armstrong's port.

The *Emmeline* had her own berth several docks down; she was state-of-the-art, with several upgrades—some standard and many not.

Because of his experiences on a case last year, he had had the *Emmeline* custom-fitted with every weapons system he could think of. He also had her defenses upgraded so that they were better than anything the Traffic cops used on the Moon. Every time a new system came on the market, he had it put into the *Emmeline*.

The *Emmeline* also had other features: She was the only place that he allowed himself to spend his fortune. Her captain's quarters were so luxurious that the first time he took her out, he slept in one of the guest cabins and worked his way up to that higher level of comfort. She had a fully equipped galley, several serving robots, and several more cleaning bots.

The ship also had her own brig (something he'd missed from the Traffic ships) and little hooks on the sides of the chairs that would allow him to easily handcuff prisoners. And the ship also had several redundant security features, each of them not linked to the other.

Someone would have to be very determined to break into the *Emmeline*, and unlike other ships he had dealt with, no one—not even the best security hacker—could break into her quickly.

Even though part of him was embarrassed by the extreme luxury, another part felt pride as he walked past the docked ships to his own. Outside, she was no glitzier than the other space yachts. In fact, she had fewer thrills.

Her hull was black and bird-shaped, with a nose that bent slightly downward. Her design was sleek, built for speed and not for impressing others.

He'd tested that speed in his early runs; she had been the fastest ship he'd ever flown—and that included some of the souped-up Traffic ships that he'd commandeered in his last years as a Traffic cop.

Even though he'd named her to honor his daughter,

he didn't have the name etched into the black frame. She was as anonymous as a space yacht could be.

The thing he loved the best about her, though, wasn't her size, her shape, or her luxury; it wasn't her weapons, her defenses, or her speed. It was the fact that she had been designed as a one-person ship, that no copilot was needed to run the helm, no assistant had to monitor the engines. She was meant to fly solo, and that made her perfect for him.

He walked up to her side and pressed a small depression near the oval-shaped main door, and a ladder eased out. The depression had responded to a preprogrammed command, triggered by his DNA and his warm fingertip, to let him climb into the ship.

If he tried the other door while the ship was docked—what most folks would call the main door—and opened it in the conventional way, all the ship's internal defenses would turn on. If he didn't shut those down as he stepped through the airlock, the ship's internal and external weapons systems would rise to alert status.

And if he still did nothing, he would have two minutes before the ship locked him inside, shut off the environmental controls, and did its best to isolate any intruder.

He climbed the ladder, entered through the maintenance hatch, and pulled himself into the engineering section of the ship. It smelled of too-fresh air and new chips in here, with a touch of plastic added in. He loved that scent. He hoped never to lose it.

He closed the maintenance hatch and used the auxiliary command center to request an immediate departure and to fire up the engines.

Even on the quickest days, an immediate departure took at least half an hour to verify. This was the part of the trip that made him the most nervous. If the police had decided to start looking for him already, they would keep a watch on the *Emmeline*. Any request she had for disembarking would reach their files.

He left the engineering section and walked past the storage compartments to the main part of the ship. The storage areas and engineering themselves had no real luxuries—just the same smooth black material that also encased the hull.

But once he walked through the door to the main part of the ship, the upgrades began. The air had a tinge of lemon to it, to keep him alert and to keep the sense of freshness. The floor was carpeted, and a sound system pumped in soothing music—which he had shut off at the moment.

When he was in flight, the walls disappeared, showing instead a star field—or the current space around the ship, whichever he preferred. In addition to the guest quarters, he had a formal dining area, a game room, and a luxurious main cabin where he and guests could enjoy any one of a million digitized movies, plays, and entertainments. He also had games and books and more music than he knew what to do with.

If he wanted to, he could leave Armstrong forever, live on the *Emmeline*, and land in space docks only for refueling and repairs.

He kept that as a backup plan, one that seemed more tempting on some days than on others.

This was one of those days.

He sealed the ship, turned on her external shielding—mostly to keep any intruders out—and sat at the pilot's chair. The approval had come in quicker than he expected: He was free to leave.

One other benefit of docking in Terminal 25 and paying her exorbitant fees was that he didn't have to log a flight plan. He was leaving Armstrong, and that was all the port had to know. They weren't required to check his destination or figure out how he was going to get there.

The ship rose effortlessly toward the roof of the terminal. It had opened, revealing his small section of the dome, which was also open. Above him, ships sped through Moon space—little blips on his navigational array.

He placed his hands on the controls, and shut off the automatic pilot.

He was flying the *Emmeline* now, and she would go where he commanded her.

37

DeRicci was just thinking about taking a short break for dinner when a team of techs invaded her office, led by Barbara Passolini.

"Move away from your desk, Noelle." Passolini's too-thin body looked formidable in the enclosed space. "Back up quickly and step away."

DeRicci resisted the urge to raise her hands, as if she were under arrest. "What's going on?"

"Tracers," Passolini said. But DeRicci couldn't tell if the word was directed at her, or at the team of even skinnier techs, most of whom she hadn't seen before.

All of them had eyes too big for their face and skin that was the lumpy consistency of bad cheese. They clearly ate poorly and didn't care much about their appearance. And none of them had muscles—the kind needed for beat officers or anyone who joined the force on the physical-enforcement side.

DeRicci continued to back up until she hit the windows. The see-through plastic was warm against her back. She glanced out—dome daylight was continuing, even though she would have thought it time for dome twilight already.

"What's going on?" she repeated.

"You got markers in your system," Passolini

snapped. She had already moved behind DeRicci's desk and was poking her finger against DeRicci's screen. Two of the other techs were underneath the desk, and a third had taken a small portable computer and attached it to some wires in her wall unit.

"Markers?" DeRicci asked.

"Someone is tracing your every movement on here, and it's not from inside." Passolini sounded irritated. "Now shut up and let us work."

"No." DeRicci surprised herself. She usually let the techs do what they needed. "Not until you talk to me. Are all these people crime scene?"

"Computers, mostly." Passolini was still poking the screen. DeRicci wondered if it would take the force.

"How did you find out about these so-called tracers?" DeRicci asked.

"Some of our backup alarms went off. We found the link, saw a few other markers, did a search. It's been a quest all afternoon, but the only other place we found anything was leading into your system."

"I don't let anyone else in my office," DeRicci said. The lock was coded to her handprint, and she had a combination above it for added protection.

"They didn't come through your office." Passolini sighed, stepped away from the desk, and gestured at one of the thin young men to take her place. She walked over to DeRicci.

DeRicci took a step forward. She didn't like standing with her back against the window. "What do you mean?"

"Someone knew your codes and broke into your system from the outside. The tracers are very sophisticated, and our only hope is to follow them from the inside back."

DeRicci frowned. Why would anyone put tracers in her computer?

"How many cases are you working on?" Passolini asked.

"Just the one we've been working on together. The rest of my work is review and evaluation," DeRicci said. "You don't think someone from inside the department—"

"The only people inside the department with these skills are with me right now," Passolini said, "and none of them is under investigation or review. I already checked."

DeRicci nodded. But she scanned the crew anyway, turning on her internal link and downloading their faces into the networked police files. She got all the names in an instant, playing across her eyes in the way that she hated, and recognized none of the techs.

"I told you," Passolini said, not trying to hide her irritation. "I already checked."

DeRicci shrugged but didn't justify her action. A double-check was always worthwhile. It did bother her, though, that Passolini knew she had checked the internal link database.

"Your partner know your code?" Passolini asked.

"I don't have a partner," DeRicci said.

"Really?" Passolini sounded skeptical. "Because there's this Detective Cabrera who's been hounding my office every hour wanting updates on the Lahiri case."

DeRicci felt her cheeks heat. She had forgotten about Cabrera. "We're only partnered on this case. And as you can probably tell, he's not happy to be working with me."

"So would he feed into your system maybe and get what he needed that way?" Passolini asked.

"Check him," she said, "but I doubt he has the skills. I've had only one partner with the kind of skills you're talking about and he . . ."

She stopped herself, but too late. Passolini's dark eyes sparked with interest.

"He?"

DeRicci sighed. "Miles Flint."

"He was good," someone said from under the desk. "You know he designed most of our fail-safe systems."

Passolini stared at DeRicci.

"That's twice, Noelle," Passolini said softly.

"Twice what?" DeRicci asked.

"That you're not following the rules of evidence."

"How do you mean?" DeRicci asked. "I had no idea there was a problem with my system until you showed up."

"Everything changes if this was an inside job," Passolini said.

"It can't be inside," DeRicci said. "Miles hasn't worked for the force in two years."

"But he designed the systems."

DeRicci nodded, feeling tired. "He didn't design them exactly. He improved them."

"You knew this?"

"Yes," she said.

"So when I asked you about your partners—"

"Don't try to implicate me in anything, Passolini," DeRicci snapped. "I outrank you and I could have your job."

"Provided you still hold the rank when you try to take the job," Passolini said. "You're not working with Flint, are you?"

"Hell, no," DeRicci said.

"You alerted him to your investigation." Passolini shook her head. "Noelle, you alerted him and he put tracers in your system. He's done something. He's guilty of something, and now you let him get one step ahead of you."

DeRicci felt her mouth go dry. She wanted to beg Passolini to keep this quiet, to make certain Gumiela didn't know about it, but DeRicci couldn't bring herself to say the words.

Besides, the other techs would hear her. They would know.

"We don't know he put the tracers in," she said.

"That's true, we don't," Passolini said. "And if we follow the DeRicci method of investigation, we don't make assumptions. We find facts. But if I find out that he put those in, Noelle, I swear to you this will be on your record. I know—"

"That you would never make such a mistake." De-Ricci had had enough. "You would never trust a friend. You would never ask someone to work with you if you thought they had specialized knowledge. Hell, you wouldn't even think twice about busting into a chief investigator's office and commandeering her entire office system, even though you don't have the authority to do so. You want to put stuff on the record? Go ahead. You'll have more charges of investigation tampering than you'll know what to do with."

Passolini had paled. Everyone else in the office had stopped working. They were all staring at DeRicci.

"How do I know that there is a tracer?" DeRicci continued. "I have no proof. I didn't call you people. I'm letting you do this out of the goodness of my heart. But if you find that this is an inside job—as you say—and you decide to blame it on Miles Flint, who is decidedly not inside, and then you decide to take me on, well, I will have to talk to my bosses about what 'inside' really means, and how could someone who hasn't been near this precinct in two years actually get through the so-called firewalls to the system? Who failed then, Barbara? Certainly not me."

Passolini crossed her arms. "Do you want us to stop working?"

"Of course not," DeRicci said. "I believe you when you tell me that my system is compromised. I just don't believe you when you tell me who did it without any proof whatsoever."

Passolini sighed.

"Finish." DeRicci waved a hand at the other techs. "I'm heading to a different office. I have to write a report on this incident, thank you very much, and I'll inform Gumiela that you came in here with the culprit already decided. I'll also inform her that you allowed this breach, and that you threatened my position here. You want to play games, Barbara? Well, good luck. Because I don't play them. I just tell the truth."

"You think you're invincible because you have that hero thing going, don't you?" Passolini asked.

"I think I'm a target because I do." DeRicci pushed past Passolini, stepped around the techs, and left her office. She pulled the door closed behind her and stood in the hallway for just a moment.

She was a target, and Passolini did hate her. But that didn't stop Passolini's accusations from having a grain of truth. If Flint felt threatened, he just might put some kind of tracer into a computer. He'd done it before, on a case that she had worked on with him.

That was the case that had somehow made him wealthy.

DeRicci was shaking. She was angry and unsettled, and she felt wildly out of control of this investigation.

But she needed to take control. Her actions in her office had been correct. She didn't dare let Passolini know that the woman had upset her.

DeRicci went to a nearby desk and sat down. Then she wrote the report, just like she said she was going to, making certain that all her bases were covered.

She had a feeling that the interdepartmental struggles in this case were about to get a lot worse.

38

The trip from Moon to Earth was an extremely short one, especially at the speeds Flint traveled. To avoid calling attention to himself, he programmed the ship's autopilot to slow several thousand miles outside of Earth's orbit.

He also made a few other critical decisions. He wasn't going to dock his ship on the space station. Instead he would take it into the atmosphere, and pay for a berth at one of the ports. He wanted his own ship as close as possible. He didn't want his ability to leave the planet contingent on someone else's travel schedule.

Unlike some space yachts, the *Emmeline* was designed to handle trips through atmosphere. That was one of the many features Flint had insisted on when he had ordered the ship.

While the ship flew herself, he remained in the cockpit, monitoring the autopilot and doing more research. He couldn't find more on the assassin—there was no trail on Earth at the moment, although he suspected he'd find it when he landed.

But Flint also wanted more information on Carolyn Lahiri. With a tie to Etae, with the pardons coming when they had and the assassin finding her just after

Flint had, then it was clear that she had done something—or she had been part of something—that someone didn't want out.

He had a lot of information about her stored in the ship's systems. He had done some of his primary research here, in a much slower trip from the Moon to Earth a few weeks before. Then he had been concentrating on finding her, and using her past as a blueprint for her present.

Now he saw her past as a blueprint for her murder.

He went all the way back to her school records, trying to find how she had gotten interested in Etae in the first place. When he had initially done the research, he had scanned this part. The information was dense and not all that interesting. Mostly, he found school papers, sent through links, about various political subjects. Most of them involved the dangers of colonization and the problems caused by intergalactic corporations.

The writing was mediocre, the arguments childish—everything had a black-and-white component: Corporations bad, independence good. There were also a lot of studies that seemed directly aimed at her father, as if his work with the Multicultural Tribunals was responsible for the mess some of the outlying areas found themselves in.

Over time, her work had focused not so much on the outlying areas, but on Etae. At that point, Etae had just received intergalactic notice. The slaughter of its native peoples, the Ynnels, by the Idonae had become justification for the original human colonists' ruthlessness.

These people had come in, killed any Idonae that got in their way, and established a human government—one that allowed no input from the Idonae at all. Nor did the human government try to rehabilitate the few remaining Ynnel tribes. Instead, the humans sent the Ynnel off-world, to "protect" them from the Idonae.

Carolyn, of course, hated all of this, and used it to prove that the human government was worse than the

Idonae had been. It didn't hurt that her father had been on the Tribunal that had ruled that, since Etae was not a member of the Alliance, its internal politics were not subject to Alliance jurisdiction. The killing could—and did—continue, and apparently Carolyn laid much of that at her father's feet.

Flint looked over at the screens. They showed only the blackness of space. He seemed to be the only one out here, even though he knew he wasn't.

Flint leaned back in his chair. All of this begged the question, the one that Carolyn had never really answered to his satisfaction: Why had she come home? Not that it would have mattered for her. Hank Mosby or whatever his name really was would have found her on Earth and killed her.

But he would have left her parents alone.

Had she known she was being followed? Was this one final act of revenge against her parents?

He turned his attention back to the research. She had moved to a college not far from home, and there she had gotten involved in some political organizations bent on stopping colonization by large corporations. Initially, Carolyn had signed on to spend a year protesting in the Outlying Colonies, her expenses paid.

And somehow that year had become not about protest, but about Etae.

Flint dug deeper into the material. He found nothing on Carolyn, but a bit on the organization that had brought the protestors out to the edges of the known universe. Apparently the organization recruited from colleges all over the solar system, finding willing young people to block certain projects proposed by intergalactic corporations.

It didn't take a lot of digging for Flint to find that the organization was a dummy corporation for one of the rival intergalactics, trying to block the competition.

He wondered if Carolyn had found that out. If she had, he knew she would have reacted badly. But he saw nothing of that in the official reports.

Only a letter from the organization to the Lahiris,

stating that Carolyn was no longer under the organization's auspices, that she and four others were heading out on their own to fight for justice in Etae.

Flint had seen the letter before, but he had never searched for the names of the others. Now he did, looking for copies of the same letter sent on the same date.

It didn't take long to find them, along with the dossiers of the others. Two of them looked younger, but familiar—the Disappeareds who had been assassinated in the weeks before Carolyn's death. The other two didn't look familiar at all.

Flint traced them and found that one of them had died shortly after arriving on Etae—slaughtered by Idonae as he was trying to minister to a tribe of them. The other, a young man, had no records after six months in Etae.

Flint looked at several photographs of him, and did not recognize him. Still, Flint had his system run some comparison checks—and some aging programs, just to see if the young man had turned up elsewhere.

Flint even searched by the young man's name, Ali Norbert, hoping to find something, but there were no records—not of his life after he arrived on Etae and not of his death.

That was the most curious detail: Three young women and two young men traveled from one of the Outlying Colonies to Etae to "freedom fight." One died. The three women Disappeared, and then ended up murdered.

The remaining young man completely vanished. He more than Disappeared. He became no one.

Flint flashed on the ruins of Carolyn's face. She had become no one too, in the end.

Flint had his system cross-compare Ali Norbert's images with Hank Mosby's, not expecting much. Even if they were the same person, the enhancements would alter the recognition patterns, and Flint didn't have enough information on Norbert to compensate.

The system would, in the end, only guess.

The key, then, was what these five had done on Etae. Flint wasn't certain he'd be able to trace what had happened, not from such a long distance and not with the limited records available over the nets.

But he was going to try.

He was going to see if he could discover why Carolyn Lahiri had Disappeared.

39

Of course, the tracers led to Flint. The way DeRicci's day was going, they couldn't have done anything else.

At least one of the techs had told her, not Passolini. DeRicci couldn't have dealt with Passolini's superior attitude, her condescending way of looking at DeRicci, as if DeRicci didn't deserve the promotion she had received.

At the moment, DeRicci didn't feel like she deserved that promotion either. She felt like a rookie, bamboozled by someone with a few more tricks up his sleeve.

Beneath the anger, she felt a sense of loss so deep that it was almost crippling. She was closer to Flint than she had realized—or perhaps it was simply that she had so few friends that the loss of one made it seem like the world had ended.

To make matters worse, Flint was not in his office. Because she could no longer trust him, she checked the outgoing records at the Port to see if he had fled Armstrong.

The fact that the *Emmeline* was gone made her feel even more betrayed. He had left a few hours before, about the time that DeRicci had been studying the hallway security vid, the one that showed a man who shared too many physical features in common with Flint.

DeRicci had left the office, claiming she was going to get dinner. Instead, she found herself in one of Armstrong's newest neighborhoods. The people who lived here were so far above DeRicci in pay scale that she felt like she was soiling their sidewalk just by standing on it. Even the Lahiris probably would have felt out of place here, in the latest trendy neighborhood for Armstrong's super-rich.

Still, DeRicci couldn't force herself to turn away. If she couldn't talk to Flint, she would talk to someone else who knew him, someone else who might be able to give DeRicci an insight into whatever it was that made him lose his grip, possibly kill two of his clients and their daughter, and flee Armstrong.

The very thought made her eyes burn.

She squared her shoulders and headed for the main entrance to the center high-rise. She used to think she hated these places. But she had found, as her salary had grown, that what she had considered hate was merely another form of envy. Now she looked at them with half an eye toward living there someday—maybe when the police department didn't steal her speaker's fees, and she felt jaded enough to sell the media rights to the marathon story for more money than she could even imagine.

To get to the main doors, she had to walk up several flights of clear glass stairs. She had to state her business, and then she found herself in the lobby.

It was an eerie place, with a black floor, expensive furniture, and too many plants. The far wall was floor-to-ceiling windows, with a clear view of the lunar landscape.

She used the automatic doorman feature next to the elevator to find out what floor Flint's old mentor, Paloma, lived on. As DeRicci scanned the list, she realized she had never learned Paloma's last name.

Fortunately, she didn't need it. Paloma had registered only under the one name, which made things much easier for DeRicci.

The automatic doorman also told her that Paloma was in, which felt like the first break DeRicci had had all day.

She got into the elevator and spoke the number for Paloma's floor. The doors closed, but the elevator didn't move. Instead, an androgynous voice said, "State your name and business."

"DeRicci," she said. "I'm here about a homicide investigation."

The voice didn't answer her. Instead, the elevator started its ascent. The elevator walls were also made of glass and gave her a floating view of the regolith and the dark rocks beyond. It was a lunar day, which she hadn't realized, and the shadows the rocks gave stretched for kilometers.

She had never floated above the lunar landscape before, at least not like this, and it was a novelty. She almost didn't notice as the doors pinged open behind her.

"Officer DeRicci?"

DeRicci turned, her heart pounding. She had left her back vulnerable, something she hadn't done in years. Behind her, an elderly woman stood. She hadn't had obvious enhancements—her skin was thin, revealing the blood vessels beneath the gently wrinkled surface. Her hair was white and floated around her face like a cloud.

Only her eyes seemed young; they were bright and intelligent and filled with a hardness that made DeRicci nervous.

"I'm an assistant chief of detectives now," DeRicci said.

She hadn't seen Paloma in nearly a year. They'd spent very little time together in the past—mostly because of Flint. He had introduced them, and had seemed to hope that they would get along.

The fact that Flint had tried to facilitate the friendship hadn't helped. If anything, it made things seem even more awkward, and whatever relationship De-Ricci and Paloma might have had fizzled even before it was born.

"Such a grand title," Paloma said. She stood in a doorway, her hands resting on its frame as if she were blocking DeRicci's way. "And now you've come to investigate me?"

DeRicci hadn't expected the paranoia. "Actually, I came to ask you a few questions about a case I got today. If you don't mind."

"Questions only? Am I or will I be under suspicion?"

DeRicci hadn't realized before that Paloma's attitude came from her distrust of authorities. Had she instilled that in Flint? He had already been leaning that way when he had left the force.

"The case has nothing to do with you," DeRicci said. "I'm merely looking for your expertise."

Of course, she had thought that the case had had nothing to do with Flint either, and she had been wrong. But she didn't say that.

"Expertise in what area?" Paloma hadn't moved. Those eyes seemed even sharper than they had a moment before.

"As a Retrieval Artist."

Paloma shrugged. "I cannot help you. I can't talk about my former work. I keep confidentiality."

DeRicci was handling this badly. She shook her head. "I'm not here about past cases or anything like that. I want to ask a few questions about how it works being a Retrieval Artist."

"You should ask Miles," Paloma said.

"I can't." DeRicci was still standing in the elevator and it made her feel awkward, like a supplicant who wasn't being heard. "He's fled the Moon."

"Fled?" Paloma raised her wispy eyebrows. "Miles Flint? I didn't think he knew that word."

"Maybe he doesn't know the word, but he sure acts on it." DeRicci's tone surprised even her. She sounded bitter.

"So this is about Miles," Paloma said.

"I guess." DeRicci shrugged. "More about theory than anything, really."

"Theory," Paloma repeated.

DeRicci nodded. "You know, theory. Maybe you could explain why a Retrieval Artist might do a certain thing."

"As opposed to why Miles might do it."

"Yeah," DeRicci said.

Paloma let her arms drop. "I must admit, I am intrigued, but I doubt I can help you. Miles and I are very different people. And just because you're angry at him doesn't mean yelling at me will make you feel better."

"I'm not . . ." But DeRicci stopped the sentence long before she got to the end. She was angry at Flint. Was that why she came to Paloma? So that she could yell at someone?

Paloma stepped away from the door. "Come on in."

DeRicci walked out of the elevator, past Paloma. The entry turned slightly and then opened to a large living room. The moonscape covered the entire far wall, but here it looked like a skillful painting rather than a view from the window.

"Miles thinks it indulgent," Paloma said, coming up behind DeRicci.

"What?" DeRicci asked.

"This apartment. He doesn't believe in spending money on luxuries."

"I get the sense he doesn't believe in spending money," DeRicci said.

Paloma smiled. It made the wrinkles on her face deeper, but gave her a pixyish look. "See? You do know him."

"I never said I didn't." DeRicci stood in the center of the room, not willing to sit down until Paloma invited her to.

Paloma leaned on the back of a brown couch, which blended into the brown rug. The drab furniture made the view seem even more powerful.

"Miles has been indicted for something?" Paloma asked.

"No," DeRicci said.

"But you said he has fled the Moon."

"It doesn't look good," DeRicci said.

Paloma nodded. "He and I are very different, you know. We run a different kind of business."

"Run? I thought you were out of it."

"I've retired," Paloma said. "I doubt you're ever out of it."

DeRicci waited for her to expand upon that comment, but Paloma didn't.

"What has he done?" Paloma asked.

"I can only give you the broad facts," DeRicci said. "But here's what I know: Some people hired him to find their adult child. He did, and shortly thereafter all of them were murdered here on Armstrong. The weapon is his, and I have a security vid with someone who looks like him at the time of the murder."

"Hmm." Paloma nodded, as if she had heard this before.

"I talked to him when the investigation started and his name came up, asking him to share information from his research. He wouldn't. And apparently at that point, he put some tracers in the police department's computer system, focusing mostly on my files. In fact, the techs tell me that his system got alerted every time I logged on."

"Miles always did have impressive computer skills," Paloma said.

DeRicci let that pass. "When I found that security vid today, he was ghosting me. He saw it too. An hour later, he had taken the *Emmeline* and left the Moon. He didn't even file a flight plan."

"He wouldn't have to," Paloma said.

"Because of all that money he pays to the Port," DeRicci said, and heard the bitterness again. "It doesn't seem like Flint to spend the money on something like that."

"He spends his money on necessities, Detective,"

Paloma said. "That ship of his may look luxurious, but she's a necessity too."

"For escape," DeRicci muttered.

"No," Paloma said. "For investigation and defense. He's going to be a lot more aggressive than I was, especially in going after people he believes have done something wrong."

DeRicci sat, and nearly lost her balance. The chair was softer than she expected. She caught herself with the armrests. "You think he killed those people? He knows better than to commit murder in Armstrong. We have laws here, whether or not his profession encourages him to obey them."

Paloma didn't seem to notice the dig. "You're looking at this wrong."

"Really?" DeRicci asked. "The evidence points to his involvement in their deaths."

"The evidence," Paloma said, leaning back, "points to his caution—unless there is more that you aren't telling me."

"I'm not telling you identities, and that's about it." For which she could get into a lot of trouble. Coming to Paloma was a risk, just like going to Flint had been.

"Miles would never leave a weapon at a crime scene," Paloma said. "Neither would you."

"In the heat of the moment, anyone might miss something."

"But you're looking for other explanations, otherwise you wouldn't be here. You want to know why he killed three people and betrayed you by not telling you."

When it was put that coldly, DeRicci wanted to disagree. But that was why she had come to Paloma. In DeRicci's mind, Paloma was the next best thing to Flint.

"Let's take the corpses out of this. Let's talk about Miles," Paloma said. "He's not your partner anymore."

"No, he's not," DeRicci said. "But we have worked together."

"Have you?" Paloma asked.

"On the Moon Marathon," DeRicci said.

"It seems to me that you were each working your own cases there, from what little he's told me," Paloma said. "He's finally learning that Retrieval Artists work alone."

"Whatever that means," DeRicci said.

"It means he couldn't confide in you. It means he couldn't reveal confidential information. And it means he knew you would investigate him, and he wanted to see what you had before you surprised him with it."

"Putting tracers in my office is illegal," DeRicci said.

"It's illegal for private citizens to do that anywhere, but I'll wager you find some of Flint's tracers in the dead people's security system. It's one way Retrieval Artists get information." Paloma folded her hands together. "Everyone lies, you know. That's why we investigate our clients. Everybody lies, so make sure you learn the truth before taking the case."

"Flint couldn't be thinking that I lied," DeRicci said, and she tried to remember what she had told him. Had she lied? How much had she left out? The conversation was a blur, culminating with his refusal to work with her, and the sad look on his face as she left his office.

"But he knew you," Paloma said. "He had refused to help you, and he knew you would have to investigate him."

"So?" DeRicci said. "Why would he care if he had nothing to hide?"

"Why indeed?" Paloma asked. "Maybe he cared that his clients were dead."

DeRicci started. Of course he would care about that. Of course he would care and want to investigate. That was Miles Flint, the man she had known. How come she hadn't seen that either?

"So why not help me?"

"Confidentiality." Paloma leaned back in her chair.

"Or maybe he knew his involvement was too great, that he'd compromise your investigation."

"I thought Retrieval Artists aren't altruistic," DeRicci said.

"Retrieval Artists aren't," Paloma said. "Miles is."

DeRicci stared at her.

Paloma smiled slowly. This smile didn't make her seem puckish. It simply made her seem sad.

"He *helps* people," Paloma said, "whether they want it or not. He's the only Retrieval Artist I know who started his career by helping a large group of people remain Disappeared."

"I'm not supposed to know about that," DeRicci said, holding up her hands. Helping Disappeareds wasn't illegal unless you knew their crimes, which was how Disappearance Services skirted the letter of the law. But Flint had been the law when he helped those Disappeareds—or just newly retired. DeRicci had tried to ignore that for two years.

"You're not supposed to know a lot of things," Paloma said, "which is why Miles didn't work with you. But you should know that he's not the kind of man to murder three people in cold blood."

"The evidence says otherwise," DeRicci said.

"The evidence says that someone used Miles's gun."

"He might have been there."

"Which is not a crime," Paloma said, "unless he was there when the murders took place."

"He followed my investigation," DeRicci said.

"And left when he got a piece of information," Paloma said.

DeRicci nodded.

"What you see as guilt, I see as research. He's looking for the killer too, even though that's not his job."

"He told you this?" DeRicci asked, feeling a bit of hope.

"Of course not," Paloma said. "He can't confide in anyone anymore. That was your main mistake, you know. Believing you could have worked with him on this case."

DeRicci swallowed. She had been thinking the same thing, but it felt different hearing the words from someone else.

"You shouldn't have gone to him. You can't go to him in the future. He can't work with you. Retrieval Artists work alone. Sometimes they die alone. That's what the job is. Do you understand, Detective?"

"Are you saying he might get himself killed on this investigation?" DeRicci asked.

Paloma studied her for a long moment, and then sighed. "I'm saying that whatever you've felt for him in the past, you must set aside now. He can't be a true friend to you, nor you to him. Too many conflicts. Just like he would have conflicts with me or anyone else. He's chosen to be alone, Detective. Completely alone, and nothing you do can change that."

"I don't want to change that," DeRicci said, but she knew she was lying. She did want to change it. Flint was the best partner she'd had, and the one person she had actually liked in all her years of working on the force.

When he set out on his own, he still seemed like the same man. Then they had worked together one more time.

One last time.

"I might have to arrest him if the evidence still points in his direction," DeRicci said.

Paloma shrugged. "Do what you have to. He'll vindicate himself if he can."

"And if he can't?" DeRicci asked.

"It's part of the job, Detective," Paloma said. "He's ready for it. Are you?"

40

Even the ports were brighter.

Flint had noticed that the first time he had come to Earth, and it struck him even more this time. Of course, this time he'd brought his ship through the atmosphere and to one of the oldest landing sites on the planet—a place called Cape Canaveral in Florida.

The Cape held a group of interlocking buildings, all of which served as a port. It seemed odd to Flint to enter a dock without going through a dome. It was strangely freeing.

It was also difficult to land in bright sunlight. Usually he landed in darkness, going from the blackness around the Moon to the artificial light inside the dome.

This time, he went from a clear blue sky into what the locals called a hangar bay. His ship leveled straight downward—he'd kept it on autopilot, since his experience with atmosphere and real-gravity landings was only on flight simulators.

The terminal was larger, cleaner, and more private. He had wired credits ahead, asking for the best accommodations in the closest landing site to Louisiana—the coordinates he had gotten gave him Cape Canaveral, a recommendation for air rentals and airtaxis, and a list of dozens of hotels along the way.

Flint set his coordinates to land in Cape Canaveral, rented an aircar, and booked a room for that night in the Cape and the following night at a hotel in New Orleans.

While the ship went through its decon cycle, and while the computers bickered about paperwork, he hacked into Earth's portside system, looking for information on Hank Mosby.

He found that Mosby had entered via transport two days before, but found no other record of the man. No aircar rentals, no hired taxis, no bullet-train tickets.

Hank Mosby had vanished. Or, more likely, once he left the port, he assumed another identity and became one of ten billion humans overpopulating the planet Earth.

Flint had hours of decon to go through himself, along with security scans and identification verification. The last time it had taken him nearly a day to get through Earth's complicated entry procedures. Of course, the last time, he had brought a small laser pistol, and learned just how stringent Earth's no-weapons rule was. Not even a Moon-issue permit, stating that he had once been law enforcement and therefore entitled to carry the weapon, worked.

The pace of his investigation would slow here. Nothing moved as quickly on the home planet as it did on the Moon. He would start where he had found her, in New Orleans, talk to her friends, see if he could find the family she had abandoned for that odd little jazz career. Maybe, too, he might hear of a man who had lurked nearby and asked too many questions—a man other than himself.

Maybe that might lead him to Mosby.

He hoped it would. Because Flint couldn't think of any other way to track the assassin down.

41

Everyone looked at her strangely as she walked through the front door of her restaurant, and it took her a moment to understand why. Nitara Nicolae touched the drying blood on her cheeks, frowned ostentatiously, and said to anyone who would listen:

"I got caught in the riot."

People nodded, made sympathetic noises, and returned to their meals. She staggered a little as she headed toward the back; just a touch of drama to divert their attention from her strangeness.

She didn't feel like herself—at least, not her Armstrong self. She felt something like a girl she used to be, long ago and far away, when the place she lived had a real night sky and air that wasn't manufactured by some machine.

A home she no longer claimed. Where she had lived with a family she no longer had.

The restaurant smelled of thyme and ginger and roasted garlic. Her stomach growled, but she ignored it. She would have time for food later.

The clank and clatter of silver against the dishes she had so carefully chosen sounded like atonal music, something she could not abide. Once she had found this place comforting.

Once it had substituted for home.

Amazing how much pain a person could put away, and think they were done with, only to have it rise up bit by little bit as the memories returned.

As the need for revenge rose with it.

Maybe she had been planning this all along. Maybe her rational mind had sent her to Armstrong, so deep in the Old Universe that she had thought her buried memories might not get resurrected.

Yet her subconscious mind had worked on vengeance anyway, hoping—maybe even praying—it would get the chance.

She could stop now. She knew that. But she didn't want to.

That amazed her the most.

She pushed open the double doors that led into the kitchen she had designed. Her employees worked the ranges. The sous chef was just finishing with his preparations for the following day, and the pastry chef had already left.

The two main chefs were cooking dinners for the various patrons outside. Both men smiled at her as she entered the kitchen, their smiles fading when they saw the blood on her face.

She waved a hand toward it. "Riot," she said, and one of them came to her, slid an arm around her back, and asked her if she was all right.

She was sure she was fine, she said to him. Positive. No need to worry.

"We have to get you cleaned up," he said to her, and she nodded. Let them think what they needed to. Let them do what they had to.

They would leave soon, and so would the patrons, not knowing they had enjoyed the last night in her famous restaurant. Such a small dream, one she had put such importance on.

And who cared, really, if a restaurant succeeded or failed? People found food somewhere else. A good meal was a pleasure that couldn't be repeated, but another good meal could take its place, and then another and another, until the first good meal was forgotten.

The smells shifted: less ginger and thyme, more garlic, a few onions, and a beef broth that seemed a little heavy on the salt. But she said nothing.

Nor did she speak when someone—one of the waiters?—wiped the blood off her cheeks, speaking to her gently, as if she were a child.

Amazing that everything she needed to be the best chef in Armstrong, she would also need to exact her revenge. All those permits she had signed, all that bonding she had gone through. Decades of crime-free living so that she could own materials in her restaurant that the government considered dangerous inside a dome.

Flammable things. Destructive things.

Explosive things.

She sat at the table and waited for her best crew to finish their last shift.

Then she would begin hers.

42

The next morning dawned clear and hot. The variations in the weather here amazed Flint the most. The night before, when they had finally let him out of the hangar, he'd noticed a damp chill. As he had walked from the hangar to the public areas of the port, the air felt like it swirled around him, almost as if it were water, a sensation he remembered from his last trip, but hadn't completely believed.

A lot about this place was unbelievable—the vegetation, green and lush and so much bigger than it seemed in the vids he'd seen of it; the smells of mildew and damp and what his ex-wife used to call freshness; the way the air actually had a texture, as if it were made of a slightly different substance than air on the Moon.

He also had trouble believing in the ocean. The blue water matched the color of the sky, and seemed to go on forever. Until he came to Earth, he had never seen a limitless blue horizon. It caught his attention each time he looked at the water.

Flint had the option of driving on land roads, something he had done for only short distances in Armstrong, or driving an aircar. He took the aircar, only because the roads looked mean and uneven, as if the material used to cover them could barely handle the differences in the weather.

The car picked the route after Flint programmed in his destination. The map informed him he would fly over the center of Florida, southern Mississippi, and into Louisiana. Flint planned to double-check his research as he flew, but often he found himself looking out the windows, absorbing the sights.

Sometimes the reflections on the water were so bright that his eyes hurt. At least this time, he had known to buy sunglasses; his Moon-based eyes weren't used to the variety and intensity of the actual light through the thick atmosphere.

He also wasn't used to the heat. Even with the environmental controls on in the aircar, he felt the humidity. The scanner at the port, a woman who double-checked every record as the person who owned it passed her desk, remarked that Flint might have been better off if he had come during the winter.

"People from the Moon seem to hate our summers," she said, as if she took it personally.

People from the Moon didn't suffer through seasons. Only changes in daylight, and a few variations in temperatures programmed into the domes for the sake of variety.

New Orleans, at least, was familiar to him, only because he had spent a few days here while searching for Carolyn. The city sprawled in a bowl surrounded by water. The city was lower than the water, which Flint hadn't found odd until someone explained the concept of flooding to him—something he'd only read about and never seen.

He had no idea if the city had charm—people said it did, but he would have found it charming by its age alone. He'd never been anywhere so old, where most of the buildings had been standing for so many centuries that he couldn't imagine the time in which they were built.

The city had its own smell, too—a mixture of mildew and alcohol—a smell that somehow seemed lighter than it should, until he realized there was no dome to hold it in, and no inefficient air filter to try to screen the scents out.

He landed the aircar on a specially designed pad in the mouth of the French Quarter. This section of the city had been famous for centuries before Neil Armstrong landed on the Moon. The first time Flint had been here, he had had to force himself to stop staring at the tiny plaques attached to each building stating when they were built, and follow the street signs to Carolyn's bar.

Now he walked the streets with a little less curiosity, although he kept his eyes open.

The Quarter had its own smells—horse dung (they still had horse-drawn carriages here, for the tourists) combined with the fresh, doughy smell of beignets and a whiff of beer that seemed to come out of each and every open door.

The Quarter had homes tucked behind wrought-iron railings, but mostly it was a place of curiously small shops, restaurants, and dark, aromatic bars that promised sin as old as the city itself.

Carolyn's bar was like that. Up front, a mahogany bar had been built across one wall, with bottles of liquor stacked behind it, just like he'd seen in the old 2-D vids. The bar was polished and had a brass railing along the edge and another at the feet, so that it looked older than it was.

Carolyn had given the bar to its manager, a hard-edged woman named Delilah. Delilah was thin and tattooed on every available patch of skin; her dark hair was braided tightly and fell flat against her beautifully shaped skull.

It was late morning by the time Flint reached the bar, and Delilah was already inside, washing glasses by hand. He could see her through the dirty window. She wore a blue tank top, shorts, and sandals—not work attire by any measure he knew, but probably more comfortable than the clothes bartenders wore in Armstrong.

Here, everyone seemed to have environmental controls cranked to frigid, but kept the doors open, letting in the god-awful heat.

As he walked in, blinking to let his eyes adjust, Delilah said, "I never expected to see you again."

He didn't know how to respond to that. Being flip and witty wasn't the right approach, but he also didn't want to tell her about Carolyn.

"Unfinished business," he said, and slipped onto one of the bar stools.

She set a glass on the pile behind her, then splayed her hands flat on the polished wood. "Get you something?"

"Iced tea." He'd developed a taste for it the last time he was here. On Earth, it was made with real tea leaves, as, theoretically, it was in Armstrong, but here the teas had a more robust flavor. Or perhaps it was the coolness slipping down his throat after a few minutes in that staggering heat.

She poured from a large pitcher that she kept behind the bar. He'd watched Carolyn the first day he was here; they always kept making tea fresh, rather than pouring it out of machines the way that Moon restaurants did.

The ice jingled in the glass as Delilah set it on a napkin in front of him. The napkin still had a musical-note logo and the word *Claire's* across the top. Carolyn had used the name Claire Taylor when she lived here.

"She with you?" Delilah asked.

Flint shook his head.

"She coming back?" It made a difference to Delilah: Carolyn had left a clause in the contract that allowed her to take back the bar within the first six weeks, so long as she repaid the monies that Delilah had paid her.

"No," Flint said. "She's not coming back."

He had to work to make that sound less ominous than it truly was.

Delilah grunted, grabbed another glass, and stuck it

into the water in the small sink. She rinsed the glass, wiped it dry, and set it on a rubber mat, just like bartenders had been doing in this place for centuries.

Flint couldn't touch his iced tea. "There's a couple things I need to find out though."

"I thought you was done with your finding out."

He suppressed a sigh. He hadn't thought this part through—explaining to people who had known Carolyn what he was doing back and why he needed the information.

"I did too, when I left," he said. "But I was wrong."

She nodded, rinsed another glass, and set it on the mat. "Her son's been here, you know. Mad as a split pig that he didn't get the bar."

"Her son?" Flint hadn't expected that. For some reason, he had thought Carolyn's son was still a child.

"Had some lawyer look at the contract. Good thing it's tight. He didn't go to her, now, did he?"

Flint frowned, wondering what exactly Carolyn had told Delilah about her departure. Obviously not the truth.

"No," Flint said. "He hasn't seen her."

"Okay, good. Because my lawyer said the only one who can break up the contract is her."

"You're safe," Flint said. "I thought her son lived with his father."

"Years ago, yeah. But kids, they grow like everyone else. He's been on his own for a long time now. He still thinks she owes him though. Money. That's what he's about."

Flint took all that in, but didn't push. He finally picked up the tea, took a sip, and closed his eyes, savoring the sharp flavor. Everything seemed more vivid here, the sounds, the smells, the tastes. Almost overwhelming.

And yet, he felt like he could get used to it.

"About the time I was looking for Claire," Flint said, "did some other man come in here looking for her?"

"Not the same time," Delilah said. "Just after,

though. Ugly cuss. Something wrong with his face. Not just off—enhanced bad or something. Was real glad when he was gone.''

Flint slid her a flat picture of Hank Mosby. "Him?"

"Sure thing. What's with him anyway? Barely could have a civil conversation. Damn near got into a fight with one of my customers.''

"He's dangerous," Flint said. "If you see him again, you send for the police through your emergency links.''

"Even if he didn't do nothing?"

"Even if," Flint said. "You're right about enhancements. Only his are illegal.''

"Real brass knuckles, huh?"

"What?"

She smiled, shook off the glasses that had been drying beside the sink, and set them behind her. "Gangs here got into trouble a few years back. Had their knuckles enhanced so that they was hard as brass. You know, like that weapon old-timers used to use?''

He wasn't familiar with the weapon but he pretended he was. "A little more dangerous than that, but the same principle.''

"Great." She dried off her hands. "I'll do that. Anything to keep him out of the bar again. What's his tie to Claire?"

"I'm not sure it is to Claire," Flint said. "He's looking for someone, and I'm pretty sure he thought Claire knew who that person was.''

"Too late now, though, huh?" Delilah said.

"Maybe," Flint said. "I think if I can figure out who that person is, then maybe I'll find him.''

She looked at the flat picture one last time, then slid it back to him. "Don't know anyone outside the norm who's a friend of Claire's. She stayed pretty straight and narrow, which is strange, considering this town and her business. Usually you gotta have your hands in someone's pockets, you know?''

Carolyn had told him a bit about New Orleans's fabled corruption. She had laughed about it, saying it was as normal here as the mildew and the humidity, and just about as old.

"No one asking questions since she's been gone?" Flint asked.

"No one 'cept Ugly Puss there, and her kid," Delilah said. "And Ugly Puss left right fast, and the kid . . . well, my lawyer's got his number."

Maybe the family would know something. "May I have it too?"

"You wanna find the kid?" Delilah asked. "Won't do you no good. They've been estranged since she run out on her husband. Her kid won't know nothing."

"Except whatever it was that made her leave," Flint said.

"You thinking maybe it's tied into Ugly Puss?" Delilah asked.

Flint shrugged. "You never know until you ask."

"Don't tell him I sent you," Delilah said. "I want him to forget about me."

"Don't worry," Flint said. "I'll keep your name out of it."

Delilah rewarded him with a wide smile, and then she gave him instructions on how to find Carolyn Lahiri's adult son.

43

They put her in a hotel called the Lunar Lander and posted a guard outside her door "for her protection." Anatolya Döbryn didn't feel protected. She felt imprisoned, which was what she had been from the moment she had arrived at this awful city.

She sat on the edge of the king-size bed, which was too soft for her tastes. Of course, the bed wasn't why she hadn't slept all night. She hadn't slept because she kept trying her links, hoping to contact her team, and getting no response—not static, not bounced messages—just nothing at all.

That had never happened before, and it frightened her. It frightened her even more to discover that on the paneled wall, the public links were wide open, just like they would be if she weren't a prisoner.

She had become so desperate, she tried her team on the public links, hoping that someone would respond. No one did.

She knew that the Armstrong authorities were monitoring her, and she didn't care. Her people might be dead out there or in hiding or injured. The media wasn't making any reports about Etaens, and the liaisons from the Executive Committee claimed they didn't know what had happened to her team.

All the Alliance's almighty Executive Committee
would tell her was that they had decided that she
would meet with them later, give them the speech
she'd been planning all along, as if nothing had
changed.

Of course, everything had changed. She wasn't stupid enough to fall for their games. She just didn't
know what games they were playing any longer. The
Old Universe had its tricks, and they were wily, even
compared to hers.

Part of her didn't want to speak to them, and part
of her knew her people, all of them back on Etae,
needed this chance.

Even though it wasn't really a chance anymore.

The news already had spread the word of her presence through a million links. They called her the Terror of Etae, the Butcher of Etae, the Crown Princess
of Murder. They called her the Pretend Sovereign of
a Dying World, a woman who had come to share
power with a group of rebels who proved themselves
more corrupt than the government they had replaced.

The subtext was there, subtle and yet so important:
It was okay for humans to kill aliens—particularly
aliens like the Idonae—but it wasn't okay to kill other
humans, particularly not for power.

Not even to save millions of lives.

Anatolya rocked back on the bed and covered her
eyes with her arm. She had come here as a supplicant,
yes. She had known she would be without power—a
new position for her—but she had the strength of the
new government behind her.

"New" only in terms of the Old Universe, of course.
A decade of changes, improvements, of doing everything possible to see that a people survived against a
devastated landscape—ruined by the Idonae and years
of war.

The known universe had supported her rebellion,
particularly after the Child Martyr incident, and she
had gained sympathy. Gianni had urged coming to the
Alliance then, but it would have been premature—

before the government really got set up, before they had a chance to prove themselves.

Then she had made no real slipups, even pardoned the war criminals and the Disappeareds, and finally, she had approached various races, asking them if the time was right. Even the humans—Pilar Restrepo in particular—assured her it was.

And Anatolya had come. She had come with her team, and made a few mistakes, but certainly hadn't planned to be branded a terrorist. Nor had she planned on that riot outside—the attack on them. Someone had known the Idonae would set off any human who had grown up on Etae, particularly a human who, like Gianni—like Anatolya—had been a victim of Idonae cruelty.

Gianni. He had to be somewhere. He wasn't the kind of man who just vanished.

Unless they killed him. How ironic would that be? They killed him here—in the civilized part of the universe—when no one had been able to kill him in the Outlying Colonies. Where people had seen the folly of continuing to try.

She blinked hard. Her eyes ached, but they were dry. Sixty people wounded and a dozen killed; names, of course, not to be released until next of kin were notified—if they ever got notified. No nationalities, no identifiers at all.

She had a hunch—more than a hunch, really; damn near a certainty—that her team was part of that dozen, maybe one or two left alive as part of the sixty to be a scapegoat come trial.

Or she would be the scapegoat.

She had to get herself out of this bed. She had to eat something, maybe get a real nap, and plan what she was going to say in front of the committee.

She knew what she wanted to say. She wanted to tell them off, to look at their high-and-mighty faces and remind each and every one of them of the horrors in their own worlds' pasts, the fact that none of their hands—if they had hands—were clean.

But she wouldn't do that. Gianni would have argued against it. So would the others. And she owed it not just to them, but to all those people her "rebel government" was trying to care for, to give them a chance at being part of the intergalactic corporate system, to get technology to rebuild their land and to remove the mines left by the Idonae, and to help the children survive.

For it was the children that caught her the most. Their big eyes, their dark faces too thin with want, their bellies round as their stomach consumed itself.

All the medical technology in the universe couldn't stop that. It came down to something as old as time: People had to be able to feed themselves before they could care for themselves. But in order to feed themselves, they had to have some kind of income. Which usually came only from caring for themselves.

Anatolya sat up. That was what she would argue, as forcefully as she could.

She would throw out the carefully prepared speech and tell them all the truth about Etae.

Her planet was inhospitable over two-thirds of its surface. The remaining third had been poisoned in war, first by the Idonae as they stripped the northern-most continent after defeating the Ynnels; then by the original human government as it slaughtered the Idonae—who were so tied to the land that the land had to be destroyed to destroy them; and then by her own government as it fought a ground-based war with an equivalent enemy. An enemy that remained equivalent until Gianni and his doctor perfected the military enhancements, the ones that the Alliance was interested in purchasing, the ones that came from once-condemned studies of Idonae physiology.

Yes, most of what she had to tell the Alliance were stories of horror. But they were also stories of survival, just like her speech was. And now, her people had moved away from war, and the only thing they had to offer was the very thing the news was condemning her people for.

The elongated arms. The fingers like blades. The body as a weapon more potent than any other. One that could slip through any form of detection used in the Alliance. One that was lethal because it looked so very innocent.

The Alliance had exposed her when they had promised her anonymity in Armstrong. They had allowed this attack to happen; they had allowed the loss of her people.

She would make certain that the Alliance lost the same amount of face. She would make sure the people who heard about the Butcher of Etae would also hear about the fact that the Alliance—the pristine, pure Alliance—wanted assassin technology as the price for letting Etae into the club.

She knew how to play this game. She simply hadn't wanted to.

But the Alliance was leaving her no choice.

44

Noelle DeRicci needed coffee.

She staggered out of her office and went to the communal food table. The coffee sitting in the pot was at least a day old, thick as sludge, and covered with a film. But it was hot, and it had caffeine.

Someone kind had brought doughnuts—which she had sworn off a year ago—but as of this moment, she was back on them. She took a glazed and a napkin, planning to make it back to her office, but the doughnut was gone before she had even turned around, the buttery sweetness perfect against her tongue.

DeRicci hadn't realized how hungry she was; it had been more than twelve hours since she had eaten anything.

She had come back to her office after meeting with Paloma and dug into the systemic research herself. DeRicci stayed late, fiddling with systems she never normally thought about. Finally, at one A.M., she called one of the computer guys in Tech and asked for some assistance.

If Flint was on the up-and-up, DeRicci had decided on the way back, he would have left something for her—a message, something encoded, something that would allow her to believe that he wasn't involved with the murders.

Maybe even something small.

She had found nothing in her own system, and neither had the tech. He had gone back to his own office, and DeRicci had continued to look, feeling discouraged.

Then the tech had called her through the departmental link. He said he'd found a note that seemed like an internal memo, although everyone in his area denied writing it. Attached to the note was a version of the apartment building security vid, stripped and analyzed.

The tech took his version of the security vid, did his own stripping, and decided the note was correct.

All of this sounded mysterious to DeRicci, so the tech sent her the vid himself.

"You gotta watch it a few times to understand it," he said.

He uploaded the same damn security vid that she had been looking at—the one with Flint or his look-alike cousin—going to the Lahiri apartment dressed in all black. She watched it until her eyes grew tired. Finally, she had transferred the image to her wall screen, and that was when she saw it—the shaky image at the beginning, the changes in the elevator door that couldn't have been caused by a continuous loop recording, but had shown, quite clearly, that the vid tape had been tampered with.

Everything, then, on the vid she'd watched was fake—or at least recorded over something else. Or screwed up in some way.

Which made the ties to Flint suspect at best.

Someone did want him out of the way.

That got her even more focused, and made her think about the security in the Lahiris' building. If the security in the building had been so fine, how come the Lahiris themselves hadn't had good security?

DeRicci had spent the next five hours searching all

the downloads stored in the department files for the Lahiri security vids. It wasn't until Passolini had arrived at seven A.M. that DeRicci had finally gotten some satisfaction.

"There aren't any," Passolini said. "The Lahiri system shut off."

"It what?" DeRicci had asked.

"Weeks ago, before anything happened."

DeRicci then told her about the tampered hallway vid, and Passolini cursed, promising to get back to her. DeRicci hoped Passolini's team could find something, after DeRicci pointed them in the right direction.

It took time, but Passolini finally returned with a partial security vid from the Lahiri apartment. The vid came from one camera and had no sound—showing an assassin that DeRicci would have thought impossible, except that she had seen a few of them at the riot the day before.

That was when she had staggered out for some coffee and something to eat, to give her mind a chance to review everything.

DeRicci took another doughnut, then poured herself some sludge and drank it as if it were fresh-brewed. She leaned against the table, her hands shaking—not from the caffeine, but from exhaustion.

Passolini figured that Flint had tampered with all of the security vids, but DeRicci didn't. She'd make a report to that effect. Flint was talented with computers, but he wasn't stupid. He wouldn't make one vid to implicate himself and another to vindicate himself. And he certainly wouldn't make the vid that vindicated him hard to find.

What DeRicci didn't like was the suggested tie to the riot the day before. Had the killer been at the riots? Had he started it? Was all of the Etae stuff happening in Armstrong connected to the Lahiris, and if so, how?

She had no idea. Her brain was moving as slowly as the sludge she was calling coffee. She was going to keep this part of the investigation from Gumiela for as long as possible.

Gumiela was already upset about the political implications of the murders. She would certainly hate any ties to the riot—and maybe to intergalactic politics.

DeRicci took one more doughnut, then headed back to her office. She would make a personal report and log it into the private area of her server, password-protecting it. The only reason she was logging it in was so that she could prove to Gumiela what she knew and when she knew it.

But she needed to keep the information to herself. She wanted to control how the department responded to this crime. She didn't want Gumiela taking off and going after Flint, or making some kind of press announcement and scaring the city about the Lahiris' killer.

And, DeRicci hoped, without stating it aloud (even thinking it made her nervous), that Flint had gone somewhere to prove that someone else had killed the Lahiris.

That was how she decided to live with all that she had learned in the last few days.

She was tired of believing that Miles Flint would run.

45

The chef part of Nitara hated what she had done to her kitchen. Liquids, flammables piled on top of her two ranges, the smaller cookstoves scattered about the room like tiny bombs.

Such a mess.

No one would ever cook here again.

If her estimates were right—and she was rusty; she could be off by quite a bit—then no one would cook anywhere on this entire block again.

If the dome survived.

She turned around and around, a tiny dervish in a room that was filled with the work of her long night. The restaurant didn't look like hers any longer.

She didn't look like herself any longer.

She wasn't herself, not really.

Or maybe she was more herself. She didn't know.

And it didn't matter. Her staff had tried to take her home. For a while, she had thought she would have to go with them, to coddle them, let them believe she was all right.

Her lie about the riot—was it a lie? She had been there, after all, and that was where she got the blood on her cheeks—had convinced them she was injured or in shock or at least not thinking clearly, when she was thinking clearer than she had in a long, long time.

If she hadn't been thinking clearly, she wouldn't have been able to reorganize an entire restaurant in the space of a night. A long night, but an important one.

She had only a few more things to do.

First, she had to let everyone know why this happened. She wanted them to know these were the dangers the Alliance faced if the current Etaen government joined up. She wanted to stop Anatolya Döbryn, and this was the best way to do it.

Nitara had stumbled on her new plan yesterday, through all the news coverage. Blame the Etaens, the current ones. Some of them were missing, the "terrorists," as they were being called.

Such a small word for the horrors these people had inflicted on others. Terror was finite, an emotion which ended.

What she had learned about herself in the last few weeks was that some things never ended. They just got buried, to be called up later, when they could no longer be suppressed.

Her family was dead, everywhere but in her heart. Just because they had been part of the government, part of the government that Döbryn had destroyed, didn't mean they had to be destroyed. But they were.

And she had survived it—so that she could get revenge.

She walked into the main part of the restaurant—lights dimmed, windows shaded, door locked—and over to the public link. Eventually, they'd trace where the message came from, but it would make no difference. Anyone could send a message on a public link.

She had been thinking of the wording all night. She punched in the message rather than speaking it, keeping the vid screen off, and then timed the message to be delivered one hour from now.

It would be sent immediately, but the recipients wouldn't know it had arrived for an hour. She so loved technology.

Technology would help her now.

Then she went back into her kitchen—or what was left of her kitchen—and took a deep breath. She climbed the chairs she had stacked beside her favorite range, then grabbed the lighter she had placed on a rafter near the top.

She studied the lighter for a moment. It was long-handled, ornate, something she'd bought on many of her cooking trips to Earth. *Every chef needs a lighter,* one of her teachers had said. *Patrons love dramatic food.*

That was when she had learned that drama caught the attention like nothing else.

She clenched the lighter in her right hand, waiting for the remorse, the guilt, the moment when she would change her mind and become the Nitara Nicolae that everyone in Armstrong knew.

But that moment never came. And after a good five minutes of waiting, she extended her arm, placed the lighter next to the fuel she had poured so liberally over her combustibles, and flicked her thumb.

The flame seemed so tiny at first, so powerless. One tiny soul against the darkness.

Then it grew, traveling across the fuel until something ignited in a pile of sparks.

So beautiful. So destructive. So tempting.

She was reaching for the flame when the bomb she made out of her kitchen finally blew.

46

The entire building shook.

DeRicci stumbled and fell to her knees, the coffee sloshing in her cup and spilling on her thighs. At least it wasn't hot. Just lukewarm and thick, uncomfortable—a horrible mess. The doughnut she'd been holding slipped through her fingers, and it rolled along the floor.

The building continued to shake, and she heard something—a concussion? Something loud—and then the lights went out.

She caught the edge of her desk with her now-empty doughnut hand and pulled herself up, wiping at the wetness on her thighs.

A thud resounded so loudly that it shook the building a third time. And then a fourth, and a fifth and a sixth.

Someone screamed down the hall, and that released a cacophony of screams. DeRicci wanted to yell at them to shut up, but she didn't.

Instead she sent an emergency message along her links, only to realize that the odd clarity she felt was because her links were down. That silence she heard was something she had missed these last few months when Gumiela insisted DeRicci keep her emergency links on at all time.

DeRicci tried to reestablish her links, but nothing worked. They were off, and it wasn't even her fault.

She thought she heard more thuds, but they didn't shake the building. It was so dark inside that she couldn't even see her hand. She couldn't see shapes. She thought she had been facing the window, and then she frowned.

It didn't matter if she had been facing the window or not. If the window was sending light into the room, she'd see it, no matter what direction she faced.

"Son of a bitch," she muttered.

She tottered toward her window, felt the cool plastic. No blinds were drawn, no privacy shades had automatically closed against the fake glass.

The dome had gone dark—and it was dome day.

A shiver ran down her back. Something had gone very, very wrong.

DeRicci wiped her hands on the side of her pants, then extended them in front of her, moving like a blind person through her office.

Her left thigh hit her desk, and she cursed as pain ran along the muscle. Then she stepped on something squishy and backed off, afraid the squishy thing would cry out in pain.

It didn't. It couldn't, of course. It had been her doughnut.

That made her smile. Absurd. She had always thought people acted absurdly in an emergency and now she was doing it.

She continued to cross the room, and got to her door, pulling it open.

The screaming had quit, for the most part, except some hysterical shouting a floor down from hers. What worried her was the moaning from the center of the main room.

"It's okay," she said, "I'm coming."

And she walked toward the pile of desks that the

baby detectives used, hoping she wasn't going to step on anyone, hoping that everything would be all right.

The floor was covered with debris—things that had fallen from desks, maybe ceiling tiles—she couldn't tell, not in this darkness.

Then, as if the gods above had heard that thought, the lights came back on—not all of them, and not real well. They were a sickly gray, making the entire office look like something from a badly recorded security vid.

That thought made her even more nervous, and she continued to head toward the whimpering.

"It's okay," she said again. "I'm here."

Here turned out to be two desks down. A cabinet had fallen on a pair of legs. She was sure the legs were attached to someone, but she didn't know who, and she didn't try to figure that out. Instead, she levered the cabinet, raised it up just enough that the whimperer could get out.

"Can you roll?" DeRicci asked, but the whimperer crawled instead, pulling herself forward on her arms until her legs were free.

"Oh, God," the woman said. DeRicci didn't recognize her—a woman with streaky makeup and the look of someone who didn't belong. "Are we going to die?"

"No," DeRicci said, but she didn't know. She'd never seen the lights go out in the dome before. She didn't even know what would cause it.

Or would cause something as big as this building to shake, not once, but repeatedly.

For the first time in her life, DeRicci hated not being hooked up. She wanted information at the touch of a thought, and she wanted it now.

But she was alone in her head, and she didn't want to be.

She wanted everything back the way it had been just a moment before.

Somehow she doubted that would happen anytime soon.

47

The blackness was so complete that Anatolya could see nothing. Debris rained on the bed each time the building shook.

She stopped counting the shakings, even though they were being caused by something exterior—not an earthquake or something belowground. She'd experienced enough of those on the volcanic islands near the Idonae's original settlements on Etae to know the difference.

These shakes were being caused by something big, something powerful, something designed to make things shake—some kind of concussion, maybe. A series of bombs landing nearby. Weaponry.

A bombardment.

Which, she suddenly realized, shouldn't have been possible unless the dome had been breached.

Wouldn't that have caused a sound all by itself? An explosive decompression, the way that ship sounded when something breached its hull?

She took a tentative sip of air, tasted nothing different, and then rolled over on her stomach.

The shaking stopped.

She lay still for what seemed like hours but had to be only minutes. No more shakes. No lights, no environmental controls—the air smelled stale—but no shakes either.

Slowly she got to her feet, hands out, prepared for anything that might fall on or near her.

Then something banged, and she heard shouting—voices, a dozen voices. They came toward her with a violence that had her shaking.

She was wrapped in arms before she realized what happened, bundled forward and out of the room, her own arms clasped at her sides.

The bodies were unfamiliar, the voices too. It wasn't until she heard them issuing commands back and forth that she knew who had invaded her space.

The guards.

They blamed her somehow and they were taking her out of the room—not for her own safety, but for everyone else's.

She let herself be dragged. No sense in fighting. They'd realize their mistake soon enough.

48

Orenda Kreise crawled through the broken art, her hands reaching and often discarding sharp pieces of metal and glass. She tried to find the least destructive path, but she knew her knees and palms would be badly carved up before her trip was over.

The worst part was the way the darkness had descended.

First there had been that hideous noise—to call it a bang was to minimize it; something tremendously loud and violent—and then the building had shaken.

The lights went out, and for the first time, she had been grateful for the sunlight filtering in from the Moon's day.

Then the building shook again. And again. And the next thing she knew, the sunlight was fading.

She looked up at the dome attached to the cultural center, and watched as darkness spread across it, the way that clouds would cover the sun back on Earth.

That was when her heart started pounding too hard. Before that, she hadn't been frightened, despite the falling statuary and the crashing picture frames.

She shouldn't have come here. She had been getting ready for the meeting later in the day with Anatolya

Döbryn, making sure the security was good, after the riots of the day before.

She was alone in the building, except for the security team, and they had left her alone in the main area while she tried to decide where to put the tables.

Was the security team all right now? They were in the entry, which was filled with just as much artistic junk. These buildings weren't designed to be earthquake-proof—so far as she knew, the Moon wasn't subject to quakes.

But she wasn't sure.

She wasn't sure about anything.

The dust from the shattered sculptures rose around her like a storm, swirling.

She stopped crawling, bowed her head, and wrapped her arms around her face.

Too late, of course. Her eyes were already burning, and her lungs ached.

She was going to die here, among broken art she hated in a city she hated even more.

Alone.

In the darkness.

For a reason she might never, ever understand.

49

The lights weren't supposed to go out in the City Center.

Arek Soseki sat at his giant desk and clutched its edges each time the building shook.

The building wasn't supposed to shake either, and if something went seriously wrong, there were supposed to be sirens and notifications across his links and all sorts of emergency backups—generators and fail-safes and tons of technology he never really wanted to get to know on any kind of personal level.

As his chair tried to dance across the room all on its own, he found himself wishing he hadn't taken the train back from Littrow. If he'd just stayed there one more night, he would have missed the riot and now this, whatever the hell it was.

The lights flickered on, only they were brown instead of the familiar yellow. Backup generators kicking in from somewhere. He felt a gust of air on his cheek and realized that environmental controls had kicked on as well.

His office was a mess. Decorative statues had fallen off his shelves, chairs had toppled, and glass was everywhere. Only his desk remained standing—or so it seemed.

One of his windows was cracked, although the only way he could tell was by the reflection—along one side his body seemed normal, and on the other, it seemed slightly crooked.

Or perhaps that was the way he saw himself now.

He gave a shaky laugh and forced his fingers off his desk, one by one. The muscles in his hands ached. He had never held on to anything so tightly in his life.

Then he stood, keeping one hand touching the desk for balance, afraid there would be more shakes.

He walked to the door, avoiding piles of fallen objects, and had to kick some plants and accumulated dirt aside to pull it open.

The front office was a disaster as well. Piles of equipment and papers and plants all littered the floor. Soseki's assistant, Hans Londran, still sat at his desk, slamming his palm against the screen on the desktop.

"I almost have something." Londran's voice was flat. He was in some kind of shock.

"The power's off, Hans," Soseki said. "We're on backup generators."

But Londran didn't seem to hear him. He kept hitting at the screen like a man possessed.

"Hans," Soseki said as he picked his way to the desk. "Stop that."

Londran didn't move. Soseki finally reached his side and was stunned to see that the screen had shattered. Londran hadn't noticed, which scared Soseki more.

Soseki put his hand on Londran's shoulders and slowly eased the man's hand away from the hole in the desktop. Londran's finger was bleeding, and as Soseki turned his assistant toward him, he realized that the man had blood down one side of his face.

Something had hit him.

"We're going to need to get you help," Soseki said.

"Nonsense." Londran's voice sounded just as flat as before. "I'm fine. If I can only get this screen working."

Soseki felt panic burble up inside him. Londran was the one who kept him organized, kept him from panicking, kept him sane. What was he going to do without Londran?

Then Soseki took a deep breath. He was going to have to do this alone. He crouched in front of Londran.

"Can you stand?" he asked gently.

"Of course I can stand, sir," Londran said. "What kind of question is that?"

"Humor me," Soseki said.

Londran sighed, and put his hands on the arms of his chair. Then he pushed upward, hovered for a moment, and sank back down.

"We're going to have to check the filters," he said. "The oxygen is going bad. I'm getting dizzy."

Soseki nodded. There was nothing wrong with the air—not yet, at least.

"It's not affecting me yet," Soseki said. "Let me see if I can find someone to check the office, all right?"

"That's my job, sir," Londran said.

"Technically," Soseki said. "But we can help each other out, right?"

Londran frowned, then winced. He brought a hand to his face, touched the blood-covered cheek, and said in his normal voice, "Something's wrong here, isn't it?"

Soseki nodded. "Stay here, Hans. I'll be right back."

He stood and made his way to the outer door, afraid of what he would find. As he tugged the door open, he faced half the office staff, covered in dirt and streaks of some kind of black substance, trying to push desks and chairs and shelves away from the door he had just opened.

"Sir!" someone said. "You're all right."

"I am, but Hans isn't. We need medical attention right now."

"We've already sent for someone," someone else said. "I don't know when they'll arrive, though. The links are down."

"Yes, I know," Soseki said. "We have emergency power, though. We need to get something hooked back up and find out what's going on. And anyone who knows first aid has to get over this mess and help me with Hans.''

They redoubled their efforts. Soseki could do nothing from inside, so he went back to Londran's desk. The man was still staring at his blood-covered fingers as if they belonged to someone else.

"It's all right, Hans," Soseki said, putting his hand on Londran's shoulder. "We'll all be fine."

"Really?" Londran asked.

"Yes," Soseki said, and hoped he sounded more convinced than he felt.

50

Carolyn Lahiri's son lived in what Delilah had called a shotgun house, named, Delilah said, because you could fire a shotgun at the front door and the bullet would go out the back without hitting anything along the way.

The shotgun house was in one of the older sections of New Orleans, and the house itself looked like it had seen better days. The roots of some kind of tree were digging up the front sidewalk, and the tree's thin branches bent downward, almost as if the little tiny leaves on the sides were too heavy for the wood.

The house itself had a sagging front porch that looked like it had been added after the house was built. It had once been white, but time and lack of upkeep had caused the paint to peel.

Flint picked his way around the roots, stood on the sagging porch, and knocked. The door's wood felt soft against his knuckles.

From inside, he heard a thud and a curse. Then someone said, "Just a minute," in that soft drawl Flint was beginning to identify as purely New Orleans.

The door slammed open, and Flint found himself looking up at a man with reddish hair that curled around dark skin. His eyes were a disconcerting green, but it wasn't just the color that made them disconcerting.

It was the fact that Flint had seen those same-shaped eyes on Carolyn Lahiri's face.

In fact, the face that looked down at Flint was a masculine version of Carolyn's, with stronger bones, broader lips, and an unfriendly glint in the eyes.

"What?" the man said.

"Are you Ian Taylor?"

"So what if I am?"

"My name is Miles Flint. I'm a friend of your mother's."

"Like I need to listen to that," Taylor said, and started to slam the door.

Flint caught the door with his foot. "I have some news. You might want me to come inside to tell you about it."

Taylor studied him for a moment, then stepped back and swept out a hand as if he were inviting Flint into a mansion instead of a ruin.

The hallway did run all the way through the house, and from the front door, he could see the back. The rooms seemed to grow off the hallway, almost like afterthoughts. The main room would have been attractive, with its expensive (at least by Armstrong standards) hardwood floors and plaster walls. But the furniture was ripped, and clothing littered the floor, along with beer bottles, open cartons that had apparently once held pizza, and half-smoked cigars tamped out on regular plates.

The stench was incredible—rotted food, cigar smoke, and stale beer, combined with soiled clothing, and that ever-present mildew smell that seemed so much a part of New Orleans.

Flint had to work hard not to grimace as he stepped inside.

Insects buzzed over the pizza containers. Flint guessed from the insects' shape that they were flies, but he didn't know for sure. He had discovered just how unpleasant bugs were on his first trip, when he went home covered with small lumps from mosquitoes and having been terrorized in his hotel room by a creature the size of a dinner plate that everyone called "just a cockroach."

He really didn't want to get near these creatures either.

Taylor closed the front door, crossed his arms, and leaned against it. "What's Mama done now? Burned down her bar so ain't nobody gonna make no money off it?"

"Your mother went to the city of Armstrong on the Moon a few weeks ago. You knew that, right?" Flint said, hovering near the mess. Even if Taylor invited him to sit down, he wouldn't.

So instead Flint walked around the small space, staring at the old, flat photographs on the wall. Some were still-lifes done in the style of the old masters of photography, but a large number were modern shots, done flat and black-and-white.

"Delilah said she run off with some guy," Taylor said. "Didn't care where."

Flint supposed that description was accurate enough. He turned. "She actually went to Armstrong to reunite with her parents."

"They're dead. She told me."

"I'm sure she did," Flint said. "They were dead to her for a long time."

Taylor had tilted his head back against the door. "You're the guy she run off with."

Flint nodded. "I'm a Retrieval Artist."

Taylor let that sink in for a moment. "Next thing you're gonna tell me is that Mama disappeared."

"She did," Flint said. "Thirty years ago."

Taylor frowned, bowed his head, and bit his lower lip. The resemblance to Carolyn had faded, and something in his stance made him seem a lot more like the judge.

A grandfather Taylor would never meet.

Flint blinked, then thought: Carolyn had been the only surviving child, and Taylor was her only child—

at least so far as he knew. That meant Taylor would inherit the Lahiri estate.

"You don't seem surprised," Flint said after a moment.

Taylor shrugged, his head still bowed. "Her and Daddy always fought, you know, said weird things. Stuff about surviving. He would say she couldn't survive without him. Not, you know, like you say to a girl. That she can't live without you. But that she wouldn't survive. Like someone was after her. At least that's what I used to think. Told my daddy once. He laughed like people do when they're lying, said I had an imagination. But he wouldn't let me stay with Mama, not once after they split up. He was scared too."

It was Flint's turn to frown. Had Carolyn's husband known she was a Disappeared? That broke all the rules of disappearance. Unless . . .

"How old are you, Mr. Taylor?"

"Twenty-nine," Taylor said by reflex. Then he looked up. "She been Disappeared for thirty years and . . ."

His voice trailed off; then he shook his head. "I was born here. I got the certification and everything."

That could be faked, but Flint doubted it was. Not in the name of Ian Taylor. When people Disappeared, they usually kept as much truth as possible. A baby born elsewhere would get a new identity and a similar birth date, without shaving any years off it.

"And both your parents are on the certificate?" Flint asked.

"Oh, hell, yeah," Taylor said. "Mama and Daddy known each other since they was in school."

Flint frowned.

"My daddy's my daddy," Taylor said, as if it insulted him that Flint might even think otherwise. "You see? The hair and the eyes, they ain't tricked up or enhanced. Ain't got the money for that."

He tapped one of the flats. Only this one wasn't black-and-white. It was one of the family portraits done in the style of centuries-old commercial photography, with a blue background and the family poised stiffly in front of it.

Carolyn sat there, looking much younger, her eyes even sadder. On her lap, a young Ian waved a small fist at the camera. And beside her, a man stood, his hand on her shoulder, his face so familiar that Flint's breath caught.

Ali Norbert. The last missing member of the team that had gone to Etae. Ali Norbert with his auburn hair and bright green eyes, hand possessively on his wife's shoulder, almost as if he were trying to hold her down.

"Don't surprise me that my Mama ran," Taylor was saying. "She was always a runner. Maybe she talked my daddy into it. He's just solid. Old military. The kinda man you need in a crisis. Been there for me, even when I don't want him."

Flint had to force his attention back to Taylor.

"My mama, she was just colder than cold. She never did want me, I think, and then I go to her, you know, ten or something, running away from Daddy like kids're supposed to do, and I tell her I can live with her now—she's in the Quarter, playing music, all glam, and I'm thinking she's like the perfect mom—and she says to me, 'You don't want me for a parent, little boy. I'll be just like my father, and you'll end up broken and hating me. So just start hating me now and we can skip the broken part.' "

Flint swallowed. He could almost hear Carolyn saying that.

"I tell my daddy after she sends me home, and he says, 'She's right. Her father was a son of a bitch.' And now you tell me she's run home to him, this son of a bitch she hated that much?"

I have nowhere else to go, Carolyn had said.

Flint nodded.

"I thought she liked it here," Taylor said. "But what do I know? She didn't even leave me her bar. Hell, she didn't even tell me she was going."

Flint studied the picture. It looked so fake, and so

old, and yet the faces that stared back at him seemed impossibly young.

"So now she sends for me because she's got news?" Taylor asked, and Flint heard hope in the man's voice. The same hope that Carolyn had tried to squelch when this man had been ten years old and yearning for a mother.

Flint had seen this sort of thing before, back when he was working as a cop. If he told Taylor about Carolyn now, he wouldn't get anything out of the man. He had to save the news for after the questioning.

"Let me ask you a few things first," Flint said, "and then I'll tell you what's going on."

Taylor leaned back, and the wary look reappeared on his face. "What do you want?"

"Just a few answers, nothing more," Flint said. "Have you seen anyone around here, maybe when your mother left? Anyone strange?"

"You ain't been to New Orleans much, have you? Everyone's strange."

"Out of the ordinary then," Flint said, and as Taylor opened his mouth clearly to repeat what he'd said before, Flint added, "New Orleans ordinary, I mean."

"No," Taylor said. "But I never had much to do with my mama. No one'd come to me looking for her."

But maybe they'd come about the father. Although Flint didn't say that. He didn't want to alarm Taylor.

"What about for any other reason? Just something out of the ordinary?"

Taylor shook his head. "How come you're still here? If you retrieved her and all."

Flint sighed. That was the question he didn't want to answer, and the one he had to, even though, technically, it wasn't his job.

"Is there someplace we can sit?" he asked, looking pointedly away from the soiled living room. "Somewhere comfortable."

"I ain't gonna like this news, am I?" Taylor asked.

"No," Flint said, "you're not."

And he didn't enjoy telling it. All of it. In Taylor's equally messy kitchen in the back of the dilapidated house.

51

Three hours after the shaking stopped, the lights came back up at full power. DeRicci was never so glad to see anything in her life.

Her joy at seeing real light was one of the few emotions she allowed herself. She knew if she thought about anything, really let it in, she wouldn't be able to function.

And in the last three hours, she had functioned as well as anyone else in the division.

She had set up furniture, helped the injured to a safe hallway where, if anything fell again, they wouldn't be hurt, and tried futilely to reestablish link contact.

The elevators were down and she couldn't get into the stairwell because the locks, designed only to let in the right people—people with a higher rank than hers—had gone down with the links.

She couldn't even let anyone know that they had injured on the fifth floor. There were probably injured throughout the building, but emergency protocol stated that she had to inform someone about the situation on her floor, and she couldn't.

Fortunately, none of the injured seemed too badly hurt.

Although she wasn't counting out internal injuries. Those had her worried the most.

So when the lights came back on full, and the environmental systems kicked in, the first thing DeRicci did was check her links.

She found garbled and half-finished messages, a strangled system, and a lot of silence from the main network. But inside the building, the links were back up.

She sent emergency messages to everyone she could think of, begging them to get medical help here quickly, and then she sent more messages, explaining that the doors were down.

That made her wonder, actually, if the doors were still down. She walked to the closest stairwell and tried the door. It clicked twice, and then turned.

Behind her, a handful of people cheered.

She let out a breath she hadn't even realized she'd been holding. Part of her had been terrified. She had thought of breaking out of the building—smashing a window, climbing into the street—but she hadn't seen any point.

The streets were still dark. The dome wasn't functioning, and someone—someone she wished had remained quiet—had wondered if some part of the dome had been breached.

Because if it had, only the tightness of the building was keeping them alive. That person thought, anyway.

But DeRicci knew that a breach would have caused a lot of problems that would have been readily apparent—at least a large breach. A slow leak, on the other hand, would take out the atmosphere bit by bit. The building would protect them, for a time, and then it would all be over.

She had wanted to make fun of the idea, but she hadn't. It still made her nervous.

Never once in her entire life had she heard of the inside of the dome going dark.

Now that the doors opened, she was going to be able to get off the floor, but she wasn't sure she would like what she found when she got down to the street.

52

Security got her out. Somehow they had remembered she was inside, and they got her through the doors.

Orenda Kreise was so grateful, she wasn't sure how to express herself. She had never been the supplicant before, at least not in this kind of situation. Bloodied, terrified, barely able to breathe—she still wasn't sure how the air had gotten so bad.

It wasn't until the lights flickered on, and she saw the extent of the devastation, that she began to understand. The dust she'd been covered with hadn't come from the destroyed statues. Something had damaged the dome and the filters had quit. The dust, always a problem in this part of Armstrong, took over—quickly, pouring into the cultural center—a building completed without thought to weather or temperature differences. A building that needed the city's dome to survive.

The center didn't even look like it had before. The ceiling had cracked—it wasn't attached to the dome after all—and above it, something dark had fallen, like a steel grate over an open window.

She coughed and spat and tried to catch her breath. The security guards were covered with dust just as she was, but had somehow escaped the blood and bruising. Apparently the main security area had few artworks and almost no furniture.

The security team's links were up, but hers weren't. Buildings were damaged all over town, and no medical relief would reach her for a long time. No one knew if it could reach her. The streets were dark, and no one knew what had caused the problems.

One of the men on the security team gave her water from a nearby sink—the water mains hadn't broken at all, if indeed Armstrong had mains; Orenda had no idea how this city in the middle of the Moon got its water. The water cleared her throat but not her lungs.

Her breathing was shallow, but another member of the team, who claimed to have medical training, said she would be all right. He kept apologizing that they didn't have oxygen to give her. She kept repeating that it was all right.

But it wasn't all right. Something terrible had happened, and until a few hours ago, she hadn't realized just how vulnerable everyone on the Moon was. Living in domes. Who had thought of that? And what did they plan to do if the dome somehow failed?

She wanted to go back to Earth, where there was sky and easy-to-breathe air, and it was safe to go outside, even when the ground quaked.

For the first time in her life, she wanted nothing more than to go home.

53

With the lights back on and the primary links back up, Soseki felt some semblance of normality. His assistants had cleaned up his office while he got damage reports from all over the city.

There had been an explosion in one of the trendier shopping areas not far from the university. The explosion had been serious enough to damage the dome, which set off all the safety protocols.

That part of the dome became isolated. Dome walls fell all over the city, not just the walls surrounding that section of town. Each wall landed with such force that it caused the shaking sensations, which were worse the closer one was to a falling wall. The main shaking at the City Center had occurred when eight different walls fell, isolating the city government and its services from computer-perceived threats.

Then the dome cover crept its way across the permaplastic dome. The cover worked faster in some areas than in others—in the newer areas, the cover operated within seconds. In the older areas, it took nearly fifteen minutes. It took nearly twenty minutes for the cover to protect the entire dome from more breaches.

And the cover left the entire city in darkness—something the engineers had always warned about, but no one had experienced.

And no one had expected a power failure. As yet, Soseki didn't know what caused that.

He felt like he had lost thirty pounds in the past three hours. He was covered with sweat and dirt, and he was moving faster than he ever had. He was also thinking harder, because he felt like he had to do the thinking for two people.

In the past, Londran had helped him. But Londran had a head injury, and, the medical team said, wouldn't be helping anyone anytime soon.

That news, more than anything else, had panicked Soseki. But he didn't dare show it. The entire city had panicked, and he had to calm them somehow.

He had to calm himself.

His links were open, processing more and more information. As soon as the citywide net reestablished itself, he would make announcements, keeping people informed about the current activities and telling them not to panic.

At the moment, he was trying to solve the problems created by the fail-safes. So far as the engineers could tell, the dome had been damaged only near the explosion, and the cover prevented continued atmosphere breach. The walls could come up everywhere except the explosion section.

And yet the walls weren't coming up. The city's chief engineer informed Soseki that was because of the power problems and the computer system glitches, not because the rest of the dome had failed.

Soseki believed it. He had been to the briefings. He knew what Armstrong would look like with a serious and continuous dome breach.

It wouldn't look like this.

It might not even remain standing.

As it were, the most damage came from the shaking as the dome walls came down. The walls were thick and heavy, and in the older sections, not even see-through. The entire dome got sectioned off in a matter of minutes.

A few people were killed when the walls slammed

on them, an image he really hadn't wanted in his head, but one which was now there permanently.

Soseki sank into his chair at his desk, which still felt like the only safe place in the city, at least to him. He would have to do more than tell the people not to panic. He would have to tell them that he was going to find and rectify the mistakes. He was going to be upbeat and positive, telling them that this was a warning bell. If they had truly been attacked from the outside, then they might not have survived.

But now that they knew so many systems malfunctioned, those systems would get fixed.

Something had exploded, someone had accidentally lit the wrong thing in one of those tony restaurants, and the dome got damaged. From the inside. The dome had been built to withstand problems from the outside. All those meteors, big and small, that fell onto the Moon's surface didn't damage the dome because the dome engineers had designed it with strength.

Now they had to improve the earlier design, make certain nothing like this ever happened again.

Soseki took a deep breath. Coming to that decision had cheered him up. He wished Londran were here to bounce the idea off of, but Soseki had the idea that Londran would approve.

One of Londran's assistants, some woman who had been hired only a few weeks ago, stopped in front of Soseki's desk.

"Sir," she said, "there's something you have to look at."

There was a lot he had to look at, probably more than some new hire realized, but he humored her. This was a crisis in his mayoralty and he had to handle it well, better than he had handled the Etaen crisis.

A few people had already accused him of starting that riot, when he had only been trying to protect his city. He and Londran had a variety of ideas on how to defend him.

Ironic now that a defense probably wouldn't be necessary.

"Sir?" the woman said again.

"Yes," he said. "I heard you."

She put a hand-held in front of him. "The public links are just coming up. This was sent across them a few minutes after the explosion, but we're only getting copies of it now. The public links aren't up in this part of the building, so I thought you'd want to see it."

He picked up the hand-held and stared at the small screen. The message was text with a symbol behind it that he didn't recognize.

But he recognized the words.

This Bombing is for Etae!

Bombing. Etae.

Soseki closed his eyes. He had been right after all, and the governor-general had been wrong. She had let the terrorists into his city and they had nearly destroyed it.

"Sir?" the woman asked again. He wanted to snap at her, but he didn't.

He opened his eyes. She was peering at him, her small face pinched with concern.

"See if you can trace where this came from," he said.

She nodded, and started to leave. Then she stopped.

"Sir," she said for the fourth time, "do you think they'll do it again?"

"What?" he snapped, already angry that she wouldn't leave him alone.

"Set off another bomb," she whispered.

He hadn't thought of that. He hadn't thought of that at all.

"I certainly hope not," he said.

And, seeing the terror on her face, he shooed her away, calling over another assistant to contact all the emergency services personnel in the city to tell them that things might actually get worse.

54

Flint had been downloading information on the Lahiri murders from Armstrong news sites, so that he could prove to Taylor that Carolyn was dead, when all contact with Armstrong quit.

The dome had been bombed.

At first, Flint didn't believe it. Then he saw the coverage coming from everywhere but Armstrong. The bullet trains between domes were shut down, and Armstrong's dome itself had turned black.

It took two different commentators to explain why: The dome had a shield that automatically activated when the dome had been breached.

No one knew how bad the dome breach was. No one had been able to contact the city at all.

That didn't stop Flint from trying while he was inside Ian Taylor's house.

Taylor was watching the downloads on the murders, occasionally asking questions—such as why his mother wasn't mentioned—and then looking at old images of Carolyn Lahiri and comparing them with Claire Taylor.

It was clear to Flint that Taylor was beginning to see who his mother had been.

Not that Flint cared. At the moment, he was more

concerned with his friends back on Armstrong. He tried to reach DeRicci first, figuring police links would always be up.

They weren't.

Then he tried everyone he knew in the Port, and those links weren't working either.

Finally he tried Paloma, thinking that perhaps she had gone to her new space yacht, the *Dove II,* and had gotten out of there.

But she hadn't either.

No one could answer him. No one had contact with the dome.

Finally, he got permission to use one of Taylor's wall screens. Flint watched reports from every dome except Armstrong's, from several ships in orbit, and from outside commentators, including a few from Mars.

No one knew what happened, although a few had gotten footage of a hole blowing out of the dome. The hole was small and had to be magnified several times just to present a good image, but when it was, the image showed something being expelled from the dome.

Whatever had happened to Armstrong had happened from the inside.

Flint resisted the urge to get into his yacht and head home. There was nothing he could do, not until Armstrong's dome was accessible again. With the dome shielded, the Port was shut down.

No one was going in or out of the city.

No one was even sure if anyone inside of Armstrong was alive.

Flint kept the news coverage on even after he left Taylor. A small feed ran along the bottom of Flint's right eye, and he had another running inside the aircar.

He went back to his hotel, having lost the spirit of the investigation. He also didn't like seeing Taylor's confusion, learning that he had a family he hadn't realized he had, and that the new family was dead.

Flint wasn't sure Taylor understood that he might inherit everything the Lahiris owned—provided, of course, that what they owned hadn't been destroyed with the dome.

When Flint got back to his hotel in the French Quarter, he went to his room, switched on as many feeds as he could find, lay on his bed, and hoped that his city would survive.

55

Andrea Gumiela did not look like her normal self. Her clothes were torn and stained, and her skirt, usually turned to reveal her slender legs, tilted sideways, as if someone had tried to take it off and failed.

She stood near the side exit in the foyer of the main law-enforcement building, and ran a finger through her messy hair. Her eyes were glassy, she was clearly exhausted, and she was looking for someone.

Noelle DeRicci had a hunch who.

The uniformed officers had gathered in the foyer, along with as many detectives as could be rounded up. Emergency notification had come across the links—the thing that started this whole mess was a bomb, set off by the Etaen terrorists who had been let into the Port the day before.

DeRicci wondered whose idiocy had caused that. She couldn't remember the news reports—thinking, at the time, that they had nothing to do with her.

What had nothing to do with her any longer was the Lahiri case and the feeling of betrayal she had carried for the past few days. Flint was out of Armstrong, which meant there was one less person for her to worry about, and the Lahiris were dead. No one would remember that case now.

DeRicci could barely remember how she had felt earlier that day, or why she had even cared enough to stay up all night, searching through computer files.

Gumiela pushed her way through the crowd of officers. No one looked good. Everyone was dirt-covered or bruised, wearing ripped clothing or scratching dried blood off their skin.

But it was a measure of their professionalism that no one had suggested leaving the building or asked for help or wanted to go home. Everyone knew they had a job to do.

They just weren't sure what.

Gumiela finally reached DeRicci's side. "I need you, Noelle," Gumiela said without preamble.

"I was ordered here with everyone else," DeRicci said, not sure she wanted whatever minor political task Gumiela was going to assign her.

But Gumiela grabbed DeRicci's arm, finding a bruise DeRicci hadn't even realized was there. "I'm ordering you elsewhere. Come on."

DeRicci let herself be led to the corridor just outside the main hall. It was cooler here—the environmental controls were on strong. In the foyer, packed with hundreds of nervous cops, the heat had grown intense.

"Looks like the engineers have a way to open the walls that shut down the domes," Gumiela said. "Most of the cops are gonna go through, help people calm down, make sure there's not other crises to deal with."

DeRicci glanced over her shoulder. Behind her, in the foyer, the chief of police was starting the meeting.

Gumiela pulled DeRicci farther away from the crowd. "They're gonna check for the bombers as well. Rumor has it that there's a dozen spread out throughout Armstrong."

"Rumor," DeRicci said.

Gumiela shrugged. DeRicci got a sense of exhaustion from the woman that she'd never seen before.

"Everything's rumor right now," Gumiela said. "All

we've got is word of mouth and panic through the links. And that damn threat."

"Threat?" DeRicci asked.

"Someone took credit for the bombing. For Etae—you know. Those terrorists sent in yesterday. I've seen it. It's legit. We have techs working on it now, trying to trace it, but with the systems in such bad shape, we don't have a lot of hope."

DeRicci felt her stomach twist.

"I need someone good, Noelle. I need someone who can keep a clear head in a crisis."

"That's what cops do," DeRicci said.

Gumiela shook her head. "Not like this. I need an investigator. Someone who'll track down the source of the explosion, maybe even the person who caused it, in record time. I've only got one investigator who I know can investigate while the world's crashing around her. That's you, Noelle."

DeRicci's mouth was dry. "Other people—"

"Other people haven't survived one other crisis like you have. And I gotta admit, this is political too."

Of course, DeRicci thought.

"If you say so-'n'-so did it, people are gonna believe you, where they might not believe Kinyone or Stevens. You've got the experience behind you, and a record for doing good work."

DeRicci shook her head.

Gumiela's hand tightened on her arm. "The public knows you. They know you saved the dome once. They're gonna think you can do it again."

"I don't want to be a publicity stunt," DeRicci said.

"No stunt." Gumiela brushed hair out of her face. Her skin had scratches and cuts around the browline. DeRicci wondered what had happened to Gumiela when the lights went out. "I'm not even going to mention an investigation until it's done. But when it is done, no matter how long it takes, we need a voice the people will trust. Like it or not, that's you, Noelle."

DeRicci sighed. "I'm not trained for this."

"No one is." Gumiela let go of DeRicci's arm. "You can put together your own team. First thing you need to do is look for leads, see if you can track down whoever did this or maybe where they're going to strike again. As many people as you need, Noelle. Just let me know."

"I don't even know who's functional," DeRicci said.

"We have a list. I'll download it into your system. You gather them outside. We have a specific aircar for you, one that'll be escorted through the walls. You're gonna have your own guards in that section, and you'll need an environmental suit."

"A suit?" DeRicci's breath caught. "I thought the breach wasn't serious."

"They don't know," Gumiela said. "Only a few guys have been in there, and they're suited. It's a mess, Noelle. You're gonna need arson investigators and folks who're used to working in zero-G. I've got a few names I think'll be good, but if they can't work with you, get someone who can."

DeRicci felt that same sense of dislocation she'd felt when she'd come out of the marathon case. The universe wasn't the same. Gumiela was being sincere. She actually believed DeRicci would do a good job.

DeRicci made herself take a breath.

"I can't promise results by any deadline," she said.

"I'm not asking for that. I would hope you can figure out who did this quickly, but if you can't, then we'll muddle through. We're gonna have eyes all over the city. But what's really important here, Noelle, is thoroughness. Everyone in Armstrong's been touched by this. We've got more dead than we probably know about at the moment. We're gonna need answers, solid answers, ones we don't revise when things calm down. I don't know anyone better to get them than you."

DeRicci stared at her boss. Now wasn't the time for casually accepting an assignment. DeRicci couldn't go without saying one more thing.

"You know," DeRicci said, "you used to think I was a fuckup."

Gumiela smiled. The smile was tired, but sincere. "No, Noelle. I never thought you were a fuckup. What I knew was that you didn't have a political bone in your body. You still don't. And what I never realized before last year was how valuable integrity combined with good policework could be. That's what we need now, Noelle. Your blunt, brash self. You'll do it?"

DeRicci sighed. There was no way to refuse.

"Of course," she said. "I'll do my best."

56

Flint dozed off somewhere in the middle of the night, and at first, he thought he was dreaming. Voices told him over and over again that contact had been made with the dome, and that for the most part, the people of Armstrong were fine.

Tired, bruised, frightened, but fine.

What concerned them the most, however, was the possibility of another attack. Etaen terrorists had set off a bomb inside the city, promising more for Etae.

Flint wished the voices would stop. Blending his case with that tragedy seemed wrong to him, even in a dream. And then he realized that he was thinking too rationally for a dream.

He opened his eyes and watched more coverage—seeing that yes, indeed, Etae was involved. His internal link actually ran the message, and he saw the words along with the symbol for Etae.

Etae. It kept coming back to that place. Carolyn Lahiri had ties to Etae, and had died in Armstrong. Now Etaen terrorists had set off a bomb in the city.

Flint didn't believe in coincidences.

That completely woke him up. He no longer felt like staying in the room, watching as a tragedy occurred in his home.

He actually had something to do.

He got up, had breakfast, and was out of the room before dawn. He was going to follow the one lead Ian Taylor had given him—the address of Taylor's father.

Taylor's father, Alan, who had been born with the name Ali Norbert, lived on a ranch in West Texas, which was, apparently, quite far from New Orleans.

The aircar followed a distinct route and was fortunately built for long distances. Flint wasn't. He had to stop the car at least twice just to move around. He had never traveled so far by car before. Bullet train, yes, to go from dome to dome, and on the *Emmeline,* but never in such a cramped space, with nothing to do but watch more news reports.

And the scenery as well. The water and lushness of Louisiana disappeared behind him, until there was land as far as the eye could see. The vegetation changed. It was no longer green and overwhelming. Eventually, the land became something like the Moon, only not as devastated—a vast sea itself of brown and green, of repeating landscapes dotted by small homes.

He didn't even see many other aircars, even though his car took him on an established route. Most people seemed to travel by ground car, driving over roads that had existed longer than Armstrong.

Eventually, he shut off the news—it kept repeating information he had already heard—and simply watched the countryside go by.

He didn't entirely understand Earth. It worked together as a unified planet, but it had continents too that weren't united, and countries that were. But there were subsets even within the countries—places like Texas (and those seemed to have subsets too, like West Texas, although he wasn't sure how that fit with the concept of Texas)—that seemed as nebulous as the idea of country.

Flint understood cities: He had lived in one all his life. The cities on the Moon were unified under the governor-general's auspices, and representatives spoke to their council. But other subsets—countries, states, counties—didn't exist at all.

At least Flint understood enough this time not to ask if he needed special documentation to go from one state to another. The last time he had come, he had asked that in the port, and everyone had snickered.

What they didn't seem to realize—what he was learning slowly—was that rules changed from planet to planet, place to place.

His car announced their proximity to the Taylor ranch in West Texas by slowing down considerably. West Texas looked like the most desolate place Flint had seen outside of the Moon. It had flat brown land, and kilometers of nothingness. Some buildings rose out of the dust, but they looked old and ragged, like permaplastic after too many centuries.

There were black dots along the landscape, which his car informed him (when he asked) were remains of old oil wells. He also saw animals moving in packs—cows, mostly, which he'd never seen outside of the vids.

From the sky, he could see roads and fences that seemed to mark off huge parcels of land. Nothing seemed to delineate the land other than the fences— no hills or trees or vegetation. Just fences that marked boundaries that wouldn't have otherwise existed.

Flint's car had to announce his presence just to get into Taylor's airspace. And Flint had to speak to Taylor's security devices, letting them know that he had just come from Ian Taylor, and that Flint was there to talk about Carolyn Lahiri's death, and issues surrounding Etae.

He figured if that didn't get Taylor's attention, nothing would.

Taylor's security cleared the airspace, and Flint's aircar crossed the invisible boundary, marked on the ground by one of the fences. The car flew only a few meters above a dirt road. People on horseback rode toward another group of cows, and Flint wondered if each of them had to be cleared when they entered Taylor land. He doubted it; the land was too vast for sensors on all portions of it.

Airspace was something else. Direct routes, like the one Flint took, could be easily monitored, as could main ground roads.

Eventually, the car crested a small rise, and Flint saw the ranch house itself. The building was long and high, made of reddish adobe, or so it appeared, with barred windows and a raised roof of a type Flint had never seen.

The house's front was covered with plants that looked like they didn't need much water, and pots that had the same type of decoration Flint saw near the roof of the house.

The road became paved nearby, and several cars were parked in a circle before the house. For all the security measures, Flint saw no bots, no human guards, and no security buildings. Just the house itself, the cars, and the empty land beyond.

Flint's car landed on the far side of the paved circle. The car's doors remained locked. An androgynous voice warned him that this location was not considered friendly. If he did not return to the vehicle within twenty-four hours, the car would return itself to Florida, and his account would be charged extra for unmanned travel.

Flint had to acknowledge the message before getting out of the car.

He walked around the circle, toward the house, expecting something—someone—to intercept him, but no one did. Perhaps it wasn't worthwhile to keep guards in such an isolated place. He climbed the red stone steps that led to the main building, saw more plants that he couldn't identify, some climbing the outside wall, and knocked on the ornately decorated iron that covered the door.

For a moment, he thought no one knew he was there. Then a voice said, "You're Miles Flint?"

"Yes," Flint said, expecting to have to give more identification.

Instead the door opened. Flint stepped into cool darkness. The door closed—

And Flint's links shut off. All of them, even the ones he had designed to stay on.

"Hey," he said, and as he did, a clear cage fell around him, imprisoning him.

He put his hands up and touched the walls. They were glass or clear plastic, something that he could see through but couldn't get out of.

He made a fist and pounded; then, knowing that wouldn't work, he reached in his pockets for anything that would serve as a weapon. He found nothing.

Then something hard shoved into the side of his head.

"Welcome to Taylor Ranch, Miles Flint," that same voice said beside him. "That pressure you feel is a gun I've shoved through the dome. This is a real gun, Texas style. We fire projectiles here, not beams of light. With the velocity and power of this weapon, I expect your head will become a mass of brains and blood on the far side of my trap in a matter of seconds. Care to test it?"

"Not really," Flint said. "Do you greet all of your guests this way?"

"Never said you were a guest. You're the one who came here, talking about Etae and my ex-wife, who you claim is dead."

"She is," Flint said, "through no fault of my own. I can prove that to you if you give me my links back. I'm not even asking you to let me out of here."

"Glad to hear it, Mr. Flint, because I'm a cautious man. That's how I've lived this long. And nope, no links. You tell me how to find out."

Flint sighed. "Without my help, you'll get only part of the story."

"Part's better than none," the voice—which obviously belonged to Alan Taylor—said. "Tell me how."

Flint told him to look up the Lahiri murders, warning him that most of Armstrong was off-line.

"What a quaint way to put it," Taylor said. "Considering it was Etaen terrorists that nearly destroyed the city."

"No one knows if the city was nearly destroyed," Flint said. "But yes, Etae is involved. I'm not involved with Etae, though. I'm a Retrieval Artist. Unfortunately, I'm the man who brought Carolyn back to Armstrong."

"She'da gone anyway," Taylor said. "She believed the pardons."

"You didn't?"

"I know how Etae works. She was always a tad too idealistic for that."

The hardness left the side of Flint's head. The spot where it had touched ached.

Taylor moved away.

"A projectile, like a bullet, will pierce that glass, Mr. Flint," Taylor said as he crossed in front of Flint. "So just because my gun isn't pressed against your head don't mean that I can't kill you in the space of a heartbeat."

Flint let his hands fall to his sides. "I'll just wait until you check my information."

"Good man," Taylor said, and disappeared into the darkness.

Flint's eyes were beginning to adjust. He was in a large entry. The floor was covered with a stunning brown tile done in a patterned design. The walls were made out of the same material as the exterior. The colors were light, and the décor painted onto the wall was as unusual as the tile.

Flint could no longer see Taylor. Flint had only caught a glimpse of him anyway. The man had seemed taller and beefier than Flint expected, but that might have been distortion from the glass.

After a few minutes, Taylor came back. He did have the same startling green eyes his son had, but his hair had turned from auburn to a dusty gray. His face had a leathery texture Flint had seen only on old spacers.

"All right. Now you tell me who killed my wife, and maybe I'll talk to you," Taylor said. "But no matter what, your links ain't coming back on."

"I don't know the name of the man who killed your

wife," Flint said. "I have part of a security video that shows the murder. One of his aliases is Hank Mosby. He's a killer-for-hire with ties to Etae. He's been enhanced so that he's more efficient at killing than anyone I've ever seen. He's got elongated arms and his fingers can become knife blades. His senses of sight and sound are enhanced as well, and I'm sure he has other upgrades that I don't know about. When he finished with the Lahiris, he came back to Earth—"

"Back?"

Flint nodded. "He was here before, but I think I got in his way. After Carolyn died, I found out that everyone in your little team, with the exception of you, is dead now—the last few assassinated in just the last few months."

"What team?" Taylor asked.

"The ones who left Armstrong to fight for better things on Etae. So far as I can tell, Mr. Ali Norbert, you're the only one left alive."

Taylor let out a hissing breath. "Why should I believe you're not one of the assassins?"

"Well," Flint said, "if your equipment is as sophisticated as I think it is, then it's already figured out that I am who I say I am. It should also tell you that I'm not carrying a weapon and I'm not enhanced."

"No reason you can't signal someone else to come in the moment I set you free," Taylor said.

"Except that you're going to keep my links down," Flint said.

"And the gun trained on you." Taylor touched the back of his hand, and the glass cage sank into the floor.

Flint looked down, saw several rings, and then looked up. There were more corresponding rings.

It didn't matter where anyone stepped once inside the entry; if Taylor wanted them imprisoned, it would happen.

"You have quite the defense system," Flint said.

"That assassin you described is only one of many," Taylor said. "They're made for close-up combat, and they generally win. I been hearing reports about strangers making inquiries, so I'm on extra alert. I figure if I catch them before they can snake out those arms, I've won ninety percent of the battle."

"So you've seen them," Flint said.

"Hell, I fought with them side by side in Etae, back when I was a believer."

"You're not anymore?" Flint asked.

Taylor raised his shaggy eyebrows. "Would they be trying to kill me if I were?"

"I don't know," Flint said. "I don't understand any of this. You've been pardoned. All the Disappeared connected with Etae can come into the open."

"Where it's easier to kill them," Taylor said.

Flint stepped away from the rings. Taylor backed up. He held a long-nosed pistol in his hands. The gun appeared to be made of steel and looked more formidable than any weapon Flint had ever seen.

"I still don't understand," Flint said. "I thought you worked with the current government, back when they were the rebels."

"I did," Taylor said. "We all did, all of my old friends."

"So what happened? Why did you have to Disappear? Did you betray them somehow?"

"On the contrary," Taylor said. "I was such a good little soldier that they paid me to Disappear."

"Then why do they want to kill you?"

"I guess now that they're trying to join the Alliance, they're afraid I'll tell the truth," Taylor said.

"About what?" Flint asked.

"About the Child Martyr," Taylor said.

57

In the hours it took DeRicci to gather her team, over-head light returned to much of the Dome. Even though the program that rotated the stages of light from dome night to true daylight hadn't yet rebooted, seeing the sun through the uncovered dome made DeRicci—and countless other Armstrong citizens—feel like things might become right again.

The city was awash in destruction. The filters had been off for hours in some sections of the dome, and the dust piled ankle-high in some places. People were instructed to sweep as much of it away from filter openings as possible to prevent clogging, but no one was doing so.

Most people were trying to clean up their homes, apartments, and businesses. So many things had fallen and broken that the entire city seemed like one big garbage dump.

As DeRicci crossed from one closed wall to another, she also saw a lot of people wearing bandages, or walking around with bruised faces and arms. She suspected people had other bruises as well, ones she couldn't see.

The hospitals and doctors had begged the city to ask people to triage; if their injuries were potentially life-threatening, they needed to come immediately. Otherwise, they were to wait for a day or two. People who had only cosmetic problems—bruises, scratches—were to live with them; no enhancements or artificial coverings for the bruises this time. People with cuts or disfiguring but not life-threatening injuries were to make appointments for the following week, with the understanding that those appointments might be moved to the following month.

So far, DeRicci hadn't heard anyone grumble. Most people in Armstrong seemed happy to be alive.

Many of the dome walls had gone up by the time she took the chauffeured aircar to the disaster site. She was arriving well after the first members of the team she had assembled. The rest of her team would arrive in a few hours, as soon as they could find transport to the site. Very few departmental aircars were working in the unfiltered air.

Emergency medical units had been on-site since the engineers got the wall door open. A few fire squads had been there too, taking care of the chemical fires that still burned in the damaged area.

DeRicci slipped on the environmental suit she'd taken from Gumiela's closet—amazed at its quality and its strength—and tried to quell the nerves in her stomach. DeRicci had been to a lot of dangerous places, and she'd worn environmental suits outside the dome many times, but she had never worn one inside.

As the car wove past the tilting buildings and the damaged street signs, DeRicci tried to not think about all those dead pioneers whom she'd learned about in school. Dome technology, her teachers had proudly told their classes, had come about thanks to the courage of the original settlers and the ingenuity of those who followed. After each disaster, the dome got stronger.

And the disasters were hideous: dome fires in which much of the city burned, and those who didn't die in the flames died from lack of oxygen; dome collapses that had taken out entire sections of the city—literally made them whirl around the interior until they were sucked into the vacuum of space.

The dome hadn't collapsed here—although what she was hearing on her interior links led her to believe it was a near thing—and the fire was survivable, at least for anyone in an environmental suit, but this disaster would probably rank with all the others when it finally hit the history books.

And she was on the front line.

The car had to stop just inside the double wall. The second wall had been brought down by the dome engineers when they saw the level of the disaster. It was an older wall, almost never used, but the engineers had felt they needed the added protection.

DeRicci got out of the aircar and found the engineers who were monitoring this section of the dome. Like her, they were wearing environmental suits, and, like her, they had the helmets strung around their necks, waiting until they got somewhere close before putting them on.

"How bad is it?" DeRicci asked.

"Worse than going outside in real night," one of the engineers said. "We're gonna double-check your suit for leaks. You got good lights built into that thing? Otherwise, you're gonna have to borrow a suit from someone out here."

DeRicci had already checked the lights. She'd heard about the darkness problem, and wanted to be prepared.

"My lights are fine," she said.

"Then helmet on. Run your own diagnostic, and then we'll run ours."

DeRicci slid the helmet over her face, and flicked the artificial environment on. The suit was so sophisticated that she didn't feel the usual puff of air the cheaper suits used to convince the wearer that everything was fine. Instead, she grew just a little more comfortable—the temperature was regulated to her body so that the thin sheen of sweat that she'd had since she rode over dissipated in just a moment.

Her diagnostic beeped. The suit was fine. She gave a thumbs-up to the nearest engineer. He held up a finger while another engineer put a device on her hip. That device made her suit whir. For a moment, she thought it had screwed up the environmental controls. Then she realized it was just double-checking them.

The whirring stopped after thirty seconds, and the engineers sent a message along the bottom of the helmet's visor. She was good to go.

DeRicci sighed, hoping no one would see her shoulders rise and fall as she did so. The engineers led her to the first door. A porta-airlock had been assembled around it, so that accidental loss of atmosphere wouldn't occur in this section of the dome.

DeRicci had never used a porta-airlock before, and it made her stomach clench. Still, she went inside, waited until the portable door closed behind her, and opened the door built into the dome wall for just this type of emergency.

She felt nothing different as she stepped through, but then, she wouldn't. She always had a fantasy, though, that she could feel the changes in atmosphere as she moved.

The distance between the old wall and the automatic one was only about two meters. DeRicci felt claustrophobic. She also worried about the inky darkness ahead of her.

The engineers weren't kidding: The darkness inside the ruined section of the dome was formidable.

DeRicci closed the first wall door behind her, waited the requisite thirty seconds, and opened the next door. Wafts of smoke were being sucked into this section— not blowing, just billowing as if something (a fire still burning?) were forcing it this way.

And if it were a fire how could it burn without oxygen? She wasn't an arson specialist and she didn't know the answer.

Maybe there was more oxygen in this section of the dome than anyone realized.

She stepped inside, and started when a hand

grabbed her arm. Someone pulled her to the left. She found herself in a small tent, surrounded by other people in environmental suits. These people seemed as anonymous as she felt—all gray suits and tinted helmet visors.

DeRicci sent a text message introducing herself and got another back: She was to talk to the head of the fire unit near the bomb site.

She nodded, then let herself out of the tent on the far side. There she saw that the interior wasn't as black as it seemed. Blackness coated the dome wall and many of the buildings, probably from the force of the blast, but she was in a gray twilight filled with dust and debris and floating ash.

There was some kind of atmosphere here; she just wasn't sure how much. She didn't ask her suit to tell her, preferring to remain ignorant of some things.

People moved like uniformed ghosts through the swirling dirt. Lights illuminated pockets of the mess—showing truly destroyed buildings, many of them shattered as though a giant fist had punched through them.

DeRicci looked up at the dome. The cover stopped halfway across, revealing a hole that seemed—from this distance—human-sized. The hole had blown outward, preventing the cover from sliding across it, and someone had plugged the hole with a makeshift cover that seemed as fragile as the dust that was floating inside.

Even if a small crack still existed in the makeshift cover, the atmosphere would leak out of here at a rate DeRicci didn't have the math skills to determine. Engineers were probably outside the dome now, working on the edges of that hole so that the cover could completely protect the insides.

Nothing here would be safe until they did.

It wasn't hard to see the bomb site. A blackened crater in the center of the mess seemed to be the origin of the dust spew. More people gathered around that, all in suits similar to hers—or cheaper versions, the kind she had worn when she was a mere detective.

She walked over, careful not to hit her boots on anything sharp. There was a path of bootprints—probably from people who had had the same thoughts she did.

Ambulances stood beside several dome doors, but she didn't see any wounded. Of course, it had been hours since the blast: The wounded should have been evacuated long ago.

If there had been wounded in this eerie place. Maybe all the officials found were bodies. She didn't know that, and wouldn't, until she was farther into the investigation.

She reached the main site, surprised by a warning from her suit along the base of the helmet:

Surface temperature abnormally high. Check for fire.

"Is it safe to come over?" she said across the audio links. "I'm Noelle DeRicci. I'm an assistant chief of detectives, handling the investigation for the city."

"Safe enough," a male voice answered her. "But watch out for hot pockets. There was a hell of a fire here when we got here, and the embers still flare from time to time."

She walked toward the group of investigators. "I'm looking for the head of the fire unit."

"That'd be me," the male voice said. "I'm Peter Brajkovic."

He held out a gloved hand, and DeRicci shook it. "I'm supposed to start investigating, to see if we can figure out who did this."

Brajkovic's laugh sounded loud in through her links. "Sorry," he said after a moment. "But I'll be surprised if you'll find much."

He swept a hand toward the crater. She saw crisped things rising out of the mess, twisted and blackened and completely unidentifiable.

"Here's what we know," he said. "We know that the bomb blew up in the kitchen of this building, which, we know, was a restaurant mostly because parts of the stove are still intact. We have found evidence of accelerant, which may mean that the bomb wasn't one thing but several things that combined make an explosive."

DeRicci wanted to slow him down. This wasn't her area of expertise. But she decided to let him finish first, recording everything, as she always did, for her personal log.

"We did find some DNA and part of a foot, but that's all we've found so far. One person was either in there when it blew or nearby—we can't tell which— and we don't know if more people were there and vaporized."

DeRicci looked at the mess. The ash floating around her seemed almost white in the light from Brajkovic's suit.

"I know you want to catch the people who did this—and nothing would please me more, frankly," he said, "but I gotta tell you, this is going to be a job for the science guys, not for eyeball types. It's gonna take weeks, maybe months, to piece all this together."

DeRicci had been afraid that it was too soon for her to visit the scene, but she hadn't known how to tell Gumiela that. So instead, DeRicci had come here. At least she had assembled the best forensic team from the department and maybe, if Gumiela gave her enough power, she might send for some other specialists from around the Moon.

"So what can I do right now?" DeRicci asked. "Besides stay out of the way?"

"Record the scene, I guess," Brajkovic said. "It'll all be yours when the hot spots are cleaned up and the dome is secured. Otherwise, there's not much to be done. I suspect most of your evidence either burned or got sent out of the dome. Sorry about that."

DeRicci shook her head. "No one ever said this was going to be easy."

He moved away from her, and left her standing in front of the ruined block of buildings, where she knew she'd be spending the next few months of her life, trying to piece together exactly what had happened here.

58

"Come into the kitchen," Taylor said. "I have fresh coffee—and a lot more weaponry in there if need be."

Flint smiled. He appreciated the other man's caution. It called to something in himself.

He crossed the entry, staying as alert as he could, and followed Taylor into the hallway. Mirrors were discreetly placed along each curve, so that Taylor could see what was going on behind him.

There appeared to be no place in this house that lacked defenses.

The kitchen was a large, homey room—or would have been if the windows weren't barred and covered. The ceiling had skylights that were also covered, and the artificial lighting in here was nowhere as good as the artificial lighting on the Moon. The room felt dark even though it was not.

Taylor poured a cup of coffee from a pot on the tiled countertop, then shook the pot at Flint. Flint nodded, and was surprised to receive coffee that tasted like it had been made with real beans.

He wrapped his hands around the mug and sat at the kitchen table, his back to the cabinets. Taylor set his cup on the table and sat so that he could see the entrance to the kitchen from the hallway and the other entrance from the side.

The gun rested near his right hand.

"Why would the government of Etae try to kill you over an event that happened three decades ago?" Flint asked.

"I started wondering when I first got word of the pardons," Taylor said, "so I did a little research."

"You put in all this defensive stuff in the last few months?"

Taylor shook his head. "I've always lived like this. I figured they'd come for us. I just didn't know when. Claire—Carolyn—said I was being paranoid."

Flint sipped the coffee, enjoying the rich flavor. Still he kept his guard up. Just because Taylor seemed to have relaxed didn't mean Flint could.

"What did your research tell you?" Flint asked.

"That the former rebels of Etae want into the Alliance. They don't have a lot to bargain with, since war has pretty much ravaged that entire planet, but they've got a few corporations willing to go in, if the Alliance approves."

Flint had heard some of this before. "Corporations often go in without the Alliance's okay."

"Yes, but in this instance, the corporations know they'll need some of the Alliance's legal protections, particularly the courts. Everything on Etae is still in a state of flux, and if the corporations lose money due to Etae's internal conflicts, they're going to want to recoup. They can't do that without Alliance aid."

"Why go in at all?" Flint asked.

Taylor shrugged. "Probably military knowledge, weaponry. Those enhancements that I've been guarding against are exceedingly effective, no matter what your body style is. It puts humans on par with the Rev, if you can believe it."

Flint had faced down Rev. He had trouble believing any human—even an enhanced one like Hank Mosby—could take on a Rev.

"But that's not what matters. To get into the Alliance, you have to convince not just the monetary wing but the diplomatic wing. And the diplomats have a vested interest in keeping the peace in the Old Universe."

"Looks like they have a point," Flint said, setting his mug down, "considering what just happened in Armstrong."

Taylor nodded. "We'll get to that. I know how the Etaen government operates. They'll do anything to get what they want."

"Even kill supporters?" Flint asked.

"Former supporters, not that I've ever spoken out," Taylor said. "And yes, considering the knowledge we have. If they hadn't needed us—hell, if I hadn't been on top of it, even then—we'd be dead already."

"On top of what?" Flint asked.

Taylor held up a hand. "I got the government to clear us, to buy our Disappearances right before the Child Martyr footage hit the intergalactic news."

"Before?" Flint asked. "Then how could you know the truth?"

"Because," Taylor said. "I wasn't just helping us all disappear. I Disappeared the Martyr too."

"What?" Flint asked. "I saw that footage. That poor child was killed."

Taylor's smile was bitter. "That poor child was never harmed. A few months before, some kids were killed outside the capital, and that raised a small outcry, giving support to the rebels. Anatolya Döbryn—the media mastermind of the group—figured out that the death of a child, a hideous, very public death, might actually give the rebels the edge they needed—if they could convince the rest of the universe that it was a rebel child who died at the hands of the then-government troops."

Flint leaned forward. His coffee mug was empty, but he didn't ask if he could have more. He was too intent.

"Döbryn figured we didn't dare risk killing one of our own—something like that might come back to bite us—so instead, they staged the entire thing. The outside reporters got what they thought was distant live footage of the child being killed, then someone—no one ever said who, but it was Claire who did the actual work—released a vid of the stuff that you've probably seen: the child begging for mercy, then being hideously slaughtered by the government's troops."

"We're all sophisticated enough to recognize a doctored vid," Flint said, not sure he believed what Taylor was telling him.

"Really?" Taylor asked. "After the original setup? Those reporters were from all over the known universe. They just never got close-up footage. No one thought to look for doctoring after that. No one dared."

"The Child Martyr is alive?" Flint asked.

"Well, she was when we got her off Etae. She Disappeared like the rest of us."

"Did the Child Martyr travel with you?"

Taylor picked up his gun and carried it to the counter. Then he grabbed his cup off the table and poured more coffee. "Want some?"

Flint nodded.

Taylor poured the rest of the pot into Flint's mug.

"Carolyn and I insisted on Disappearing together because we believed we were in love," Taylor said. "She was pregnant and I wanted to raise a child in a peaceful place. I had a hunch, even then, that Claire couldn't settle down for long. But I thought maybe I could tame that. Ian was about five when I realized I couldn't. But if we hadn't Disappeared together, I wouldn't have seen my son, let alone raised him. He's not perfect, but he's got a good heart. You're lucky you didn't hurt him."

Flint held out his hands, palms up. "I had no reason to hurt him. I'm just here to get information, maybe see if I can figure out what happened to Carolyn."

"She was killed by the government she helped create for the secret she helped bury," Taylor said. "If news that the Child Martyr was a fake comes out, then Etae will never have a chance at the Alliance, at least not while Döbryn and her crew are alive."

"I don't get it. If the child wasn't hurt—"

"The Child Martyr was the turning point, her so-called death the moment when the rebels became legit. We got weapons, we got support—through back doors—we got everything we wanted to defeat the government. If the Alliance finds out the rebels manipulated them, then Etae won't ever get a chance to join. And, even worse, if the factions on Etae find out the Child Martyr is a fake, the war will break out all over again."

Flint nodded. The situation was beginning to make sense. A cynical, twisted sense, but sense nonetheless.

"So," he said, "the current government pardoned you—"

"To make us easier to kill," Taylor said. "I mean, how perfect is it? Disappeareds come out of the woodwork, and then they're murdered. Hmm, the death must be caused by the very reason they Disappeared. Of course, no one knows why most people Disappear, so the deaths will remain unsolved. And using hired killers . . . well, that makes it even easier, really. It's brilliant, just like Döbryn."

"She was in Armstrong when I left," Flint said. "They're blaming her or her people for the bombing."

"I heard," Taylor said. "It's too crude for Anatolya. She's a master of subtlety. This may have something to do with Etae, but it wasn't her idea."

"You seem convinced."

Taylor shrugged. "I worked with her. You don't forget a woman like that."

"And you don't think she's forgotten you," Flint said. "If you're so worried she'll kill you, how come you've left your son undefended? Aren't you afraid they'll get to you through him?"

Taylor shook his head. "Until you blundered in there yesterday, my son had no idea his family came from anywhere but West Texas. I suppose I'll have to call him home now, help him a little, but he won't mind. He said on the link that he finally understands my caution. He'll be cautious now too, and I convinced him to wait until things die down before collecting what's left—if anything—of the Lahiri estate."

"I can give you the name of good people in Armstrong who could help you with that," Flint said. "You wouldn't have to leave Earth."

As he spoke, he wondered if those people were still alive. The urge to get back rose in him once more.

"We'll see," Taylor said. He sat back down at the table, keeping the gun close. "Ironic, I think, the way this all turned out. Etae comes back into my life whether I want it to or not. Claire finally goes back to see if she can get Daddy's forgiveness or approval or whatever it was that drove her in the first place, and does it at the exact moment Etae comes to Armstrong."

"The pardon caused the timing," Flint said.

Taylor's eyes narrowed. "Of course. But you gotta wonder about that old man. He was so corrupt. He took bribe after bribe on the Tribunal. Ever since you showed up, I've been wondering if Döbryn or someone contacted him, told him about the public relations mess, and offered to pay him if he helped them kill his daughter. All he had to do was get her to come home after her pardon, something that'd please his wife at the same time."

Flint felt a chill. "The judge didn't want to hire me. He didn't want her to come home."

But the judge had searched for her himself. His wife had wanted to hire Flint, but the judge had exposed Carolyn long before that.

"Don't kid yourself, Mr. Retrieval Artist." Taylor leaned his chair back. "I've met people like old man Lahiri all over this universe. Sometimes I think that's what's at the heart of places like Etae—people like Döbryn and Lahiri, people who believe more in themselves and what they want, people who, for one reason or another, never learned compassion. Döbryn I can almost understand. Her entire family was massacred right in front of her by Idonae, and the man who saved her, the one who gave her his name, taught her that the best defense is a good offense. She was killing Idonae by the time she was six. She had no hope."

"And Judge Lahiri?"

"Who knows?" Taylor said. "All I know is that the minute Claire figured out she couldn't purge his parenting habits from her system no matter how hard she tried, she left. She wouldn't see Ian no matter how much we begged. Finally she told me the best thing she could do as a mother was to forget she'd ever given birth. And it took me another year or two to believe her."

Flint set his coffee mug down. He didn't know what to say. He had come to Earth for answers. Now that he'd found them, he wasn't sure what to do with them.

"Here's the thing no one on Etae knows, Mr. Retrieval Artist," Taylor said, his finger running along the length of his gun. "If I get killed, I got a couple of lawyers in various places instructed to release a lot of information on the Child Martyr. Footage taken as she Disappeared, some other stuff that'll do the very things the Etaen government worries I'll do when I'm alive. So if you are here as a representative of Etae, being subtle and secret the way that Döbryn likes to play her games, then you know. I die, it all comes out. And you can't stop it."

"It'll throw that part of the universe back into chaos," Flint said.

"You don't think that's happened already?" Taylor's grin seemed flat this time. "Someone got Anatolya's number, they really did. No one's gonna recognize Etae now that Armstrong's been bombed. Anatolya's been defeated at her own game, maybe for the first time in her life."

59

Anatolya Döbryn finally got her meeting with a member of the Alliance, but not in the way that she had initially imagined. Orenda Kreise came to the secure room where the guards had taken Anatolya.

Kreise looked like she'd been through hell. Anatolya had seen vids of the other woman. Kreise had always been possessed, even under stress. Now she was covered with cuts and bruises, and she wheezed as she spoke.

The meeting was short.

"You're getting a choice," Kreise said to her, "which is more than some of the diplomats think you should have. You can stay here and face charges as an accessory to the bombing, or you can leave. You will not, of course, get any consideration from the Alliance. Any thoughts of a meeting are off. But it's pretty clear to us that you didn't order the actual bombing, since you were trapped in the hotel and your links didn't work. If your people decided to do it after the riot, then that's for the Armstrong police to determine. No one objects all the way through the Alliance to your being sent home, so long as no one from your government ever contacts us again."

"We had nothing to do with that bombing," Anatolya said.

Kreise's eyes narrowed and she crossed her arms, revealing more cuts and bruises along the skin. "You're welcome to stay and prove it, but you'll probably end up in some prison somewhere, serving a life sentence for the hundred dead that the city's found so far."

Anatolya felt her breath catch. This entire trip had been one disaster after another.

"The Alliance feels the one thing we can give you is this opportunity to leave, so long as you tell your people that we want nothing to do with you. We're going to let those intergalactic corporations know as well that anyone who uses Etaen enhancements will be prosecuted. That's the message we want you to take back to Etae. Can you do that?"

Anatolya ran her hands along her legs. She had never been in this position before. Before, she had always run things.

"My people, my team, they—"

"They'll get justice," Kreise said. "Whatever that means. Personally, I think you're getting more than you deserve, but I was overruled."

She glared at Anatolya.

"So if I were you, I'd get out the moment the Port opens, because I doubt this'll be a popular decision on Armstrong. You do have a crew to fly your ship?"

"Not everyone disembarked," Anatolya said.

"Good. I'd hate to have to provide you with one." Kreise gave her one last look, then headed for the door. "Fifteen minutes to make up your mind. Otherwise, I'm going to let Armstrong's police know that we have you here."

She left, closing the door behind her.

Anatolya let out the breath she'd been holding. Part of her wanted to stay, to clear her name and the names of her people. But she could do nothing from prison, and she had seen things like this before. Once or twice, she'd manipulated them herself.

The only way she could help her people was to go back to them. She had no idea how she would turn this around, but she would have to.

If the Alliance was going to prosecute anyone enhanced the Etaen way, then maybe Etae should take its cue from the Alliance. People always made more money on the black market than in the legitimate one.

Money would help Etae. It wouldn't solve all their problems, but it would be a start.

Anatolya stood, went to the door, and knocked on it. A guard pressed his face against a small opening.

"Tell Ms. Kreise that I'm taking her up on her offer," Anatolya said. "I want nothing more than to get out of this place and go home."

60

The conversation with Taylor left Flint shaken. He walked out of the ranch house and was surprised at how much warmer it was outside than in. The sunlight still caught him; its richness seemed to be something the dome engineers couldn't duplicate.

He wondered if there was any word from Armstrong. He would check when he got in the car.

At least his links had come back up. Every single computerized function, everything the chips attached to his hands and skin did, had shut down inside of Taylor's house.

Flint walked around the paved circle, still not certain where the conversation with Taylor had left him. Flint had answers, and he wasn't sure he liked them.

The Lahiris were dead, not because Flint had found Carolyn and put this into motion, but because it was already in motion when they had contacted him.

He had reached the side of the car when something snaked around his rib cage. The pressure was hard and painful, knocking his breath out of his body.

He grabbed at the thing that held him, feeling warm flesh, and looked down, seeing skin elongated and wrapped around him like rope.

Suddenly he was jerked off his feet and dragged

backward. He sent for help along his links, but he couldn't get enough air to cry aloud.

Something else—another fleshlike thing—wrapped around his arms, trapping them against his torso. The pain was excruciating. Even though the flesh-rope didn't cut into his flesh, it might as well have. His nerves were pinched against the bone, making his eyes tear.

Then he slammed into a hard body. A face looked down at him, a face that didn't surprise him at all.

Mosby.

Flint didn't have a chance. This man had more weapons built into his person than Flint normally carried—and he wasn't carrying anything at all because he was on Earth.

Even if Flint got away, he wouldn't be able to escape. Mosby had better eyesight and better hearing. He could capture Flint again with those ropelike arms before Flint made it halfway to the car.

"I like that yacht of yours," Mosby said in accented English. "We could negotiate—your yacht for help getting Norbert outside."

So he had found Taylor and was ready to kill him.

"Can't . . . breathe . . ." Flint managed, his words so soft he could barely hear them.

"All right." Mosby loosened his grip around Flint's torso ever so slightly. Flint got a little air, and it made him dizzy. "That yacht of yours—it's keyed to you, isn't it? Living flesh, right? Blood flowing through the veins, warm skin? Can that be changed?"

Flint had no idea why Mosby was talking about the *Emmeline*. "I have to . . . authorize. . . ."

"Figured." Mosby cursed. "You help me get Norbert outside and I'll pay you to deliver me off-world. Deal?"

He was offering Flint a chance—probably the only chance Flint would have to survive this attack. Flint certainly couldn't fight him. But if Flint got him to the *Emmeline*. he would have a chance to kill him.

"Take . . . transport," Flint said. "Like before."

Mosby let out a dry little laugh. "You Tracked me. I'm sure someone else will. They won't Track me on that little gem you own."

His grip around Flint's middle grew tighter. Black spots dotted Flint's vision.

"Not gonna help me, huh?" Mosby said. "Never met an ethical Tracker before."

The word *Tracker* got through to Flint. Mosby didn't realize he was a Retrieval Artist. Instead Mosby thought that Flint found Disappeareds for anyone who paid him enough money—in other words, Mosby thought Flint could be bought.

"Didn't . . . say . . . that." Flint barely got the words out. He was fighting to remain conscious. Something snapped on his right side, sending pain skittering through him. He latched on to the pain, hoped it would keep his eyes open just a moment longer. "Talk . . . deal . . ."

Mosby had dragged Flint to the side of the building, near the tall plants.

"You take me anywhere after you get Norbert outside. I'll pay you. Deal?"

"No . . ." Flint's voice was a ghost of its former self. "Sell . . . you . . . yacht . . . Money . . . up . . . front . . . I'll . . . reprogram . . ."

"Not worth it without Norbert. No deal unless you get me that Disappeared," Mosby said.

"Don't . . . need . . . him . . . outside," Flint said. "Can't . . . breathe . . ."

Mosby loosened his grip a little more. Both sides ached. Flint couldn't run if he wanted to.

"What do you mean, I don't need him outside? This place is a fortress."

"Yes." Flint coughed, tasted blood. That wasn't good. "But . . . I've . . . seen . . . you . . . kill. . . . Don't . . . need . . . to . . . worry."

"You've seen me kill?" Mosby's dark eyes were too close to Flint's. They made him dizzy.

"Security . . . video . . . Lahiri . . . apartment . . . You . . . missed . . . one . . . visual. . . ."

Mosby swore again.

"Arsenal . . . yes . . ." Flint said. "Conventional . . . weapons . . . and . . . old . . . ones . . . He . . . had . . . a . . . projectile . . . gun . . . on . . . me. . . . Lots . . . of . . . guns . . . steel . . . barred . . . windows . . . probably . . . encased . . . walls . . .."

"Which still does me no good," Mosby said. "I need him out here."

"Or . . . you . . . in . . . there," Flint said. The black spots had grown bigger. Even with Mosby's loosened grip, Flint was going to pass out. "Then . . . you . . . can . . . wipe . . . the . . . vids. . . . All . . . traces . . . of . . . us . . . No . . . one . . . will . . . suspect . . . we . . . know . . . each . . . other . . .."

"I like how you think," Mosby said. "But I can't just barge through that front door."

"I . . . can . . . get . . . you . . . inside," Flint said, hoping that was true. "I'll . . . knock . . . talk . . . to . . . him . . . Then . . . you'll . . . enter. . . ."

Mosby's grip loosened even more. "Don't double-cross me, Tracker."

Flint coughed, spat blood. "Couldn't . . . if . . . I . . . wanted . . . to."

Mosby smiled; then his elongated arms shoved Flint forward, holding him up as Flint stumbled back toward the door. Flint tried to assess the various pains he was feeling.

A few broken ribs, maybe a broken arm. His lungs burned so badly that he could barely breathe even without the pressure. Coughing blood probably meant that one of them was punctured.

He wasn't sure he could pull this off without passing out.

His legs wobbled as he tried the stairs. Mosby's arms let him go, and Flint nearly toppled over.

For one brief, heart-stopping moment, Flint thought of running, maybe using the plants to block Mosby's incredible reach. But he didn't have the strength, even if he had the cunning and the luck. He could barely stand.

He swayed as he walked to the front door. He wouldn't be able to warn Taylor. He would have to hope that Taylor used his damn cage no matter who came inside. If Taylor didn't . . .

Flint would be responsible for another death.

He raised a hand, saw blood running along the back, realized that Mosby had cut into him after all. Then he wasn't just having trouble breathing, he was bleeding too.

Flint knocked, like he had before, sucking in as much air as he could so that his voice would sound normal.

"Thought you left." Taylor's voice was small and annoyed through the outdoor speakers.

"Forgot I had one thing to show you," Flint said.

The words came out breathier than he wanted and faster than he normally spoke.

A click meant the door unlatched. "Make it quick," Taylor said.

Flint opened his mouth to answer, but Mosby's arms wrapped around him so fast that he couldn't even get the words out. The arms squeezed extremely tightly this time, and Flint heard more snaps, followed by stunning pain.

Mosby flung him aside as if Flint were made of cloth. He soared over the steps and landed on the pavement, his body bouncing twice. He couldn't even reach out to stop his fall.

He managed to turn his head, to see Mosby walk through that door, and the door close.

Then Flint leaned back on the pavement, and shut his eyes.

A muffled gunshot echoed across the parking lot.

Flint swallowed. He had probably been wrong. Taylor had probably trusted him enough not to use the cage, and Mosby got the gun out of Taylor's hand the moment Mosby entered the house.

Then Mosby had turned the gun on Taylor, and completed his mission in one shot.

Could the ambulance and police that Flint sent for

even get onto Taylor's property? Probably not. Not on conventional roads anyway. Would they be smart enough to go off-road, like Mosby had?

Probably not.

Flint would be at the mercy of Mosby.

If he didn't die first. If that whole thing about the *Emmeline* was true.

A hand touched his face, cool and competent.

Flint's eyes opened.

Taylor's face floated above his, eerily calm against the blue, blue sky. "Good thing I didn't trust you," Taylor said.

Flint tried to answer him, but couldn't. Not that it mattered. Taylor probably thought he was in league with Mosby. It would end here.

"I never shut off the defenses. I kinda liked seeing you in that cage. If it pissed you off, you could've cursed me all you wanted. It wouldn't've mattered to me." Taylor grinned. "You're one quick thinker, you know? How'd you keep him from killing you?"

"Offered to sell him my yacht," Flint said, or he thought he said. He wasn't really sure if the words came out of him or if he just intended them to.

He closed his eyes, and finally realized how wonderful the warm, hard ground was on the planet Earth.

61

Six months later, Flint sat at his desk in his office on Armstrong. The building listed even more to the right than it had in the past. The shaking, which happened during the bombing while he was off-world, had caused a number of buildings in this old part of town to collapse.

Fortunately, his wasn't one of them. But when he finally got out of the hospital and got cleared for return to Armstrong, he came home to discover nearly a meter and a half of dust covering his floor.

He'd had to completely revamp his security system and his computer system. Everything had been ruined—fortunately ruined enough so that no one could steal his records. And even more fortunate for him, he had those records backed up on the *Emmeline*.

Of course, it had taken Flint a long time to need those records. For the first month after the attack, he hadn't done much more than heal and argue with Alan Taylor.

Taylor had paid for Flint's hospitalization and reconstruction. No matter how much Flint had protested, Taylor wouldn't change his mind.

He figured that Flint had probably saved his life.

Eventually, Taylor would have had to leave his fortresslike ranch, and Mosby would have killed him. Taylor admitted to Flint more than once that he had no contingency plan for surviving away from the ranch; he had just figured that Mosby—or any Etaen assassin—wouldn't try killing him in public because it was too risky.

Taylor hadn't counted on an attack in the parking area in front of the ranch.

Neither had Flint.

He had gone over that scenario a million times in his mind, and slowly realized that nothing could have prevented Mosby's attack.

Flint could have done his reconstruction treatments on Earth, but he wanted to come home, and he was happy he had. He got to see his office and his old friends.

In between treatments, he had contacted DeRicci. They had been in touch briefly—Flint had heard from all of his friends when communications to Armstrong got reestablished—but he hadn't told her what he was doing on Earth.

When he got back, he thought he could tell her and help her close the Lahiri case. After all, there really was no more confidentiality to protect—all the Disappeareds were pardoned and most of them were dead.

But DeRicci hadn't wanted to hear about it. She had already found the security vid and had planned to follow up on it when the bombing occurred. At that point, she got assigned to run the investigation team, and Gumiela closed all of DeRicci's other pending investigations.

DeRicci promised to hear Flint's story when the bombing investigation was done, which, she figured, would be sometime in the next three thousand years. To say the investigation was going slowly was an understatement: Although the team had reconstructed some events, they couldn't be certain of much from inside the blast area.

They had found DNA from the restaurant's owner

near the bomb site, and speculated that she had triggered the explosion when she had come into work that morning. They had also traced the bomber's message to a public link in the restaurant, but that link had been so thoroughly destroyed that they couldn't tell when the message was coded, let alone who had done so.

The current theory was that some of the Etaen terrorists who had gotten into the dome the day before had built a makeshift bomb in the restaurant. No one had seen them arrive, but many people remembered Nitara Nicolae, the restaurant's owner, coming in late, looking terrified—maybe she had run into the bombers at the riot, and they had followed her back.

But even that theory was on shaky ground. Only two of the terrorists had survived the riots—the rest had been killed by rioters or Armstrong police—and no evidence of those two had shown up anywhere else.

Etae was calling for an intergalactic investigation, claiming that its people, who had arrived on Armstrong in good faith, were being blamed without cause, but no one took that denial seriously.

The entire mess just continued, and Flint doubted that parts of it would ever end.

He had been thinking about that as his new security system kicked into life. Clear screens—making the images see-through—rose as new visitors walked toward his office.

He felt a flash of irritation when he recognized one of the visitors as the reporter Ki Bowles.

She hadn't bothered him about her friend since he'd come back from Earth. From all the news vids, he guessed she had been tied up with the bombing investigation, the rebuilding of that section of the dome, the reports of the dome engineers on all the electrical malfunctions, and all the other scandals that had come from that day.

Flint had thought he wouldn't see her again.

He was disappointed to see that he was wrong.

At her side walked a woman with a vaguely familiar

face. She was short and heavyset, unusual for this part of Armstrong, where people paid greatly for enhancements to keep themselves thin.

Flint unlatched the door before Bowles even knocked, and had his system look for the other woman's ID. Remembering Bowles's earlier visit, he also had the system compare the woman's face to those of known Disappeareds.

The system was working as Bowles stepped inside. She seemed thinner and tired, her delicately tattooed face not hidden this time by a hat.

"That was easy," she said as she ushered the other woman in. "I thought you'd be as much of a pain as you were the last time."

Bowles didn't seem as startled this time when her links cut out. The other woman looked surprised, though, and Bowles said to her softly, "I warned you about that, remember?"

The woman nodded, and Bowles pushed the door shut.

"Remember," Bowles said, "you said I should bring her here? You said I'd be a real friend if I brought her with me. It's taken a while, but she's finally agreed to come."

Flint could lie and say he didn't remember, but he did. This was the woman who Bowles thought might be a Disappeared. She stood with her hands clasped in front of her, her head bowed. Her hair shone darkly in the artificial light, and her clothing, while tasteful, was cheap.

This woman didn't have enough money to investigate her past, even if Flint wanted to.

"You believe you might be a Disappeared?" Flint asked. He hadn't moved from his desk, partly to intimidate his potential new clients, and partly because he hadn't fully healed yet. All of his ribs had been broken, and his lungs punctured. It would take time, the doctors assured him, for his reconstructions to integrate into his body and gain their own strength.

"I'm having strange memories," the woman said, her voice soft. "And I don't remember my childhood before the age of ten. I'm pretty sure I can recover it, and that there's something back there, something awful."

"People don't Disappear children for no reason," Flint said. "If something is back there and it's serious enough for someone to want you to forget your past, then I suggest you do just that."

"But the memories are coming on their own—worse in the last year. The bombing . . ." Her voice broke. "The bombing made things even worse."

"I'm sure," Flint said. "It brought up buried memories for a lot of people."

"I think you should investigate," Bowles said. "As I told you before, I'm willing to pay for it."

"It doesn't work that way," Flint said. "Besides, you'd want to report whatever we find, and I can't agree to that."

The woman frowned. Bowles was shaking her head. "You don't understand. I—"

Flint's computer beeped. Bowles stopped speaking and looked at him.

"Is that important?" she asked.

Flint's main screen had gone opaque, so the person behind it couldn't see the same information he did.

The computer had found a match to the woman before him. The match was, on flat vids, one-hundred-point, provided she had aged the way the computer believed she would. Flint would need old records to see if she had.

But he hoped he wouldn't have to ask for them. His stomach twisted, and he finally understood Ki Bowles's interest. She had done the same scan he had long before she had contacted him, and she had seen the same shocking images.

The woman's hundred-point match was with vids of the Child Martyr.

"How old are you?" Flint asked the woman.

"Forty," she said.

Flint didn't nod. He didn't do anything at all. It felt, for one brief moment, as if his heart had stopped.

Finally he made himself take a deep breath. He looked at Ki Bowles, his expression as neutral as he could make it.

"Ms. Bowles," he said, "the only way I'll take this case is if you have no involvement in it whatsoever. Remember? I told you that if you brought her back, you'd wait outside. Now I'm revising that. I want you gone."

"But my friend can't pay for your services." Ki Bowles flashed him her million-credit smile. "You're pretty expensive, Mr. Flint."

"I'm expensive so that I can pick and choose my cases. I choose to work this one without you or not at all. What do you say, Ki?"

It was the first time he'd used her first name. Her cheeks colored.

"What do you say?" Bowles asked the woman.

The woman was watching Flint. "Why would you want to help me?"

"Because I have a hunch Ms. Bowles is manipulating you for her personal gain and I find that offensive. So I'm offering to make your life a little easier."

The woman swallowed. Then she looked at Bowles. "Do you mind if I just hear him out?"

Anger flashed across Bowles's face, but disappeared almost as quickly as it arose. She was probably figuring she could get the information out of the woman when she left the office.

"No," Bowles said after a moment. "I don't mind at all. I'll wait in the car."

"I'll take her home," Flint said.

"It's not necessary," Bowles said.

"Yes," Flint said, leaning back and crossing his arms. The movement caused now-familiar pain to run from his elbow to his wrist. "It is necessary."

They stared at each other for a moment, then Bowles sighed. "All right. I'll go. Call me."

That last she said to the woman. The woman nodded, miserably it seemed to Flint, and then Bowles let herself out of the office.

Flint watched on his screen as Bowles hurried across the dust-covered street toward her aircar.

Brilliant woman. She knew what a coup it would be if she had found the Child Martyr, and if she had gotten a Retrieval Artist to confirm the identity. The search that Bowles had done wouldn't be enough for an entire universe, which had once believed in the current government of Etae, but with a Retrieval Artist's backing and all the work he could do, the universe would have to believe.

"Why don't you trust Ms. Bowles?" the woman asked.

Flint glanced away from his screen.

"It's a long story," he said, and he knew he would have to tell it. All of it, from the importance of the Child Martyr, to the fact that she didn't really die, down to the changes it would cause across the known universe if there were proof she was alive.

Provided she lived long enough for the proof to be obtained.

Flint sighed. This would be a long day, without any real compensation.

"You don't have any money, do you?" he asked.

"So that is important," the woman said. "You just told Ki—

"I know what I said, and I meant it," Flint said. "But humor me. How much money do you have?"

"Enough for this month's rent," the woman said.

Flint nodded. He had expected as much. He punched a few keys on his computer, wondering how to approach this.

He would have to be as manipulative as Bowles. It wasn't every day a Retrieval Artist convinced a potential client that she needed to Disappear yet again.

He doubted he would be able to convince her quickly. But he hoped he would be able to.

She needed to in order to stay alive. Bowles

wouldn't keep this secret very long. If Flint didn't take the case, then Bowles would go to someone else who could.

And this dumpy, lonely, nameless woman standing in front of him, a woman whose bad memories were driving her crazy, whose life was about to be turned upside down one more time because of something someone had done to her—because she was the key to a government she didn't remember—would die for a cause she didn't even understand.

Fortunately, Bowles had come to Flint, and fortunately, he did have the ethics she had once credited him with.

"Come here," Flint said, getting out of his chair. He shoved it toward the woman. "Sit down. I'm going to show you a few images, tell you why Ki Bowles thinks you're important, and then I'm going to help you."

Whether she wanted him to or not.

It was the least he could do for Carolyn Lahiri. He might have failed her, but he wouldn't fail in this.

The woman sat down and then looked up at him, her round face innocent and childlike.

"Images?" she asked.

Flint nodded. He tapped his screen and slowly, carefully, started to introduce the Child Martyr to her past.

ABOUT THE AUTHOR

Kristine Kathryn Rusch is an award-winning writer in several genres. Winner of the 2001 Hugo Award for the novelette "Millennium Babies," she has also won the *Ellery Queen* Readers' Choice Award for best mystery short story. She is also a winner of the *Asimov's* Readers Choice Award, the *Locus* Award, the World Fantasy Award, and the John W. Campbell Award.

She has published more than fifty novels in almost a dozen languages, and she has hit bestseller lists in the *Wall Street Journal, USA Today,* and *Publishers Weekly.* Her science fiction and mystery short stories have been in many year's-best collections.

The Retrieval Artist novels are based on the Hugo-nominated novella "The Retrieval Artist," which was first published in *Analog.*

Roc Science Fiction & Fantasy
COMING IN MAY 2004

CHOICE OF THE CAT
by E. E. Knight
0-451-45973-3

In Book Two of *The Vampire Earth*, David
Valentine, a member of the human resistance, is
sent on his first mission—to investigate a new
force under the alien Reaper's control.

COVENANTS: *A Borderlands Novel*
by Lorna Freeman
0-451-45980-6

This exciting new series features Rabbit, a
trooper with the Border Guards. But this
trooper is different than the others—he is the
son of nobility and a mage who doesn't know
his own power.

NIGHTSEER
by Laurell K. Hamilton
0-451-45143-0

New York Times bestselling author
Laurell K. Hamilton's spellbinding debut
novel—a tale of a woman known as sorcerer,
prophet and enchantress.